DETAIL MAN

THERE'S A PILL FOR THAT.

also by
KENT McINNIS

SIERRA HOTEL
CLEAR AND A MILLION
SEMPER FLY

DETAIL MAN

THERE'S A PILL FOR THAT.

KENT McINNIS
AUTHOR OF SIERRA HOTEL

HAT CREEK

HAT CREEK

An Imprint of Roan & Weatherford Publishing Associates, LLC
Bentonville, Arkansas
www.roanweatherford.com

Copyright © 2024 by Kent McInnis

We are a strong supporter of copyright. Copyright represents creativity, diversity, and free speech, and provides the very foundation from which culture is built. We appreciate you buying the authorized edition of this book and for complying with applicable copyright laws by not reproducing, scanning, or distributing any part of it in any form without permission. Thank you for supporting our writers and allowing us to continue publishing their books.

Library of Congress Cataloging-in-Publication Data
Names: McInnis, Kent, author
Title: Detail Man
Description: First Edition. | Bentonville: Hat Creek, 2024.
Identifiers: LCCN: 2024939048 | ISBN: 978-1-63373-956-7 (trade paperback) | ISBN: 978-1-63373-957-4 (eBook)
Subjects: | BISAC: FICTION/Medical | FICTION/Historical/General | FICTION/Humorous/General
LC record available at: https://lccn.loc.gov/2024939048

Hat Creek trade paperback edition July, 2024

Cover Design by Casey W. Cowan
Interior Design by Staci Troilo
Editing by Anthony Wood & Don Money

This book is a work of historical fiction. Apart from the well-known actual people, events, and locales that figure in the narrative, all names, characters, places, and incidents are the product of the author's imagination or are used fictitiously. Any resemblance to current events or locales, or to living persons, is entirely coincidental.

To the Tornadoes & the Party Van

Chapter One

"ARE YOU SURE you want to see him?" Mary offered Stu Roy a chance to return on a better day.

He looked around the neatly appointed waiting room with no patients. That was a good sign for a new detail man because the doctor wouldn't be busy—more time to discuss medicine.

"Well, yes, of course, I'll see him." After all, it was his job to call on Doctor Addicus. The nurse sighed in resignation.

"Okay... come this way." Mary acted strangely as she walked him down the eerily quiet hallway to the open door of his office. "Doctor, Mister Roy is here to see you."

Stu nodded to Mary, who looked at him with an I-told-you-so smirk. Stu stepped through the doorway with his sales bag filled with visuals, medical studies, drug samples, and giveaways.

He shuddered at the sight. The room filled him with utter panic. Not easily moved by strange behavior, Stu stopped his forward movement and stood still in absolute terror. Doctor Addicus sat in the chair behind his barren desk, both fists tightly gripped on the front edge as if he would fall backward if he let go. He sat like a bug-eyed mannequin, staring straight ahead. The doctor appeared unable to recognize that Stu was in the room. The pupils of both eyes were the size of his eye sockets. His breathing was staccato. His expression was frantic. Stu feared he was dying. It was a hell of a memorable sales call for a brand-new drug rep.

Finn Trottel, Stu's boss, gave him an assignment that morning to call on this doctor because he was known to do what detail men told him to do.

"It will be good practice for you. Different doctors respond in different ways. You can easily win him over and he'll do what you ask. Go see for yourself."

Stu's first lesson was clear. He now knew what hooked-on-speed looked like—impending death. But Stu was new to the job and proceeded to make his sales call. *Just following directions. They pay me to do it their way.* Since the wired doctor did not offer him a seat, he stood in front of the desk, placed his bag upon a nearby chair, and pulled out three different visuals of pharmaceutical products he intended to sell.

"How are you today, Doctor Addicus?" He couldn't think of anything else to say. His question was foolish. Normally he would extend a hand to shake, if offered. Addicus was too busy gripping the desk.

"Fine!" He managed to make a one syllable word sound staccato, as a variance to his rapid breathing. "Wh... what k... k... can I do fo... or you?"

He continued looking straight ahead. Stu moved over to his field of view. The doctor flinched.

"What patients are you seeing today?" Finn Trottel taught him that this was a good opening. Find out what was fresh on his mind. Stu hoped it involved something related to a drug he was selling.

"I don't... ah... ah... ah ah ah...."

The young man now grasped that his doctor call would proceed without the doctor's feedback. New drug reps feared feedback, so this was fine with him. He opened his first visual and tried to paint a word picture of a patient with gas and bloating. Selling a solution for excess farting, Stu found demeaning, but he described the embarrassment that occurs to patients with gas. A simple solution could be the use of his digestive enzyme Flatulaide.

"Would you prescribe Flatulaide on your next ten bloated patients?"

"Ye... yes."

"Thank you. You won't be disappointed. Remember the dose. One tablet thirty minutes before each meal."

"Yes... yes."

Every breath the wired doctor took was a struggle. Stu opened a second visual.

"I know you are in General Practice, so you must see pregnant women out here. Surely you find many of them constipated. Do you use laxatives or stool softeners in these circumstances?"

He waited in vain for a reply. Doctor Addicus appeared to be straining hard not to explode. He commenced to babble rapidly and incoherently. Stu knew he wasn't listening, so he tried a new tactic. He pulled out a file card and laid it on his desk.

"Here, doctor. I want you to read up on this and please keep it on your desk until you remember its name. That's Soulag XL at bedtime. She will be happy, but her husband will be even happier."

Doctor Addicus didn't respond. Stu was now at the place in his call where he should leave with a reminder of a third product. Company rules did not allow Stu to pitch the third drug on his list, although it was the big seller for hypertension and an extremely technical product. Not yet trained on it, his manager told him to remind people on the way out and hope they didn't ask questions. After laying a third file card on his desk, Stu turned to leave and thanked Doctor Addicus for his time. Passing through the doorway, he turned to look at him one last time.

"Oh, Doctor Addicus, don't forget that Destense has a new dose of 10mg tablets once a day. I left a file card on your desk."

He continued to grip his desk like a twin vice, again unaware of Stu's presence. He was back in his own world of uninterrupted ecstasy or hell. There was no way to know which. Stu stared at him.

What have I done? That was stupid to bother with him. Mary must think I'm an idiot.

He returned sheepishly to the waiting room. Mary was waiting in ambush.

"So, what do you think? Want to make another call next month?"

Stu lowered his head, ashamed of his actions.

"I should be calling an ambulance, not making a sales call. Do we need to call for help?"

Mary's face turned solemn. She pursed her lips and shook her head in revulsion.

"It won't do any good. Everyone in town knows already." She expressed little sympathy as she pointed down the hallway. "The only one who can help him now is the same man that you just left."

Stu's face mirrored hers—a mix of sadness and disgust. With a shrug of his shoulders and a light click of his tongue, he stepped to the outer door.

"I'm sorry. I hope you can get through this yourself all right."

She only nodded, her expression not changing. Her sad eyes said it all.

Stepping out into the dry air of another hot summer morning, Stu unexpectedly realized he was holding his breath. He exhaled as the energy drained from his body. He returned his detail bag to the trunk, opened the door to his car, and got in. The heat inside was blistering. The cheap vinyl seats of his company car were especially hot. Quickly starting the ugly brown Chevy Malibu, he put the air conditioner on full blast and revved the engine to kick start the blast of cool air. Only then did his mental stress let go. His heart pounded rapidly. Respiration increased. He realized that his adrenalin had hit top gear. All he could think of doing was to drive away slowly and wait for his body to calm down.

He drove from the parking lot onto the main drag of the small town. The community was in deep trouble if bad things ever happened requiring emergency medical attention. As he drove, it became evident just how naïve he was. Stu Roy had not led a sheltered life, but he was going through a phase. In his new job he discovered that there was a whole new world out there and perhaps there was more dysfunction in the world than he presumed. He could only imagine that watching a murder would be more traumatizing than seeing someone high on speed. In his first month on the job after his initial training, he was already cynical about these highly educated physicians. While once he may have looked up to them, in a brief time he concluded they were quirky, odd, and down to earth just like normal people. He had quickly removed the doctor-in-the-ivory-tower presumption from his imagination. They were flawed. That horrified him. If he got sick, Stu now feared to go to any of them.

They are all incompetent... and they won't use my drugs. Since I got my training, I know mine are superior.

The problem with this logic was that every one of Stu's competitors thought the same thing about their own product line. Competent doctors had to deal with that reality every time they talked to a drug rep. Some doctors handled it with patience and poise. Others handled it poorly. That was the art of selling Stu had yet to master. Given a few years, the good and seasoned reps knew already that everyone's drugs were adequate solutions for patients. It wasn't always the drug, but the rep that the doctors bought. Doctors bought reliable information, friendship, and a rep's willingness to tell the truth. Often the truth came with the words, "Doctor, I would encourage you not to use my drug in that patient. Here is why." Stu Roy, as he pensively drove out of town, had not yet learned that.

The rest of the day, Stu drove to other small towns in his rural sales area in western Oklahoma. All of the doctors he called on were new to him. They were as curious about him as he was of them. They would ask him what he did before joining Plushaut Uclaf? He was an English teacher in high school for eight years before becoming a pharmaceutical salesman for the French pharmaceutical company. No one ever asked him if he was qualified to talk to them about patients and medicine. That surprised him a great deal. He cringed every time doctors asked him where he previously worked. Others had issues with anything dealing with France. It was still better than the Jewish doctors who told him that it was a good thing his company wasn't headquartered in Germany. Although it was thirty-five years since the end of World War Two, the issues still affected a doctor's prescribing habits.

Stu's day ended at 6:30 in the evening when the last doctor on his list called him back to his office an hour after his last patient left the building. The nurse informed Stu that her doctor liked to finish his charts before seeing drug reps. Finn Trottel told his new hire that this doctor was important to his success and that a long wait was possible. When the doctor finished his charts, it was well past 6:00.

"You're lucky tonight," his nurse said, as she showed him back to the doctor's office. "Yesterday he had three reps here who waited until 7:30 to see him."

Now Stu was driving home. It would be a frustrating drive back to his house because his wife had no idea when he would be back. Offices way out in western Oklahoma paid long distance charges for telephone calls to Oklahoma City. He couldn't just borrow a telephone. It would be at least an hour and a half if he significantly exceeded the 55 mph speed limit. Highway Patrol troopers were unpredictably tolerant. He tried to match his speed to their maximum tolerance. Today it worked. Pulling into his driveway, he had taken an hour and ten minutes along mostly two-lane highways to make it home before 8:00 pm. It was still daylight in the summer, but winter would be an issue that worried him.

He parked his car outside of his garage. He could have kept it inside, but it was a company car—one not of his choosing. Finn told him that reps should worry about the cars they own and to use the company car as much as possible. It was a company perk. And all his gas was paid for—whether for personal use or for work. He stumbled inside to see his anxious wife coming toward him eagerly.

"I thought you were never getting home," she said and planted a welcome kiss firmly on his lips.

Stu and Ana were high school sweethearts. At least that was their joke. Both English teachers, they met after Ana was hired in the summer before Stu's seventh year of teaching. By then he was head of the English department, a rapid rise based upon the frequent attrition of teachers looking for better paying jobs. He had planned to quit, too, after his upcoming year—until Ana, the new teacher, joined his faculty. It was love, and perhaps a bit of lust, at first meeting. The feeling was mutual, which Ana later confirmed. Stu liked her genuine, almost sensuous, smile and her womanly figure. Ana guessed right that he was a college athlete. She noted his graceful movements, indicative of exercise and strong self-confidence. And the way he first looked upon her melted any caution she had left. It was after their first month of classes that they had their first formal date. They went to a movie and were busted by half of the school children there. Within a day the stories were circulating. The English teacher hunk and his attractive petit newly hired teacher were now an item. Monday classes were a source of amusement for both. What they discovered about each other was that they were unflappable.

Stu had for the first time in years been anything but calm in the presence of Doctor Addicus high on speed. Of course, he was never going back there again. He wanted Finn to know. He didn't care if his boss wanted him to continue. He excused himself to use the telephone but turned with an idea to save some time.

"Ana, I'm calling Finn Trottel. You'll want to hear what happened today. It'll save going through the nightmare story twice."

He dialed Finn while Ana joined him. Finn was used to calls from reps in the evening and he was expecting Stu to be calling today. Stu was primed when he picked up the phone.

"You no good bum," Stu said. "You set me up, didn't you?"

"Stu? I set you up? What do you mean?"

"You know what I mean?"

There was a long pause. Finn cleared his throat.

"*You called on Doctor Addicus today, didn't you?*"

"You're damn right I called on Doctor Addicus. I should drive over to your house and work you over, you piece of... well never mind."

Finn replied with laughter that quickly grew louder and more uncontrolled. Irritated, Stu took the phone from his ear and held it toward Ana. Her reaction at first was shock, but Finn's laughter was contagious, and Ana found herself joining in. He stared at his wife, trying to look stern but couldn't suppress his smile. He put the phone back to his ear to shout something, but the words came out as laughter. With three people laughing now, he knew the joke was on him.

"I guess the joke's on the new guy, you dirty rat!"

He slammed the telephone down onto its cradle. Stu and Ana laughed their way back to the kitchen for a late, cold dinner and a long explanation.

Chapter Two

It wasn't long before Stu went to his first division meeting where he would meet the other Plushaut Uclaf sales reps under the management of Finn Trottel. Finn scheduled his three-day meeting in a plush hotel in Oklahoma City with single rooms for each of his ten men. It was a new policy. Other divisions had started hiring women, which made it awkward to save money by having two reps share a room. The hotel lay close to both the airport and Interstate 40, which allowed those from Tulsa and Wichita a quick exit for home on Friday afternoon. All reps had to stay at the hotel overnight, even those who lived locally. Stu soon learned why.

It was a late Tuesday afternoon when he drove into the hotel parking lot and unloaded his suitcase and hanging bag containing an additional suit, white shirt, and tie. Suits or sport coats were mandatory at these meetings. After all, Finn reminded them, they were professionals. Stu was nervous, uncertain how to conduct himself. He was more accustomed to locker room antics and jargon than a stuffed-shirt division meeting. He was on his best behavior to make a good impression.

It was another hot summer day. He had worked all day, always suitably attired. A few of the clinics encouraged him to remove his coat, but he refused. He told them all that it would be disrespectful to their doctor. One doctor that day told him that he wouldn't see him until he removed his coat and tie. Stu was learning fast.

The group scheduled a casual reception in Finn's extra-large hotel suite, to convene at 5:30 p.m. Stu wanted to ensure he wasn't late by arriving early, but without leaving the impression that he quit work early. Another car drove up that looked suspiciously like his own company car, except the car's paint scheme was more to his liking. A middle-aged man stepped cautiously from the car. Tieless and holding his sport coat in his hand, he opened his trunk, unzipped a suitcase, and carelessly stuffed his coat inside. After zipping the bag again, he pulled it out of his trunk. He turned to face Stu.

"Are you the new guy?" The man was tall and overweight with a heat reddened face, five o'clock shadow, and a wide grin. "That looks a lot like Jon Baskin's car. He was a great guy, God rest his soul."

Stu stepped over to him, hoping to make a good impression. He already knew he was driving a dead man's company car. He extended his hand in greeting.

"You guessed right. I guess I'm the rookie now. I'm Stu Roy."

"Jim Tomey... or Jimmy. Take your pick." He pulled a fine linen handkerchief out of his pocket and wiped the sweat from his brow and the back of his neck. Sweat clung to the fringe of hair below his bald head. "You better get inside. It's blistering hot in this parking lot. Grab your bags and follow me. I'll get you started inside."

"That would be great. Thanks."

Stu followed Jimmy into the Hilton lobby where he waved to several other members of the division milling about. They were all early and dressed casually, which Stu concluded meant that Jimmy and he were the only reps who had put in a full day of work. Stu started to walk up to one, but Jimmy intervened.

"I'd check in first and get your bags up to your room. Take your coat and tie off, then meet us in Finn's room... three eleven. I'll introduce you." He hailed the four early birds and asked them to pay attention. "Okay, boys. We've got fresh meat for the grinder here. Meet Stu Roy."

"I'll be with you shortly, gentlemen," Stu replied and waved a hurried hand their way.

After checking in at the front desk, he carried his bags up to his room on the second floor. The room was well appointed—at least according to his standards. His hotel experiences were limited. He could not easily make a comparison. One thing he liked was that he didn't have to pay for it. Plushaut Uclaf was picking up the tab for room, meals, and entertainment.

Stu entered Finn Trottel's suite and took his first glimpse of corporate life at leisure. Atop the wet bar were two large cardboard boxes filled with more booze than Stu had ever seen outside of a liquor store.

"Holy cow," he said quietly.

It was 5:30 p.m. Two men, reclining on the only sofa, were well on their way to an evening nap. Jimmy Tomey, talking with two others, encouraged Stu to join them.

"Wait until tomorrow to meet these other two boozers," he said laughing. Stu could see why.

Stu stuck out a hand in greeting to a rep who sported a heavy black beard and mustache. The man waved his hands in animated gestures. Everyone behind him gave him space. Oblivious of the swirling danger he posed, his loud words accompanied each punch of an arm. Stu introduced himself at his peril.

"You're Stu Roy," he said and offered a wide swing of his hand to grip Stu's. "Fred McAnich."

"Charlie Ketter," said the next man in introduction. He was near Stu's height of just under six feet with a muscular build and a bone crushing handshake.

"Charlie was a college wrestler," Jimmy said. "His glory days passed fifteen years ago, but he can still crush your hand."

Charlie's quiet voice reminded Stu of a cat about to pounce. He guessed correctly.

"Charlie's always one of the two top salesmen in our whole division," Fred said in an arm sweeping gesture at the word *whole*.

Charlie turned to Stu. "Meet my sidekick, Lance Layton."

After they shook hands, Stu had a chance to chat with the group of now five. The two sidekicks, Charlie and Lance, were opposite personalities and statures. While Charlie was soft-spoken with the compact muscles of a wrestler, Lance was six inches taller and so slender that his clothes barely fit his rack of bones. His belt was cinched tight to hold his pants on, while his pants cuffs barely covered his socks. Lance's bass voice made up for any other deficiencies.

"Who's that over there?" Stu asked the group, nodding toward a mousy introvert who appeared unhappy to talk to anyone.

"That's Blair Dill," Lance replied. "He keeps his distance from everyone else, which suits all of us."

Stu didn't ask any more about it. Blair would be one to watch over the next couple of days. On the other hand, he was more curious about the two men on the sofa.

"Who are those two bunk buddies?" he asked the group, pointing his finger at them.

"You mean Dan and Cress, our two sleeping beauties?" Fred said in a circus-like hand gesture. The others muted their chuckles. Jimmy spoke for the rest.

"That's pretty typical behavior at every meeting. Dan Anders has a drinking problem. He's married but we've never seen his wife. I went to his house once. It was devoid of furniture, except for one sofa and a bed. Dan expends all their money on booze and women."

Charlie Ketter added in his quieter voice, "Dan's sidekick, passed out next to him, is Cress Caston. He's always tagging along with Dan… a loner with a friend. Together, they'll soon sober up and try to lure you into membership in their alcoholic club."

"I think I'll be okay," Stu replied. Glancing across the room, he spied his boss, Finn Trottel talking to an older more serious man. Neither looked happy.

"Don't go over there," Charlie said. He added a note of caution. "Don't get mixed into that conversation. Did you meet Mike Austin? He just walked in."

"No, but I'll go say hi. Thanks for all the info from you guys."

"He's our steady-as-you-go rep," Charlie said, continuing to keep Stu informed. "Nothing fancy. While most of us are racehorses, he's a powerful plow horse—and imperturbable. He's low key and persistent. Of all the reps, the doctors like him the best and trust him the most."

Stu found it easy to approach people now. The mix of reps' personalities was educational. His approach to Mike Austin was a delight. He proved to be cheerful and friendly. Stu liked him from the first moment they met. Glancing again at the older man talking to his manager, Stu noted that Mike was the exact opposite of him.

"The man you're looking at is our only supersalesman," Mike said. "He will waste no time with you. That's Bill Dooley, the old man of our district. He's in his mid-forties, humorless, and still wearing polyester leisure suits. He's an obnoxious braggart who gets along with no one."

"What does Finn say about him?"

"He considers Dooley unmanageable. He is also consistently the most successful salesman, despite nearly every doctor complaining about him. He works unimaginable hours, wears out a wife every five years, and gripes constantly about wife number five. Everyone wonders where he finds these women. Nobody else can stand to be with him more than five minutes at a time."

Stu looked around. Everyone but mousey Blair Dill and unmanageable Bill Dooley were drinking and laughing. *What am I in for? Best I be careful.* Boldly walking past the yacking duo of Trottel and Dooley, Stu paused at the cornucopia of liquor and mixed himself a drink.

At 7:00 a.m. the next morning, as the reps prepared for the first full day of their meeting, Finn Trottel was in his hotel room on the phone with his boss, Regional Manager Abbott Wahl. Wahl was a no-nonsense pharmaceutical veteran of the old school. Hired in the late 1950s, he weathered many changes in his career and embraced changes in the industry with relish. He was not a manager who believed in top-down leadership. He let his division managers make decisions not allowed in other regions. Well-liked by everyone, he had a knack for commanding respect forged from his early experience as an officer in the U.S. Air Force. Quick to assess a situation, he wasted little time in making decisions or countering actions of his managers. He allowed his people to learn by their mistakes and rarely had to bail them out of trouble. There were actions he questioned, but his goal was always the bottom line. His expectations were basic.

"If it's not illegal, unethical, or immoral, then I am fine in doing it your way... unless it doesn't produce results."

Finn Trottel was fine with his reps' actions—unless it didn't produce results. He never mentioned any other stipulation. His regional manager did have one concern that morning.

"*I don't understand why you want to send money back to me.*"

"I want to show you and the other DMs that I can get maximum production out of my reps without that much incentive. I'm that good as a division manager."

"*I'll just give it to the other DMs. I'm not going to send it back to the company. They don't deserve it.*"

"Well neither do my reps."

"*Have they not performed well?*" Wahl shuffled through papers on his office desk until he found the latest sales figures for all the sixty salesmen and six division managers in his region. "*It looks like your men are doing quite well. Some top numbers among your group.*"

"Look at my ranking. Am I number one?"

Wahl studied the numbers briefly. "*Almost, Finn. Albuquerque beat Oklahoma City by... ooh, it was close. But you are in second. That's decent enough.*"

"If I can't get the biggest raise then they won't either."

"*You did have the largest sales volume. It's just that the Albuquerque division had a much larger percentage of growth. That's what the bigwigs weigh as of primary sales importance... growth.*"

"You take the money back. Give it to the other boys and I'll show you that I can finish the year number one again."

Abbott Wahl looked at the numbers again and shook his head in equal doses of frustration and resignation. This was not the only year Finn had tried this cut in his allotted salary increases. His boss grew increasingly weary after so many years of this behavior.

"*Okay, Finn. Go motivate them. No doubt the other DMs appreciate your generosity.*"

There was never a problem with this secret getting out to the reps. Every division manager who received this extra infusion of cash remained a silent conspirator. Who wanted to risk killing this goose that was laying their golden eggs?

After hanging up the phone, Finn Trottel gathered up his meeting packet and went downstairs to announce the interim salary increases his reps were getting in an era of double-digit inflation.

STU TIGHTENED HIS tie. He wore the same suit he interviewed in weeks before. Early in high school sports he learned to never act subservient to anyone in his peer group. He assumed he deserved to be in this group of men and picked a seat at the conference table accordingly. The seasoned reps like Jimmy and Bill were at the far end of the long table from their manager. The two drinking buddies, Dan and Cress, took chairs beside each other. Mousy Blair Dill chose the seat up front and to the right of where Finn Trottel would be. Others were laughing. Blair's kissing up to the boss like this happened at every meeting. Of the few seats left, Stu picked the seat farthest from the boss and across from the two drinking buddies. Fortunately, as it turned out, Mike Austin sat between him and obnoxious Bill Dooley. Bill was already whining about being out of the field for another division meeting. For everyone else, these division meetings were a delicious and sometimes raucous break from the routine grind.

When the rest of the men found seats, and the boss took his seat, the loud voices and impish laughter continued for another five minutes, until the clock pointed to eight o'clock sharp. Finn called the meeting to order with a ballpoint pen clink of his water glass. Cress held his head like a man with an acute hangover while laughing in one final interruption. Only Dan found him funny.

"Good morning, Land Runners!" Finn Trottel said. Stu was surprised to learn his division had a team name. "I want to welcome all of you to the third meeting of the year. We're doing well this year, but we still need to get ahead of those pretenders in Albuquerque. We also have a new Land Runner in our midst, Stu Roy."

The group broke into spontaneous applause, which made Stu feel much better. He relaxed a little more.

"Stu, I know you met everyone last night, but here's your chance to correct the record. Tell us a little bit about yourself, so we can get to know you better."

Stu stood up. A few at the table looked surprised. It was apparent that standing to address the men was not routinely done. He didn't care. He needed to exercise some dominant behavior from the beginning. He wanted the group to know he would be a contender. Perhaps he was a bit too cocky.

"My name is Stuart Roy, but I go by Stu. Only my mother calls me Stuart. I graduated from high school with a football scholarship to a small college in Kansas. I decided to go to Kansas State instead. I tried out as a walk-on, but you guys need to know. College ball is not like high school. I stepped away from football and I have no regrets. I got a degree from Kansas State in English and my teaching certificate and a master's degree at Central State College in Edmond, Oklahoma. I was born in Oklahoma City where I taught high school English for eight years. I actually hired my future wife, Ana, as an English teacher in my seventh year."

Cress Caston interrupted. "I thought English teachers are all homosexuals."

Stu didn't miss a beat. "Not only is that not true, but English teachers make the hottest wives and the horniest women."

That laid to rest the calculated plans of Cress, so Stu continued.

"I tried to avoid coaching but got tapped as an assistant football coach. In the eight years I taught and coached, we kicked some serious butt on the football field. So far, we have no little ball players to coach at our house, but Ana and I have a hell of a good time trying."

Stu liked how this introduction was going. He decided he had said enough. He finished with a trite, but necessary, close.

"Teaching doesn't pay as well as pharmaceutical sales. This gives us a chance to see Ana quit teaching as soon as we can make the end zone. I'm glad to be here with you guys."

Stu sat down. He was concerned if he had made the right impression. He never knew for sure when someone like Cress interrupted him. He worried his end zone closing was too corny. He knew it was, but he needn't have worried. He got a good response when he sat down from the people he hoped to impress. Things were going well for Stu.

Finn continued the meeting by reviewing the agenda for the next three days.

"Today we'll cover the new approach we want to take with Destense 10mg tablets. Mainly, we want to de-emphasize the 20mg dose. We'll cover that this morning, have lunch, and then practice roleplays until everyone has given a practice pitch to the group."

While muted groans arose and quietly ebbed among the men, Stu's heart began to race. This was his first meeting. He was not trained on Destense 10mg tablets. Would he be called on?

"Stu, as the new guy, I want you to pay attention to our roleplays. If you feel ready, I'd like you to pitch Destense 10mg to us also."

"I'll be ready. Just don't expect any miracles."

Bill Dooley began to laugh. "Heh! This should be just what we want to end the day. At least it will be entertaining... or cringe worthy. Just don't ruin my dinner, okay?"

No one spoke as Stu absorbed the putdown. "Why don't you play doctor when I give my pitch?"

This was in-your-face and the whole room knew it. Unknown to Stu, it would become the most memorable quote the Land Runners would bring up in Stu's first year on the job. The laughter among the reps indicated anticipation. Stu was either an idiot, fearless, or both.

Finn began to laugh at the thought. He liked the idea. It was brash of Stu to challenge someone so soon. Finn knew Stu had picked the worst rep in his group to challenge.

"I might like that," Finn said. "Are you sure you want to make it that tough on yourself so soon?"

"It sounds entertaining," Stu replied. "I can end the day like he said he wanted... sorry, but I forgot your name already."

When Finn began the meeting in earnest, Mike Austin leaned over to his ear and whispered.

"We'll talk at lunch, but you need me to help you with a good practice pitch before you go against Dooley. If he can, he'll put you down by making you look like a fool. I'd like to see you turn the tables on him."

"How do I do that?"

"First off, tell him you are following up on your previous call. That way he can't throw you in a direction you're not trained on, yet. Control the call from the outset. We'll talk more after lunch."

Stu nodded in the affirmative. The two looked up at the same time, realizing that Finn had stopped talking.

"You two yahoos through talking now... or do you want to conduct a private meeting with each other?"

Mike spoke first. "We're through. Sorry."

"Okay, then. Let's start over from the beginning."

The groan from Bill Dooley was intentionally audible.

The meeting droned on. For all reps except for Stu, this was a rehash of the same topics they covered at each meeting. Wearing a suit and tie made a boring meeting almost intolerable. Finally, Finn had them take out the workbooks they were to have studied before the meeting. None of the reps had read up beforehand. It didn't matter. The manager would go through the booklet in minute detail, so there was never a real need to study. Pharmaceutical industry training did not include pop quizzes.

Finn covered the reasons for a smaller dose of Destense. This relatively new drug was indicated for high blood pressure, congestive heart failure, and several obscure diseases that only a cardiologist would understand. An *indication* was a legal term for the Food and Drug Administration's approved uses of a drug. All other uses for Destense were called *off label*. This novel and innovative new weapon to control high blood pressure had taken seven years and five hundred million dollars of research and development before it came to market. In its first year of promotion, the medical world considered it so important, and so potent, that the widely respected and influential experts in cardiology were advocating it only be used by board certified heart doctors. There would never be a law to that effect, but general practitioners and family doctors became reluctant to use it. Finn explained that they would promote the new lower dose of Destense 10mg to that group of physicians. He looked to the far end of the table at Jimmy Tomey.

"Jimmy, you called on some cardiologists for me to hear their opinion of the lower dose. What did they tell you?"

Jimmy laughed. "They all told me the same thing. The new 10mg tablet is worthless. Instead, they said that we should have introduced a bigger dose. Most reminded me that the drug was too complicated to put in the hands of non-specialists."

"And what did they say about the value of a lower dose for family doctors?"

"They said it wouldn't work."

"Did they express any safety concerns at a 10mg dose?"

"None."

Stu saw his chance to make an obvious point before the others beat him to it.

"What we can say then," Stu said, putting his intended point to Jimmy's findings, "is that Destense 10mg is a safe dose… and with proven efficacy according to the FDA."

By the expression on many of the reps in the room, this was a bold move for a rookie. Stu feared he made his comments too soon for his standing. Finn looked at him with surprise on his face. Then he smiled.

"Stu here has nailed it. It's really simple. Cardiologists say it's safe and we know it works. Don't make it complicated."

"I guess saying 'it works' sounds better," Stu said. "'Proven efficacy according to the FDA' sounds too pretentious even for the new guy."

"And you'll bore the hell out of my doctors." It was superstar Bill Dooley speaking for the first time.

"I think Stu is set to kick your ass before the year is up." Lance replied.

"It might be fun to kick some ass," Stu said, laughing as he looked over at the superstar. "There's a first time for everything."

The group caught the spirit of Stu's self-effacing comment. After a pause, laughter took hold and Stu knew he had won some points.

That was the marketing plan for the new dose—to target Destense 10mg tablets to primary care physicians. The point could have stopped any need for more discussions, but Finn was not finished. The topic continued for another hour. It seemed longer to Stu. For Bill Dooley, who continued his on again off again groaning campaign until lunch, it seemed days.

Chapter Three

Lunch was lavish. If the Land Runners expected to stay slim, this was not the path to take. With all meals paid for by Plushaut Uclaf, there was no way to remain at a steady weight. When Stu looked around at the other men, he immediately spotted the correlation between tenure in the company and the degree of portliness. There was an unspoken pressure to eat like a farmhand at harvest time, although no one there would be burning enough calories at this meeting to exceed the calories in their salads, much less the full lunch buffet.

Stu sat between Charlie the wrestler and Mike, his lifeline for his afternoon practice sales pitch. Both men were close to Stu's age and size. Stu turned to Charlie.

"You didn't put much on your plate." He pointed to Jimmy at the next table of four. "Are you going to let them get ahead of you?"

"No way. They are so far ahead, Mike and I could never catch them. It's an old habit from my days of pulling weight for wrestling."

"This lunch is dangerous," Stu replied. "I've never seen anything like this since my training table days at K-State."

"You should wrestle. You hear about us having to lose weight all the time? Not true. We burned so many calories in training, we had to eat just to keep our weight up."

Mike cut in. "You jocks talk about training tables. I had a mother who insisted that I eat until I puked. She was obsessed with feeding me and my sister. I got to college and vowed to lose weight."

"That's not the usual story," Stu said. "So, you didn't gain the freshman fifteen?"

"Lost about twenty-five in my first semester," Mike said. "Frugal eating and miles of walking on campus to get to classes did it."

"What school?"

"Same as Charlie here, Oklahoma State."

Stu turned to Charlie. "You wrestle at OSU?"

"Oh, hell no! I was good, but not that good. Turns out the guy I would have been bumping off the lineup was national champ two years in a row. I didn't even try out. I studied instead."

The three concentrated on their lunches and ended earlier than the portly senior members. Still relatively young men, they finished soon because they ate at the speed of a ranch hand, just not in the same volume. The extra time gave the three a chance to walk outside and talk. All three took their suit coats off. The hazy blue skies were filled with benign puffy cumulus clouds which lent a feeling of a vast three dimensions in space. The sun burned the sidewalks and caused the three men to seek shade under a sheltered overhang.

"Let me tell you about Bill Dooley," Mike said. "He's an ass. Nobody likes him, but he has the best work ethic of any rep in the business. He told us one day that his only hobby is work."

"So, what do I do?"

"What were you thinking when you asked him to be the doctor?"

"Oh, I guess I wanted to shut him up. Call his bluff."

"He's a jerk. He'll try to embarrass you," Charlie said.

"So, tell me what he's really like. What embarrasses him? What sets him off? What college degree does he have?"

Mike said, "Oddly enough, he taught English in junior high."

"He has a wife who I think hates him," said Charlie.

"Mention his ex-wives. Charlie, don't you think that would tick him off?"
"But this is a sales call with a fake doctor. What tricks will he use on me?"
"He'll try to get technical on you." Charlie nodded in agreement.

"You guys might not know, but I actually read the meeting booklet cover to cover. And I got through my two-week training at the top of the class. There were twelve of us. I can do the technical side with ease, but my sales skills are weak."

Charlie moved closer to his ear. "Don't let him go until he agrees to write Destense 10mg, then make him write it on a script pad. That will tick him off. The rule is to ask for the business three times before giving up. Don't stop there. Wear him down. Close for the sale by nagging him until he says 'yes' just to make you go away. That's the way he does it."

THE AFTERNOON WAS oppressively boring for all the reps. Stu wasn't about to rock the boat, but from his teaching experience, he knew Finn's approach was a loser. It needed some pizzaz. Bill Dooley closed his eyes and fell asleep in his chair. Finn was all too happy to let him remain that way.

Finn was lecturing on medical data a competitor might use to chip away at the reputation of Destense. Like all drugs, it had side effects. The file card left on every call listed contraindications, warnings, precautions, and adverse effects. Some were valid. Others were not. If a drug under development had patients that caught head colds in the study, those must be listed as a possible side effect of the drug. Silly side effects often became a salesman's hammer.

All of this was new to Stu, but it reminded him of his own students, their eyes looking down and hoping they wouldn't be called.

Finn looked up from his notes. "Lance, read us the list of Destense side effects."

And so, it droned on. Stu was already distracted enough, waiting to face his first test with Bill Dooley. In marketing, anything found in a file card could be a hammer. Stu knew instinctively that Dooley would use that tactic to turn his first practice sales call into a shambles.

During a fifteen-minute break, Stu spotted one of his old high school students in the hotel's lobby as she walked over to greet him. The girl he remembered was now a grown woman. But she was memorable to Stu because she also starred for many years in the school's annual musicals.

"Mister Roy!" Bright, talented, and unafraid, she stood excitedly next to him with her husband. "You may not remember me, but you were always a favorite teacher of mine... Jean Clayton... I mean Stack."

"Oh, I remember you, sure. The star of the show." He looked at the man beside her. "Is this your husband?"

"Oh, Steve, meet my favorite English teacher, Mister Roy."

"I'm just Stu now, Jean. Good to see you both."

Jean turned to her husband to explain. "Mister Roy is the teacher who helped me get into the program at OCU."

Steve was genuinely surprised and happy to meet Stu. Jean's time at Oklahoma City University put her on the fast track for landing a lucrative job as a vocalist and a musician in Nashville.

"I found it easy to recommend you for that program. I hope you've done well."

"Oh, yes, she has," Steve said. "She tells me all the time that she wishes she could give some payback to the people who made a difference. That's why I'm happy we met. She has mentioned you before."

"I'm flattered, but I always knew she would be successful."

"I still owe you, Mister Roy."

A synapse in Stu's brain fired up, which caused him to look at the two of them with a big grin. "Do you have an hour to spare?"

With a puzzled look, Jean nodded her head. With that Stu formed a plan for his practice sales call.

Mike and Charlie had stepped aside when Stu's student came up. They were not privy to the conversation, but one phrase Stu spoke to the couple did catch their attention.

"...at my nod leave quietly."

As Mike and Charlie headed back to the meeting room, Stu in turn asked the two men for a favor.

"FINN, I WOULD like to go first." Bill Dooley looked up from his daydream to respond. Stu was right. It caught the braggart off guard.

"I'm not ready!"

Finn, too, was caught off guard. "Are you sure? I want to hear a few more pitches before I hear yours."

"I'm ready, Dooley." Stu turned to his boss. "Finn, trust me. You want me to go first."

"Okay, but first we need to cover something. It should take about ten minutes."

While Finn droned on for what seemed over an hour, but was closer to his promised ten minutes, Jean and her husband stood outside the meeting room door and waited. Stu remembered Jean Clayton as a ham when it came to stage productions. She had an uncanny knack, even at sixteen, of making her character seem lifelike.

Finn finished as promised. In another hour, this cynical group of sales reps would forget what he said.

"Okay, Stu. You're up." Mike and Charlie glanced at each other in puzzled anticipation. They had no clue as to Stu's plans. They hoped to be impressed if his gutsy move amused them at Bill Dooley's expense.

"I'm ready," Stu replied. "Are you ready and willing, Doctor Dooley?"

"Yeah, I'm ready, but I'm a busy man. I have about thirty seconds for you today."

They each pulled a chair away from the meeting table to the middle of the floor and sat down facing each other. Bill immediately slouched in his chair in a posture of disinterest. Stu held onto a letter-sized four-page visual but kept it in his lap.

"If you weren't a busy man, why would I want to call on you?" He paused, leading Bill to think he was dumb struck. In truth, Stu was not nervous at all, which surprised even him. "What patients are making you busy today?"

"You have fifteen seconds."

"Well, we better do some business then. Last month you challenged me to prove the efficacy claims for our new 10mg dose of Destense for your essential hypertension patients."

"I did not." Stu had learned in his sales training to treat all of a doctor's objections as questions. After he thought it through, it made sense. An objection is negative, but a question is a positive, so always look forward to an objection—just treat it exactly like it was a question.

"You forgot, Doctor Dooley, but I did not. I hear that you get referrals from a cardiologist I called on... Doctor Downing."

"He's a crock."

"Well, he told me that you shouldn't be qualified to use Destense in any dose... not just you, but any family practitioner."

"You're out of time."

"So, you agree with Doctor Downing?"

There was a long pause. Old Bill would have to answer in a way to keep up his bluster.

"Hell no!"

"Thus, the reason why I am back to answer your question from last month. Destense 10mg according to Doctor Banks, et al in *Annals of Internal Medicine* found that in one thousand two hundred thirty-eight patients with mild to moderate essential hypertension...."

"What's the design of this study?" Bill knew the answer. So did Stu.

"It was a double-blind crossover placebo-controlled study." Stu had to be careful with the wording. He often joked that it was a *doubly-blind, cross-eyed study*.

"What does that mean?" Stu ignored the question because he knew it was meant to divert him to another subject. For the first time, Stu held up his visual, opened to the Madison Avenue designed sales figures to show him the results of the Banks study.

"It means that the FDA used this data to determine the efficacy of Destense 10mg." He pulled a pen out of his shirt pocket and pointed to some fine print at the bottom. "You can see the p-value of less than 0.01 is five times more valid than what is considered statistically significant. And as you know, every study to be truly valid must have a p-value less than or equal to 0.05. These values are incredibly significant. Have I convinced you to reconsider?"

"No. I want to see the paper."

"Sure, I have it right here. Let's go over it."

"I told you you're out of time."

"Okay, I will leave it with you to read, but I'm not leaving until you agree I have proven the drug meets your requirements."

"No."

"So, I should go back to your cardiologist buddy, Doctor Downing, and tell him you agree with him?"

"He doesn't know diddly squat. Don't listen to him."

"I won't. I agree you are a capable doctor, but I want to hear you say you will prescribe 10mg Destense."

Stubborn Bill Dooley was never going to give him the satisfaction as Stu surmised. He turned to Mike and Charlie.

"Guys, I hear a knock on the door. Could you open it please?"

Mike jumped up on cue, opened the door, and Jean Clayton Stack, the rescue angel, stepped inside. She immediately high-tailed it over to imaginary Doctor Dooley.

"Honey, I overheard what you said to this nice gentleman. I don't think you treated him right. You should be ashamed of yourself. We've talked about this before."

With her left hand on Bill's shoulder, she looked over at Stu and extended her hand.

"Hi. I'm Doctor Dooley's wife. I'm Jean."

"Pleased to meet you, Jean. Your husband is one of the most important doctors I call on. You must be very proud of him. He's a really nice guy."

They both looked at the imaginary Doctor Dooley and waited. Laughter behind her had to die down before they could continue.

"I don't know what you want me to say."

"Tell him you'll write that prescription, for goodness sakes." Jean then bent and gave him a kiss on his shiny bald head. "Would you do it for me, Honey?"

Bill Dooley sat silent shaking his head, then looked up alternately at her and then at me. "I'll do it for you, Sweetie, but not for him."

Jean looked up. Stu mouthed a thank you with a nod of his head for a good-bye.

"Thank you, Honey. You're a sweetie. I'm going shopping now. Bye-bye!"

Jean turned and scampered out of the meeting room to the cheers and laughter of nine of the ten other men in the room. When she closed the door behind her, Finn stood up to restore order.

"What... was... that?" Bill said, looking all around him.

"That was awesome!" Jimmy Tomey said to more laughter and clapping.

Finn looked toward Stu and Bill, still sitting facing each other. "One hell of a sales pitch, Stu. You'll do just fine as our rookie, won't he Doctor Dooley?"

Bill said nothing for a moment. He was ticked off, mad that he had failed to destroy the new guy, and embarrassed to hear the laughter that was at his expense. He hated it, but he admitted to himself that Stu impressed him.

"You're all right, kid," Bill replied, devoid of emotion in voice or expression. "I gotta hand it to you. You got me... and that's not easy to do."

Chapter Four

On his first day in the field in 1980, Stu met his first detail man from another company outside of Doctor Schmidt's office. Chad Choteau was short and shaped like a bulldog. Stu's image of a drug rep did not match Chad's appearance. His shirt collar choked him with the aid of an unfashionably wide tie. His polyester light tan suit showed evident wear. He wore white leather shoes that Stu once wanted but was grateful he never bought. Chad stood in the clinic parking lot by his company car and waved at Stu.

"You must be new. Are you a drug rep?"

Stu was not yet comfortable with the protocol for dealing with other company detail men. Nonetheless, he assumed this was his way to learn.

"Hi. You must be one, also." Stu extended his hand. Chad's grip was not limp, but it was relaxed and noncommittal. Unlike someone trying to prove a point, Chad did not do bone crushing handshakes.

"I'm Chad Choteau with Burroughs Wellcome." Stu was confused by his subdued voice. Hearing the word *welcome* put Stu instantly on guard. Chad handed him his business card. Again, Stu read Wellcome. He was remembering a man who once gave him a card saying he was deaf and would welcome a handout of money. Stu looked critically at the card, too long for comfort.

"Who do you work for?" asked Chad.

Still confused, Stu answered his question. "I work for Plushaut Uclaf selling pharmaceuticals."

"Oh, you're Jon Baskin's replacement."

Stu made the connection and lightened up. "Yes, I took Jon's place."

"You have any business cards yet?"

"Oh... sure." He pulled a card out of his inside coat pocket and handed it to Chad, who studied it quickly.

"Stuart Roy?"

"Call me Stu."

"I miss seeing Jon. He was a good friend and a tough competitor. You couldn't find a better salesman."

"I've already found that out. Every doctor and nurse is telling me something great about him. I almost think he's my toughest competition."

Chad laughed at Stu. "You'll hear that for a while, but I bet it will die down. He was just so good at making the doctors write his crap, instead of my crap... come to think of it, you've got some big shoes to fill."

"Did he have a lot of clever expressions?"

"The doctors still quote him to me, if that's what you mean."

Stu laughed at this comment. Jon Baskin's notes were filled with clever one-liners.

"Have you seen Doctor Schmidt before?" Chad asked.

"No, first time. Any advice?"

"You may be too late for today. He likes to see his reps before he goes to lunch."

"Baskin's notes indicate he's quite disagreeable. He calls him Doctor Schmuck."

"That's Schmidt, all right." Chad was aware that a new drug rep successfully calling on this doctor would be a morale booster. "Here's a tip for you. He'll disagree with everything you bring up. Ignore what he says and make your point anyway."

"That works?"

"Works for me. It worked for Jon."

"Thanks, Chad, it's nice to meet you. I appreciate the info."

"Any time, Stu. I'm sure we'll meet again."

They parted company, allowing Stu to hurry in before lunchtime ruined his chances. He gave a card to the young receptionist along with an abundance of notepads and pens. She directed him to sit and wait. "Doctor Schmidt will be with you shortly."

That was a good sign. He jumped the first and most important hurdle—the gatekeeper. The office décor, as he later jotted down in his notes, was *Apocalyptic Jesus*. A King James Bible rested on each end table in his waiting room. Four patients waited with him—the Bibles untouched. The Book of Revelation was a prominent theme in the framed pictures and documents adorning the walls. Prints of a classic depiction of man's descent into Hell sent Stu into gloom. Overhead speakers played church hymns by organ, choir, and orchestra. Stu speculated how many antidepressants Doctor Schmuck prescribed. *Ten minutes more of this and I'll be asking for some.*

When Stu finally got back to the doctor's office, he sat in a seat facing the desk and waited for another fifteen minutes. Doctor Schmidt's office was slightly more subtle than his waiting room. The office had a large picture on the wall to his right of Saint Paul writing a letter while in a Roman prison. There were more Bibles and a few Christian art pieces scattered about. New Testament verses hung in frames behind the desk. Wanting to start on a positive note, Stu planned to offer some favorable comments concerning his office.

When Doctor Schmidt did walk in, he held Stu's card in his hand.

"Where's Jon Baskin?" He looked angrily at Stu. Stu quickly stood up to greet the man.

"I'm sorry to report that Jon passed away a few months ago."

"Oh…? So, what do you have?"

"I see you have a wonderful picture of Saint Paul. I have always admired his life and his words."

To Stu's shock, Doctor Schmidt stepped forward and got in his face. "Well, I take offense to that! I admire my Lord and Savior, Jesus Christ!"

The teacher in him came out. He was used to the unexpected outbursts with teenagers. He always had a good response to moderate their fragile emotions. He quickly had a response before the doctor could get another breath to continue.

"I agree with you. Jesus Christ is my Lord and Savior, but don't you admire Paul's story of redemption? He was converted by God himself on the road. I see myself in that story."

Doctor Schmidt muttered a few incoherent syllables, perhaps speaking in tongues, and sat down behind his desk.

"What do you have?"

The outburst intimidated Stu to where he raced through his product line. He remembered that Finn told him to always ask for the business before he left. "Closing the sale is the reason we pay you. Always ask the doctor to prescribe our drugs by brand name."

Stu stood up when the doctor did. "Thank you for your time. Doctor Schmidt, can I count on you to prescribe Destense, Soulag XL, and Flatulaide this week?"

Doctor Schmidt stared at him with penetrating eyes. "Son, are you born again… have you truly met Jesus Christ in spirit?"

"Yes, sir. I have accepted Jesus as my Savior."

"Are you prepared for His coming today?"

"Of course."

"God tells us in Revelation that Christ is coming back."

"Yes, sir."

"If you pay attention to the sin around us now, you know that the day of judgement is near."

"I was hoping we had more time to save a few more souls here on earth before that day comes."

"The end is near. The rapture is coming… and you want me to prescribe your drugs?"

"Yes, sir. I would appreciate it."

"Why would I do that? It seems pointless."

By now Stu wanted out of the office at the risk of his career. He was in a no-win situation. He thought again about Finn's directives for closing for the sale. "Always ask for the prescription three times before you give up." Stu stepped toward the doctor, until he reciprocated Schmidt's in-your-face move. He calmly asked the doctor one last question.

"Doctor Schmidt, until the rapture comes, will you prescribe Destense, Soulag XL, and Flatulaide?"

Chapter Five

Stu calculated that in his normal day of work, walking covered several miles and helped him keep his weight at a reasonable measure. That was fortunate because his company generously paid for his lunch. They also allowed sales reps to use their company cars as family cars, including paying for gas. The forty dollars he paid each month for that privilege was a bargain worth thousands. Ana loved it, too, because she could drive the car any time for any reason. And that was the perk that proved a problem on Monday mornings when Stu's first call was often a gasoline station.

For the next four months the weather became cold, which presented a new challenge. Stu discovered that on a typical day, he would get in and out of his car at least a hundred times a day. He would open his trunk an equal number. At first his left hip and knee were sore from the repetitive motion of entering or exiting his vehicle. Then he found his left shoulder hurting from opening and closing his trunk lid repeatedly. He learned that when his hands got cold, his fingers began to crack.

On one winter work-with, Finn gave him several other suggestions to ponder.

"Never use a finger to point out something. Fingers are dirty. Use a pen instead.

"Plan ahead by quickly learning where all the bathrooms are in your territory.

"If your doctor smokes, your call will end when he puts out his cigarette.

"Treat the receptionist and everyone in the office like you would their doctor.

"You can tell the personality of the doctor often by the personality of the receptionist.

"Always carry something in your hand to give them at the time you leave a business card.

"Learn everyone's name and write it down.

"Expect two percent of doctors and drug reps to be scoundrels.

"For the first two years, expect to be sick a lot.

"If you are going to cheat on expenses, make it for fifty thousand dollars because five dollars will get you fired just as fast.

"'I don't know' is an acceptable answer.

"If you want to challenge a doctor's opinion, do it in private, not in front of his staff or peers.

"Leave the patient alone.

"You are in the health industry, so look healthy.

"You can imitate a doctor's verbiage and pronunciation, but never mimic a doctor's accent.

"And finally, my most important rule.

"Never interrupt a physician who is writing a prescription."

The most embarrassing tip Finn gave Stu occurred on a cold winter morning as they rode together north on U.S. Highway 81 to Kingfisher. This Tuesday looked to be a perfect day to work with the boss. He had plenty of doctors lined up that were relatively easy to see. He lucked out with a schedule that would impress any division manager.

They had already called on two doctors in Okarche. It went well for Stu. Finn gave him selling tips as they drove the ten miles to Kingfisher. The sky was a bright blue. The sun began to warm the ground, melting the frost from the grass and trees. Oil drilling trucks were everywhere, heading both north and south. Drilling was near its peak in this hotspot. They were midway between the two towns when Stu's car suddenly stopped running. He carefully pulled to the shoulder. The steering wheel was stiff, and the brakes required extra pressure as he brought the car to a safe stop.

"What the heck just happened?" Stu looked perplexed.

"Is your engine running?"

"No. It's dead." Stu glanced at the fuel gauge. The words he uttered were not fit for women or small children. He turned to Finn, embarrassed and angry with himself.

"Now, what do we do?"

"What do you mean, 'we?' What are you going to do? I'm not going to do anything."

Now Stu's anger and embarrassment went off the chart. He could say nothing to make the situation better. It grated on him that Finn's words were exactly the words he would use if he were in his boss's shoes.

"Okay, so what do I do?"

"I would start walking. Head north. Isn't there a gas station just before you get into Kingfisher?"

"Not a very good one. I might try the second one."

"You're the one walking. Knock yourself out. I'll wait here and do paperwork...." Stu wasn't moving. It was cold. "Go.... Go!"

The humiliated detail man began his march of four to five miles. Fortunately for him, the winds were calm. His body heat began to warm him up. He was glad he didn't have an overcoat to burden his hike. It approached 10:00 a.m. at the completion of his first mile. His dress shoes hurt his feet. He thought of all the people with ill-fitting shoes like he suffered while growing up, when his parents tried to make his shoes last a little longer. Stu's shoes were ones he bought on a teacher's salary, not meant for long walks. He made a note to upgrade his footwear.

A small and rusty Japanese Datsun pulled up alongside him. Stu stopped with the driver. A man rolled down his passenger-side window, leaned an arm on the door opening, and gave him an offer Stu feared he could not refuse.

"Hop in. I'll give you a lift."

The man's face was dirty. His eyes looked half closed. The arm he laid outside the passenger window sported tattoos covering him from hand to bare shoulder. Stu had not seen that much ornamentation since the last television news story picturing prisoners at the McAlester Penitentiary. Stu's mind was reeling. *If I do, or if I don't... either way he may kill me... so I might as well take a chance on a free ride.*

"Thanks. You're my hero," he said and got into the car.

Stu looked for a seatbelt but failed to find one. His convict look-alike driver wore none. The man floored it back onto the highway. He wiped his eyes with a dirty hand before turning to his passenger.

"You run outta gas?"

"Yeah. I feel like an idiot. I left my boss back there to stew." Stu noticed the speedometer now read 80 mph. The car shook.

"I'm late for work," the driver said, "but I thought I'd help out my fellow man." The little car was now going ninety. "I had an all-night drunk last night. My toolpusher told me if I was late again, he would fire me. I don't think he will. Workers are in short supply."

"How much sleep did you get last night?"

"I don't know. I think I passed out." He wiped his eyes again and blinked the desperate blink of a man trying to retain awareness.

Stu thought of all sorts of scenarios that ended the same way—in a flaming car crash.

"Well, I'll keep you awake. How long have you worked in the oil patch?"

"Couple of years now. It's crazy out there. People living in cars, garages, in parks. It's crazy."

"What about you?"

He patted the dash of his Datsun. "This is home."

Stu took only a split second to decide that foregoing his favorite gas station was a decision of survival. At 90 mph, Stu was approaching Kingfisher fast. "The first gas station is about a mile and a half from here on the right. You can drop me off there."

"Gotcha," he said. In what to Stu was an eternity, but was less than a minute, he began to coast into town. Stu pulled out his billfold and grabbed a five-dollar bill.

As the driver pulled up to the gas station, Stu offered God a silent prayer of thanks—thanks for the safe journey and thanks for the time-saving free ride. He handed the man the bill.

"Hey, man. Buy yourself a beer tonight on me. Thanks for the lift. We both have boss problems now. Good luck with yours."

The driver waved the five at Stu. "You're a good man."

Stu barely closed the car door in time before it rattled off into town at a speed destined to make the driver even later for work. The police in Kingfisher were always busy. He stood a moment to watch him disappear into Kingfisher. An older man, who acted like he owned the place, approached him.

"You're all dressed up like a man who should be driving a car. Did you run out of gas?"

"Yes, sir. About halfway from Okarche." Stu tried to hide his embarrassment with a bit of humor. "I couldn't stand my boss anymore, so I left him at the side of the road."

The man laughed, not at his joke but at him. "I can give you a can of gas, but you might have to carry it back. We're swamped at the moment. That all right?"

"I promise to bring the can back and fill 'er up here."

The man scoffed at the comment. He walked back to his garage then returned with a two gallon can. After filling it with regular grade gas, he handed it to Stu.

"How much do I owe you?"

"Nothing yet. When you bring my can back, and if you want more gas, we'll settle up then."

"That's a deal. See you in about an hour." He picked up the can. It was heavier than he expected. With five miles to walk, he didn't want to waste time. He finished the first twenty-five feet before the man shouted.

"Mister! Hey!"

Stu, with his gas can, turned around.

"My son said he'll drive you back in his truck. Wait about ten minutes and he can take you."

There was not a more grateful person in Kingfisher. Stu assured them of that fact several times. He vowed he would always buy his gas there from now on. Soon he was on the road with a responsible young man of sixteen, who was not only sober, but he drove exactly the 55 mph speed limit while wearing a seatbelt. Stu in one hour had experienced polar opposite drivers.

When they arrived at Stu's car, the owner's son, in characteristic form, waited for several cars to pass before he crossed over into the northbound lanes of Highway 81. Stu would have crossed two minutes earlier. Safely parked behind Finn, he pulled out another five-dollar bill and gave it to the young man, using the same line.

"Take this with my thanks and buy yourself a beer tonight." The young man blushed.

"Thank you, sir, but I'm not twenty-one yet. Can I buy a Coke instead?"

"That's even better. Buy yourself two Cokes... and one for your girlfriend, too."

The teen let out a nervous giggle. No one was supposed to know of her existence. Stu relieved him of any worry when he stepped out of the truck and grabbed the gas can from the bed. He had his own demon to worry with. It was waiting in the car for his return. He waved the young man off and walked to the back of his car, setting down his can of gas.

Stu opened his car door to check on Finn. "How was your wait?"

"Long, but I did get some paperwork out of the way. I also have an idea of something you can do."

"Hang on. First, I have to pour this gas in the tank." It took a full minute of a slow gurgle to empty the gas. By the time he finished, he carried the smell of gas on his hands as well as a shoe. He stored the empty can in a half full sample box in his trunk. He stepped apprehensively back to the front of the car and got inside.

"We'll fill up at the first station we see and return the gas can." Stu looked at his boss. In a spontaneous bluster he added, "Well I've been busy. How about you?"

"Oh, I sure have been. I planned my next division meeting already and you are in charge of the vehicle safety briefing. I'll let you have an hour. You better start planning."

Chapter Six

Every day when Stu came home in those first early months, he had a new story to tell. Ana loved to remind Stu of his running out of gas with the boss. His first odd encounter with Doctor Addicus high on speed was still his most memorable experience. He found that doctors were just as human as the quirky patients they treated.

In a small town north of Guthrie, Stu called on an older physician who had his right arm severed at the shoulder. When looking at his handwriting, it was obvious he was not left-handed. His prescriptions were a challenge to read. When Stu talked to more experienced drug reps from other companies, they told him of the days before the doctor lost his arm. The man practiced radiology with little thought for his own safety. First, gangrene set in and he lost his fingers. Then in another year drug reps noted that his hand was missing. Over the years, more sections of his forearm disappeared, then above his elbow. There was little left to amputate after he lost the greater part of his shoulder. That was when Stu called on him in his final years. Soon Stu came home to report to Ana that the doctor was dead.

Other tales he brought home shocked her, such as the revelation that three of his pulmonologists smoked. He came home proudly one day to tease Ana with tales of fulfilling his manly fantasy.

"I finally got the wish of all travelling salesmen."

"And what would that be?"

"A nurse asked me if I would like to have a kept woman."

"Well, would you?"

"Do you remember the Oklahoma City Dolls football team five years ago?"

"Vaguely. I know there is a movie about them that just came out."

"Well, my potential kept woman was their linebacker."

They both laughed about the potential danger that might happen with such a match up. It was a month later that Stu came home and shared with her his continuing problem with being propositioned while out of town in western Oklahoma.

"I must be some kind of a hunk. I was sitting yesterday at the table in my room at the Ramada. I had already eaten dinner in their restaurant. My room was a great spot to look out at the swimming pool while I wrote up my calls and updated my expenses. One of the swimmers came up, knocking on the picture window. I looked up to see a man waving enthusiastically. I was sure it was another drug rep who remembered me, but I couldn't remember his name. I waved back and he walked on. A couple of minutes later my room phone rang. I picked it up, and a male voice said, 'What are you doing?' I told him I was doing paperwork. 'Then what are you doing?' I said I guess I'll watch some TV and then go to bed. You know what he asked? 'Alone?'"

Ana began giggling which grew in intensity into a continuous laugh until she grabbed her side in pain. She quelled her pain, but she kept up her giggles.

"You are in demand... aren't you? You must be so proud!" She grabbed her side again and cried in laughter-filled pain, until Stu rescued her with a hug.

"You'll be happy to know I said, yes… I will be alone… although I might call my wife, too. I'm through with fantasies of traveling salesmen for a while."

DOCTORS OFTEN WELCOMED a rep as a method of taking a break. Alan Blanton, M.D., a middle-aged general surgeon who had taken a liking to Stu, needed to take his mind off things. When Stu came into his office, he gave the doctor a penlight with Destense 10mg printed on it. Doctor Blanton leaned back in his office chair and propped his shoes on the desk. He put his hands behind his head on the only place where he still had hair.

"Don't mind my shoes in your face," he said to Stu. "I've been standing up all day."

"What cases wore you out?"

"Had a few students with me this morning. They all want to be surgeons. It takes practice. It's not like in my day. Too many rules now."

"What was different back then?"

"Back in the day when I was a fourth-year medical student, I was interested in taking every opportunity I could to practice stitching up patients. So, I hung around the emergency rooms. The attending physicians always let me practice and perhaps admired my motivation. Sometimes I got more than I wanted.

"A patient came into the ER and talked to the resident physician, who gladly let me take over his treatment. The man was ill at ease as he explained to both of us that he had a foreign object in his rectum that he couldn't get out. I got the unenviable task of finding it." He held up the Destense penlight. "When I dilated the anal sphincter a beam of light hit me in the eye. It was from a penlight just like this one."

ON ANOTHER AFTERNOON fellow Land Runner, the mousey introvert Blair Dill called Stu on the telephone in a rare moment of glibness to share his marital problems.

"What's going on?"

"My wife locked me out of the house yesterday." He was crying. Stu waited patiently for the man to compose himself.

"I returned home this morning to pick up a few work-related items. She was hurling leave pieces, research papers, and drug samples out of our upstairs bedroom window. I picked up what I could until… until my car couldn't hold anymore. It's humiliating."

"Have you called Finn?"

"No."

"You need to call Finn. If you don't, this is how you lose your job. He's the one who can help you."

"I know." He was crying again. "I'll call him right now."

"Blair, I can't help you with your wife, but you call me anytime. We can even meet somewhere for lunch… talk it out."

"Yeah, okay."

"I'm sorry, Blair." The phone clicked off.

Months later Blair had his lunch with Stu. Stu noted his upbeat attitude. Over a meal at Taco Bell, he told Stu about calling on a family practice physician.

"Doctor Slaughter. Do you know him?"

"Sure."

Frank Slaughter, M.D. was a new doctor, fresh out of his residency in Kansas City. He opened his practice in a new building, which meant he had money or knew a generous banker with a great deal of faith in him. He was young and overweight with a barely noticeable scraggly thin mustache. His wife, whose photo rested on his desk, shared her husband's obesity.

"Well, after three or four calls, the two of us hit it off well. One day shortly after my wife evicted me, Doctor Slaughter noticed my downtrodden face. He said, 'Blair, you want to tell me what's going on? You aren't yourself today.'"

Blair teared up, gathered his emotions, and spilled his guts about the man he now called Frank.

"Frank listened to me with empathy. He talked about the wife he loved and shared that there were women out in the world who could make me happy. He suggested that moving on sounded like the only reasonable solution. But mainly, Frank just listened."

"So, having someone to listen to you helped?"

"A lot, I called on him three more times. Each time Frank asked me how my divorce was going. After letting me talk, he always ended our call with encouragement that there were women who could make me blessedly happy someday. 'Don't give up out there, Blair.'"

"Are you selling him anything?"

"Well, that's the problem. On my fourth return visit, I found a note on the front entrance to Frank's office. It stated that Doctor Slaughter had left his practice. I learned from the town's pharmacy that Frank had skipped town and left no forwarding address."

Stu could see the pain in his eyes. Blair was devastated to lose his trusted confidant, but he had some good news he wanted to share with Stu about a new lady friend he met.

A week later Blair joined his fellow Land Runners to share this story, but he had a punchline that surprised them all. After giving them his sad tale of Frank Slaughter's kind counseling and listening, he pulled out a copy of the morning's headlines in The Daily Oklahoman. The front-page below the fold read, Wewoka Doctor Arrested for Wife's Murder.

"That's who counseled me!" Blair was uncharacteristically loud with the pronouncement. "Frank Slaughter, M.D., of Wewoka, Oklahoma."

He opened the newspaper to the second page and read.

"Oklahoma State Bureau of Investigation officers stated that the medical examiner determined Missus Slaughter's death a homicide, after evidence showed up that her husband, Doctor Frank Slaughter, allegedly poisoned his wife, a diabetic, with cyanide-laced Anacin capsules and excessive doses of insulin."

Blair's dramatic reading from the newspaper showed a human side of him that few had ever seen. It pleased the men to see Blair coming out of his shell, if only for a morning.

"And to think, his counseling is how I survived my divorce."

Stu asked, "Did you ever tell him you wanted to kill your soon-to-be ex-wife?"

Blair thought about the question. He started to speak, then paused again. That made the men laugh.

"Slaughter told me one day that wanting to kill your wife in a divorce was normal. Then he asked me if I ever had those thoughts."

"And...?" The question came from several.

"Yes." Laughter returned—a primal response by all the men in the room who could share stories of wives and girlfriends who committed acts of betrayal.

STU ALSO LEARNED that nurses were not always reverent of their physicians. At a large hospital in town, he met the Director of Nurses, Norma Vazquez, RN. It was always a good idea to meet the department heads before roaming the hallways in a hospital. She gave him useful tips for talking to different people from the pharmacists and lab techs on down to the lady who polished the floors. It was a surprise to Stu that the floor polisher was also in charge of scheduling the infrequent and valuable hospital displays. In three hours at a hospital display, a drug rep could see and talk to a week's worth of doctors.

To his surprise when he asked her about calling on a certain general surgeon, she answered the question in a shocking way.

"You mean Crash-Cart Appleby?"

"Is that what you call him?"

"All the nurses call him that."

"Why?"

"Just don't let him perform surgery on you."

"Well, I heard good things about Doctor Appleby."

Director of Nurses Norma Vazquez stared at him in stoic self-control without saying another word.

Stu encountered the same medical concern in a small town in Oklahoma. On his first call in the newly built clinic, he learned from two very proud osteopathic physicians that they were creating a medical complex, soon to be a local empire.

Gas stations were frequent places to encounter other detail men. Stu frequently shared where he was headed, the idea being to stay out of each other's way.

A dermatology rep named Tom spotted Stu and came over. "You going to D.O. Mayo?"

Stu was puzzled. "What's the D.O. Mayo?"

"You know Crafty and Big Red, don't you?"

"Oh, those guys. D.O. Mayo. That's a great name."

"I just came from there. Big Red is pissed."

Stu finished pumping gas, but intel in the pharmaceutical industry was helpful. Tom was good at sharing information with others. Stu stood by his car and soaked in the news. He intended to go there next.

"So, what happened?"

"You know Rusty, that big fellow? The one who won't stop talking?" Stu nodded his head. "Well, be careful how you talk about their clinic."

The Oklahoma Oil Boom was in full swing and investments in oil wells were all the rage. Doctors Crafty and Big Red had been lucky and were in great shape. One doctor enhanced his naturally red hair. His car tag read, Big Red. The other doctor was not as flamboyant, just crafty. Life was good to them. They had converted a small hospital into a four-sided empire of an additional clinic, pharmacy, and nursing home. They were overly proud of it.

"Did Rusty step in it again?"

"You know how we meet the docs in the exam rooms? Rusty was in the next room. I could hear everything."

"I hear half the patient conversations most times," Stu said.

Tom continued. "Rusty was talking to Big Red and made the mistake of trying to make a joke. He told the doc, 'Your town is really coming up in the world, isn't it?' Big Red is really proud of his hospital complex. Doc asked Rusty... I'm sure expecting a compliment, 'Oh? What do you mean?'"

Tom began to laugh. "Get this. Rusty said, 'You finally got a Pizza Hut in this town.'"

"So, what did Doctor Big Red do?"

"He stormed out of the room into mine, shook my hand, and got on the phone to the hospital and ordered the pharmacist, 'If I ever write one of Rusty's drugs again, you call me or substitute another drug.'"

Stu was not stupid. This was not a good day to visit the D.O. Mayo.

Chapter Seven

Stu Roy knew from experience that teachers get sick more in their first years. Then with experience and proper precautions, they build immunity to most child borne pathogens and they learn to duck all the coughs launched their way. The germs and their means of transport were different in physician's waiting rooms. Over half of the patients in a doctor's office were likely contagious. In schools, by contrast, students stayed home. In fact, students were most likely going out of their way to stay home. And teachers didn't have to sit between coughing patients. Stu exposed himself to sickness in waiting rooms ten to fifteen times a day. When autumn came, he was surprised to find that the immunity he built up as an English teacher was not a hundred percent.

Stu looked fashionable in his dark well-tailored new suit, as a five-year-old boy continued to cough and sneeze all around him. He had been waiting in the doctor's office for almost forty-five minutes. His usual rule was to wait no more than thirty minutes before leaving. This doctor was different. Unlike most physicians, he was a monster of a writer, so the wait would likely be a good investment of time. This was his second attempt to see this high prescriber, the first attempt ending in failure and the loss of more than an hour. It was possible to wait too long and end up throwing away the hour. Or it was possible to wait so long that getting coughed on would make Stu so mad and frustrated that he would want to complain to the doctor. In either unfortunate situation, nothing was sold. He was at the point where he might be better off to leave and fight another day.

The little boy continued to hack away, which forced Stu to commit to an action. As he stood up to leave the office, the nurse stuck her head out the door. She was not a happy woman, although comely enough in her green scrubs.

"Mister Roy," she said. Her manner was impersonal. "Come on back. You'll have to wait though. He just started a physical on a new patient. It's probably going to be another hour."

He looked at her and back at the coughing kid. He had learned from other drug salesman that Doctor Upton had some bad traits that were not rep friendly.

"He never will see me, will he."

She sighed in a momentary expression of sympathy and sadly replied, "He's never going to see you. You should know that." Then she motioned him closer and, in a whisper, added, "He made you wait out here on purpose, until he started his physical. Give up on seeing him. It's not going to happen."

Trying to control his anger, but grateful for the truth, he thanked the unhappy and honest nurse and walked with dignity away from her, past the hacking five-year-old, and out the door of the family practice clinic.

The fresh air outside was devoid of children's microbes. He hoped he had survived another contagion. He would live to fight another day, but decided this morning never to call on the clinic of Doctor Upton again.

Stu had a thousand new friends, since he started his job six months ago, and a hundred other clinics to call on. But those other clinics would have to wait. Stu Roy fell ill. His manager was not happy.

A DOCTOR'S JOB is not glamorous, as any patient who gets a physical will tell you. The physician has a hard job. It is often smelly, dirty, bloody, and catching. But doctors derive their respect through outcomes, not the process.

DETAIL MAN

Stu had been selling pharmaceuticals long enough to conclude that no doctor was qualified to take care of him. He now knew that they were regular human beings, just like everyone else. They had human flaws. Being brand new and underpaid, he had no money to spend. With two weeks of vacation to use up that summer, he decided to paint his newly purchased house and to start a compost pile. When his painting arm got tired, he would step down from the ladder and stir up the compost heap, which he piled high with rotting vegetation, grass clippings, assorted types of dirt, and small limbs.

Aside from painting the house, his only real accomplishment that summer was developing severe pneumonia. He became fevered and ached all over. His chest hurt in a way he had never experienced before. He found it hard to describe, except that as he stood outside talking to a neighbor, he wanted to sit down in the grass. To make it even worse, he now thought he knew enough about doctors to be scared of all of them. They did not listen to him. They were constantly writing those ineffective substitutes, instead of the superior drugs he sold. When on the off chance they did listen to him, they would ask the most basic questions. They did not know about some of the things he knew. He was thirty-one years old and some doctors with thirty years of experience were asking him questions. Some physicians valued his information. To his utter amazement they had lives outside of medicine that were highly suspect. How could a doctor be competent if he loved riding Harley-Davidson motorcycles on weekends? Without a helmet, no less! Some had marital problems. Others had the opposite problem—too much marriage in the office, which created chaos among the staff. The doctors Stu called on were terrible businessmen. The few women physicians he called on at that time were extremely aggressive to sales reps. These women, by necessity, asserted their place in the boy's club by overachievement and independent mindedness.

Confronted with the need to select a doctor to treat his illness, which could not wait, Stu panicked. He couldn't pick anyone. The doctors in his mind were all incompetent morons! In less than a year of selling to them in their offices, he had mentally kicked every one of them off their pedestals. They were incompetent. Why else would they solicit his advice? They smoked but wanted to treat his lungs. They were all just like Stu—flawed and imperfect. So, he held his nose and picked a doctor—one who seemed to like him and who prescribed something he sold. What better qualifications than those? He called his office only to learn that the doctor no longer took new patients. He called another physician. Once again, this office did not take new patients. Stu was by this time quite ill. Out of desperation, he called an office whose family practitioner was no admirer of Plushaut Uclaf. Doctor Hull was always short with him on sales calls. Besides not seeming interested in what Stu had to say, he was often sarcastic with both medical doctors and detail men. Stu feared the worst but had a pleasant shock. Every preconception he held of the man was wrong.

The first difference Stu noted as he sat in the exam room with Doctor Hull was his face-to-face attention to him. It was not like those sales calls they had endured together. He asked Stu lots of questions, seemingly had all the time in the world. He asked about Stu's family, now only a wife—no children, yet. What did he do on vacation? The doctor's seemingly unrelated questions aroused Stu's interest. For a moment he had a flash of awareness. *Maybe he likes me after all.* He got a chest x-ray which the doctor gazed at briefly. Pointing to the illuminated picture of Stu's lungs, he showed him the spots of pulmonary infiltrates that suggested pneumonia. He listened to his lungs for a long time and then said something that was not exactly proper medical terminology. "Your chest sounds cruddy!"

Finally, he said something that made Stu feel better. "I'm going to call another physician... an Internist. Wait here." He left the exam room carrying the X-ray.

Great for me. He is at least aware that I need help.

Ten minutes passed before Doctor Hull came back into the exam room. "Do you know Doctor Crowder?" he asked.

"Yes, I know Doctor Crowder. He won't talk to me, but I know who he is."

Doctor Crowder was an internist/oncologist who wouldn't see sales reps. His nurse always kept Stu out of his way. Contrary to his earlier reasoning about other doctors, this specialist did not value Stu's opinion. Obviously, Doctor Crowder was a moron.

Doctor Hull then informed him that Doctor Crowder, hearing the symptoms described, recommended Stu enter the hospital for treatment of pneumonia. Doctor Hull noted Stu's worried look. With a wife who needed him at home, Stu asked to stay out of the hospital.

"I understand. I'll work to keep you with me… if I can." Doctor Hull surprised his patient by his willingness to accommodate his wishes. "I want to try treating your pneumonia if you'll come back to my office daily for a checkup?"

With a promise that Stu would come back to see him the next day, he let him go home on *erythromycin*. The antibiotic *erythromycin*, he later learned, was an appropriate choice, but unfortunately it worked like an unsympathetic laxative. The next day Doctor Hull switched him to *tetracycline*, which was easier on his patient, but also was less effective on the bacteria causing his pneumonia. On day three, Stu presented with lungs that sounded more like a boiling pot than the near silence of normal human breathing. His doctor was back on the telephone with Doctor Crowder. The word came back that he had *Eaton Agent* or *PPLO*. It was new information to Stu, so the doctor explained what an atypical pathogen was—a primitive cell that has no cell wall. He mentioned another word—*Mycoplasma. Three names for one bug? What else did he know with such ease?* Stu started a third antibiotic. His memory failed to record what it was this time. He was in a mild delirium. In a few days, the boiling sound in his chest was gone, but he was not much better. This increasingly competent physician in Stu's mind was calling Doctor Crowder again. His doctor related to him in minute detail the thought process of their conversations. He wanted to do another x-ray and get more lab work. He had Stu come back the next day, where he informed him that the tests confirmed his suspicions. He also had a fungal pneumonia called *Histoplasmosis*.

"How did I get that?"

"People get it from working in barns or around pigeons."

Stu was a city boy. He didn't realize the connection.

Hull asked him again. "Where were you on that two-week vacation?"

They talked for a long time before Stu mentioned his compost pile. All week while painting his house, he used his feet to stir up and tamp down the rotting vegetation into compost. Bingo! He had the source for the *Histoplasmosis* infection. He put him on an antifungal medication which made Stu improve rapidly.

Six weeks from the day of his initial presentation to Doctor Hull, he returned to work with a new appreciation of physicians, what they did for a living, and how they dedicated many hours to patients without anyone knowing. Treating patients was more complicated than Stu realized. There was interaction among physicians. They were much humbler in real practice than patients might think. They did not know everything, but they did not pretend otherwise. The system worked and Stu was impressed.

Back at work he concluded that his previous image of physicians being on a pedestal was unrealistic. With his new assessment, they were now people just like regular folks. They had families with both problems and joys. They made mistakes like everybody did. They were smart but did not always have the answers themselves. For the first time in his short career, Stu realized why pharmaceutical salesmen were of value to doctors. In mentally bringing them down to mere human levels, Stu's respect for physicians went way up and was never to waver. With this change in attitude, his career began to blossom into a partnership of mutual esteem. The physician's respect for him and what he offered them continued to grow.

Chapter Eight

It didn't take long for Stu to notice that the division meeting tradition of alcohol consumption was taking its toll. Military life was a training ground for future drinkers. It was no different in Plushaut Uclaf. From Finn's boxes full of booze to the company's interest in fine wine, Stu learned early that careers risked destruction from a tradition Plushaut promoted.

After eight years with Plushaut, the Land Runners began training in proper manners—everything from basic etiquette to knowing the best wines and how to discuss them expertly.

"Hey, Lance," Stu whispered at the last meeting of the year. "You notice how fat Dan and Cress have gotten recently?"

"Finn has turned into a fat ass, too," Lance replied. "The button on his pants is so tight, it might pop off and put your eye out."

"Too much wine training, I would say."

"Last January at the national meeting, did you notice the top execs? They've put on about fifty pounds over the past five years."

Among the Land Runners, Dan Anders and Cress Caston were heading for self-destruction. Dan was a successful salesman. Finn left him alone. Cress was more of a problem.

That night in the hotel, Stu continued his tradition of sneaking Ana up to his room where they would pretend to play illicit lovers for a night.

"Do you see this?" Ana was looking at the vast parking lot out of their hotel window. "Stu, I see two of your friends bringing interesting women into the hotel. It's pretty late at night."

"At least we're married."

"And intend to get a good night's sleep."

"Why do you say that?" They both giggled at their little joke.

When morning came and Ana had slipped out before sunrise, Stu got a call from Cress at 6:15 a.m.

"Stu, you have an extra toothbrush and toothpaste?"

He grabbed his dentist sample pack he carried for emergencies and went to knock on Cress's door, which was already open a crack. Cress was standing in the doorway pouring himself an eight-ounce glass of bourbon for breakfast.

"Thanks, buddy," Cress said in hoarse tones. Then he looked nervously behind him. A tall woman wearing a leopard print leotard and matching bra continued to dress. "Don't tell anyone about the girl. I don't want to get in anymore trouble."

"Good God, man. That's a terrible breakfast."

"I'm okay... just don't want Finn to know."

The moment that Stu saw him womanizing and drinking so indiscreetly, he realized Cress was lost. Cress's life ended a year later with cirrhosis of the liver and pancreatic cancer.

Chapter Nine

Since that first day when Stu crossed paths with his first competitor, Chad Choteau, they had become good friends. Stu found many friends within the industry. At first, he was leery of talking to competitors, but he chose to treat his competitors as brothers who sometimes squabbled. They were the right instincts. It was a fraternity of men and increasingly of women.

The first time he worked in Enid, Oklahoma, he acquired more knowledge in one day than he had learned in a month of working with Finn. There was a clinic of three internists next to the big hospital.

They only allowed sales reps to call on them at noon on Wednesdays. Reps called it The Lineup because every drug rep in town tried to be there first. Starting at 11:00 a.m., the crowd would grow. By noon there were usually a dozen detail men and women. They lined up in chairs against the wall in proper sequence and waited. When the first doctor got loose to talk, the assembly line of sales pitches began moving. Of course, when a second doctor was ready, sales rep number one would be engaged with doctor number one. Soon after, when the third doctor called for a rep, the system of order would break down. Gentlemanly behavior always prevailed, except for one fist fight the reps told Stu about involving the unmanageable Bill Dooley.

"How can you stand that guy being on your team?" asked the rep behind Stu at The Lineup. The wait before noon was always a source of useful information peppered with friendly chatter.

"Dooley? Oh, he doesn't bother me. He's just kind of different, that's all."

In truth, Stu was just like the rest of the Land Runners, who did not call him a friend. But Stu had learned one thing about teamwork. Dooley might be an unlikeable Land Runner, but he was *our* unlikeable Land Runner. He wouldn't badmouth a teammate.

"You can't beat his work ethic. He never quits."

"He's a jerk, and you know it," the rep said. "Last month Dooley had made a call on Doctor Fleck. I waited next to see Fleck. Dooley followed him into where I was waiting. He proceeded to bad mouth my drugs. You know what a big man Fleck is... with a flair for the dramatic. He hurled Dooley out the front door of his clinic... like you see in a good Western."

Chad Choteau, six reps behind Stu, wanted to add his own experience.

"I'm sorry, Stu, but Dooley is no team player." Chad was not one who complained about any rep.

"Go ahead. Tell me what he's done now."

"Dooley drove up to my favorite service station near Hydro, while I was gassing up my car. He jumped out, put the pump nozzle in his tank, then asked me where I was going. Like a dummy, I told him. Dooley's eyes got wide. He pulled the gas nozzle back out and reseated it at the pump."

"I know what's coming," another listener said.

"He said, 'Oh, that's a good idea. I'll go there, too.' Then he jumped back into his car without ever filling up and peeled out of the station."

"That's the Dooley I know," someone said with disdain. "He always has to be the first one to the office."

LUNCH AFTERWARD AT the nearby cafeteria afforded Stu a wealth of accumulated wisdom. Richill's Cafeteria was the place to be at lunchtime in Enid. Nearly every influential businessman in town ate there. The food was good and reasonably priced. It served the best chicken fried steak in Oklahoma. A parrot greeted you when you entered. Depending on the year, the parrot was mechanical or real. A mural depicting historical Enid covered one wall. From the ceiling, two large 'O' gauge electric trains rumbled along on eight hundred feet of track. Both trains operated on the same track, kept from colliding by computerized power switches.

At Richill's there were sales reps' tales of small-town nurses' and doctors' affairs, even a few tales of good deeds and caring doctors.

Stu was sitting down with his tray of chicken fried steak and gravy with a smattering of a vegetable to make Ana happy. A competitor greeted him with a question.

"Are you the guy who went calling on methamphetamine-doped up Doctor Addicus?"

"Am I the only one?" Stu said.

They all knew Addicus, but Stu was the first to try to sell him while he was tripped out on speed.

"Yeah, that story is legend... that and you working with that dirtbag Bill Dooley."

At the far end of the table someone yelled out, "If Dooley ever has a wreck in his car, I hope Doctor Addicus is the doc in town on emergency room call."

"Or maybe," another rep shouted, "a proctologist."

STU SHARED A story about his first mistake in correcting a young doctor fresh out of his family practice residency. He was with Finn waiting in the clinic's lab when young Doctor Hester came in. He, too, wanted to make a good impression. He looked at one of Stu's Destense file cards and mentioned a patient he had on the drug and praised it in glowing terms. Stu asked him to describe the patient.

"She's only sixteen, poor girl. She's obese... always out of breath... and already has severe hypertension. She suffers from weakness, some neuropathy. I thought it was type-2 diabetes, but her blood sugar is normal. Thank goodness we have her blood pressure down. Destense has been a life saver."

"Doctor Hester, I would take her off my drug right now. Destense is contraindicated in children under eighteen. It causes serious arrythmias because of elevated serum potassium. You've described hyperkalemia to me."

Doctor Hester looked up at Stu, then at Finn. "Is that so!" He stood up abruptly and exited the lab.

Assuming Doctor Hester was calling the sixteen-year-old's parents to discontinue Destense, Stu and Finn waited for him to return. After thirty minutes, Stu asked a nurse what was happening.

"I don't know what you said, but Doctor Hester said you are not welcome to come back again," she said sternly, "and to stop playing doctor."

There were other times when criticism ended in humor. When Stu hosted a catered lunch in the kitchen at a four-doctor clinic, he noted Doctor Peter Tacon, one of his favorite doctors to call on, was already in the adjoining lab and eating the sack lunch he had brought to the office that morning. What bothered Stu was that he had a sandwich in one hand and a specimen cup of a patient's urine in the other. He deftly poured a portion of the urine into a test tube, took a bite of his sandwich, and after laying his sandwich down, licked his fingers. For ten minutes he repeated the process of pouring, biting, and licking. Stu was relieved when he finally finished the sandwich. Watching Doctor Tacon was cringeworthy. When he came in the kitchen to talk with Stu, a chance to criticize his obvious poor protocol was too tempting.

"Pete! Watching your lab technique has been the most entertaining thing I've seen all day."

"What do you mean?" It was always hard to determine his word's meaning because of his dry humor.

"I didn't mind the urine and the sandwich together so much, but watching you lick your fingers between bites seems to be bad technique."

Doctor Tacon was not a man sensitive to criticism. He looked at Stu and smiled in his impish way.

"Where did you graduate?"

Stu was confused by the question's relevance. "You mean college?"

"Yeah."

"Kansas State… and a master's from Central State."

"Okay, Kansas State will do."

His grin continued. Stu sensed another good story he was about to share.

"Two men walked into a public restroom and used the two urinals at the same time. One was a graduate of Harvard. The other was from… Kansas State. Do you get it?"

"I get it… Kansas State, so go on."

"So, when they finish their business, the Harvard man goes to the sink and proceeds to wash his hands. Expecting to see the man from Kansas State beside him at the sink, instead, he sees him walk to the bathroom door and go out. So, the Harvard man finishes handwashing and goes out, too. Standing nearby is his new acquaintance. He walks up smartly and says to the man. 'At Harvard they taught us to wash our hands after we urinate.' The other man takes the admonition to heart and replies, 'At Kansas State they taught us not to pee on our hands.'"

STU WAS LEARNING valuable lessons every day. His insights were growing exponentially. He understood that he was now a seasoned rep, whose decisions were bathed in a mix of experiences.

Stu dreaded each time he called on a cranky doctor in Enid named Cal Boerne, M.D. This day started with a rare conversation.

"How is your day going?" It was always good to have some brief small talk before the meat of the matter. It also gave Stu a chance to learn what was on his mind medically, so he could tailor his comments to a doctor's concerns.

"I just got back from Santa Fe. I enjoyed an Italian opera. You know in Italy they boo the tenor. I can't do that in America."

"That might be good practice to boo one of my competitors."

"Or I could tell you you're singing like that fat lady. That would mean it's over for you."

He was being his cranky self, chuckling at his barb at a drug rep. Like many smokers, he began to choke as he laughed. But this time it was different. He kept choking, gasping for air, and grabbing his chest. He fell out of his chair unconscious. Without a nurse in the office to advise him, Stu went into action.

"Help! Quick, I need your help. Heart Attack!" He commandeered two sales reps in the hallway to help. Not knowing what else to do, they carried the unconscious Doctor Boerne from his office across the street to the adjacent hospital emergency room.

A young emergency doctor, Art Benny, M.D., went into action.

"Gently now, let's carry him into this first room." Stu was not happy that the doctor wasn't more urgent with his directions. "Okay men, if you can, lift him on the table."

Stu and the two reps backed off to get out of Doctor Benny's way. Stu turned to the doctor in charge, expecting him to immediately go into action. To his surprise, Doctor Benny stood there doing nothing but looking at the lifeless cranky Doctor Boerne. Stu wanted him to do something.

Don't just stand there. He's dying... or is dead already. Do something!

Instead, Doctor Benny studied the patient, took his time to survey the big picture, and gave an order to his attending nurse. Then he turned to the three reps.

"Gentlemen, leave, now!"

Only then did he turn his back to them, step forward, and slam a fist firmly on the sternum of his patient. Doctor Boerne reacted by gasping for air. His chest heaved in recoil off the table. The action began in earnest. A nurse came in to escort Stu and his friends from the area.

"Boys, you need to get back outside now. Stay in the waiting room if you want. Go. Go!"

I waited in the lobby until word came of Doctor Boerne's condition. Cranky or not, Stu remained loyal to his customer with genuine concern.

To everyone's shock, Doctor Boerne recovered and was soon back at work, making the job of sales reps miserable again. The joke running around was that Doctor Benny did his job too well because it didn't fix Doctor Boerne's personality. For Stu, the takeaway was that keeping one's cool and analyzing the situation before acting made Doctor Benny a hero. It was another lesson learned.

Chapter Ten

THE YEAR WAS 1990. Stu Roy was now a seasoned and well-respected pharmaceutical salesman who enjoyed his job. He was not the same person doctors knew ten years before. He understood how they thought and worked. He no longer sold pharmaceuticals. Instead, he sold patient solutions. Most often, his solutions involved some product he sold, but not always. Doctors respected him because he would recommend a competitor or would tell them that his drug was not a good choice.

The change had come early in his career. He had two epiphanies. The first was to treat the doctor the same way the doctor treated him. The second was to start acting like he deserved to be there with the doctor.

He was on another early morning trip out to Elk City in western Oklahoma. A quick shot along Interstate 40 took a hundred and ten miles and a little under two hours to get to the two-doctor clinic of Doctor Smith, a Family Practitioner, and Doctor Brown, an internist and gastroenterologist. Doctor Brown did more Family Practice in Elk City than he preferred. Stu put in a card for his 8:00 a.m. drug rep appointment. Doctor Brown was ready for him. That was not always a good sign, as this internist was not from Oklahoma. Coming from New

York, he had his own impatient manner that made a sales call difficult for Stu.

"Come in and sit down." Stu stepped inside his office to take his designated chair. Brown picked up the telephone and punched in numbers, leaving Stu to sit down and wait. The call lasted almost ten minutes, which caused Stu to wonder why he was called back before the doctor was ready to see him. The call finally reached a crescendo.

"I don't care what you tell me," Brown said. "If I tell you to buy a stock, it means I want it… no… no, that's not going to happen, so buy the damn thing or I'll find a better broker."

He slammed the phone onto its cradle with a dramatic flourish, then looked at Stu.

"So, how are you going to piss me off?" He sported one of those goatees seen on caricatures for the devil. A small-boned man, he looked angry on every call Stu had tried. He glared at Stu over reading half glasses.

"I see it's bad timing for me from the start."

"Just tell me about whatever crap you're selling and get out of here."

This was a typical call with Doctor Brown. He talked fast and was rude on every call. It was intimidating to any polite Oklahoman. Native citizens tended to talk slower and live life in less of a rush. Stu tried to speak, but he was pulling a sales visual out of his detail bag. Doctor Brown eyed this motion and stopped him cold.

"Don't show me that trash. If I want to read it, I'll do it on my time, which will be never, I'm pretty sure."

"Well, I might instead show you this research recently published that addresses a patient your partner told me about."

"What journal?"

"*A Journal of Medicine*."

"AMA Journal is crap. Bring me something from *New England Journal* or *Annals of Internal Medicine* and I might look at it. I don't trust your rigged AMA studies."

"I'm sorry. I picked the wrong one then. I do have a related and verified study from New England Journal that is closely related." Stu reached in his bag and quickly pulled out the article.

"You forgot one thing."

"Yes, sir?"

"You said it related to a patient of Doctor Smith's?"

"Yes, it's concerning...."

"I don't have time to treat his patients and mine both, so I don't give a rat's ass about how to help him."

Stu was totally flustered by now. He considered Brown a challenge and was relentless in winning him over. This, however, he knew was a loser of a call.

"I'll be on my way then," Stu said. He quickly laid three file cards and the New England Journal study on Brown's desk. He had failed to mention even a single product or patient type. It was a sales call of utterly no value to either one of them.

"Yeah, we're done here. Have Smith sign for any samples I need." He picked up the telephone and immediately began talking to his broker. Stu was quick to realize that he had not hung up on his broker, but had put him on hold to wait, just as Stu had waited. Slamming the telephone down had only been for dramatic effect. Stu stepped out into the hallway but turned back for one last look at Doctor Brown. Sure enough, as the doctor continued his harangue on the telephone, he took each one of Stu's leave pieces and dropped them one by one into his waste basket.

The routine in this office was to go next to the other physician's private office. For Doctor Smith the routine was to wait in a designated drug rep chair just outside his office door. Doctor Smith's habit was to write up each chart in the refuge of his office after each patient. He would then call Stu in for a chat—or a rant. After a twenty-minute wait, Doctor Smith joined him with his customary courtesy.

"Good morning there, Stu. How are you doing?" He shook his hand with a firm and callused grip. He had farmer's roots.

"Well, not so good."

"Oh? Why is that?" He leaned forward, putting his folded hands on his desk. For being in his fifties, his hair was remarkably dark brown, with only a hint of gray in the waves covering his ears.

"I just called on your partner, Doctor Brown."

"Gave you a rough time, did he?" He reacted to his own comment with a chuckle and an impish grin.

"The only thing he agreed with me on was that I was leaving his office."

Doctor Smith paused to look pensively at his pharmaceutical guest. Other salesmen had shared similar experiences with his partner. It was not his first time giving a drug rep some advice.

"Let me help you out here, Stu." He removed his eyeglasses and began wiping the lenses clean with a wrinkled handkerchief. "First, he is from New York. Enough said. Second, he treats me the same way… and we are friends."

"That sounds impossible."

"No, it was easy. Now it's a little different if you are a detail man calling on the jerk. I'm a doctor. We are peers, so he couldn't really pull it off with me. I soon learned that he was never going to respect me until I dished his rude manners right back at him. Ever since that day, he started to like me more."

Smith signaled an expression that meant, *you understand?*

"You want me to act like a Damn Yankee."

"Yes, and that's one word by the way… *Damnyankee*."

"Well, thank you. I can do that. Not much to lose."

"Trust me he will respect you for it. You'll win him over. Just go in there like you are another doctor. You're not going to treat his patients, of course, but go in there like I would. If he cursed me, I would curse back. If he calls you a name, call him a jerk. Act like you think a New Yorker acts. I guarantee he'll start to like you. He simply misses the interaction with people he grew up with."

Stu finished his call with Doctor Smith after a good discussion of three different patient types and left three file cards on his desk. He noted that Smith put one of the three in his white coat pocket. That was a sign of success. Doctor Smith wanted to remember it. He would be courteous and not throw away the others until Stu was gone.

Treat the doc like he treats me and act like I deserve to be there. Fifteen years on the job and Stu was still learning.

FOUR WEEKS LATER Stu was back for another 8:00 a.m. appointment with Doctors Smith and Brown. This time he spoke to the courteous Doctor Smith first. They discussed patients and drugs. The subject of Doctor Brown did not come up until Stu stepped out his office.

"Thanks for your advice you gave me last month. I'll try for some respect from Doctor Brown this time. If I don't come out alive... well at least you tried to help me... call the morgue."

He laughed quietly but said nothing. Stu paced the short walk to Doctor Brown's office. To his surprise, the New Yorker was already there writing in one of a stack of charts he kept perpetually on his desk. Stu dropped his sales bag just outside the door. His sales pieces were already in his hand. Doctor Brown looked up in his typical snarly fashion.

"What do you want? And make it fast."

"First off, you need me."

Brown looked up in shock. "What in hell does that mean? I need you like I need a burr on my ass."

"Why in hell do you schedule an appointment to see us? It must be because you want something. I want to know what that is because until today you've been the burr that's been on my ass the past two years."

"Get out of here." It wasn't convincing. His expression was more hurt than anger.

"Not until you tell me what we have that will benefit you. Today is the last day I'm taking any New York razz-berries from you. I'm here to help you... not be your punching bag. So, cut the crap and tell me what you need from us."

The silence that ensued was agonizing. Doctor Brown looked at him curiously for an uncomfortable period. Stu continued to stare into his diminishing glare of intimidation. Then the dam broke.

"Well, you are feisty this morning."

He expected a response but did not get it. Stu continued his silent stare. The wait this time was shorter.

"I don't want my time wasted."

"That's why I am asking what you want?"

"Brevity."

"Okay, you've got it. What else?"

"I'm an internist. Talk science."

"I'd love that. I might even learn something from you."

"What? Am I the detail man now?"

"I don't want you to play detail man. You don't want me to play doctor. But we can both get something out of this."

"Like what?"

"How about we discuss the landmark study that just came out about treating spontaneous bacterial peritonitis? You're a GI doc. Have you read that article in the Annals?"

He said nothing at first. Then he said what Stu hoped to hear. "Nobody cares out here that I'm a board-certified gastroenterologist. You bring me that information and I will gladly talk to you."

"Okay then. Until next month, that's all I wanted to do today."

Stu didn't leave any literature this time as he stepped into the hallway.

"Mister Roy," Brown said from his desk. "Show a little respect next time you call on me."

Stu turned around and stepped back into his office. "Are you going to call the material that I bring to you a bunch of crap?"

"Yes."

"Call me a burr in your ass?"

"Yes."

"Then you won't mind if I call you a sanctimonious Damn Yankee?"

"No."

"All right then. See you next month."

A smile crept onto Doctor Brown's face. It was the most fun sales call Stu had been on in years.

Chapter Eleven

STU WAS PUZZLED. He was calling on an osteopath in the small town of Signal. Finn Trottel traveled with him. The parking lot, usually over-parked after lunch, was empty. Stu walked to the clinic entrance to read a note taped to the office front door which gave directions to his temporary clinic. Doctor Lane's office was in the town's outdated former hospital, built by the community in the early years after World War One. He had converted it into a combination home and clinic. With nine children and a wife, the doctor had found a home that kept work and family close together. But so was his nurse. Eventually, a look became a touch, became a hug, became a kiss. The inevitable sexual affair began. Months later, his nurse began to make demands for more commitment. When Doctor Lane's response failed to meet the needs of his lover, she began making threats. Not wanting his wife and nine children to learn of his dalliance, he went on a quest for a hitman to solve his problem.

Since Stu's recovery from pneumonia, he revered the job the physicians did, but he still knew that they were all too human. Paying a hit man was bad enough for a physician dedicated to saving lives, but Doctor Lane was highly intelligent. Hiring a hitman seemed to be beneath the dignity of his station in life, an enterprise reserved for low

IQ individuals. Like most unintelligent activities, the doctor's hired assassin failed to kill his nurse. The county sheriff did not fail to apprehend the second-rate assassin. It is easier to be bad if the victim doesn't know the hired gun. From her hospital bed, she named the man, a frequent clinic patient. The lousy hitman informed on his client Doctor Lane in complete detail.

When Doctor Lane surrendered to the officers with the Oklahoma State Bureau of Investigation, they housed him temporarily in the Washita County jail. Once word got out, patients began to show up there. The small metal building had a good-sized parking lot, only half-filled with trucks the county used for the town's maintenance needs. On this day, as Stu and Finn drove up, they found the usually half-empty parking lot jammed full. About twenty people lingered by the jail entrance. Finn was curious. Stu was trying to do whatever the boss wanted him to do. This was definitely outside the box.

"Pull over there on the street. We'll park and go see what the story is."

"Should I bring my sales bag?" Stu was also curious but uncertain if Finn expected him to sell anything. He found similarities here to his call on Doctor Addicus who was high on methamphetamines. He feared ever again appearing to be naïve.

"No, this is definitely not a sales call. This is a jail. You don't want to carry any large bags in here. Let's just see what's up."

"You think something happened in his office and he's here temporarily?"

Finn stopped and turned to his rep. "Let's just call it research." He pointed to the crowd outside. "That's a waiting line if I'm not mistaken. Why don't you lead the way?"

Stu walked ahead. Pulling out a business card to have at the ready, he walked to the front of the line with Finn in tow. The door was closed but Stu entered like he worked there. There were no other people standing inside, except for a plump gray-haired lady, serving as a radio dispatcher and receptionist. He walked up to the reception desk and placed a business card on the counter.

"You must be wanting to see Doctor Lane."

"Yes, ma'am."

"Are you a detail man?"

"Yes, ma'am, Stu Roy with Plushaut Uclaf. What's the story here? Is he seeing drug reps today?"

"He is sort of busy seeing patients. You really want to talk to him behind bars?"

Stu carefully pondered what to say. The situation deserved flippancy. He looked at Finn as he responded. "I guess it depends upon what side of the bars you put me."

It wasn't a new joke to her, but she was kind enough to ignore it. "You know, don't you? Doctor Lane was arrested this week for attempted murder."

The answer to her question was clear in the surprised expressions of Stu and Finn. She began laughing at their reaction.

"He... allegedly... tried to kill his nurse," she whispered.

"And you're letting him see patients?"

She looked at Stu with exasperation. "We're in Signal, Oklahoma. We have one doctor. Everybody in this town is either diabetic, elderly, or crazy. Nobody's going to tell us how to run this town unless they supply us with a new doctor."

"I think we need to see him then." Stu looked to Finn for his approval.

"It might be fun."

The dispatcher took a card from Stu and carried it to a deputy in the back hallway. After a brief discussion, the business card went farther down the hall. A minute later the deputy came to the front desk and lifted the countertop passageway.

"This way," he said with a wave of his hand.

Stu and Finn followed him to the back. To his left, Stu noticed the open door of a closet packed full of pharmaceutical samples.

"Does Doctor Lane take samples?" he asked the deputy.

"No. All that is evidence, but if we have a patient that really needs something, we might borrow some."

"Will he need some fresh that is not evidence?"

"If you want to join him in jail. Otherwise, don't leave anything... and no hands or papers put inside the bars."

The three reached Doctor Lane's cell. "Doctor Lane, I believe you know these two boys."

The doctor looked up with a bright smile on his face. "Stu, great to see you." He looked next at Finn. "Who's your partner here?"

"Doctor Lane, this is my friend Finn Trottel."

"You mean your manager."

"I confess to being his overseer, yes."

"Well, he's a good detail man for us. You treat him right or I'll crawl out of this cell and get you."

The laugh was genuine, but uncomfortable. Doctor Lane did not miss noting the mixed reaction. In his mind it was still small-town politics. He was in jail, but still vital to the community. In his mind, his incarceration was a necessary gesture to keep the investigators happy. He was optimistic that it was only temporary. In the meantime, he was seeing his patients for free, getting meals paid for, and out of range of his wife, who was truly out for blood. He happily accepted his sheriff's protection.

"So, what are you boys selling today?"

"It depends on the people coming in the door. What's the disease of the day?"

"Today?" Doctor Lane pondered that for a minute. "Crazy people."

"What kind of crazy people?"

He looked at Stu with a puzzled frown. "The kind who are crazy enough to come to this jail to see their doctor."

"I think it's a fairly smart move on their part. What complaints do these crazy people bring to you today?"

Doctor Lane looked up at Finn. "You need to give this boy a raise. He's good like a bulldog."

"You mean he won't let go?" Finn said.

"Exactly!" There was a long pause. Silence was Stu's friend at the moment. "Tell me more about this new agent you introduced. What's it called?"

"You mean Flofral?"

"That's the one. It has an unpronounceable generic name."

"Flofral is *heptoxifylline*."

"That's it! A new hemorheologic agent for intermittent claudication and diabetic microvascular disease, right?"

"Yes, sir. You even said hemorheology correctly."

"Well, I could use it here. I have a significant Indian population, you know. Seems like every one of my Indian patients is diabetic or will be soon."

"Other doctors have said the same thing. You know I call on the Cheyenne Arapaho Clinic in Clinton."

"What do they say besides 'it's not on my formulary?'"

"Does that cause problems if you prescribe it here?"

"You mean besides being behind bars?" He laughed at his own joke.

"I'm thinking more of your patients' compliance."

"If they have to pay for it, they won't fill my prescription. The Indian hospitals all have the same formulary. *Heptoxifylline* isn't on it."

Stu stared at him in frustration through the bars. "That's my problem, too. They don't fill the script. They don't do anything. All three of us lose… you, me, and the patient."

Doctor Lane looked up and shook his head, his face showing his frustration with Indian Health. "I know. Nothing we can do."

"Doctor Lane, I see a line out there. Your patients might get impatient if I don't leave. Good luck to you on this ah… situation. I'll see you back at your office perhaps next time."

He nodded a sendoff. Finn and Stu strode quickly out of the jail hallway, through the front door, and into the open air. Finn stopped and called to Stu.

"Why didn't you sell him our other drugs? It's not like he could run out on you."

"Finn, he's in a freaking jail, that's why. That place gave me the creeps. And you know that his career is probably toast. Besides, it's lunchtime. We need to find a town that has more than a tired-out Dairy Queen."

The rest of the day was boringly routine. They called on four more physicians after putting cards into eight different offices. The job had many days of great call frequency followed by other days where Stu feared Finn would think he hadn't gone to work.

Stu stayed in Clinton at the Ramada Inn, while Finn drove home to work with another sales rep next morning. He couldn't wait to call Ana and share with her the most bizarre sales call of his career.

Chapter Twelve

THE INDIAN HEALTH Service was a mess. The ultimate example of government bureaucracy, many of the physicians shared their frustrations with Stu. Others embraced the system and defended it vigorously. Every three months he called on the Cheyenne-Arapaho Clinic in Clinton, Oklahoma. This large, combined clinic and hospital incorporated many aspects important to the two tribes. Most prominent was a sweat lodge out back behind the facility, which men of the tribes used almost continuously. It was tribal medicine in a modern setting.

Stu arrived late for his 8:00 a.m. appointment to see four physicians. He walked up to the front desk and presented his business card.

"I'm sorry I'm fifteen minutes late. I have no excuse. Have I lost my chance to see your doctors?"

The Cheyenne receptionist, now on good terms with Stu, began laughing. As she continued her diminishing chuckles, Stu was thinking that she meant that the doctors would never see him because of his late arrival. Instead, she gave him an unexpected answer.

"Are you kidding? This is an Indian clinic. No one's on time at an Indian clinic."

So, Stu put in three more cards for the physicians and waited to be called back. Sitting down he thought about her words and how flexible the system had to be. When he parked his car in the parking lot, there were several large families patiently sitting in their cars or milling about outside. A patient's visit often included everyone in his family, occasionally a day early. The clinic accommodated this cultural norm, as much as was reasonable.

Physicians were a revolving door. Working at Indian Clinics was often a part time job for local physicians. Other physicians were working off their medical school loans, serving in the uniformed Public Health Service, or running out the clock until retirement.

Another aspect that angered Stu was the Indian Health Service national formulary committee. Plushaut Uclaf had successfully climbed to the national level in the hierarchy with a proposal to use Flofral (*heptoxifylline*) in the Indian Health System because of the high prevalence of type-2 diabetes among Indians nationwide. The price of Flofral was reasonable. Its benefits in increasing patient life expectancy were enormous. For diabetic patients, the risks of heart disease, kidney failure, stroke, and amputations were huge. Adding the genetic components of native tribes, amputations were a frequent outcome.

Stu's company described to the national formulary committee how the use of Flofral in diabetics could prevent gangrene and amputations, usually beginning with their toes. The cost of the drug was equivalent to or less than the cost of a surgical amputation. Rehabilitation costs for patients in recovery would be less, if not zero.

The formulary committee turned down Plushaut Uclaf's proposal, while agreeing that they preferred avoiding amputations. They recognized that surgical amputations were more costly. It sounded good for Flofral until the concluding paragraph of their letter of rejection.

Although overall cost savings appear an advantage, the departments of surgery and of rehabilitation are separate entities with separate budgets. Coordinating these entities would not be to the advantage of the Indian Health Services Drug Formulary. Budgetary restraints currently placed upon the drug formulary require a comparable therapeutic agent to be displaced when a new drug is added. Flofral does not match that of any other drug on formulary.

To Stu it looked like the Indians were once again being put on the chopping block. The Indian Health Services decided it was more for their convenience to amputate toes and limbs than to try a proven and effective pill—nothing humane or healthy in that.

A nurse called Stu's name.

"Mister Roy, the doctors will see you now. If you're worried that you were late, the first doctor just got here."

Stu stood up with his large sales bag and walked down the hallway to the back kitchen. After a few months of calling on so many clinics, he was like part of the staff, even in this sometimes-hostile environment. He knew the rules, where the doctors preferred to see him, and how long he might have to wait. It was now after 9:00 a.m. He had waited for an hour. Of the four doctors he expected to talk with, only one waited for him in the kitchen. Doctor Smith greeted Stu warmly. Stu knew him from two previous calls.

"Come in here, Stu," he said, leading him in the hallway to his private office. He looked at him with a curious smile. "You look dressed up today. Someone die or something?"

Stu looked down at his suit. "Only because I had to work with my boss yesterday. This is not for you."

They both laughed. The two hit it off beginning with Stu's first call months earlier. Smith was unusual at this Indian Clinic. He cared for and worried about his patients beyond their medical needs. He received his medical degree from Tufts, joined Public Health Service, and enjoyed his job in Indian Health. He found it challenging. His initial encounter with the Cheyenne and Arapaho tribes had puzzled him. He spent close to a year working to gain their trust and understand the culture. He attended powwows. He attended tribal meetings when asked. When he learned that another physician in town was taking lessons in the Arapaho language, he joined him. The tribe appreciated his interest in their traditions. It was through his efforts that the bureaucracy in Washington, D.C., officially approved a sweat lodge for the medical treatments of the tribes.

"I'm sorry about the decision with Flofral," Smith said. He sat in his office chair, awkwardly trying to find room for his legs. A tall man, who easily stood out in a crowd, his legs constituted two-thirds of his height. He talked with Stu sitting sideways to his desk. "I've tried it on several diabetics to get them to buy Flofral from the pharmacies in town, but they just won't do it."

"I think its criminal, what they're doing to your patients. So yeah, I'm disappointed, too."

"Compliance is always a problem with patients anywhere, but this is worse. If the drug isn't free, they won't fill the prescription."

"You ever talk to a retired veteran? I learned the same thing from VA patients. They won't buy something better when they can get good-enough-for-free from the VA hospital pharmacy."

"So, is there anything on our formulary that you can sell me now?"

"Well, do you still use our Soulag XL for constipation?"

"Sorry, but it's on our formulary now as a generic."

"Same with Destense, 10mg and 20mg for blood pressure?"

Smith ran his finger across the page of the new formulary booklet. "No, sorry. It's gone generic also."

"Well, shoot. There goes my call."

"We gave Flofral a good run for it though. I kept hoping we would get that. I probably irritated a few dozen bureaucrats along the way."

"I do appreciate your help." He reached out a hand to shake Doctor Smith's. "Should I wait for the other three while you go to work?"

"Don't bother. I'm the only one here today that you would want to see."

Stu thanked him for his time and was not even out of the back room when Doctor Dipity blocked his exit. Irritated, he gruffly asked Stu, "Are you leaving?"

"Yes, sir."

"Good! I don't write your crap anyway—wouldn't if I had to. So, you can go on your way."

The doctor stepped aside and let Stu pass. Finn would be happy with his reported activity. Stu would count that brief insult as a second sales call. One for Doctor Smith and another for the doctor he called Doctor Dipshit.

Chapter Thirteen

When Stu began his job in pharmaceuticals, he thought an internist was a first-year resident after medical school. He was unfamiliar with osteopaths. When his boss referred to pharms, he pictured corn, wheat, and cattle. He once asked a cardiologist, "In your practice, do you deliver babies?" He had gone from zero knowledge to respectful ability, welcomed by his doctors and esteemed by his peers both within his company and among his competitors.

As a fifteen-year veteran, Stu was now a senior member of his new division. As the company expanded, it carved out additional divisions as the stakes for success or failure grew higher and higher in the industry. He was delighted that the unmanageable Bill Dooley stayed behind in this carve-out. Dooley was happy because he didn't like change. Stu loved change. His new division manager was a young and overdue breath of fresh air, Mike Austin. Mike was an average sales rep, but Finn Trottel had seen something brilliant in him that most managers would have ignored. Mike knew how to lead. It took some hard selling for Finn to convince upper management that a man with only average results should get the promotion. For the sales force it was a welcome recognition that from experience, great sales reps did not always translate into good managers. There were countless cases already that proved the point.

For the first time, Stu realized that competition had become all-out war. The number of new drugs approved by the Food & Drug Administration dropped dramatically. The sense of the FDA was one of extreme bureaucratic caution. The cost to approve a new major entity in the pharmaceutical industry grew from three hundred million to over a billion dollars. Even after investing that amount of money, only a third of the new drugs received FDA approval. To pay for the expanding cost of getting a drug approved, companies raised prices, bolstered their sales force, and merged with other pharmaceutical companies. Mergers and acquisitions became a recurring theme for the next twenty years. Plushaut Uclaf was not immune to the trend. Although they kept their name, they bought certain smaller chemical companies. With district meetings coming up, Stu's company sent out a letter to all employees announcing the purchase of a chemical company. To the surprise of everyone, the announcement to both companies included information about the retirement of the entire management staff in Plushaut Uclaf. To replace them were the managers of the acquired company. Ironically, the new Plushaut executives rehired one manager. Nearly every Plushaut sales rep wondered why they kept that one guy whom they perceived to be a doofus.

To everyone's surprise the company became better to work for. Rules of engagement with doctors loosened up. Stu was glad to get more giveaways, but less happy to have more samples than he could give away. The problem arose when the federal government began introducing more regulations and laws. They mandated sales reps to follow certain guidelines that the new management ignored, not out of malice but out of ignorance. Where reps once ordered the drug samples they needed, now they received standard orders of samples. That was great if the rep's territory was in the wild west of drug towns. In most of the cities, corporations were buying out a physician's office practice and placing restrictions on the use of samples and drug rep visits. It made more sense when Stu realized that these same corporations also owned the pharmacies. But that wasn't the main reason. The clinic managers were controlling the practice, not the physician. Their belief was that the numbers and frequency of drug reps were out of control in their clinics, which Stu knew to be true. Many doctors, who enjoyed the presence of their favorite reps complained—sometimes aggressively. But doctors grudgingly grew aware that the company owned them, and the clinic manager was their boss. Increasingly the doctors gave up their resistance. Their bosses fired from their own practices those doctors who wouldn't comply. Stu decided to begin calling on these managers and to treat them like another doctor. He sought out their advice and made sure they got special treatment with high quality giveaways that he could buy for their office or bring from his company's stockpile.

WITH THESE CHANGES to the industry and to their company, the new division convened their first January meeting to launch a new year with its newly installed upper management. There was a handful of new reps to meet, including three females. Finn avoided hiring females for the past ten years. Mike Austin hired two of the three. The third lady was Finn Trottel's first female hire, which he only did because she would go into another manager's division. Mike asked Stu if he would sit with Finn's hire and lend his calm support during the three-day meeting. He shared that, since he had not hired her, he wanted him to assess how she would fit in. Stu agreed, sight unseen, because he enjoyed doing anything different that broke the boring routine of a division meeting that Finn replicated four times every year. When Stu told his wife Ana what his assignment was, she laughed.

"Is my husband assigned to be the division stalker?"

He chuckled, but in the back of his head, he did wonder what he had gotten himself into. He was also curious. *Was she attractive? Smart? Naïve?*

"Let's just say that I may call you for some advice."

Chapter Fourteen

THE FIRST PLAY Meeting occurred the summer before at Shangri-la, a lake resort on Grand Lake in far northeastern Oklahoma. Each year the top Division within Abbott Wahl's region won a no-holds-barred-knockdown-drag-out meeting, where money was no object and no training was in evidence, unless it was to teach a new rep how to drink heavily. For four days they could raise hell, risk their lives, and celebrate their sales success. Many things could go wrong at these meetings. Stu shuddered at the behavior fueled by alcohol and a seemingly unlimited expense budget. Golfing, boating, or any daring sport occurred from sunrise to sunset. After a day of studying this behavior for the first time, he dived in.

An initiation of sorts, Play Meetings did serve one important benefit to managers and reps alike. They learned how people behave when away from home. Some passed the test. Others did not. Finn Trottel's antics disappointed Stu, but he still took advantage of his largess.

Dinner the second night was a group meal, of course starting with an hour of drinks at the bar. Knowing the names of mixed drinks he had never had, Stu ordered several odd cocktails. The bartender had no clue what they were. Neither did his division mates. After ordering a mint julip, and getting the same response from the bartender, Stu out of desperation asked for the only one left he had read about.

"How about a Grasshopper? I don't know what it is, but can you make that?"

"Yes." The bartender was as relieved and amused as was the whole group of partiers.

Stu was surprised to learn that this version took ice cream along with whatever else they told him. A waiter brought it out to the end of the long table of twelve and asked that they send it down to Stu at the other end. By the time it got to Stu it was empty. Everyone had a big laugh. So, Stu ordered a second.

Finally, the bartender personally passed it to the middle of the table closer to Stu, but to no avail. For the second time, it arrived empty. He got a little testy and stormed out of his seat and walked to the bar to order and receive his Grasshopper in person. While Stu waited at the bar, his division mates continued to heckle him. Eventually, they lost interest and turned their attention to each other. When Stu returned to his seat, Grasshopper in hand, the joke was over—so they thought.

The usually soft-spoken Charlie Ketter was the first to cry out. "Oh, no! What have you done?"

Others turned, and pandemonium raged as the bartender delivered a dozen more Grasshoppers to the table. Finn turned to look at Stu with a combination of irritation and admiration. He had learned something about his rep. Stu was one to be reckoned with in the future, and he admired his initiative.

Stu held up his glass. With the use of someone else's money, he became a legend for the day.

"Drink up boys and girls. The drinks are on me."

That was in the summer, but there was a new sheriff in the company town for the new year. Meetings from now on were likely to be a lot different.

"All right, boys and girls. Let's take our seats and get started." It was 8:00 a.m., and Mike Austin looked as relaxed as Stu had ever seen. He was in his element and Stu hoped that his reign would start successfully. Stu's new manager was also his friend. He wanted to make sure he made it easy for his boss.

He gazed at the middle section of the conference table where he always preferred sitting. In the old division with Finn Trottel, the older reps sat as far from the boss as they could. Stu needed no hierarchy of placement, preferring seats in the middle where he was closer to the younger reps. Sitting in the seat closest to the boss was Finn's young female hire, Cissy Bordon, in all her feminine glory. Stu contemplated calling her Lizzy if she turned out to be a good team player. Any nickname was a compliment if the new rep was easy going. Stu took his seat next to her. Across from him were the other two female hires that Mike personally hired. All the reps had introduced themselves to each other in the fifteen minutes of milling about before Mike called the group to order.

Cissy turned to whisper in Stu's ear at the same time as Mike began talking. "Thank you for sitting with me. I truly value your experience."

Stu nodded courteously, but kept his attention focused on the boss. Mike began his first meeting seated with the old team, a pleasant smile indicating his level of comfort.

"Welcome to all of you. Thanks for being in your seats in a timely fashion." He stopped to look around the room at each person facing him. The men were in coat and tie. The three newly hired women wore their own definition of business attire. "Before we get started with the work of the day, I want to go around the room and introduce each of you individually. We have four new members of our team that I think will fit in quite nicely." He glanced to his left at the three new hires sitting across from Stu, then to his right at Cissy.

All the others were seasoned reps from the old division. Fred McAnich, Charlie Ketter, Lance Layton, and Jimmy Tomey. The boss still had one more hire to select to reach his full contingent of ten reps in the division. Fortunately for the four veterans, Bill Dooley remained in his old division. Management had either fired or run off the other reps Mike previously worked with over the past few years. Alcoholism and poor work ethic were root causes of termination for many reps.

The surviving older reps eyed each other with meaningful looks. Sitting closest to the boss was Christy Fowler, young, baby-faced, and poised. Next to her was Lorelei Lolly, in her mid-thirties, unmarried, and a seasoned rep from another drug company. Sitting by Lorelei was new hire Benton Wickingham IV, who was nobody's fool. Even as a new hire, he had a commanding presence about him that was oddly appealing to everyone.

"Let's start with Cissy Bordon." Mike extended his right hand in her direction. "I'm sure you have already met Cissy, but I'll add a few notable facts and then, Cissy, you might want to share some things about yourself with the group."

She looked to her right at Stu and the others, then nervously nodded her head.

"Then let's begin. Cissy grew up in...."

Cissy stood and interrupted. "Mike, if you don't mind, I'll talk about myself. I would feel more comfortable."

"Okay." Mike stayed cool about it, but to his core, he was irritated. It served to confirm the reason he asked Stu to evaluate her. And Stu knew why Mike picked him. He had a happy marriage and never talked about the joy of conquest as did about ten percent of the reps.

"I just wanted to say how honored I am to work with such a well-respected group of men." Cissy glanced around the table with a sweet smile for all the men, but locked her gaze on new hire, Benton Wickingham IV.

Fred McAnich, sitting to Stu's right, leaned into his ear and whispered. "How in hell would she know how well-respected we are?"

Stu discreetly nodded while keeping his attention on what Cissy was saying.

"I grew up in a small town outside of Shattuck…." Fred interrupted.

"I thought Shattuck was a small town, too! You can't get much smaller than Shattuck." He punched the air with every other word in his unique animated manner. The other men in the room looked down, not wanting to be associated with Fred's juvenile remark.

Rather than flustered, Cissy focused on Fred with a pinpoint intensity. For Cissy, it wasn't because she was put off. Cissy had hooked her first man for the day. Her focus was all about lust.

"I grew up in Gage. Compared to Shattuck, it's definitely a small town."

She stared at Fred for an awkward extra second too long. Lance Layton chuckled nervously in his deep resonant voice then asked a question.

"Where is Gage?"

"Go fifteen miles northwest and you would be in the top of the Texas panhandle." Her grin widened as she spoke. "Growing up there, Shattuck had a big medical presence. I got to know several of the doctors and knew that the medical field was what I wanted for a career. I went to OU in Norman…." A couple of cheers and a like number of boos erupted. Then the rest of the room piled on. Lorelei looked at her fellow new rep in surprise.

"Cissy! You're an OU Sooner? Oh my God, why am I sitting here?"

The laughter that followed was a testament to good fellowship, proving briefly that meetings could and should be spontaneous and fun.

Cissy continued. "That's about all. I got a degree in nursing, met a lot of doctors and detail men, and now I am here, thanks to Mister Dooley who recommended me to Mister Trottel."

Cissy sat down. For a short second, every seasoned rep pondered the same fact. *Bill Dooley is a poor source for anything.* Any newly hired rep, who stayed with the company for a year, landed a four-figure bonus in the pocket of whoever recommended him. Bill Dooley's bonus-hire track record was high volume but poor outcome. Yet, in that split-second Mike Austin started clapping, and like a yawn, the others automatically did the same.

Christy Fowler came next for introductions. This was her first job out of college. The division's nearly universal skepticism was no surprise. With no work experience prior to this job, the group assumed it must be her looks that got the job. It wasn't Mike's style to hire someone on looks alone, so the tenured men were keenly interested in what she said—and how she looked. She was easy to fall in love with. Her smile drew men away from their usual torso survey. With a stunning figure, Christy had this magnetic attraction in her eyes that made men forget to look lower. Baby-faced with long auburn hair and bright blue eyes, she left the impression of a graduating high school senior—young, comely, and happy. Women don't always appreciate men's attraction to a happy female. Christy reminded them all of another by the same name, Christy Brinkley, the swimsuit model in *Sports Illustrated* from the decade before.

Mike began his introduction. "After finishing her master's degree in human physiology from Stanford University, Christy Fowler came to us with a pristine resume and a recommendation from Doctor Christiaan Barnard."

"The Christiaan Barnard?" Jimmy Tomey asked.

"Whoa! The transplant guy?" asked Fred McAnich.

"That would be the guy," Stu said. "I met him once at Baptist Hospital. He was there in the mid-1980s with the heart transplant doctors. Did you work there, Christy?"

"I was a patient there," she replied.

After a few seconds of stunned, yet polite, silence, Mike continued his introduction. Christy said a few words but did not offer to fill in the blanks of her association with Doctor Barnard or her reason to be a patient there. No one paid attention to what she said. Her bearing, her voice, and her smile impressed the group more than the words she spoke. How she got to Stanford University was clear. The robust clapping was satisfactory to match her accomplishments.

Doctor Christiaan Barnard was at Integris Baptist Medical Center serving as Scientist-in-Residence at the Oklahoma Transplantation

Institute for two years. Stu had brought to his office a Plushaut check of $10,000 to support the transplant institute. While Stu talked to the office manager, Doctor Barnard walked into the room, listened to Stu and the manager talk, then walked out of the room without saying a word. A thank you would have been nice. Stu was unimpressed and disappointed.

Next up was Benton Wickingham IV. At the mention of his name, the men began suppressed laughter. Mike continued.

"Benton Wickingham the Fourth spent six years as an Army infantryman. He then used the GI Bill to get a bachelor's degree from Central State University in marketing. Benton, you're up. Let 'em know what you want 'em to hear."

"Well, first of all, I am happy to be here in a job where my college degree might be helpful. I am a proud veteran. I put the IV at the end of my name for whimsy. I am indeed the fourth, so my friends have always called me Four. If I earn it in time, I hope you will too."

Four sat down to claps and shouted golf jokes from his teammates calling, "Fore!"

"You may already know our last new hire," Mike said. "She has been our competitor for years—and a damn fine one at that. Lorelei Lolly—I love that name—previously worked for Merck for... how many years?"

"Ten years."

"Well, take it away, Lorelei, and tell us something about yourself that we don't already know."

Lorelei Lolly was a great catch for Plushaut—the crown jewel of Mike's hires. Everyone who encountered her in the field thought the world of her. She was a tough competitor.

"Since I know most of you already, I don't feel the need to dwell on myself. I see Jimmy over there. It will be a pleasure to work with you. My job will be easier now. What a great help you were to me when I started out."

Lorelei, with expensive tastes, was sharply attired. Unmarried, but always looking for Mister Right, she was wise enough to be comfortable with who she was and where she was. Stu knew from talking to her that several doctors had asked her on dates in the past, but she was never interested in someone who was well-to-do but worked all the time. She wanted a friend, not a fat portfolio. She proceeded to turn to each individual and introduce them, not herself.

"Fred? I always knew when you were around. I could see you talking before I heard you talking. What a good friend you are. Lance, on the other hand, with that voice of his, I could hear him before I could see him. What good advice he always shared with me. Charlie? Well, I fell in love with Charlie, until I found out how good he was at selling against me. He is one of the best salesmen in this area, if you ask the doctors. Stu is one of those reps that surprises me sometimes. He used to give me tips on how to see those tough-to-see specialists. I asked him once why he would share that information with me, a competitor. Stu, your answer was wonderful. You said that you would still outsell me but knew that I would always return the favor. I'll never forget that. I have to say something nice about my new boss. Mike, I chose to leave Merck when I heard you were promoted to manager of this division. I have that much respect for you."

Lorelei paused and looked around the room to the three new reps she was joining.

"The four of us are lucky to be here with this great group. Enough said. Thanks, Mike, for hiring me."

The clapping was louder than before as nine pairs of hands clapped just a little more enthusiastically. With Lorelei's introduction, everyone in the room understood why Mike hired her. She cared about people. Lorelei was good for morale.

Chapter Fifteen

THE MEETING CONTINUED with Mike having each of the seasoned reps give a short background about themselves for the benefit of the new reps. They were all used to the exercise and usually peppered the information with jokes about each other's skills, foibles, and odd habits. Stu, who was a master of quick one-liners, contributed his share of gigs on his teammates.

"Stu, you are so funny... so gifted," Cissy whispered, her lips close enough that Stu felt her breath mixed with her words. It took him by surprise. *Only Ana should do that.* The gesture was unwelcome. It had the opposite response she expected.

"Funny? Not usually." Even he didn't know what he meant. It was a brushoff line.

At lunch, the atmosphere was festive. There was plenty of banter between bites of food about the bounty of the buffet. It was common for everyone to pile more on their plates than was necessary for a day constantly seated in comfortable chairs. All the reps overate and fought sleep an hour later. Fred would never have issues. Constantly in motion, Fred would have a plateful of calories burned off before 3:00 p.m. He was gyrating as he ate, with Cissy sitting between us. She turned to speak to me.

"Is Fred always so funny? He's nice and all, but I'm glad you'll be my mentor. You are so knowledgeable. It's a much better arrangement."

Stu was no fool. He knew what a line of false flattery was. Besides, he was married—and happy about it. *How would Cissy know what knowledge I have? Can't wait for her next come-on.*

To Stu's relief Fred interrupted them. When Cissy turned to him, Stu overheard her as she piled the same fawning on his teammate. Fred, for once not gyrating, went for all her sweet talk like a fish to a hook. As she reeled him in, he swallowed her sweet talk—hook, line, and sinker.

The group waddled back to the meeting room at 1:00 in the afternoon and prepared for roleplaying. It was routine for one sales rep to make a sales call on another rep pretending to be a doctor. The more veteran reps usually made their role as doctor more realistic than would a new rep. Because of that, Mike called on Cissy to be the first up to demonstrate a call on make believe Dr. Stu Roy. She was noticeably nervous as she gathered her sales visual and giveaways that were part of the company's recommended promotion for the quarter. This was her first time practicing in front of the division. For several weeks before this moment, she had practiced the same sales pitch with Mike and Mike's managerial mentor, Finn Trottel. They were pleased with her progress.

With two chairs pulled out from the conference table, Stu and Cissy sat face-to-face in full view of the others as she began to sell one of the older and easier drugs to talk about.

"Good morning, Doctor Roy." Cissy began by shaking Stu's hand as he glanced at his watch to note it was early afternoon.

"Good afternoon. You're new. What's your name?"

"I'm Cissy Bordon and you are my first ever call."

"Oh, my goodness, another one to train."

Cissy giggled and went on. "I note that you are an internist."

"I am?" Stu couldn't help being ornery. "For you today, I will be an internist—so... yes."

"And what patients are you seeing today. Any interesting cases?"

Stu knew it was time to help her out. "My day has been a constant stream of patients coming in because of constipation."

"I've heard that it's a recurring problem in pregnant women."

"I'm an internist, not a gynecologist."

"Of course." Cissy's face flushed at her freshman mistake but recovered quickly. "But you do see plenty of elderly."

"Now you are in my specialty. Nearly all my patients are over fifty-five."

"So, you've seen and heard the complaints of discomfort, embarrassment, and worry in these patients. Are they mostly women?"

"I would say so." Stu was through with whimsy. He wanted her to have that shot at looking good in front of her peers.

"My mother and grandmother both complained of that as they aged. They tried every product the Rexall had in our town of Shattuck. Bulk didn't work. The phenolphthalein products were uncomfortable. Stool softeners took forever. Sound familiar?"

"Yes, all day today. Nothing works, but the patient keeps coming back. Can't you fix it?"

It was a genuine question familiar to Stu—a line once asked by one of his doctors. He still couldn't decide if that doctor was serious or pulling his leg.

"I may have a fix for you if you find that contact irritants are ineffective long term. Would your patients benefit from something that systemically stimulates bowel motility while additionally regulating the patient's daily habits without causing the discomfort associated with more effective, but harsh, laxatives?"

"That's a mouthful, but sure, I want to know. What do you have that can do this?"

"Let me introduce to you Soulag XL for chronic constipation in your elderly patients." She pulled out a sample of Soulag XL, neatly packaged as seven tablets in a heavy clear plastic card. "This is a week's worth of relief for both your patients and for you as their doctor. Will you give it a try for this week?"

"How much does it cost?"

"My mother paid about five dollars for a week's therapy. You dose it once a day at bedtime. Will you prescribe it this week and give me a report?"

"I will do just that."

"Thank you, Doctor Roy."

She shook Stu's hand, then nervously slumped in her chair.

"Hell," Doctor Roy said. "My wife and I will have our own pill party tonight with this sh… stuff."

Chapter Sixteen

BY THE END of the first day, Mike assumed that his managerial debut was successful. His new reps had all performed well in their first presentations. Benton, or Four, his army veteran hire, was meeting the challenges of civilian life as he had hoped. He now would hire more veterans like Four in the future.

He had worried that Christy would need some help at first because of her youth. She surprised him with her poise and unflustered handling of her practice doctor. It was obvious that Doctor Jimmy Tomey was smitten by her youthful beauty and treated her like a China doll. She needed no help in teaching Doctor Tomey that she was no novice sales rep.

Lorelei was a manager's delight. Her only need was for the meeting to be over. Then she could go back to work doing what she did best. She cared for patients and helped them by working with the physicians she influenced every day.

The reps were milling around in the hotel lobby. Mike looked over at the two big leather easy chairs in the back corner. Seated and talking with his hands was Fred. Standing in front of him was Cissy, feigning fascination with his conversation. She finally sat down in the other plush seat, put her elbow on the arm and rested her chin on the back of her hand and fixated on Fred. Watching Fred talk long enough would exhaust the most attentive listener, yet Cissy continued to hang on to his monolog. Cissy impressed Mike with her practice pitch to Doctor Roy. The irritation from her initial interruption of his introduction was all forgiven after her performance. Her overtly flirtatious personality puzzled him. Doctors would be either put off by her antics or put upon. He would have to watch for that.

It was routine for all members of the newly named division, The Boomers, to stay the night in the hotel even if they lived in town. It was the company's way of building a cohesive selling spirit. That afternoon Mike had worked through several names for his division. The week before, he had asked for suggestions. They only came from the older reps. Some were serious. Most were not. The rejects included *Pretend Doctors, Okies, Okie Dokies, Local Yokels,* and, because the division was finally hiring women, *Asses and Assets.* That one Mike chose not to bring up. It most likely would come out anyway at dinner, after a couple of cocktails. The name Sooners got many early votes, but, because it was the state's nickname and more importantly the University of Oklahoma's nickname, it got the boot. There were fans of rival Oklahoma State University who would have made a mockery of it. Sooners were claim jumpers who sneaked in early before the Oklahoma Land Run of 1889. Boomers referred to claim jumpers who a decade before tried to settle in Indian Territory prior to the Land Run.

To sway the vote, Stu said, "Sooners and Boomers were both felons, so they would both fit how we view ourselves as drug selling bad-asses. Why not go with Boomers?"

And so, it stuck. Soft-spoken Charlie Ketter surprised the division by declaring that for this meeting he would call the new hires Baby Boomers.

Dinner began at 6:30 after the Boomers shed their business attire for more casual wear. Jeans, shirts or blouses, and sweaters were the norm. When a waiter came by to take drink orders, it was Mike's first chance to observe how the Baby Boomers adapted to company paid drinks. In

Plushaut Uclaf there were no rules on drinking except the obvious one—*don't be stupid*. As Dan Anders and Cress Caston had learned years before, drunkenness and womanizing will get you fired. If a rep nonetheless could sell like a champion, even that behavior might be overlooked, just not forever. For the next half hour, the Boomers were on their best behavior. But not everyone was there.

"Hey, where's my buddy Fred?" Jimmy Tomey asked. "He never misses happy hour."

"He's not the only one missing," Stu whispered to Mike. Stu, after all, was in charge of forming an opinion of the only Baby Boomer Mike had not hired. This was Finn Trottel's doing.

Five minutes later Fred came down the stairway to the lobby. He raised both arms in a gesture of triumph, after finding where his friends sat waiting. Jimmy and Lance made a space between them at the table and pulled out a chair. Fred sat down with a dramatic exhale of air and smiles.

"What are we having, boys and girls?"

A minute later Stu spotted Cissy descending the same stairs. He nudged Mike and motioned with a nod in her direction.

"Crap!" Mike held his voice down. "What in hell is she doing?"

Cissy, with a look of supreme confidence, dramatically stepped down to the lobby wearing extreme high heels with a pure white body suit that looked like she had painted it on. Every male in the restaurant was aware of her approach.

The deep voice of Lance said, "Good Lord, what have we here?" She smiled for his benefit alone.

Cissy noted a look of jealousy in Fred's eyes after Lance spoke.

"Hello boys!" she said on her approach. Stepping over to the side of the table opposite Fred, she asked Four and Christy if she could sit between them. Lorelei made no effort to conceal her shock at the poor manners. Four politely moved over a seat to the end of the table and found another chair to pull up.

After another round of drinks, two waiters came to take dinner orders. Things began to settle down. It was another free meal for the Boomers, and they ordered five or six appetizers—meals in themselves. Most of the men ordered steaks, always popular in the Southwest. Christy, already proving herself to be the sharpest of the lot, ordered a salad. Apparently, Stanford University taught her some nutrition facts that everyone else at the table ignored. Lorelei was like one of the boys, bringing Christy along with her in the fun. To Four, this dinner was like being back in the Army without KP. Cissy pulled out a cigarette, held it up to her lips and looked across the table. In a Hollywood-inspired pause and waiting for a gentleman to offer her a match, Cissy postured in vain. With her coquettish moment ruined, she spoke. "Do any of you boys have a light?" Fred immediately pulled out a hotel matchbook and did her bidding.

Lance looked at Fred. "I didn't know you smoked."

"I don't."

This brought on quiet looks all around the table. Christy was horrified to see a cigarette. The cloud caught Mike's eye along with his nose. He looked over at Cissy, quickly got up from his seat, and approached her.

"Cissy, we don't smoke in meetings. We are in the medical industry. If you want to smoke, you need to go outside."

Cissy quickly snuffed out her cigarette. Ignoring Mike, she turned to Fred with a sultry smile and said, "Thank you."

Back at his seat, Mike turned to Stu. "Didn't I make nonsmoking clear?"

"You did. That was a prop."

Mike didn't get the point. A lot was going on. The rest of the dinner went off with fun all around and a lot of joking and laughter. It was an hour later that Stu noticed when people left the dining room that Fred followed Cissy into the lobby. Mike headed to the adjoining bar to continue more Boomer bonding with the others. Lorelei proved her value as she had the others captivated with her stories, jokes, and her ability to hold her alcohol. A few, like Jimmy, ran out of steam early. As the reps departed one by one, it ended after Mike, Lorelei, and Stu declared that they had enough and shut down the bar after midnight. Stu and Lorelei lingered in the lobby after Mike headed upstairs.

As both looked down to the end of a long hallway off the lobby, Cissy rounded the corner with Fred following like a stud dog pursuing a bitch in heat. The closer they came up the hallway, the more Fred's eyes looked glazed with visions of conquest. Cissy made no effort to turn around. Instead, she approached the two with a Hollywood movie smile and walked right past them.

"Did you see the leash on him?" asked Lorelei.

"This is not good," Stu replied.

"Isn't Fred married?"

"Yes, he is."

"Stu, I don't want to tell you what to do, but you're going to have to save him from Miss Bad News. I'm in no position to help him."

"I'd be crazy to try tonight."

"You think Mike knows what's happening?"

"I don't know, but he asked me to keep an eye on her. This is bad."

"We better split up before she invites us to join them."

"Not much chance of that. Can you keep a secret?"

Lorelei gave him a nod. "Sure."

"My wife Ana is waiting for me in my room. For at least one night at every meeting, we play this game. We take off our wedding rings and have an affair. Then she sneaks out early in the morning. We've done it for years."

"Well, you sneaky little boy. I'm proud of you."

"Good night, Lorelei."

"Good night, Stu. Sweet dreams—and don't hurt yourself."

Chapter Seventeen

STU WAS UP early for coffee before breakfast when Mike entered the hotel café. Stu caught his attention. Mike eagerly joined him.

"Good morning, Boss!"

"I figured you would be here."

Stu and Mike had roomed together in earlier lean times in the company. Both were early risers which made for a compatible match up. This year the money was flowing, and reps again had separate rooms.

"What do you think of your first day as our leader?"

"I thought it went well. I had fun."

A waitress interrupted them to pour their first cup of coffee. She left them a sizable pitcher of cream at their request. They began their morning's wakeup ritual—one sip at a time.

"So, what do you think about Finn's hire. How is Cissy doing?"

Stu looked at Mike for a long time before he spoke.

"Mike. We are in deep trouble."

"You think?"

"Cissy Bordon is bad news."

Stu took another sip of his cream laden coffee and sighed in pleasure. Only then did he return to the unpleasant subject.

"Fred is a married man—and I'll be blatant. I don't know what's gotten into his head."

"It's Finn's hire. That makes it awkward."

"At least now we know his reluctance to hire a woman. He sucks at it."

"I need to talk to him first."

"I'd tell him after this meeting is over. He has his own to deal with this morning."

"Maybe in the next couple of days, Fred will come to his senses."

"I could talk to him, I guess. That would keep you out of the loop… at least at the first."

Mike took his own pensive sip of coffee, as he mulled over his options. He could lower the hammer on the two lovers. He could ignore them and hope the problem went away. That had worked in the past for division managers. Their behavior was so obvious, he assumed everyone at the meeting was tuned in to it. The Boomers would certainly be watching their actions this morning for clues. It would disrupt the flow and focus of his first meeting as a manager.

"Okay, here's what we're going to do. Let's watch this either unfold or unravel today. Tonight, I want you to glom onto Fred. Talk to him when you can but make it hard for them to discreetly pair up. Let's see what happens."

"Thanks for the crappy assignment."

"Is it going to interfere with your own secret love affair?"

"What love affair?"

"The one you have with Ana at every meeting when we have separate rooms."

"Never done anything like that. I have no idea what you're talking about."

"Of course you don't. What was I thinking?"

The waitress interrupted to take their breakfast order.

"You ready to order, Stu?"

"Yes, thank God."

Mike's second meeting day began again at 8:00 a.m. sharp. Stu was there early but found that Cissy and Fred had beat him to their seats. Except it wasn't Fred's seat. Stu took his first stab at following the boss's orders.

"Good morning, you two. I thought I was the only early bird in this outfit."

"I needed to study," Cissy said, "and Fred said he could help me with some questions I had."

"I thought that was my job."

"Oh?" Cissy's mind began cranking to find a possible response. She focused her gaze at each man in turn. "I didn't mean to put Fred in trouble. I'm sorry, Fred."

"No problem. I was glad to help out."

"Thanks for helping me out, Fred, but you are sitting in my seat. Mike wanted me to do this mentoring, not you."

"Sure." Fred stood up and moved one seat to his right, which put Stu in the chair between them. That irritated them both. The rest of the day's meeting was a somber and uncomfortable experience for all three. Fred was silent and brooding. Cissy continued to pour fuel on the fire. She kept up a steady stream of compliments directed at Stu about his intelligence, experience, and teaching skills. By the end of the day, he concluded that if Ana complimented him every day to the extent that Cissy was doing, he would likely kill her one day in midsentence. It was grating, syrupy adulation that only a teenager could fall for—except for Fred.

The remainder of the day involved more roleplays with make-believe doctors. It was helpful for every rep to hear how their peers sold to doctors—word phrases, questions, and patient types they might find noteworthy. The division shared issues of success and issues of impediment that might help another. Sometimes a rep shared a story of success, which always bordered on bragging. They were told sparingly and only to show another rep how they could address certain difficulties. The only rep who ever violated the rules of humility was Bill Dooley, who fortunately stayed with Finn Trottel's original division. Every

DETAIL MAN

doctor's and rep's personality dictated a different strategy. Selling to physicians with towering egos, which was a minority, required months and years of discussion.

One oddity of this meeting was Mike's announcement about the word *division*. The Plushaut Uclaf home office received word from the newly educated political correctness police that *division* was too divisive a word. From now on, the Boomers would be a *district*, not a *division*. It was the home office's desire that this move would bring Boomers closer together. Mike and Stu knew there was too much closeness going on already. The Boomers agreed it was a pile of smelly manure. But it was the new way, no matter what the sales force thought.

The company's recommended sales calls were always wordy, often not helpful, but mandatory to follow when home office guests joined their meeting. One such person was coming into Oklahoma City to monitor Mike because he was the newest manager of the Southwest Region. The Boomers would have been happier to have their regional manager as a visitor. Abbott Wahl was a great guy to the sales reps and their managers. Instead, a midlevel woman from the marketing department in New Jersey joined them for Friday's final day.

Cissy and Fred settled down to their fate of separation from each other. Stu made sure of it. Even at lunch the two sat far apart. Mike was relieved to see the change and was encouraged further when the two went in separate directions at the end of the meeting.

The lady from marketing arrived by airport shuttle just as the Boomer District sat down for predinner drinks in the hotel bar. This was unlike ten years before, when Finn's division gathered after meetings in his room suite with a box load of hard liquor, paper cups, and ice. Plushaut Uclaf eventually learned that it was a magnet for alcoholics and banned managers from supplying liquor at meetings. Going to the hotel bar was better for controlling overindulgence, but not by much. Managers still could pick up the bar tab for the district. Only when Mike Austin paid and left the bar would moderation take hold of the team.

The home office lady was someone new to Mike. Rose Astor was in her mid-thirties, tall, and athletic. She wore her ruddy brown hair in a stark bun that made her look more like a sadistic prison guard than an innovative marketing genius. Her stingy use of words and her cold handshake upon meeting the group made most Boomers grateful she was visiting for only a day. Thirty minutes and two martinis later, she turned into the life of the party. Her loose lips began a steady flow of accounts of life at headquarters in New Jersey, the site for many drug companies where there were favorable laws of incorporation. Her unflattering descriptions of sexual liaisons, backstabbing, and boot licking were not new to the sales force. It was, however, surprising to hear it firsthand and with no polite filter. She described in detail a fist fight between two high ranking executives in the parking lot on a recent morning. She not only named them but named their wives who were in a dalliance with each other's husband. She shared her opinion of who was stupid, which turned out to be everybody. In a fatal slip, Rose began bad mouthing the sales department for not listening to the marketing department. In her inebriated state she mentioned that the sales force, meaning The Boomers, was likely too stupid to understand why marketing was so helpful. By then her listeners were looking for a way out.

Mike asked those who were not drinking much to load up passengers for a trip to a restaurant outside the confines of the hotel. The Boomers were eating at Molly Murphy's, an establishment known for its outlandish architecture. Reminiscent of Russia's onion-shaped domes of St. Basil's Cathedral in Red Square, the all-wooden restaurant was an appealing curiosity that drew large crowds. The waiters were known for their irritating lack of manners. More than one waiter had angered a customer, but their rule was to keep up the role-play, even at the risk of going too far. People loved it or hated it. The buffet salad bar was a white Jaguar XKE with holes cut out of the hood with all the salad fixings inset. It was a wonderful place for a bunch of salesmen to let their hair down.

Upon entering, Rose continued to raise eyebrows as her conversation turned into a monolog in the Molly Murphy's dining hall. After some rearranging, the eleven pharmaceutical reps settled down at two big tables. Then the action began.

Stu noted that Cissy and Fred had managed to sit at the same table, but not next to each other. There was an even chance that would happen anyway. At their table also sat Rose, who was soon into her third martini and droning on about some pervert in her office complex. She caught the attention of the waiter, Captain Hook, and it was game on. Stu's table of five included Mike, Jimmy, and Baby Boomers Four and Lorelei, which was by far the saner table, especially when they found out that they got Tinker Bell as their waitress. One look at Tinker Bell, and Lorelei could not keep quiet.

"You boys hit the mother lode with Tinker Bell, or whatever she is. Or should we ask her to trade tables?" She was laughing at the other four men, knowing that Tinker Bell came equipped with the most marvelously exposed breasts.

"Tinker Bell? I thought she was Dolly in a tutu," said Four. "This is great. Tutus and tatas."

"Spoken like a real soldier," Jimmy said.

Four grinned knowingly. "Were you Army?"

Mike cut in. "Four, you are it. You're the only veteran we have in The Boomers. Think we need more?"

"Hell, yes. Make sure they're Army, though. All the others are either too crazy gung-ho, drunk half the time when on dry land, or whining about the color of the napkins clashing with their flight suits."

Tinker Bell came back with drinks for the table and told the five about the specials they could order. They first ordered two appetizers for the table while they looked over the menu. Stu and Mike had been here before with Jimmy. They all agreed that having Captain Hook would have been bad luck. As the waitress returned with appetizers, Lorelei began laughing at the men trying to be discreet in their peek down into the depths of her two heavenly mounds.

"If I didn't like men so much, I could be turned on right now."

"You're going to fit into this division just fine, Lorelei."

"Stu, we're not a division anymore," Mike replied with an affected haughty pose. "We don't divide. We district."

Jimmy looked over to see Four cautiously laughing, still getting used to fitting into the group with his manager present.

"What do you think," Jimmy said. "You think Sergeant Four here will fit in okay, too?"

"He better fit in. I hired him." Mike raised his glass of pure soda water. "To the newbies."

"To two Baby Boomers," said Stu.

A dustup at the other table shortened their toast of the newbies, as Captain Hook slammed down a mug and barked a command to Rose in a most convincing pirate dialect. Rose was both unamused and drunk.

"A-a- r-r ye goin' ta shut the bilge pump so I can take o-r-r-ders or must we walk the plank h-e-e-r-r?"

Lance, who by now was fed up with Rose, shut her up with his loud resonant order to do just that, "Shut up!"

Charlie, on the other side of Rose, looked like he was ready to take her down in one of his college wrestling pretzel-holds. With Captain Hook back in command, he took each person's order for dinner, while insulting each one of them for ordering what he declared was the wrong thing, considering their looks.

Tinker Bell was back with appetizers. Mike had to make a comment.

"We're sure glad you're Tinker Bell and not Captain Hook over there."

"Thank you. Are you sure?"

All five in unison called out, "Yes!" which brought them to the attention of Captain Hook. He came straight over.

"A-a-r-r! I see this lady is bothering you. I will find a replacement for you. I believe Frankenstein's Monster is available. I'll get him for you."

"No, no!" Four was out of his chair. "At ease, sailor. You're not taking my Tinker Bell."

"I'll get the monster right away. I'll be back." Captain Hook stepped away. They hoped he returned to Rose's table.

The dinner went downhill from there. Frankenstein's Monster did show up. He was actually quite understandable for a monster. He sounded just like Boris Karloff, who never had a speaking part in the movie. Lorelei mentioned that to him, but he staggered away without a retort. Tinker Bell came back with dessert. The table of five was having a blast. The table of six was having a blast, too, because Rose, the home office marketing executive, was asleep in her chair.

Chapter Eighteen

THE NEXT MORNING the meeting started thirty minutes later. It was Mike's gift to his waning Boomers. The last day was always tough on everyone. Most reps on a typical Friday shut down their day early. A few like Stu tried to make Friday their best day by working late. His theory was that fewer reps on Friday afternoon would give him better access to doctors. Plus, he hoped they would appreciate seeing him working then. After all, doctors had to work long hours on Friday, so why not be there with them. That did not apply to district meetings. Everyone, including Mike, wanted to go home.

Rose, now sober, was back to her reserved and cold manner. When she spoke to the Boomer district in the morning about what was going on officially in the company, she was condescending in her answers to questions.

"I think she truly believes the sales force is stupid," Charlie whispered to Stu. Charlie never offered critiques of people. Rose was his first exception.

The seating was different today, which attracted the attention of Mike. Cissy was again in her assigned seat on the end next to Mike. Fred, never one to sit near the boss, chose this morning to sit next to Mike, which put him conveniently across the table from Cissy. Stu was still sitting next to Cissy as her mentor. Next to Stu now was Charlie. His buddy, Lance, suggested he might enjoy the show that Cissy was putting on so he sat as close as he could to her. She did not disappoint.

The meeting droned on. Then the Boomers practiced their final role-plays with their fake doctors. They were more realistic calls by Friday and included discussions involving all three products that the company wished to stress. Destense 10mg was over ten years old but still an important drug behind Flofral. The third drug, suitable for a reminder only, was a topical steroid cream that had already flopped in the marketplace because it was the tenth steroid cream introduced in the past five years. The entire sales force knew it was a bust, but the home office marketing department in New Jersey was not listening. It was quite common for upper management to be five years behind reality—that was according to the salesmen. With Rose in attendance, no rep dared mention the futility of selling a new but similar drug in an already saturated market.

The meeting broke for lunch with extra time for checking out of the hotel and bringing any suitcases down to the meeting room. Cissy was having trouble checking out of her room. Mike noticed and went over to help, but Cissy claimed she had it under control. The men traditionally hung around the lobby on these days. Lorelei by now was considered one of the guys. She and Christy had hit it off well. The men were relieved to find that Christy fit in well as just another guy in the group. No one said that about Cissy. She had not socialized with the rest. When she entered the lobby, Mike asked her where her bags were.

"Oh, I've already put them in the car."

Mike looked at his watch. "Oh? That's a good idea. We have time." He turned to the guys in the lobby. "If anyone wants to put bags in their car, you have ten minutes to do it."

Four and Jimmy took him up on the suggestion, but nobody else moved. Ten minutes later the whole crew was in the meeting room and seated—eager to get the meeting wrapped up.

As the afternoon session started, the less than subtle foot play of Cissy and Fred began under the table next to Mike. Stu already had his suspicions from the morning, but the physical contact became too animated for the room to ignore when the meeting resumed. Cissy and Fred were each slouched in their seats with eyes fixed on each other. Their bodies' slight movements occurred simultaneously as their feet and calves embraced.

Charlie finally intentionally dropped a pen and some paper on the floor for the purpose of seeing what was going on under the table. After he came back up top, he grinned across the table at Lance, then at Stu. Mike was not happy with what Charlie had done.

It was after three o'clock when Mike began his final review of the three-day meeting. He reviewed in agonizing detail what they had covered on the two previous days. He stressed the importance of following the company program. He reminded the team, mostly for the new members, of the importance of asking for the business, not to simply give a sales call. He thanked Rose for taking her time to fly from New Jersey just to be with his district. As was tradition with Finn, Mike put in another hour of review that the Boomers would not remember past the meeting room door closing behind them.

When the meeting did end, the reps were so eager to start their weekend that no one stayed around to help Mike clean up the room or wait long enough to see what was happening next. They missed plenty.

Chapter Nineteen

MIKE AUSTIN WAS happy about last week's district meeting with his Boomers. He woke up early the next Monday, filled with anticipation that his efforts would be as motivational as he thought they were. Only time would reveal the answer. Motivating a basketball team or a sales force was often a crapshoot. He parked his car in the familiar hotel parking lot where he had post-meeting business to straighten out concerning some room charges. Managers were responsible for paying the hotel bill for all reps, meals, and meeting equipment.

Stepping out of his blood red Buick, he was happy about the day. Mondays were always the day for managers to stay at home and work in their office, which was usually a grueling twelve hours of paperwork and irritating regional manager calls. Getting to run an errand was a refreshing break in an otherwise tedious workday.

With a folder in hand, he cheerfully stepped over to the front desk, presented his problem to the clerk, and waited for his chance to speak with June, the event manager. She was an attractive, polite, and efficient event coordinator who had worked with Finn Trottel for many years. Mike liked her because she made Finn's job so much easier. Today it was not so easy.

"We have a disparity in the room charge here," Mike said, "and I can't understand why my bill has a charge for five days for one of our members?"

June picked up the itemized list that Mike showed her then looked carefully at the large computer screen at her desk. As she checked, Mike had trouble seeing her expression because of the bulky computer equipment. Computer towers and 19-inch screens were all the rage these days.

"Here it is," she replied. "It looks like the lady who arrived a day late, Rose...?"

"That's the one." Mike paused for a moment to let her reply, but he could see she was fixated on the screen. "First off, she is supposed to pay for her room herself, but she was here only one night."

"That's not what I see here. It shows that she stayed over this weekend and is due for a Tuesday noon departure."

"Really?"

"You're welcome to look at this." She pushed her chair back from her desk to give Mike room to step around and check the screen up close.

He looked at June and assessed the situation honestly. "I think we have something that I don't like going on."

"We do have her card on file, so it'll be easy to drop this charge and put it on her credit card."

"That would be great. Thank you."

Mike left June to sort out the bill. He decided it might be interesting to take breakfast in the attached café again like last week. He liked the food, and he recognized the same faces working there. He asked for a seat where he could look out to the lobby and see clearly anyone coming down the grand stairway or entering from the elevators. He ordered a big breakfast of eggs over easy, pork sausage, grits, pancakes, and coffee. Now it was a waiting game.

He ate slowly because he spent most of his time looking up to watch movement in the lobby, not face down looking at his plate. An hour later, he was full to the gills with breakfast and his fifth cup of coffee. The coffee, chased by his glass of water, had filtered through. He couldn't leave for fear of missing Rose, but he couldn't stay either. He was determined to wait her out. He asked the waitress to bring him his bill. When she came back with it, he gave her his credit card, not even checking the tab. When she brought the card back to him, he quickly added a tip. Standing up to place his card in his billfold, he began a desperate rush to the bathroom. He was out of time and the will to wait.

He stopped suddenly in front of his table and froze where he stood. He forgot about the bathroom. He was shocked. There, at the top of the grand stairway, was Rose. She had that condescending smirk on her face as she came slowly down. She was holding on to the arm of a man who sheepishly looked left and right. Adding to Mike's surprise, the man had another woman clutching his other arm. Mike knew of men's fantasizing about a *ménage à trois*. He was looking at such a man in an indiscreet triumphant display of conquest. Parading down the steps with Rose Astor, full of laughter and smiles, came Fred and Cissy.

Chapter Twenty

MIKE WAS QUICK to exit the café to confront Rose and her two companions. He stopped them at the bottom of the stairs with regret in his heart. He would have to do something he didn't like. For their part, Rose looked at Mike with a mix of anger and fear. Fred, to his credit, lowered his head in shame and didn't look up. Cissy was haughty and defiant, standing proudly smirking before her boss with a so-what attitude.

"Fred. Cissy. You're fired. You need to go home now. At the proper time I'll come by to pick up your car, your samples, and everything else that Plushaut owns. You will park your cars and not drive them again. Do you understand?"

All three looked stunned. Fred nodded affirmatively. Cissy said nothing but put on a show of disbelief. Rose, for her part, quickly regained her composure and went on the offensive.

"You will not involve me in any of this. Understand?"

"You may be from the home office, but you are in my arena when you mess with my people. I can promise you that the whole company will know about this within the hour. I hope you can get a flight out of here before they cut off your expense account."

For a moment there was a standoff of silence. The growing anger in Rose did not exceed the force of authority from Mike. He knew the company would be on his side. Rose looked first at Cissy, then at Fred.

"You two, come with me!" It was a command, not a suggestion. Cissy made a defiant turn on the stairs to follow Rose. Fred was undecided.

"Mike, I'm sorry. Do I have a say in this—a chance I can talk you out of firing me?"

Mike stood his ground in silence. Although he was crying inside for a friend that he had worked with for more than ten years, he knew he had no choice. Company policy was clear, allowing no leeway for being out of the field with obvious intent to defraud. Finally, he spoke.

"I will make only one promise, Fred. I won't tell your wife. You can do that yourself." Mike paused to think about his own wife and how much it would hurt her to have one she trusted so completely betray her.

"Thank you," Fred replied feebly.

"I feel a lot more sadness for your wife than I do for you, Fred. You let me down, too."

Fred stood in a posture of humiliation. There were no more of his typically wild arm gestures. People who walked by were staring with curiosity at the two, before politely averting their gaze.

"I need to get some stuff from the room."

"Do whatever you need to do. Then go home and park your car. I will call you in a day or two."

Without another word, Fred turned and climbed up the grand stairway like a man ascending to the gallows.

The new boss, christened with his first calamity, wiped a tear from his cheek. He waited to regain his composure and urgently headed to the men's room before looking for a telephone.

He remembered that June was not through with his issue, so he went back to her office to use his new phone. He dialed the familiar number of his mentor, Finn Trottel. He was at home at his office desk and picked up on the first ring.

"Mike, how goes it?"

"How did you know it was me?"

"I have that Caller ID. It shows me your phone number. I have all your phone numbers in that Rolodex in my head."

"I have bad news for you."

"Oh?"

"I just fired your new hire."

"Cissy Bordon?"

"Yes."

"Well, I'll be damned!"

"I just caught her and Fred coming down for breakfast at our meeting place with our home office guest."

"That was Rose, wasn't it?"

"Yes, that Rose."

"I've heard stories about her. I should have warned you."

"I've heard my own stories. You never know about rumors. This time, it isn't a rumor."

"We managers know her as Medusa."

"You gotta give me some advice on what to do. I have two problems. First, how do I handle Fred and Cissy? I told them both they were fired. Next, I can't fire Medusa, but I want to report her. What do I do?"

"First, you must document the hell out of this. There is sure to be some pushback unless you call their bluff."

Mike's brain was in fight or flight mode. Ideas, obstacles, and consequences were swirling in his thoughts in a mishmash of anger, sadness, and fear. He briefly visualized being fired himself for reacting so swiftly. He feared the repercussions of legal action against Plushaut, which would include a risk to his own career. He began to sense that the company, to avoid a lawsuit, could turn on him. All manner of fears poured out of his inner conscience. He stood holding the phone, talking to Finn, while June looked at his beet red face flushed with emotion.

Mike asked Finn, "You mind if I stop by your place, so we can talk?"

"I'm here. I'll look for you."

Mike hung up the phone and turned to June. That's when he noticed her concerned stare. She offered some motherly advice.

"Your billing problem is solved. That's off your plate. If it's any consolation to you, that woman is just what I heard you say. She's a snake in the grass. Whatever you did shook her up. Good for you."

"Thanks." Mike grabbed his folder off her desk, gave her a last nod, and walked out of the building unsure of what lay ahead for his career.

It was a year later at Christmas. Plushaut Uclaf in America had completed an unexpectedly successful year in an otherwise suppressed pharmaceutical market. Stu was looking forward to the two weeks of time off. Doctors hated to get sales calls in December. They, like those children in Moore's Santa Claus classic, had visions of sugar plums dancing in their heads—just like the sales reps. Patients, determined to see doctors before their health insurance deductibles returned in January, made December an unwelcome frenzy of activity.

Mike also looked forward to the holidays as he cleared out his desk to hand over management duties to his replacement. He was stepping down to again become a sales rep back in Finn Trottel's district with his past teammate Bill Dooley and a whole lot of reps he did not know well. Although his Boomers were successful, he was unhappy in a job that demanded so much of his time, which often exceeded eighty hours each week. He was so unhappy that even the prospect of working in the same district as Bill Dooley was not a deterrent.

Fred McAnich now worked for a new drug company at a salary, so he claimed, of one third greater than with Plushaut.

Cissy remained with the Boomer District in a capacity that the other reps with her described as bullet proof. She claimed that her firing was not reasonable, since it was early in the morning before breakfast. She also said that when confronted by her manager, she was dressed for work and consulting with Rose in her official marketing capacity. The personnel department in New Jersey were cowards. It was a kettle of worms in an era of equal rights for women to be swept under the rug. Subsequently, no one, including other women, would associate with her. When forced to deal with Cissy Bordon, all sales reps and their managers were scared to death.

Chapter Twenty-One

IN THE SPRING of 1995, on a crisp and sunny April morning, Oklahoma City changed forever. A bomb exploded at the federal building downtown, killing 168 men, women, and children, injured another 680, damaged 324 other buildings, and put the name of Oklahoma City in every newspaper in the world. Oddly, from ten miles away it made a sound at Baptist Hospital like a giant steel pallet being dropped from a truck, followed one second later by another higher pitched whang! Stu, distracted by a phone call, thought no more about it as he worked his territory until three and a half hours later.

He met a gardener who asked him, "Have you heard any more news about the bomb?"

"What bomb?" Stu asked.

"Somewhere downtown. The radio says a bunch of people got hurt."

Stu drove his car to the top of the parking garage at the hospital. From his vantage, it looked like the ruddy brown smoke came from the Oklahoma City University campus. The enormous pillar of smoke he saw was another three miles away from the campus. That's when he returned to his car, turned on the radio, and listened for something he could do. Blood and plasma were already in short supply.

He drove down to the street and headed to the Sylvan N. Goldman Oklahoma Blood Institute a mile away to donate. He found there was no place to park. A line of volunteer donors, only four hours after the blast, was a block long—or so he thought. It stretched west deep into a residential street. Stu knew it was already too late to make a difference. So, he did the only thing he could think to do. He went back to work to share the grief with his customers, hoping they would have a job for him to do.

Over the course of the following several weeks, the number of missing grew smaller. The number of confirmed dead grew larger. For Ana, her greatest hope came true as she read in each morning's newspaper the list of possible deaths, which grew smaller as missing people were found either in hospitals or back home and untouched by the tragedy. In two weeks, Stu and Ana attended five funerals for people of his acquaintance.

In time, Oklahoma City would rise from the ashes to a new place of prominence. It did, however, change the lives and attitudes of everyone. Many regained their hope for a bright future. Others failed to shake their anger. For Stu, always an optimist, the year was still good to him. Ben Hodge, Stu's new district manager, was changed in a different way, unable to shed the weight of his anger.

STU STEPPED OUT the front door of his new upscale home that Ana and he built the year before. He gazed with pleasure at his new 1996 Buick LeSabre Sedan, the product of his in-house promotion the company set up for the sales force. He finally reached the pinnacle of sales force status with its upscale company car, special lapel pin, and respect from management that stretched all the way to the company's president in New Jersey. His salary jumped by thirty percent, allowing Ana to build her dream home. Stu got his dream garage, big enough to handle every box the company might want to send him with room to spare after parking two cars.

He looked at Buicks before he placed his fleet service order. The company did not offer the bigger Buick Roadmaster, so he settled for the LeSabre. He had parked it in his circle drive and loaded it to the gills with samples and giveaway items that came to his house in an endless parade. Because he wanted the Buick Roadmaster, but it wasn't an option, he nicknamed his car the Loadmaster. It was a beautiful golden metallic, a paint color he had wanted for fifteen years. He was moving up in the world and continued to enjoy what he did. He was picking up his manager in twenty minutes for a half day work-with and a free lunch.

For four years, Ben Hodge managed the Boomers. He spent most of his time at home and away from the sales reps. Most reps in his district liked it, knowing that in other states the managers were more hands on. They assumed he was lazy, which gained him no respect. Extremely short, all of his district salesmen and women looked down on him.

It was easy to beat the system. Cissy had done it for years including one year when the company moved her to a new territory in Enid, Oklahoma, where she sat and waited for a list of doctors grouped by zip codes to come in the mail. Every so often she would call Ben asking him to come up and work with her. He never would drive up there. She continued getting paid to do nothing. He, too, was afraid to be alone with this pariah. Ben no longer managed a division or a district. In the infinite tweaking of the company nomenclature by no-name home office geniuses, he now carried the title of Zone Manager. The Boomers in an informal gathering decided to be the first zone to call themselves Zombies. And so, it stuck—just not officially.

Stu looked briefly at his house and thought of Nathaniel Hawthorn. His cottage-style house had more than seven gables. It was deceptively large on a two-acre lot, with a three-car garage, and with a large backyard that was perfect for children and a dad to romp. After years of practice, children had arrived. It took seven years to grow from conception to three boys. Ana quit teaching to be a full-time mother. Stu's sales rep promotion and large raise made it possible. The oldest boy was six, with each boy being two years apart in age, and three birthdays in the same month of May. In a clever deception, Stu told them they had the exact same birthday and enjoyed a single birthday celebration they calculated would work until the second boy learned how to read a calendar. Each boy had a room to himself, although they all managed to finagle more time in the master bedroom than either Stu or Ana wished. The parents savored the time because they knew that, starting at age twelve, each boy would shun them during their insanity phase of puberty.

Stu stepped into his Loadmaster and drove forward out of the circle drive on his way to pick up Ben. Over the four years, he had enjoyed Ben's days with him. They would meet at 8:00 in the morning and eat a big breakfast and drink lots of coffee until as late as 9:30. It was a late start each time, but they both knew that doctors were not in their offices more times than not before 10:00 a.m. The bigwigs in New Jersey and most regional managers had no clue of the real world of doctor calls. When a rep would get that dreaded call from home office executives, requesting a day in the field with them, the rep often prearranged his schedule around the few doctors who either were early birds or those who would come in early as a favor. It rarely worked out, but the real world was not what they wanted an executive to see. Executives were always five years behind the times. It was better to fool them than to explain the truth.

Ben Hodge was an avid golfer who loved country club life. He first joined The Greens, but soon switched to the older and bigger Quail Creek Golf & Country Club. He always met his rep there for breakfast. Besides being a pleasant place to eat, he could quickly meet his club dining obligation without a sweat. He was a numbers guy, which became the bulk of the topics for the hour and a half. No matter how good the year was, Ben made sure the reps knew they were behind last year's numbers and that they needed to step it up. He liked to focus deep into the data to show where sales were less than stellar. This might include a single doctor or an entire area zip code or hospital pharmacy. If he found any good sales numbers, he had an irritating habit of pointing out another Zombie who was outperforming the rep. It could be helpful. It could be irritating. It was always predictable.

After ordering their breakfasts and engaging in idle chit chat, Ben brought interesting news for Stu. He revealed what jolly and practical joking old Finn Trottel had done to his reps for years.

"For at least the past ten years before the new Boomer Division came into existence, Finn has held back salary raises and bragged to the other division managers about how he could get his reps to work for less than what the other managers paid to their people."

"I don't understand. That makes no sense."

"Each year he took a portion of the money allocated for Land Runners' salary increases and sent it back to the region."

"Stu, you and the rest of the reps in your division were screwed out of thousands of dollars for your first ten years. Think of it this way. If you got a thousand dollar raise each year for ten years, that would be an extra ten grand per annum every year for the rest of your career. Finn sent a quarter of that money back to the region for no reason that I can come up with."

"What happened to the money?"

"What do you think? Abbott Wahl divided the money up and gave it to his other five division managers for their reps."

"But we all thought he was a great boss to work for. It's hard to think he really did that."

"Oh, he did. He screwed all of you and you'll never be able to recoup what he kept from you guys. I've tried to make it up to you all, but it won't happen. The company is not budging."

"What does Finn say?"

"He laughs it off. I remember in the past he bragged about how he could get his reps to make him a winner for the least cost of any division in the company. He made that his ticket to getting himself big fat raises."

"They haven't promoted him above manager either."

"Why would they want to? Once he had a position at the top, think of how many people he could cheat out of their rightful paycheck then?"

The two men pondered in silence after diving into their breakfasts that were starting to get cold. Ben knew that managers tended to play one-upmanship with each other. If the company allowed a manager to buy a chair, some other manager would take the allotted money and buy a sofa—supposedly, to make the others envious. The sofa manager could prove his better skills, apparently, via furniture selection.

Power posturing also worked for those who played golf. Stu attended a meeting where golf was mandatory for the entire region of seventy reps and their managers. He joked about what he could do if he got lost in the rough while looking for his ball in the adjoining fairway. Charlie Ketter had countered that if he drove his golf cart to the highest part of the green, he might be able to find it. Two managers approached Stu and Charlie, forcefully informing them that golf was a serious sport and that joking in the clubhouse would not be tolerated. They then invited them to leave. Stu and Charlie, feeling manly themselves, refused to leave. Nothing more happened to them, but Stu never forgot how serious the managers were about impressing each other. From then on, when something silly went on with management, they would say to each other, "Well, you're not allowed to have fun playing golf."

Even reps had their practices of posturing to each other. If the hotel had a workout facility, you could find the men all lined up at the weight benches, pumping iron, looking overly serious. No one laughed in the gym. They sweat a lot. They looked tough enough. It was ten years later that Stu noticed the same body builders were still bulking up, but this time it was blubber, not steel.

Others ran in the evenings. But they didn't smile either. Stu, too, tried out the gym and found the perfect exercise. He bragged about it for years, after a meeting in Miami, Florida. Going to the resort's gym, he managed to wait for a stationary bike to come available. These were the type with a resistance belt. When riders tightened the belt, it added resistance. That burned more calories.

Shortly after he began pedaling, a group of young women from a modeling agency entered. It was his luck that they stopped at an open area ten feet from him, laid down exercise mats, and began all manner of postures, contortions, and movements. There were a dozen pairs of legs swirling around. Then came the crunches. They were obviously in good condition because the exercises seemed endless. Stu didn't want to miss the show, but he grew tired of peddling. What he planned as a twenty-minute ride became thirty minutes. He was about to quit from exhaustion when a little devil hopped on his shoulder and suggested a remedy.

Take the tension off the bike. You won't have resistance. You can peddle and leer forever.

For another hour Stu peddled away in the longest cooldown ride of his life. In his fantasy world he imagined that the ladies marveled at his stamina and secretly wished to introduce themselves to such a hunk as he. Eventually, the game ended for the dozen models. They had performed hundreds of pushups, thousands of crunches and leg lifts, and an equal number of stretches, twists, and bends. He finished his ride with no sweat to cloak his deception. That evening the topic came up at dinner.

"Were you there in the gym this afternoon when those models came in?" It was Jimmy, who certainly was no athlete. He was not there but he knew of their presence.

"I was there," said Charlie. "I was working the machine behind Stu on the bike." He looked over at Stu and laughed. "You were one lucky son of a gun."

"I was right in front of them," Stu replied. "I had the best seat in the house—and today's bragging rights."

"How close were you?" It was Four, now leaning forward with interest.

"Ten feet. But there were a dozen models at least. It was hard to focus on just one."

The others groaned in unison at Stu's stoking of their envy.

"I thought you were going to die on the bike," Charlie said. "You were moving along pretty good. I didn't know you were in that good of a shape."

"I'm not. I just loosened the tension and peddled in neutral for an hour."

A commotion of laughter and comments followed Stu's admission.

"You cheated," Jimmy said.

Stu had his retort ready to go. "Listen guys. While you were out there pumping and peddling or who only knows what, I exercised my brain. Am I the only one who thought to do that?"

There was a moment of silence until Charlie chimed in. "You win this round but wait till tomorrow."

Stu didn't have to worry. When tomorrow came, they learned that the models had already left for home.

Chapter Twenty-Two

STU MADE HIS first call with his manager at 10:15. Drug rep appointments were blessings—usually. While most calls were walk-ins, appointments increased the chances of a real sit-down sales call. Every drug salesman had their book of physicians, pharmacies, and hospitals crammed with helpful information. The important items made for a jigsaw puzzle of scheduling for a day in the field. The book included days off, best times to call, nurses' names, hot button items, favorite competitive drugs, and a handful of other trivia. The most important item in this book was the name of the receptionist—the gatekeeper. Without being on her good list, all other information was worthless.

Stu and Ben sat in their car at the clinic's parking lot going over Stu's records of previous calls there. After so many years of calling on the same people, once every six weeks—now every four weeks, Stu had his notes memorized. He knew which doctors never changed. He knew which ones required constant review. This clinic had two constants. The big writer was predictable and the call boringly routine. The second prescriber was always someone new. Today, because Stu had a manager with him, he went through his notes. It was always good to show Ben a plan for each call. This doctor had a Ph.D. in pharmacology as well as his medical degree. He was sixty-six years old and took off on Thursdays.

His hobbies were nurses and other women. He could not keep a marriage intact but kept trying. There was an extensive list of competitive products that he prescribed. Stu reminded Ben that it is good to see competitors on a doctor like this because there was still business he could take from them. The name of the game in pharmaceutical sales was growth. If sales became flat, it would be a disaster. The only other way to grow his market share was to grow the market as a whole. It was easiest to steal a share of it from another company.

"So, what's your plan?" Ben was in his management voice.

"He doesn't stand for being lectured, but I think I can catch his attention with a visual cue I tried last week. It was successful in getting me an extra thirty seconds sometimes."

"What is it?"

"Come this way and I'll show you in there."

Ben shrugged his shoulders in an okay gesture before they stepped out of the car.

This clinic was a long-established family practice mainstay for the upper and middle classes in northwest Oklahoma City. The seasoned veteran doctor of osteopathy approached the point of his career where many physicians contemplated slowing down their practices. He ran through a steady stream of partners—young family practitioners, general surgeons, pain doctors, and psychiatrists. They lasted a year or two before they left to start their own practices. Franz Joseph Steuben, D.O. was a shot doctor, tyrant, and mentor. He was the most prolific prescriber in Stu's territory. The number one sales goal Stu had when he called on the man was to not tick him off. He had seen it happen to other reps—always good if it was a competitor. Over the years Stu had gotten more relaxed with him, although to Doctor Steuben, Stu was just one rep of a constant stream of reps waiting to see him and leave samples. Between every patient room visit, Doctor Stueben's habit was to enter the long nurses' station counter and write his notes in the chart. He would then press the button on an antiquated intercom and mumble incoherent orders to his nurses. Every patient who left his office reported quick improvement after three or four shots of any one of his five favorites. There was B-12 for memory, epinephrine for inflammation, thiomerin for fluid retention and weight loss, Lincocin to stop bacterial growth, and any injectable that would blunt the side effects of the first four. The nurses could not understand him on the intercom, so they simply guessed at what he said and shot up the patient. To add to the chaos, with every visit, the staff was brand new.

Ben and Stu stood at the open trunk of the new Loadmaster unloading several cases of Flofral, Destense in all three doses, and Soulag XL. Doctor Steuben went through an enormous number of samples each month. The drug closets were always empty of Plushaut samples. Almost always he would complain of being out of samples. Stu was glad to have Ben with him to carry the cases inside. He opened his detail bag to fill it with visuals, file cards, research papers, and sufficient numbers of notepads, pens, and other trivial toys. Most displayed the names of his promoted drugs, except for his research papers. With Ben loaded up with sample boxes, Stu grabbed his detail bag in one hand and a load of samples in the other. He then led his boss to the front door of the clinic.

In this clinic, reps did not wait to put a card in with the receptionist. Stu led his boss to the entrance on the left of her desk and entered the nurse station where aides scurried about in a frenzy. The doctor was talking to one aide who made the mistake of asking him to repeat himself. The others fled the station until the curse-filled rant ended and he went to see another patient. As Ben and Stu madly began tearing open cardboard boxes to stock the sample closet, the staff crept back into the room. The chatter among them was instant. They were saying all sorts of things they would never say in the doctor's presence.

It took a good twenty minutes to place the samples in the closet where the doctors and aides would see them. Like the battle that grocery store stockers have with competitors fighting for the best location on the shelf, there was always a battle for best eye level shelf space in the sample closet. The doctor made it worse, since every company's samples were gone so quickly. It left space for another competitor to claim. Fortunately, there was a big, beautiful space to stack up nearly all the Plushaut samples. In this clinic the doctor preferred that reps keep all his samples together by company, not by therapeutic class. It made it easier. When Stu filled the shelves as well as he could, he took the remaining sample cases, cut off the tops for better visibility, and left them on the floor.

After reaching in his bag to pull out some visuals, file cards, a stack of notepads, and a dozen ballpoint pens, he heaved a sigh of relief.

"Now, if I can avoid pissing him off, we'll be a winner." The ladies laughed quietly at his declaration. They knew it was true.

This was Ben's first time to call on Doctor Steuben. Stu cautioned him. "I know you like to say a few things to doctors, but this is not one of them. You need to stay in the shadows and offer nothing except an expressionless face."

"Okay." He looked at the aides who were eavesdropping. They nodded their heads in agreement. "Okay."

"I noted a new shingle on the building. You have a new doctor again?"

A nurse named Martha, who had stuck with the clinic for several years, answered Stu. "Yes. A very nice doctor... Doctor Bell. He came from out of state... I think Missouri or Arkansas. He's been here for almost a month now. After Doctor Steuben gets through ignoring you, you can just walk back there to his office." She pointed in the direction of the hallway. "He's not busy quite yet. He would probably like the company."

"What's his specialty?"

"Just general practice. He's an M.D., not a D.O. like our doctor."

"Any hobbies?"

"I can't tell you for sure. You'll see. His office walls are kind of bare. And one of you," she looked at Ben, "will have to stand up. He only has one folding chair to offer you."

Doctor Steuben appeared from the hallway and stormed over to his special spot. Stu stood by quietly while he jotted down notes in the patient's file. With the best of efforts, Stu could not translate into English a single scribble written down. The doctor, head down, made one brief sideways turn to find Stu, then did a double take when he spotted Ben behind him. He returned to stare at the file while mumbling his shot and prescription orders through the intercom.

"Yes, doctor."

Steuben placed the file on a growing stack in front of him and picked up the next folder, still never looking up.

"What do you have for me today?"

Stu took a cautious step forward. "I left you enough of Soulag, Destense, and Flofral to make it hard for you to close the sample door."

"It's about time."

"A quick point that you may find humorous." Stu reached in his shirt pocket and pulled out a fishing lure, still in its clear plastic packaging, and showed him the warning label."

"I can't see that... read it to me."

"It says that according to the State of California, the paint on this lure causes cancer, so don't put it in your mouth."

Doctor Steuben looked up finally and grabbed it. "Let me see that."

Stu knew that he had about ten seconds to get his message across. He had to get his message clear and precise.

"Funny they should say that about the paint. I thought the hooks would be deterrent enough. Templeton reps keep telling you that Flofral is inhibited by high fat meals and impaired by metabolic interactions with grapefruit... but check out my competitor's package insert. Templeton's drug has the exact food restrictions, exactly like Flofral. Also, Flofral's package insert says that the therapeutic effects are unaffected by food."

Stu's ten seconds were up, but Doctor Steuben turned to mumble an almost incoherent question.

"What basis is their claim?"

"Templeton quotes a *Lancet* letter to the editor about a study they conducted on Flofral. This trial was in dogs eating the equivalent of eighteen times the fat and grapefruit of a normal-sized breakfast. I think it's pretty obvious that a meal that size, if it didn't kill you, would impair the absorption and metabolism of any drug. The Templeton rep's statement is about as dumb as telling you not to put a fishing lure in your mouth or to eat eighteen breakfasts at one sitting. That's why I put this sticker on the front here. 'Flofral has no food restrictions.'"

Doctor Steuben turned away from Stu, leaving him uncertain as to his success or failure.

"Nurse... nurse!" A young nurse's aide nervously stepped in.

"Yes, doctor."

"Where's Martha? I don't want you. I said nurse. Where is my nurse?"

"I'm right here, Doctor Steuben," Martha said, coming around the corner into the nurse's station. Her voice had a condescending quality from years of dealing with him. Only she was able to get away with it.

"Take all the Templeton samples and throw them away."

"Throw them away?"

"Yes."

"All of them?"

Steuben grew angry. "I just said that. Throw them all away. Now!"

"Yes, doctor." Martha nodded to the nervous aide to join her in the sample closet. "Get a big garbage bag... quickly."

The aide slinked away as Steuben turned back to Stu. "You better be right about this, or you are next."

"Oh, I'm right, sir."

"We'll see, won't we?"

"I'll stick my head in next week. Give you a chance to chop it off... if you think I'm wrong."

"Son, by next week, you check on the pharmacies around town. I will run every pharmacy out of Flofral within fifty miles of this office. Enjoy the ride."

Doctor Steuben was through with Stu. He turned once again to his next patient chart and turned a few pages. Before he stepped into the hallway to see the next patient, he picked up the fishing lure packaged in clear plastic and put it in his shirt pocket. Ben came out of the shadows.

"Where in heck did you come up with that idea?"

"A friend showed me one he bought at Walmart. I went down there and bought a few more and had a hundred sticky labels printed with that message."

"How long do you think that your work here today will last?"

"About a week. Maybe less. That's why we keep coming back over and over."

Chapter Twenty-Three

BEN WAS HEADING into the waiting room when Stu called him back.

"Ben... we need to meet the new doctor."

"Does he have any potential or are we wasting our time?"

Patients in the waiting room were taking note of his comment.

"This is another understudy of the most important doctor in my territory." Stu was more than a little exasperated by his attitude and the place he chose to express it. "Every doc that comes out of this clinic goes on to be the best writer in my territory. You bet he has potential. We get to them while they still have time to talk to us. Come on!"

They strode back into the hallway, turning left to the back where so many young doctors had learned from the master. Within two years they all knew how to make patients feel better and make tons of money while doing it.

Halfway down the hall they found the door to Doctor Bell's office. A nurse sat on a stool at her station set up at the back. She was a middle-aged blonde with too much eye makeup and fingernails painted a fiery orange-red that were nearly one inch from her fingertips. Her slender body did not match her large, augmented chest. Stu, not a fan of manufactured faces or breasts, found her unattractive. Ben was so dazzled that he slipped up and emitted what he thought was an under-his-breath expression of lustful moaning. It didn't matter because she sat there, expressionless, listless, and bored.

"Just push the door open," she said. "Don't knock. He's probably sleeping."

"What patients is he seeing today?"

"He saw a baby boy about an hour ago."

"That's all? I'm Stu, by the way." He turned around to look at his boss. "This is my friend, Ben... and your name is...?"

"It doesn't matter what my name is, Ben and Stu. I'm a temp nurse. I won't be here after today."

Ben couldn't resist asking her a question. "Can you even type with those nails?" Stu was mortified.

"Do it all the time," she said. "It's easy."

Stu nodded his head toward her, grabbed Ben's arm, and turned to Doctor Bell's office door. He gripped the doorknob and pushed it gently. The door opened a crack where he could peek in. There Doctor Bell sat, not sleeping but staring at the opposite wall in a daydream. Stu opened the door wider which caught the doctor's attention. He greeted the two with a broad smile. Standing up to meet them, Doctor Bell became ebullient with joy to see anyone. He wore the lines on his face of a man in his fifties, but in fact he was much younger. His thinning widow's peak was well on its way to total baldness. He sported gray roots not yet retreated with hair coloring.

"Come in here, men! It's good to see you."

Stu reached for Bell's extended hand and received a vice grip that nearly crushed his unprepared knuckles. It was no different when he crushed Ben's hand. He was tall and thin, which made his shabby white cotton dress shirt and blue jeans hang loosely. Stu was immediately put off by his over-exuberance, but he marked it down to his worry for a lack of patients. New doctors always start out slow, worried, and bored, until their day of joy when they find their giant patient load to be overwhelming. This was the perfect time to mold a new doctor with habits that often lasted for a career.

"I'm Doctor Bell... and you two are who?"

"I'm Stu Roy... here's my card." He laid it on the unadorned desk. "My friend here is Ben Hodge."

Doctor Bell glanced at the card, then at the two men. "Please have a seat, Stu."

"Oh, I can stand if that's all right with you. Ben, you can have the chair if you like. He's exhausted after working with me all morning."

As the three laughed at the little joke on Ben, the doctor looked again at the business card. Years earlier, Stu's calling card listed no drugs. In the mid-eighties the card sported the three main drugs sold by reps—Destense 20mg, Soulag XL, and Flatulaide. The company eventually added the names of every drug they sold to pharmacies. What pharmacies bought was more extensive than what drug reps promoted. It created confusion. Stu had samples of three drugs but occasionally had to explain details of an additional sixteen.

"Wow! You sell all of these?"

"No, just the top three... the ones we carry samples for. I can tell you about the others, but they have for the most part seen better days."

"Let's see here... I see some cardiac drugs... a few over the counter GI products... diabetes meds... I don't see pain meds... Flofral. Flofral? I've never heard of that. What's Flofral?"

"It's a hemorheologic agent used to promote blood flow in patients with intermittent claudication, atherosclerotic heart disease, and type-2 diabetes."

"With a name like Flofral, it sounds more like a drug for urine flow or pain management."

Stu wanted to change the subject. "So, what is your practice? I understand you came from Arkansas... or was it Missouri?"

"I had a practice where I grew up in Springfield, Missouri, but went to medical school at the University of Arkansas."

Stu glanced at his diploma, the only object on his four walls. He noted the graduation year of 1982.

"Well, welcome to Oklahoma. What brought you here?"

"It just seemed like a time for a change. Oklahoma City sounded interesting. I hooked up with Doctor Steuben and he gave me a chance to learn how to be a better businessman and a better physician."

"He scares half the reps in town."

"Oh, he's not that way with me. In fact, in the month I've been here, I hardly interact with him. I get my information from the staff. They're quite helpful."

"That's good to hear."

"So how can I help you men? I'll do my best to make you look good when my patients start pouring in." He held up Stu's card and waved it at him.

Something did not seem right. It bothered Stu. Although eager to learn, Doctor Bell was not a new physician, but everything Stu said seemed to be new to him. Besides, he was slightly nervous as he asked questions—too many questions. He failed to challenge anything said to him. Doctor Bell tried to flatter him. Stu found it suspicious for an introductory call.

"I know that Doctor Steuben uses lots of Flofral. In fact, he just threw out our competitor's samples because of some false information they told him. For his patients with diabetic microvascular disease, he doses it one Flofral 60mg enteric tablet a day... with or without food. If your patients have any tummy discomfort, they can take it with food, but the absorption is the same. It's a limb saver. For your diabetics, who suffer ulcerations and possible amputations, Flofral 60mg is what they need. Are you up for giving it a try?"

"I'm in."

"Any questions?" Stu gave him a file card that contained the FDA full disclosure, a legal document all drug reps had to leave.

"No, I'll read up on it. I'm happy to know about all new drugs and this sounds wonderful." Doctor Bell paused to let that sink in. "What else can I do for you today?"

Stu brought out his other visuals and covered in detail the other two drugs he made money on—Destense and Soulag XL. Doctor Bell continued to ask detailed questions. It was a perfect demonstration of a sales call for Ben to see, as he did his duty and stayed in the back corner observing. When the calls ended, Bell again shook their hands with exuberance and told them how valuable they were to him. He added that Stu had given him more useful information than he had ever gotten from a detail man before. The praise was so over the top that both Ben and Stu couldn't wait to escape.

As they walked out the door, the temp-nurse called to them.

"Did you like Doctor Bell?"

"He certainly was happy to hear from a drug rep," Ben said.

The nurse and her inch-long fingernails stepped closer to Ben and whispered, "I should let you know. I don't think he will be with us much longer."

"Where is he going?"

"I haven't a clue."

"Thanks for that information," Ben said, and followed Stu to his car.

"What do you think of Doctor Bell?" Ben asked as he watched Stu put his sales bag into the trunk.

"Let's get inside the car first."

The sun was already heating up the inside of the car. The air inside had the stale odor of cardboard sample boxes. Stu started his car and turned up the air conditioner while rolling down the windows to let the heat out. Half a minute later the air from the dash was cool and he raised the windows. He turned to Ben.

"We just called on a doctor with a substance abuse problem. I think he's hooked on pain meds." Stu paused to let that sink in. "And I think he's been out of practice a long time... probably in rehab."

Ben looked shocked. "Really? I was going to tell you that you wasted an hour of your day and mine calling on a worthless doctor."

"I agree, but we never know until it's too late."

"So why do you think he's on drugs?"

"Well, okay. First, he came to Oklahoma City from his hometown. Why would he do that? His practice here is zero. That's not a reason to leave his practice behind. Then there is his diploma from med school. He graduated in 1982, but he had never heard of Flofral or Destense. How could he not know about those two? They've been on the market for a long time."

Stu paused for a moment, trying to remember the other clues he had. His eyes got wide as he remembered another point.

"Did you notice how he mentioned more than once that we didn't have any pain meds? He looked disappointed. And Doctor Steuben has not had contact with him. I think he knows there's something wrong, too. Lastly, nobody should be that happy to see an unknown drug rep. He treated us like we were long lost friends. He practically crushed our hands with joy. How would he know he should be glad to see us? We could be jerks."

Ben was listening and learning. It hadn't occurred to him because his focus had been on Stu.

"I never thought of it that way. Why would he act that way if he was hooked on something?"

"Because he needs us to help fill his habit."

"How could we be of help? We don't sell pain meds."

"But he doesn't know that. He's going to treat the next rep just like he treated us, until he gets hold of a live one who will do whatever it takes to make a sale."

"Well, Stu. He's leaving, so it's out of our hands. If you run into him again, don't waste your time, or mine."

"Rest assured, he will end up in the newspaper or on the local TV news."

"How did you end up so savvy about drug addiction?"

Stu laughed as he pondered the memory of his introduction to drug addiction.

"Let's just say I had my baptism of fire in my first month on the job, when I called on a meth addict named Doctor Addicus."

WITHIN A WEEK, as Stu made his pharmacy calls, he heard the same question.

"What on earth did you say to Doctor Steuben?"

Pharmacists were running out of Flofral faster than they could reorder. The wholesalers began to run short and altered their ordering plans from Plushaut Uclaf. Stu knew it wouldn't last forever, but he had illustrated to his boss why innovation and some competitive research paid dividends.

Stu was starting to see flaws in the way the company did business. With this success he decided he had enough respect so that he could help the company. He began pointing out to management where sales efforts would work better with changes. As he was soon to learn, managers, like wives, don't warm up to salesmen who point out their flaws.

Chapter Twenty-Four

THE REST OF the day with Ben went great. After calling on volatile Doctor Steuben and addicted Doctor Bell, he directed Stu to drive him to his favorite lunch counter for a debrief of his two calls and another free meal. As happy as Stu was to see him leave after lunch, he viewed his manager with sizable contempt. He was clueless about what Ben did at home in the afternoon, but it had to be wrong in the eyes of the company. Over the years Stu learned that it was nearly impossible to lose a job for not working.

Besides Ben, there was the home office marketing department's Rose Astor the Disaster. Cissy Bordon had learned how to work the system. Women were treated differently in Plushaut, and Stu claimed he knew the reason.

It was day two of working with Ben. They were at International House of Pancakes for breakfast.

"Men pretend to be male chauvinists, but in truth they are afraid of the women they work with."

"One slip-up... and the man gets the reprimand," Ben replied.

"When I was hired, there were no women. Then began the pressure to hire them. I remember Finn Trottel had a quota."

"Is it true that Finn tried hiring aggressive women?"

"Yeah."

"And they were all lesbians." Ben laughed loud enough to shake the windows.

"Then he tried hiring pretty women."

The waitress brought two giant plates for Ben of three large pancakes, biscuits and gravy, and eggs over easy with bacon and link sausages. Stu drank only coffee. Ben's meal gave Stu a chance to talk.

"Finn needed to hire smart women who did not have an axe to grind. He was terrible at it. That was why all Boomer-Zone-Zombies liked Lorelei. She wanted her teammates to treat her like one of the guys. She handled herself by the same standards as the men. She tolerated their sometimes-crude nature while keeping her own high standards of personal conduct."

It was also true in Stu's experience that the women doctors he called on in his early years were tough physicians. They resisted a rep's selling or telling them what to do. Stu explained.

"Now, older female doctors… they were novelties in medical school and had to work extra hard to prove their right to be there. They were tough nuts to crack."

Stu loved winning them to his side. Over the years he learned much from the ladies about their personal struggles in a man's world. The waitress poured Stu more coffee, while ignoring Ben, who began laughing.

"Did you see that?" Ben said. "I let out a low rumbling fart. It drove her away."

Stu, taken aback, tried to ignore what Ben said. "Like I was going to say, after fifteen years at his job, I see a difference. Most women now go into obstetrics, gynecology, and pediatrics."

Ben was obsessed with farting. Not the silent but deadly kind. He enjoyed the ventriloquist's art of projecting sounds and odors that would identify another person as its source.

On the third day of their work together, Stu confronted him.

"Ben, you need to stop that." They were in Stu's car after a call on his most important and hard-to-sell physician. Ben was anything but contrite.

"I find beans are best to supply my ammunition."

Every rep had expressed displeasure at his actions when having to work with him. No one dared tell him directly, since he controlled their paycheck. Stu was no longer afraid to call him out. The morning with Doctor Steuben had been the last straw. He had to cease with his zephyrs.

"Ben, you embarrassed me in the elevator this morning at the Mercy Tower. Farts all the way to the tenth floor in a packed elevator are unacceptable. I'm asking you to please stop farting."

Ben looked straight at Stu and let out a high-pitched peep that descended like a muted trombone down to a lower note. Stu rolled down his window and continued.

"You turned to a lady on your left and made a face at her. Was that so people would think it was she who was farting?"

"Some held their breaths as long as they could." Ben began laughing. "When the doors finally opened on the tenth floor, it was pandemonium."

Stu expressed his displeasure at Ben who responded with self-assured laughter.

"You're acting like a ten-year-old, Ben."

"Didn't you like calling on… who was it… Steuben? I gassed him up pretty good… damn, you didn't even know."

"No. I need you to stop." Stu took advantage of his seniority to press the point. "No more jokes while you're in my territory. Save it for Dooley."

STU'S NEXT CALL was on Estelle Patton, M.D., an internist with a well-established practice. While Stu and Ben waited in the hallway, where she preferred to talk with drug reps, Ben planned his next juvenile prank.

"Watch this."

"Ben, no. Stay right here with me."

"Do you notice her habit of entering her private office to write up her notes after each patient? Just watch."

Ben stepped into her office and waited until she emerged from an exam room before launching his zephyrs and stepping back into the hallway. He laughed gleefully and watched as she entered her office. Stu left the hallway and informed the front desk that he would come back later. Ben followed without comment.

Ben often carried a laser pointer with him, which was useful to loan to a doctor who gave medical talks for dinners he frequently hosted. At the next office, while sitting in the waiting room, he discreetly shined a red dot on an old lady's white blouse to see if she would jump.

"I'm bleeding!" the lady said in distress. When her daughter came to her assistance, the evidence disappeared.

"Oh, Mother!" the daughter said in frustration. "You're just seeing things again."

Ben hardly contained his laughter.

"You need to stop that," Stu whispered, then excused himself and went into the hall in frustration.

Stu declined lunch, instead took Ben to where he parked his car that morning. It seemed a hopeless battle. After repeated offenses, Stu gave up his futile expressions of displeasure. Instead, he decided to start a journal which documented the times, places, and antics of each juvenile episode. It might come in handy someday if he could convince someone else to verify similar behavior.

When Ben went home after lunch, Stu again called on this same Doctor Patton at her preferred time of 2:00 p.m. for reps.

When Doctor Patton's nurse finally called Stu to the hallway, it was evident that he would have to make it a quick pitch. He would leave it up to her if she wanted to talk for any length. Sound bites were becoming the only way to sell. Stu had begun frequently using a phrase to get the doctors to stop and listen to him. They had learned over the years that he meant what he said. *"The less I say, the more you will remember."*

He remained standing in the hallway as nurses, lab techs, and other doctors passed by. Most said hello. During a lull in the traffic, he stepped over to check the sample closet. Internists, the eggheads of primary care physicians, use few samples and seldom called a drug by its brand name. Stu went over in his head the word *heptoxifylline* and willed himself not to say Flofral.

From down at the far end of the hallway, Doctor Patton walked his way. Her eyes were fixed on Stu. She had a comfortable smile on her face, which was not always the case. That was a good sign for a meaningful sales call. She began talking to him before she was halfway there.

"I have a story to tell you," she said. "I think you'll like it."

These were the comments that Stu loved to hear. It meant that the call would not be routine. They were always opportunities to grow his market share and a window into the doctor's thought process.

"I hope I'll like it, too."

As she approached him, her hand came out to meet his in a mutually firm grip of greeting.

"How is Ana?"

Ana, at Stu's recommendation, had chosen Doctor Patton as her primary care physician. They had become great friends over the years.

"Still healthy, thanks to you."

"Let me get right to my story. I've been waiting for you to show up. I don't know if you are aware of what Templeton reps are saying about *heptoxifylline*."

"Oh, I am, trust me. It's all…."

"Don't bother to tell me again. I believe you. I gave my husband your fishing lure. He got a chuckle out of it. Now, I had one of the Templeton reps come to me last month and say he would put fifty dollars into my favorite charity if I could prove their claims were bogus."

"So, what charity did he have to pay?"

"You're getting ahead of me. Right on my desk was the paper from New England Journal that you left me from your last call. I showed it to him the same minute he made the offer. It says right in the abstract that absorption and blood levels are the same for *heptoxifylline* and their drug whether taken with or without food. So, I asked him to pay up. He said he would."

"Did he come through?"

"Well, first I should have known. He tried to argue with me. I showed him that *heptoxifylline* states in the package insert that, if there is any nausea, take Flofral with food. I showed him his own package insert that states that nausea also occurs with his, but their remedy is to lessen the dose, not take with food."

"So that's how he can make the claim that *heptoxifylline* has a food restriction and his doesn't."

"Exactly. So, the rep came back to see me this week. I asked him for the fifty dollar donation. He said he couldn't do it but asked me if I would prescribe it anyway… funny thing is I can't even remember the name of his. What's it called? Pro… or Pri… something?"

She looked at Stu, waiting for an answer to her question.

"I'm not going to help you remember the name of my competitor. That's his job."

At first, she looked startled, then began a hurried chuckle. "Oh, you salesmen. You're lucky your wife is Ana."

"I'll tell you what, Estelle." He changed to her first name because of Ana's connection and because, after five years, he had earned the right—and this was personal. "Unlike that other rep, I will donate fifty dollars to your favorite charity today. Where should I deliver it?"

Again, Doctor Patton was surprised at the offer and at first shook her head with a polite comment, "No that's not necessary."

What followed was a silence. Her expression was one of reconsideration, which Stu luckily picked up on. He was getting better at reading women's expressions and at remembering to keep quiet in the moment.

"I think I will change my mind and accept your offer."

"Where to?"

"Planned Parenthood."

This time the silence was all Stu's doing. She could see his mind turning. He was trying not to show his reaction. It was not working. Doctor Patton was not letting him off the hook. Stu decided it was time to be blunt and honest.

"I'm sorry, but I can't do that. Give me another charity."

The gears were spinning and grinding in both their heads for five seconds, but it seemed like an awkward hour. Then Estelle Patton spoke.

"How about the American Red Cross?"

"Done," he said with an audible sigh. He looked at her with relief. "Thank you."

Before he could collect his wits, she went to see another patient.

When he returned to his car, he wrote up his call. He ended his note with the comment, *"This is the most productive call I've had with a doctor in months. I hardly got to speak. She did all the talking and sold herself."*

THIRTY MINUTES LATER Stu walked out of the American Red Cross headquarters with a receipt for the generous support by Estelle Patton, M.D. Getting in the car, he was ecstatic about his success. He started his car and turned it in the direction of Estelle Patton's office. If every call went like this, he would be the greatest salesman of all time. He intended to personally hand her the receipt and let it do the selling all by itself. He would make more calls that day, but his heart would not be in it. His brain was, though. He tap-danced in his head until the end of the day, which turned out to be after 6:00 p.m. If the doctors had to work until then, so would he. He finished up the day with nine doctor sales calls. The other six doctor calls occurred in the last hour and fifteen minutes of his day. It was a typical, unpredictable day.

Chapter Twenty-Five

THE NEXT MORNING Stu woke up with Ana cuddled up to his back. He loved to feel her warmth, especially in the morning, whether summer or winter. He savored that brief time of peace and awareness of each other, before their three active boys woke up in solidarity to demand nearly full attention.

Ana had been a patient of Estelle Patton for almost eleven years. After Stu's pneumonia and his revelation of how doctors work so well in cooperation, Ana asked what multi-doctor clinic he could recommend for her. The choice was a winner in her mind.

He lay in bed. The sun was beginning its yellow glow in a sky painted by dust and humidity. It was not yet time for his alarm to go off. He pondered the day before. Perhaps he was confused by being half awake. Why had he been celebrating a good call? Standing alone, Doctor Patton's contributions to his total count of prescriptions written were moderate at best. Why did it make him happy? He wondered if he had had his own doubts. Had his competition gotten into his head? Was he really that good of a salesman?

He mentally slapped himself. *Get over it. Don't let it steal my momentum.* He willed himself to look for the reasons he had celebrated. That would cheer him up. *Patton did my work for me. She explained to me why*. Then he had his answer. He had failed to articulate the food issue to his satisfaction with Doctor Steuben. That call was successful, but he knew he did a poor job with his lure analogy. *Do not place the product in your mouth. How do I use that better?* He recalled how silly some of the FDA-listed side effects were in package inserts. Like putting hooks in one's mouth, nearly all drugs included the cure in the list of the possible side effects of a drug. Sleeping pills caused sedation. Destense caused low blood pressure. Diuretics caused frequent urination. One would hope so. Stu determined that he had to make clear the obvious in a way that would counter his competition's deceptive tactics.

He decided the answer was to practice until he got it right. To do that, he would change his schedule and call on doctors who were not critical to his success, but good for practice. He would have the words perfected when he called on his heavy hitters.

That night he crafted a sample call that could cover all the fishing lure points he wanted to get across to a doctor. He never meant to recite them verbatim, but to use them as a template for a more natural give and take conversation.

Stu also decided to quote past comments from *The Medical Memorandum on Pharmaco-Treatments*, which published every other week an unbiased critical assessment of new prescription medicines. It also would compare them to older drugs used to treat similar diseases. Drug reps considered this publication to carry more weight than any other source they could quote. It could make or break the launch of a new drug with two pages of its succinct commentary.

Medical Memorandum / Fishing Lure / Flak Pitch

Doctor, here's something you might enjoy. I have here a high-quality fishing lure. I know you might not fish, but since you are so important to my success, I went ahead and sprang for the big bucks. It cost me $1.97 to get this fine lure at Wal-Mart. As you look at the beautiful paint job, it's interesting to discover that there is a warning on the back, which says that in the state of California this paint is toxic. Please note the sentence

I highlighted in yellow. This point is critical. "Do not place the product in your mouth." Funny they should say that about the paint. I thought the hooks would be deterrent enough.

Believe it or not, this lure has a point to it. So does this old bomber pilot quote.

"When you're receiving flak, you're probably over the target."

The connection between the two will make a lot more sense when you wait for my exciting conclusion.

For us at Plushaut, being "on target" is what Medical Memo said about Flofral on April 30th last year.

"Flofral may offer the best combination of effectiveness and safety."

If you talk to my competitors, they will have trouble trying to refute what Medical Memo said about Flofral. Medical Memo is to a competitor what garlic is to a vampire. They both will recoil in horror at the sight. What my competitors are left with is nothing to say on the subject, so they will resort to flak. By "flak" I mean they will say silly stuff about Flofral—just like the warning on this fishing lure. It may be stuff that actually is true (you really don't want to put a fishing lure in your mouth), but it will be silly when you hear it.

Here is my two-fold request of you. First, listen for the flak. Lately, it revolves around food issues. The equivalent of eighteen high fat breakfasts at one sitting is a hook in their own mouth. When you hear their pitch, ask them to demonstrate eating an eighteen-pound breakfast. It's fun! Second, when you hear the flak, ask my competitors, "What did Medical Memo say about that?" The fact is that Medical Memo did not deem the flak worthy of referencing in their review of hemorheologics. It's just not important.

Will you now increase your prescriptions of the best? Powerful once a day Flofral?

PLUSHAUT WAS LEARNING and changing, too. Management now emphasized the importance of the top twenty percent of prescription writers that wrote eighty percent of the drugs. It also meant the other eighty percent of doctors were not important enough to call on. The message to the sales force was to go after the big fish, not the little ones.

Stu and Ana shared concerns for another issue. Plushaut was in financial trouble. Their stock price plunged. The FDA approved few new drugs. Research and development costs rose exponentially. Drugs lost their patent protection before FDA approval.

As Stu lay in bed with Ana, the FDA was turning down approval of Plushaut's revolutionary antibiotic, PLU-919, after spending over one billion dollars to bring it to the market.

"Certain drugs have both left-handed and right-handed molecules mixed together."

"Oh, tell me more," Ana whispered in Stu's ear with a high level of sarcasm.

"What if I told you that this issue could seriously affect your ability to shop?"

"Well then, it's best you go on."

"Then let's continue."

"I'm all ears as long as you practice… what is it? *The less you say, the more I remember.*"

"Okay. We will soon bring out a new drug that only has a left-handed molecule. Next, we have a new indication for Lystrepto to treat heart attacks. I think the company is going to do just fine."

These were often improvements to their product line, but none were blockbusters. The industry was treading water and Plushaut was sinking.

Lystrepto became a perfect example of how marketing trumps good research and development nearly always. Plushaut brought to market this innovative new drug, generic name *streptokinase*. Primary researchers discovered the benefits of certain compounds found in nature that could dissolve blood clots, primarily in legs and lungs.

Stu was pumped. "This will save lives," he said to Ana. "I can picture a doctor telling me that I'm a hero."

"Maybe you would sell more if you tell the doctor that he's the hero."

Ana was always right, but Stu vowed to study this very complex subject and be the smartest one in the room. What he forgot was that science doesn't sell a drug like Lystrepto.

Dissolving blood clots also caught the eye of Gengineerico, one of the first successful biotechnology corporations in the pharmaceutical industry. Vascular endothelium plasminogen activator or *vePA* entered the race late with the brand name, Plaseve. No one called it that. The entire world called it *vePA*. The curve ball thrown at Plushaut's Lystrepto was Gengineerico's marketing push to dissolve blood clots in the heart. In simple terms, they were going after FDA approval for heart attacks. The race was on.

In 1984, Lystrepto received its indication to dissolve clots in a heart attack by IV infusion. It worked within minutes. Pluchaut's slogan for Lystrepto, *Time is Muscle*, was used to good effect—at a low cost of just over $100. Lystrepto was on a roll.

Then came the annual conference of the Academy of Clinical Physicians in Washington, DC, at the end of May 1984. It was the first time for Stu to attend a big meeting of thousands of physicians, primarily doctors of internal medicine and their subspecialty offshoots.

Gengineerico had a display booth for the first time to promote to physicians their only drug, *vePA*. The company-issued press releases concentrated on a single indication of myocardial infarction or heart attack.

"See over there?" a Boston rep with Plushaut said to Stu. She pointed at the Gengineerico booth only thirty yards away. "They hired a handful of women with big boobs to man the booth."

Stu understood right away why it drew a large crowd.

It was on the second day of the four-day conference that he had a chance to stop by the booth and pick up literature about his competitor. Out of courtesy, he brought a Lystrepto file card to give the ladies in trade. The ladies astonished him.

"We don't have any file cards to give you. Sorry."

Stu paused a moment to enjoy the close-up view of the three endowed and attractive representatives.

"So, what are you giving to doctors?"

"We only have information about how to buy stock in Gengineerico. Would you like our prospectus?"

Their leave pieces were all projected sales numbers, stock performance charts, and glitz. Neither the name Plaseve nor the generic name *vePA* was mentioned.

Although still awaiting approval for launch from the FDA, Gengineerico was sending to cardiologists tons of information about the potential for *vePA*. Stu and other company reps were constantly assaulted by clinicians who spotted the Lystrepto panels at the Plushaut booth and informed them that their days of Lystrepto glory were numbered.

"You might have better success," one Las Vegas cardiologist said, "if you were more attractive."

"The fact that you find me unattractive I take as a compliment," Stu from experience knew to dish it back.

"Their new clot buster is going to put your company under."

"Are you using it?"

"No, it's not out, yet."

"So, currently, you're using *streptokinase* to stop a heart attack... an MI, right?" Stu knew to use generic names when speaking to doctors at an Internal Medicine convention.

"No."

"No? Why would you not use what's indicated right now?"

"*Streptokinase* is not indicated for myocardial infarction."

"Yes, it is." Stu handed the doctor a file card opened to the page on heart attacks. "I'm glad we got to talk."

The cardiologist briefly studied the facts presented. "Nice. I wish your company had told me sooner."

"That's why we're here."

"You're still going to lose until you have some women here to compete."

"Over there they've got boobs and stocks to offer. We're just here to save lives."

The man gave a stifled laugh, turned, and headed to the next booth.

Stu was not naïve. He knew that boobs and stock investments trumped science and proven success every time.

ONE YEAR LATER a Swedish drug manufacturer broke the patent on Lystrepto and began offering their generic brand of *streptokinase*. Prices dropped. Lystrepto's price was down to $78 per dose to treat a heart attack. Gengineerico's *vePA* sold for an astronomical $2300 per dose. With a differential cost of roughly thirty to one, Stu knew that Gengineerico's *vePA* didn't stand a chance—or so he thought. A talking point that stuck with the cardiologists invested in Gengineerico drove Stu crazy.

"It may cost more but you get what you pay for."

To make matters worse, Gengineerico went on a publicity campaign to gin up support from the public. News items flooded the news programs. Patients testified how *vePA* saved them from a certain death. One cardiologist informed Stu that patients entered the ER demanding *vePA*.

"When I told them that there is a drug called Lystrepto that is just as good for a much lower price, they hesitated. They didn't want some cheap drug that could not possibly be as good as *vePA*."

Stu learned a lesson that was a constant reminder to him of why drugs are expensive. Everything to the public has a perceived value. If a drug is expensive, it must be better. Every company that lowers its prices in a competitive market loses market share. Every company that sells a product based on price alone loses its reputation. Drugs became successful because of their perceived efficacy. To the patient, the higher the cost, the better it must work. In a final blow to Stu's Lystrepto sales, the hospital pharmacy managers admitted to Stu.

"The hospital makes more money selling *vePA* than we can using *streptokinase*."

Another new drug and its investment went down the toilet. It was a half a billion-dollar mistake for Plushaut that was to repeat itself many times more.

Chapter Twenty-Six

THE THREE BOYS at the Roy house began to ask their father what he did when he left home every morning. Usually, he came home in the evening, but sometimes he was gone for two or three days. Stuart junior was now almost nine-years-old. With school only one week away, the oldest boy sat in the front passenger seat of Stu's car pretending he was his father's district manager. Dressed in blue blazer and Khaki slacks with white shirt and tie, Stuart grinned as his father sped across western Oklahoma on Interstate 40 before exiting for Cordell. This was the first of what would be one overnight workday each with all of Stu's children over the next several years. It was an experiment. Done without company approval, Stu did not ask permission. Whether it hurt his sales efforts or not, Stu thought it important to let every child know what he did for a living that made their lives happy and safe.

Since Stu and Ana's first child was a junior, it was easy to affix an old nametag to Stuart junior's coat lapel. Stu wore the same khaki slacks, blue blazer, white shirt, and tie that closely resembled his son's. They had finished lunch at a Sonic Drive-in in Weatherford. Stuart was not yet bored of the drive, but his dad knew things needed to move along as fast as they could. He planned a drive on the more rural state roads to

Mangum before making the long drive back north to stay overnight at the Holiday Inn in Elk City. Unique to the hotel chain, the one in Elk City had a large, enclosed recreation area the size of two tennis courts, suitable for shuffleboard, ping pong, and other offerings designed to make a child sleep well and early.

The temperature was hot, even for August. This part of Oklahoma to the southwest had a reputation for drought and blistering hundred plus degree heat. Passing south of Cordell, Stu suggested his son look for the farmers in their pickup trucks as they approached from the other lane.

"What am I looking for?"

"When I drive down in this area of our state, the farmers always wave at me as I drive by. This is the only place where I see it. So now, we wave at every pickup truck that comes our way. You ready?"

"Yeah!"

At that moment, a large turkey vulture made a low pass directly in front of the car. The boy, focused on farmer's trucks, startled at the unidentified object approaching. At close range, the bird appeared enormous to an eight-year-old boy. Ominous in appearance with its hideous red head and sinister carriage, Stuart shouted in terror as it barely missed colliding with their car at 70 mph. He unbuckled his seat belt and crawled down into the footwell to hide.

"What was that?" He tried hard not to cry.

Stu kept calm. To him it was common to have the unexpected happen. Once before, when going home from Altus, he had seen his first ever live armor-plated armadillo. Before, they had only been dead on the roadway. After ten miles, he passed hundreds of them, all digging holes off the road's shoulder or in the center median. The drive in these parts was always entertaining.

Stu glanced at his terrified son, now in the footwell of his seat. "Don't stay down there for too long. You'll miss waving to a farmer." Stu waved at an imaginary truck. "Oops, there goes one passing by now. You missed it."

Stuart lifted his head up, got back in his seat, and once more buckled up. To Stu's relief a farmer in a pickup approached and, as if on cue, waved as he passed them. Stuart laughed aloud. He subsequently entertained himself all the way to Mangum.

They arrived in Mangum, later than was wise. Even as a small town, it was a busy place for physicians. In the blistering heat, Stu suggested they take off their sport coats and leave them in the car. He retrieved Stuart's nametag and pinned it on the boy's shirt pocket.

"They told me one day I looked too uppity wearing a jacket. One doctor said I better never wear a suit here… ever again."

"I'm for that, too. Let's get inside. It's hot." Stu grabbed his sales bag and stuffed it with samples. Then he took an empty box, filled it with a mixture of samples and giveaways, then held it out to Stuart.

"Here, you can help me carry."

The two walked into the four-doctor clinic where young Stuart handed the lady at the front counter his father's business card. Dad had earlier penned a 'Junior' after his name.

The lady, still in tight pin curlers in the afternoon, was a wiry and weathered woman in her seventies. Her husband was the always delightful Doctor Current. She looked over the counter at the boy.

"Well, hello young man. Are you working today with your papa?"

"No, I'm his district manager and I'm mean."

He said it loud enough to send several patients in the area into laughing.

"I bet you are, and I know your papa. He does need a spanking."

The boy looked at her and grinned. Then turning to Stu, he gave him a couple of whacks on the backside. He tried for more, but his rambunctious history called for swift action. Stu grabbed his wrist.

"Not here," he said sternly. "You do that at home, not at work."

Looking slightly embarrassed, Stuart relented after unleashing a final tepid tap on his father.

"I have four doctors here today, so I'll need three more cards, please."

Stuart supplied the extra cards. The two quickly found a seat to wait with the others. Stu noticed another drug rep at the corner of the room. She had not shown much interest in Stu's arrival. Multi-doctor clinics were different from a one doctor clinic. It was not necessary for Stu to ask a rep, out of courtesy, if his dropping a card would disrupt their chance to see the physicians. Besides, in rural areas, where reps drove a hundred miles to get there, it was common courtesy to have no restrictions of any kind. Common sense and necessity prevailed. He got up to say hello, after instructing Stuart to remain seated.

"Have you been waiting long?" Stu said. "I'm Stu Roy with Plushaut."

The young lady held out her hand. Well dressed and willowy, she had a warm smile and natural poise. He shook her hand and noted the delicate fingers and the controlled grip. That was a clue to him that she was self-assured. A large white diamond on her left hand overwhelmed a modest wedding band.

"It's nice to meet you. Janet Norris with Plaquarn. Your son is very handsome." She had a distinctive accent Stu could identify. Her raven hair, a result of her Cuban ancestry, touched her shoulders, framing her face. It made her look more professional—all business.

"Thank you. He's a hard worker, too."

"Have you called on this clinic often?"

"About ten years now. Same doctors the whole time."

"This is only my second time."

"Well, what would you like to know?"

"You don't mind...? I mean... we are competitors."

"Oh, of course not, I share everything I know, and I always get good information in return."

"You sure?"

"I've found that after a few years we get lazy and miss a lot of information that we would have asked about early in our careers. New reps have always helped me out, so I like to return the favor up front. All of you reps are my friends."

"Look at your son." She pointed to him talking to an elderly male patient, who seemed quite thrilled to have a companion for a while. Stu was content to leave it alone. "Tell me about Doctor Mackie. My first visit with him left me a little confused."

Stu laughed because he knew what she meant. Doctor Mackie was quiet and seemingly unresponsive to questions. Stu figured him out the same way that Janet Norris was about to. He asked for help.

"He puzzled me for a year, but my boss told me to try something. I asked Doctor Mackie a question, knowing that he wouldn't answer me. But this time I kept quiet for what seemed like an eternity… and then he answered. I was stunned. So, if you can learn to wait… don't say anything. He'll answer. He's just thinking what to say, that's all."

"Thank you. I can do that. It might even be fun to practice on him."

"I practice a lot with docs."

"So, do you always get to see all four of them?"

"Usually only one or two. Each of their days off is different, so there's always at least one out of the office. You just have to alternate your days of the week."

"I really liked talking to Doctor Nestor. He seems very nice." Her voice, smile, and relaxed manner were pleasing to the eyes.

"I'm not much of a fan of his," Stu said. "He wants to tell you what you want to hear. Don't rely on him. He wants everyone to like him, so he might exaggerate his support for your drugs."

Janet looked up when a lady called her name. A nurse at the other end stood in the doorway to the back holding her card. She graciously excused herself and headed back. Meanwhile, Stu came back over to rescue the older gentleman from his district manager. Within minutes a nurse called Stu and Stuart back. She had a motherly greeting for the boy.

"Doctor Current will see you today. Oh, he will love this. Is this your son?"

"No, I'm the district manager," the boy replied, a tad too loud to suit his father.

"Well, be careful. I don't know if Doctor Current likes district managers, so watch out."

Stu knew from experience that she was telling the truth. It wasn't uncommon for managers to wait in the waiting room until reps finished talking to a doctor. He learned to love it when a doctor shooed his boss out. They were always aware of the possibility. It was never an awkward moment. When managers did interrupt a salesman during a call, it became awkward quickly. Stu had an inkling that Doctor Current today would make an exception.

"Come in here, Stuart," the doctor said, then looked at Stu. "Not you. You're a manager today. I want to talk to the rep."

Stuart looked at his dad with some apprehension.

"It's okay, Stuart. You're a sales rep now. You know what I say? Give him a good sales pitch." He handed the boy three file cards then stepped to one side of the door. The doctor took over the call.

"Come in here, Stuart." He stood up and stepped around his desk, extending his hand. "I'm Doctor Current. Take a seat."

Stuart was unsure what he meant, so Doctor Current motioned to the two chairs which faced his desk. "What seat would your papa sit in?"

"This one." He pointed to the nearest chair and sat down. The doctor walked behind him to sit down in the chair next to him.

"So, how old are you, Stuart?"

"I'm nine... well, almost nine."

"Is this your first time to work as a detail man?"

"What's a detail man?"

"What your papa does... selling medicines to doctors."

"I guess so."

"First time, huh?" Stuart nodded. "So, you're making your first sales call. Tell me what you have."

Stu, from around the corner in the hall, was having fun. Two nurses came up to stand with him. His instincts told him that he would sell more to Doctor Current today than ever before.

"Well… Daddy says that these medicines are really good." He handed the doctor his three file cards.

"Okay, let's see. What's this Destense? I'm not familiar with that."

"It keeps your blood from having too much pressure." He paused to think. The doctor waited. "Daddy says there are gener… gener…."

"Generics?"

"Yeah! There are generics that don't work as well. I think the pills have dirt in them or something. Daddy shows a picture. I don't understand it."

"Well, this is your first call. I bet you'll get better if you keep listening to him."

"Daddy also sells Frofral. That's his favorite drug to sell."

"Why does he like Flofral?"

"Well, Fro… Flofral… that's hard to pronounce. It does things, Daddy says, for the first time. It saves… it saves…." He turned his head to the door. "Daddy, what does it save?"

"Life and limb," Stu replied with as much volume as was proper in the clinic.

"Yeah, it saves life and limb."

"And what does that mean?"

"It means people lose their legs… sometimes just their toes… and then… they die."

"So, Flofral sounds like it would be pretty important to use on people." Stuart nodded.

Doctor Current held out the last file card and put it back into Stuart's hands. "Tell me about this one. Tapilon?"

Tapilon was a new antibiotic that Plushaut promoted for another company, Connicut Labs, to supplement their small sales force as a Tapilon *rent-a-rep*. His knowledge of it was minimal.

"I don't like this one. It's a shot."

"I don't blame you, son."

"Daddy says it kills bugs… not the bugs I see in my house. It kills bugs I can't see… lots of them."

"So, the kinds that make you sick?"

"Yeah, so you should try it."

"I will."

"What about the others?" He was looking at the back of Stu's business card that listed other drugs no longer a priority.

"What do you mean by 'what about the others?'"

Doctor Current was trying to clarify where the boy was going. He showed Stuart the list on the back.

"Will you try those, too?"

"Oh, that's right. You have other drugs. I'm sold. I will try out all three upon your recommendation."

"Daddy says I might have to ask you three times before you say yes."

Laughter from the hallway was instant. The new Plaquarn rep had joined the other three in the hallway to join in the moment. Stuart seemed confused about the commotion outside the doctor's office.

"Why are they laughing?" Doctor Current was laughing, too.

"Stuart, you are so good at your job that you only need to ask me to try it once. It sometimes takes three times with your papa… your daddy. Once was all you needed to ask. You are that good."

Stuart was grinning as Stu, still laughing, stepped inside his office to retrieve the boy and to get Doctor Current's signature to leave samples. He knew the call was over. Janet Norris, his friendly competitor, was next in line to talk to him and try to undo Stuart's pitch for Tapilon.

"Stu, thank you for letting me have a little fun. You have a fine son. He might make a good doctor someday."

"Thank you. Now I know what technique works… short and sweet."

Doctor Current laughed. "My favorite kind." He picked up another business card and motioned to Janet Norris. She first stopped to say a word to Stu.

"Thank you for your advice on Doctor Mackie. It was amazing. He answered my questions. You were a help."

"You went easy on Tapilon, I hope."

"Not a chance."

"Janet Norris," Doctor Current said. "Come in and have a seat."

Stu and Stuart grabbed their bag and sample box and stepped across the hallway to Doctor Mackie's office where they hoped to undo everything the Plaquarn rep just told him.

When Stu stepped into Doctor Mackie's office, Stuart had time to walk around to relieve his nervous energy. They waited fifteen minutes before the doctor came back to his office to greet them. He was tired and not in a mood to see any more sales reps, yet he remained polite because of Stuart. Usually quiet and introspective, Stu noted his impatience through his body language. When Stu showed him the inside page of his visual, Doctor Mackie cut him off.

"I just listened to a new rep tell me over and over about the differences between her drug and Tapilon. I heard the name Tapilon so many times that I can't recall what she was selling. You don't have to continue. You're preaching to the choir."

This was unusual behavior for him to give feedback without the usual awkward pause of silence. Stu had a ready answer that made the doctor softly smile.

"Doctor Mackie, I may be preaching to the choir, but even the choir must rehearse occasionally."

Stu waited an agonizing fifteen seconds before Doctor Mackie responded.

"I suppose you're right."

"And I would be remiss if I didn't remind you that the choir needs to pick up the tempo."

For the first time in memory, Doctor Mackie let out an audible laugh. Stu, after covering all three products, was certain that he had hit a home run at the expense of Janet the Plaquarn rep. Even young Stuart was impressed.

Chapter Twenty-Seven

THAT NIGHT AT dinner in Elk City's Holiday Inn, Stu and Stuart ran into a friend of theirs from a drug company specializing in products for dermatologists. Ron Terry had slaughtered Stu with his steroid cream. Grandicort 0.2% Steroid Cream had worked well for patients, but Ron and his company that derms loved was awesome to watch. Both Ron and Stu started their careers together and had a special bond. They were virtually non-competitors. They shared a table with Stuart who ate his chicken fingers while the two men talked about a stunning event they should have known was coming.

"You're saying the feds arrested Doctor Brighton yesterday?"

"Right in front of me. It was crazy. His nurse… well there's always a nurse involved with him. She was back there wailing as they cuffed him."

Doctor William Brighton was a medical doctor best described as swashbuckling. For a small-town doctor in Anadarko, also named Indian City, USA, he didn't fit the mold. He was not a tribal member. He dressed more like a city slicker than a good old boy from southwestern Oklahoma. Reps nicknamed him Hollywood Bill. Stu once made his sales call on him while he performed a hair transplant on a patient. The rep, doctor, and patient talked together for ten minutes like they were sharing a beer at the local bar.

Hollywood Bill had three addictions—oil wells, gambling, and women. He did well with the women, but gambling and oil wells, not so well. It was ten years since the Oklahoma oil boom went bust. Doctor Brighton invested heavily in oil wells. For five years he did well at feeding his Las Vegas gambling habit with his oil revenues. Over time he managed to lose more in gambling than his oil wells could pump. Doctors are often the worst businessmen in the world. He decided the smartest thing to do was to borrow from certain men in Las Vegas. What could go wrong with oil nearly a hundred dollars a barrel? After a year of loans, his debt was approaching three million American dollars. The loan sharks began to come around at odd hours of the day and night. His nurses-of-the-week left him in fear for their lives. He tried to solve his problem the only way a bad businessman knows how. He began writing thousands of prescriptions for Valium and Quaalude. For almost three years he practiced medicine as a controlled substance prescription factory for drug addicts. Hollywood Bill was a star. But it wasn't enough. He increased his volume of illicit prescriptions so boldly into the millions of pills that, as expected, the Feds took notice.

"I was in his office with him," Ron said, "when we were interrupted by several guys... FBI, DEA, some sort of feds. They came in and politely announced that they were here to arrest him. He cooperated with them as they read him his rights and cuffed him."

"Did Brighton say anything?"

"Yeah, but they were too busy asking me who I was. I just wanted to get out of there. It scared me half to death. As they escorted me out, you want to know what Brighton said to the feds?"

"I didn't do it?"

"No! He said, 'Thank God you're here. Where have you been? I've been writing Quaaludes as fast as I can in hopes you would come and arrest me before the loan sharks killed me.'"

AFTER DINNER, RON left for his room, while Stu and his son went into the indoor pavilion at the hotel. He introduced Stuart to the sport of shuffleboard, a game not as widely played anymore. When they grew bored of that amusement, they moved next to a ping pong table. Stu spent all his time retrieving bouncing balls that rolled for miles. His hope for wearing out Stuart was surpassed by his own fatigue. Today they had covered over 250 miles driving between towns. Even with the driving they did, they managed to see seven doctors, which was a miracle.

As Stuart tried his hand at shooting baskets, Stu reflected on how glad he was that his son was not in Anadarko to see a doctor arrested for such a sad reason. It bothered him to imagine a person, so talented as to go to medical school, who then would destroy his whole life and career. With so much brain power and talent, the cause of Hollywood Bill's downfall was his own stupidity and hubris.

Stu watched his boy try one missed shot after another. He knew that the last thing he would ever do was shoot the baskets for him. Brighton never appreciated what he had. No one would let him miss the basket and learn what it was like to have to struggle. Stu knew that was the danger in being the smartest one in the room. It made one feel untouchable.

He called out to Stuart. "Try again. You can do it."

The boy began to tire. The elevation of his shots diminished with his fatigue. It was time for Stu to give his lesson.

"Stuart, try this." He took an imaginary basketball in both hands. Holding it below his knees, he launched an imaginary underhand shot at the hoop. With his left hand he traced the ball taking a high arc and landing with nothing but net. The spark of a solution came to his son's face. With renewed excitement and dogged determination, he took his dad's underhand posture with the ball. His underhand launch easily exceeded the elevation of his overhand shots, arching gently higher, then into a descent that passed over the hoop, hitting the backboard, and dropping through.

"Swish!" he said triumphantly, then sighed with relief. "I'm tired now. Can we go to our room?"

Chapter Twenty-Eight

THREE MONTHS LATER, as drug reps neared the end of the year and no one wanted to work, tensions reached a boiling point in Plushaut Uclaf. Earlier in the year the company mailed letters to all the sales force to explain the financial plight they all faced. They even developed a slogan designed to work miracles with the sales force.

Nine ninety-six in ninety-six!

Plushaut had to achieve total sales of $996 million by the end of the upcoming year or the company would collapse in ruin. Of course, the sales force presumed correctly that the goal of *Nine ninety-six in ninety-six!* was to save the home office management from losing their jobs. For the last half of the year Plushaut top executives had flooded sales reps with pep talks, voice mails, letters, and lectures about the importance of those numbers. It was no surprise to anyone how convenient it was that the number needed matched the year they were in.

As a measure to cut costs, Plushaut suspended all expense accounts. Paid-for lunches that reps charged to their expense accounts ended abruptly. Reps who ordered minivans for their company cars had the order suspended. Anyone using a minivan received instructions of how to turn them in. Sales reps who paid extra money for added features and specialty colors on their company vehicles were not paid back when they returned their vehicles before the presumed length of use ran out. It was the equivalent of a large cut in salary.

Stu was a keen observer of the way reps, managers, and home office personnel conducted their business. He was grateful to have a job that he enjoyed. He accepted the challenge to reach sales of $996 million with a personal mission in mind. He observed many activities of his company that were wasteful and ill-conceived. No one else made public note of these bad habits, so he made a list. For the time being, he kept it to himself.

Nine months later, during the October quarterly meeting of the Zombies, their guest visitor was Abbott Wahl, Regional Manager of a now expanded eight zone managers making up the southwest region of the United States. Wahl was well into twenty years as regional manager. He had no intention of moving up from what he called the greatest job in the company. His job was easy when he had good managers. He enjoyed talking to the sales reps at these meetings. It was in the evening that he got a chance to chat with Lorelei Lolly and Jimmy Tomey.

As the longest serving rep in the Zombies, Tomey was on his way to retirement at the end of the year. Wahl fully expected him to be free to say anything he wanted to the boss's boss.

"Well Jimmy, what do you think so far about the company and our mandate for nine-nine-six?" Wahl was sitting in one of the four plush, maroon leather chairs in the lobby of the Waterford Hotel in Oklahoma City. His military bearing was evident even three decades after his departure from the air force. He wore a stylish gray herringbone sport coat, black slacks, with an up to date and expensive silk tie on his pristine white shirt. The man was unable to wrinkle clothing. His shoes could still pass any drill instructor's shoeshine inspection.

"Abbott, I think it's their problem, not ours." Jimmy, who called Wahl by his first name, sat to his right on purpose. Many managers, who fancied themselves scholars of the Knights of the Roundtable, thought this meant something. To Jimmy it only meant that it would drive them crazy with speculation. "How in blazes would we know how to get to nine hundred and ninety-six million bucks?"

Jimmy had an ornery streak on occasion that contrasted with his usual mission in the company of being the most helpful rep out there. He was seldom the top performer, but nearly always in second place. Overall, Jimmy's sales over the years were the best in the region because he was never in the bottom half with any product he sold.

"I get what you mean, Jimmy, but there's hell to pay if they don't make it."

"Are we talking like… Guillotine hell?"

"Perhaps. Thank God I'm not up there with them. France is finally figuring out that they've been fudging the books in hopes of getting out of their hole by making it up in a good year."

"So, what can we do?"

"Tomorrow morning, I will give you all the latest motivational speech from the home office. Then it's off to the Tulsa zone meeting in the afternoon."

"Give me a hint in ten words or less."

Wahl laughed at the suggestion. "Oh, why not? You're a short timer. Aren't you retiring?"

"Yes sir. I'm outta here in December. I have a lot of my vacation lined up. My last official day is New Year's Eve."

"Well, good for you. Congratulations. What a way to celebrate the completion of a job well done?"

"Am I going to like this ten-word summary?"

Wahl gestured Jimmy to move closer. He whispered, "We are all in the raft together."

"We are all in the raft together?"

"You got it."

"That implies we all may die."

"Great image if you want pessimism among the ranks."

"You're not saying that in the morning, I hope."

Wahl looked at him. He envied Jimmy's ability to retire. He seldom wished to quit, but he was distressed about what could happen that might take away a job he truly enjoyed.

"Jimmy, do you know anyone who knows how to do a motivational skit or maybe do something on video tape?"

"You mean something that is funny and cheerful?"

"Exactly! I can see the lack of enthusiasm in you Zombies already."

"I don't know if that's true."

"That's because you're in the thick of it. Granted, retirement in three months would keep me upbeat. The rest of them seem unmotivated. When you tell reps they must achieve a goal or drown, that's not a motivator."

"I hear that Four… 'er Benton Wickingham did something like this in the Army. You want something like that song group, *Up With People?*"

"God no! I got enough of that in the sixties. They didn't make me feel better when I put my time in with the Army. Not that syrupy stuff."

"What if we poked fun at the company?"

"I like that idea, but you can't use any names."

"I could. I'm retiring."

"Don't you dare. They'll have us all killed, including you."

Lorelei spotted the two and came over to greet Abbott Wahl. After a handshake and other niceties were over, she sat down on the other side of Jimmy. He turned to her and smiled.

"How would you like to be in a video?" Jimmy gave her a short summary of the subject.

"I might help you," she replied, "but I don't wish to be in one."

"You think Four would help?"

"Four? Are you kidding? He would be perfect. You know he makes silly little videos for his children. He played one for me once. They are priceless. He had his two little ones laughing on the floor. And I'm sure it wasn't their first time to see it."

"Lorelei, did your previous company ever do something like that?"

"No, sir. They were fairly conservative in everything they did. But I didn't hear. What kind of video are we talking about?"

Wahl jumped in to answer her question. "I'll wait until tomorrow to give you a theme. If I tell you now, it will ruin my morning presentation. Get Wickingham to help you come up with something, I'll be very grateful."

Abbott Wahl looked up in time to see Ben Hodge and excused himself. It gave Jimmy time to reveal the new raft theme to Lorelei. Their minds' creative wheels began spinning.

Chapter Twenty-Nine

It was late the next morning that Abbott Wahl, after delivering his message from the home office to the Zombies, got back on the raft and went to Tulsa. Ben went to his easel and wrote the new motivational slogan in big capital letters on the white paper.

WE ARE ALL IN THE RAFT TOGETHER

He was not privy to Jimmy's conversation with Abbott Wahl. But Jimmy brought it up and Ben got upset and defensive. Although he was as unmotivated as the rest, he tried to put on an upbeat meeting. It was not going over well. Jimmy and Lorelei, commissioned to put together a motivational video that teased the company, met with strong opposition.

In the four years Ben had been zone manager, he had become more unpredictable in his behavior when with reps in the field. They noticed his defense of the company was often over the top. No company is perfect. All reps observed flaws in the system, mentioned managers that might need improvement, or uttered negative comments about ill-informed home office dictates. Knowing that his reps were planning a video set him over the edge, Jimmy set him straight during the meeting in front of everybody.

"We're not doing it for you, Ben. We're doing it for Abbott Wahl... your boss."

Ben pouted for the rest of the meeting.

"Whɑt ideɑs did you come up with over the weekend?" Lorelei asked the other two men.

Jimmy and Four were sitting across from her at a Denny's on the west side of town. It was Monday morning after the disaster of a zone meeting. By Friday, according to Ben, the Zombies had already left the raft. In truth, the three of them hadn't been this motivated in months. In their minds, the phrase, *'Don't just stand there. Do something,'* couldn't be more applicable. The whole company was on edge as the weeks counted down.

Part of Abbott Wahl's raft talk included a one-page handout of the progress of company sales through the end of September. With one quarter to go, the odds that the company would reach that 996 million number was unlikely. At first the three puzzled over the audacity of a video depiction of Plushaut's officers from the chief executive officer all the way down to the lowliest product manager in charge of fart medications.

"You guys weren't with me one night at our last national meeting in Miami." Jimmy said. "If you remember, that was the meeting where we first heard about needing to cut costs, increase sales, and reach that nine-ninety-six number. Some of us went to one of the gentlemen's clubs nearby...."

"Why you bad boy," Lorelei said. Four, no sheltered child, laughed.

"I know what you're going to say," Four said. "Stu told me."

"About the Plushaut bigwigs there?" said Jimmy. Four nodded. "Yeah, what's amazing is they were the same people who were on stage presenting their concerns about how in this coming year every dollar counted."

"Have you heard this before?" Four asked Lorelei. She shook her head.

"Anyway. To my story. I noticed five or six of the top Plushaut directors, including our CEO drinking up a storm, having multiple lap dances, and who knows what else. A couple of wannabes were hanging with them. I wasn't there long… those places actually give me the creeps, but it was late. They paid their tab about midnight."

"Whoa, Jimmy. That's late for an old man like you."

"At ease, soldier, and let me finish." Jimmy was on a roll and didn't want to be interrupted. "The CEO and his minions were leaving. So, I motioned to one of his wannabes to come on over. I never can remember the guy's name, but he's always sidling up to the big shots. You know the type."

Four and Lorelei both nodded. The Army and other drug companies all had their suck ups.

"I asked him directly, who paid for that? He said one of the east coast regional managers put it on his corporate card. He volunteered that the tab before any tip was around eleven grand. All paid for by the company."

Four and Lorelei let out groans of disgust at the amount.

"And they want us to sacrifice," Four said.

"I'm not impressed that the leadership would put a tab like that on a company card," said Lorelei.

Jimmy chuckled. "Why do you think they had a regional manager pay for it. The name of the place is on his tab, not theirs."

The three paused for a moment to regroup their thoughts. They finally went back to Lorelei's original question of what ideas they had to suggest. For an hour they bounced ideas back and forth with no real plan that was sending them into stitches of laughter. It was Four who finally grabbed their attention with an idea that started them talking excitedly.

"Why don't we make a video that no one has to be in. We'll only feature a narrator's voice asking one question… What Hollywood movie would best describe 'we are all in the raft together?' Then let's take movie clips with boats in them and put them together one after the other. Think of disaster movies."

They started saying the names of movies they could use.

"I've got one. *African Queen!* Remember Bogart and Hepburn going down the waterfall?"

"*Huckleberry Finn* on his raft."

"The sea battle in *Ben Hur.*"

"Is there a movie about the Titanic?"

The names kept coming. It would require many movie rentals from Blockbuster Video to pull it off. Four assured them that he had the equipment to do it. But they were unhappy that a better movie hadn't come to mind for their grand finale.

They silently ate their breakfast and drank more coffee, when suddenly Jimmy blurted out a movie that made Lorelei spew coffee and Four choke on a link sausage. They had their solution for their video—the hook it needed to make the entire company laugh with them.

"What Hollywood movie best describes 'we are all in the raft together?'" Jimmy asked. "What else? *Deliverance!*"

Chapter Thirty

BEN LOOKED STERNLY at Jimmy and Lorelei, who sat on his home office sofa that he had paid for himself to impress the other managers. Four was already at Blockbuster renting video tapes and laser disks. Ben bristled at their idea to motivate the company with a mocking depiction of the company's *in-the-raft-together* slogan.

"You won't do that on my watch."

Jimmy was feeling his oats. He wanted Ben to have a better attitude but realized that trying to be helpful got nothing done. Besides, he was a short-timer. If Ben fired him, he would get an extra severance package. Nobody ever understood why the good guys who retired couldn't get compensation, unless they were bad enough to get fired.

"We work for Abbott on this project, not you. This is only a courtesy call."

Ben turned to Lorelei in a tactic meant to intimidate her. "What do you say, Lorelei? I want to know where your loyalty is."

Lorelei paused in her response, looking back at Ben and burning a steady confident stare back at him. She reached across his office desk and casually picked up his office phone, turned it around, and dialed a number.

"Sure, you can use my phone," Ben said sarcastically. "You don't ever have to ask."

Lorelei still said nothing. Jimmy could hear the telephone ringing in the earpiece. He had no idea what she was attempting. When the voice said, *"hello,"* he failed to quash his smile.

"Mister Wahl, this is Lorelei Lolly. My zone manager would like to talk to you."

She handed him his telephone. Ben, surprised and angered, looked at her with scorn then cupped the mouthpiece. He whispered to her.

"You already told him about this, didn't you?"

Lorelei only smiled.

Ben reluctantly put the telephone to his ear. "Who is this?"

"Ben, what did you need me for?"

"I'm not sure, Abbott. Lorelei dialed you up and handed me the telephone."

"I did talk to her this morning after your group came up with an idea for a video about movies with rafts in them. I loved the idea of ending with scenes from Deliverance. I nearly laughed my ass off when she told me that."

"Yeah, that's what they just told me but…."

"That's pretty clever, don't you think?"

"Well, I…."

"I think it's going to be a perfect way for our folks to relieve some of this stress at our next regional meeting."

There was another awkward silence as Ben calculated what was most appropriate to say.

"Ben, I know they were a little nervous about it, but you go ahead and tell them that it's okay. I guess Lorelei just needed to hear it from you."

"Will do, Abbott." He put the phone back on the cradle. Looking up at his two sales reps, he sneered.

"Don't you ever pull that stunt with me again."

"What did he say?" Jimmy was enjoying this.

"He said to tell you that you can do it, but you have to pay for it yourself. I better not find any items charged to your expense accounts."

Jimmy leaned forward and placed both hands on his desk. With close eye contact he said, "Ben, you have never understood that my hearing is very good. I heard every word you and Abbott just said to each other."

Lorelei was not so blessed with good hearing after ten years of dancing at discos in the 1970s, however Ben's half of the conversation was clear.

"We must follow what Abbott wants, Ben. You know that."

"You want to get my approval? Follow the chain of command and come to me first," he replied. "I think your idea is disloyal to Plushaut and it won't get my blessing."

When Jimmy and Lorelei hurried out Ben's front door to get to their cars, they had a chance to speak out of his presence.

"What do we do about our expenses, Jimmy?" Lorelei was worried about spending her own cash.

"I'll tell Wahl that we'd like to charge it to his account. We don't have to tell him why. No need for us to be jerks like Ben."

Lorelei shuffled around in her purse to find her car keys. The hunt took a while. Jimmy waited patiently for her to respond.

"In six years with Plushaut, I've never seen Ben like this. He's become defensive and critical." She paused to pull out the keys and jingle them in full view for Jimmy's amusement. "We can't propose any idea without accusations of being disloyal to the company. Have you noticed that?"

"When we were both sales reps, we used to pal around together at national meetings," Jimmy replied. "He changed some, of course, when he became a manager. I never expected him to get transferred here. When he arrived with his family, my wife and I tried to help him settle in. I told him what realtors were good... what area of town to live in."

At this comment, Jimmy began to laugh at his own daring.

"I told him I wanted his neighborhood to be way far from my own house."

Lorelei joined him in laughter.

Chapter Thirty-One

STU ROY LEARNED of the video a few days later. It was Friday when Ben Hodge called him at the last minute and announced that he would work with him that day. It was a lousy stunt to play on a rep. Stu's plan for the day was ruined.

"Sure, if I must. I have junk piled all over the car, but I can carve you out a space."

"I'll be waiting at the usual place."

Stu's original plan was to rearrange the massive pile of boxes in his garage before he left. It was a perfect time since it had snowed overnight. The sun would soon melt any ice. It was common sense to be safe until that happened. The caution was not for his car. The danger was in the distance between the car and the office door. He always remembered the three doctors who broke bones on the same icy morning years before, including the elite internist, Doctor Crowder, who had helped in treating his severe pneumonia earlier in his career.

Littered everywhere were cases of drug samples for four different products, including different doses of the same drugs. Boxes filled with miscellaneous giveaways lay in odd places. Ana was in the garage with him. In a discussion of the company's plight, she suggested that Stu would benefit from some extra organization. She volunteered to help him. For her it was like opening presents on Christmas. While Stu was never enamored with the items he gave to doctors, nurses, and pharmacists, Ana found some of them too tempting to pass up. Some made great toys for their three boys. She would grab a handful of ink pens, notepads, and trinkets to put in her special collection box. She claimed it as wages to her payment box for being a loyal rep's wife—a Plushautette.

Now the chaos must wait for another day. Knowing Ben would leave him after lunch, he pulled the clutter out of his car and packed his trunk and backseat lightly. If he had to, he would return home and finish the garage organization in the afternoon. Fridays were beginning to be poor days for doctor calls.

When Stu made it to Quail Creek Golf & Country Club, the morning was again overcast. Whatever snow had melted had refrozen in spots. The ice in the country club parking lot was bad, but even worse on the steps leading to the front door. Stu carefully made his way, looking for granules of ice melt to step on. The club staff was unaware of the refreeze.

Ben was in a foul mood. He opened up as soon as Stu shook his hand and said his usual, "how are you doing?" It was never meant to be anything but rhetorical, but today it unleashed a flurry of grumbles.

"Did you hear what your buddies are threatening to do?"

"What buddies?" The question further irritated him. Stu pulled out his chair to sit down across from him. His back was to the golf course, but this morning Ben was not doing his usual wandering gaze over his head at the fairways.

"Your idiot friends, Jimmy and Lorelei. I think Four is involved, too." Ben gritted his teeth before continuing with more of a threat than a question. "You're not in on this disaster, are you?"

"Ben, I have no clue what you're talking about."

After expressing some doubt, Ben proceeded to outline the plan for a motivational video that the three had proposed, including the alleged insulting use of the movie *Deliverance*. He mentioned that Abbott Wahl was an idiot. Jimmy Tomey was a bad influence on Lorelei and Four. Lorelei was a bad hire. Four bent the rules like he was at war with the competition. Then he turned on Stu.

"You are the most negative rep I have on my team. You find fault with everything."

"Ben, I would disagree with that statement. I worry about this nine-ninety-six thing the company is doing, but that's not being negative."

"You have already questioned the list of doctors you have to call on by saying that some weren't worth the effort to call on."

"Three of them were dead, Ben."

"But you had to tell people about it."

"Another doctor on my list is a veterinarian."

"Just the other day you griped about the new Destense pens."

"I mentioned that to you because the doctors couldn't get them to write. I quit giving them away because they left a negative message. How about, 'Destense doesn't work, just like these pens.'"

"There you go again, being negative."

"That's a silly thing to say."

"You also comment in meetings that the Plushaut selling plan is a disaster. You won't follow the sales direction...."

"Are my numbers bad?"

"Your attitude is bad. You even complained about the samples you get."

"I used to be able to order the samples as needed. Now, in the great wisdom of the French in Paris, they tell me how many samples I get. How do they know? They're five thousand miles away."

"It's above your pay grade. You don't have the right to run the company."

"I can't give away all the samples the company sends me. Come to my garage and see for yourself. They talk about cutting costs. If they listened to me, they could save a bundle."

"There you go again, being critical of the system. That's all you ever do... find fault."

"So, you think everyone is wrong about the nine-ninety-six in ninety-six campaign and that we're-all-in-the-raft-together slogan?"

Stu looked at Ben with an icy stare. He had had enough.

"The raft is sinking. They have everybody rowing, but nobody is fixing the hole."

A waiter waited patiently for their strident conversation to wind down, but he grew impatient and interrupted the two.

"Mister Hodge, were you wanting to order anything else?"

For the first time, Stu noticed that Ben had eaten breakfast before he arrived.

"No thank you. I think we're through."

Ben stood up. Signed a ticket for his breakfast and walked out of the dining room before Stu was out of his chair. He followed him to the exit, where Ben waited in a fury.

"Where's our first call?"

"Come with me and I'll check my schedule. It just got altered by an unplanned departure from breakfast."

THE FIRST CALL on the icy morning was with an extremely sensitive physician, perilously on the edge of deciding to never see reps again. Stu had convinced him to make a bargain. Stu would not mention certain drugs he sold, nor would he bring up competitors for comparison. He would never ask him to prescribe anything. For his part, Doctor Neuman would allow him to call on him and leave samples. If there were any new developments, Stu could explain them to him. It had worked to Stu's advantage for years. Doctor Neuman had rewarded him nicely.

Stu explained the rules to Ben as they drove into the clinic parking lot.

"Doctor Neuman sees only two or three reps anymore. It took me years to gain his trust. One day he announced that he was no longer seeing reps. Somebody pushed him over the edge."

"But you can still call on him?"

"So far... if I don't screw it up. You must be careful what you say. I know we are always supposed to ask for the business but closing the sale will get us kicked out permanently."

Ben folded his arms across his chest. "I'll sit back and watch."

"Good, let's go do all the wrong things. That's how we sell here... and by the way, he takes samples of only one thing. Flofral."

They carefully stepped out of the car onto the icy parking lot. The wind surprised them with its power, nearly blowing Ben off his feet. An unexpected cold front was blowing through, stopping the snow from melting. They carefully paced their way to the office entrance. Doctor Neuman's clinic was pristine on the outside. Professional landscapers managed for each season to be fresh with new plants, flowers, and pots. His tan brick building with light yellow trim looked new. It had looked this way for a decade. The doctor did not tolerate many people. He had never had a partner at his clinic and told Stu once that another opinion would only make him unhappy. He did not like nurses, drug reps, or other doctors telling him what to do.

Ben opened the door and let Stu walk through first, since he had his hands full with his detail bag and one case of Flofral samples. Although drug reps were masters at opening doors while encumbered with mountains of boxes in each hand, help was always welcome.

Once inside, Ben was blasted with the overly warm air in the waiting room. Stu had forgotten to mention the odd temperatures that Doctor Neuman preferred year-round. The humid air was stifling. Sweat formed on the double-paned windows. Stu took a card to the nervous young lady at the receptionist's window. Once again, he explained to her that he was one of the few drug reps her doctor would see.

"You might give that to Joan. She knows who I am and will know what to do."

She slightly relaxed and took his calling card to the back hallway. Ben, with time on his hands, first let out a prolonged and loud barrage of flatulent. Next, he looked around the area. He was struck by the sterility of the waiting area. Everything was in perfect order. No furniture looked used. A dozen magazines were all current issues, placed artfully on tables and magazine racks. Several vases of fresh cut flowers from a local florist adorned the reception desk, sconces, and end tables.

"Where are the patients?" Ben said to the empty chairs.

"Doctor Neuman doesn't like to keep anyone out here. You are looking at a display room, not a functioning one."

A door to the waiting room opened. Nurse Joan stood there smiling at Stu. Suddenly, her face dropped. A second man stood there. She looked at Stu.

"Who is this?" It was not a question of curiosity, but an assault.

"This is my friend Ben. He works with me occasionally. Can he come in if he promises to be good?"

"Doctor Neuman would not like that."

"I promise to be good," Ben replied.

Joan stood her ground by blocking the doorway. She looked at Stu sternly. She trusted Stu and decided to let him take a chance.

"You can bring your friend back because we have known and trusted you for years now, but I think it's a mistake."

"We know the rules, Joan."

"Okay then. You know where to go."

"Anything we should know before we go back?"

"His son graduated with a chemical engineering degree from college this month and got accepted to Kansas University Medical School."

"Thanks, Joan. That should get us started. How about you?"

"Same old me. Nothing new… I hear him coming out of a room. You better hurry."

Stu quick-stepped to the back kitchen where Doctor Neuman visited reps. Once inside, he pointed Ben in the direction of a corner where he was to remain out of the way. Hurriedly pulling visuals out of his bag along with one patient sample of four Flofral capsules and three file cards, he laid them on the counter. Stu would not use them for anything except as a visual reminder of his four products.

Everything was ready. Doctor Neuman stepped into the hall and gave some directions to Joan for the patient he left the moment before. She mentioned that there were two Plushaut reps in the back. Ben chose this moment to pass another smelly gas bomb in the kitchen. The doctor stepped through the doorway of the kitchen, looked at Ben, and sighed. The heat in the room made Ben's zephyrs all the more pungent.

"Good morning, Stu." He was not looking at Stu, but at Ben.

"Doctor Neuman, this is my...."

"Stu, what-a-ya got?"

"Well, first, I hear your son is starting medical school soon. Congratulations."

"Thank you. We're certainly thrilled at our house."

"You think he'll join you here someday?"

"Not a chance. You have anything new for me?"

"Yes, actually. Today, I need to tell you an area where I want you to stop using Flofral."

"That's a refreshing thing to hear from a detail man." He briefly looked up at Ben who had a shocked look.

"I'm going to let you read this from the most recent Annals of Internal Medicine by Chandler at Johns Hopkins. There's a metabolic site in the liver that Doctor Chandler found to interfere with the elimination of some of the newer macrolides. You need to discontinue Flofral if you treat any infections with one of those antibiotics. It's all there in the paper."

"May I have this copy?"

"It's yours to keep."

"This is why I let you see me. You tell me the good and the bad. I never hear detail men tell me the side effects of their drugs."

"Doctor Neuman, our job is to tell you the good things about our drugs. If there are problems, that's the job of my competition to tell you."

"But I don't let your competition call on me."

"That's why I have to do both jobs."

Neuman laughed. "Anything else to tell me?"

"No, that's it." Stu pointed at his visuals laid on the counter. "You know what I sell. Any issues you have?"

"Yes. I have one question. A lady told me this week that she has been on Destense for years, but now it causes her nausea."

"How old is she?"

"Sixty-eight or nine."

"Is she on the 20mg dose of Destense?"

"No, 40mg."

"How is her blood pressure?"

"It's controlled at that dose."

"Do you think her renal function is at the point where you could cut the dose back to twenty? I know that at age sixty-five, most patients may have lost forty percent or more of their kidney function… a normal part of aging."

"She had trouble swallowing the 40mg tablet, so I told her to cut it in half and start taking it twice a day. That's when the problem started."

"Okay, I think I have your problem solved. The 40mg is a delayed release tablet with an inner enteric coating. It's not meant to be broken in two. It's dose dumping the whole 40mg directly in the stomach. That's the cause of her nausea."

"Stay right here. I'm going to make a call and find out." Doctor Neuman walked out of the kitchen to consult Joan. Stu turned angrily to Ben.

"No more farts, Ben." His boss responded defiantly with one more rip. Stu marveled at the seemingly unlimited supply Ben kept on hand.

Stu moved over where he could get fresher air and watch his doctor get the patient's telephone number from Joan and call her. Doctor Neuman began a conversation that Stu and Ben were unable to hear. When he hung up, he turned to look at Stu in the kitchen doorway, pointed an index finger at him, and followed it with a thumbs up. He added a note to the lady's chart then returned to the kitchen.

"Stu, good call. You nailed it. I'll be a little more careful from now on. I'm stepping her down to 20mg once a day. We'll see if she's controlled. If not, I'll bump it up to twice a day. No more 40mg tablets." He raised his hand to add one more thing. "Joan says that we don't need any Flofral this time."

For Stu this was one of the better calls he had ever had with Doctor Neuman—and Ben was here to witness it. But Ben was still angry with Stu over their morning conversations and couldn't stay quiet any longer.

"Doctor Neuman, perhaps you should consider using lower doses of Destense routinely. Twenty milligrams is the most common dose. Could I get you to prescribe Flofral 20mg more often in the future?"

The kitchen grew suddenly silent except for an audible sigh from Doctor Neuman. He stared daggers at Ben for a moment, then looked at Stu.

"Doctor Neuman, I disagree with what my friend asked you." The exasperation in Stu's voice was evident. "You and I have an agreement about this, and I am sticking to it. Disregard what you just heard."

Without another word, Doctor Neuman glared again at Ben then turned to walk out of the kitchen. Stu stepped over to watch him storm up the hallway to Joan's station. He spoke a few curt words to her then took a chart into an exam room. Joan turned to Stu with an angry look, like a mother does with a hopeless child.

Stu gathered up his visuals to stuff in his detail bag. With bag in one hand and his samples under his arm, he led Ben into the doctor's pristine waiting room. After apologizing to Joan and waving goodbye to the nervous receptionist, he exited outside into the cold wind and ice of the clinic parking lot. He was halfway to his car when Ben shouted in a loud voice.

"Stop right where you are!"

Stu turned around. "What?"

"Stop right where you are!"

"Let me put these things in my trunk first."

"Turn around and come right here!"

Stu ignored the command and proceeded to open his trunk and place his detail bag and Flofral samples in their place. He closed the trunk and turned around.

"Come. Right here!" Ben was pointing at his feet like a father does with a child. Stu stepped forward but refused to get as close as *right here* would require.

"Ben, what is wrong with you?"

"Come. Right here!"

"Ben, I'm not going to let you treat me like one of your children. Tell me what you want."

"Nobody corrects me in front of a doctor like that." He stood in the middle of the lot fuming. The wind blew his tie almost horizontal. Stu was cold.

Stu pointed at his car. "Why don't you step into my office? I'm not talking to you in the middle of a parking lot, Ben."

To emphasize his point, Stu walked defiantly to the car, got in, and started the engine. He quickly collected his thoughts and decided in the spirit of taking no prisoners to attack first. When Ben sat down in the passenger seat and closed the door, Stu let loose.

"You were not supposed to say anything, especially to try a close on him. What in the hell were you thinking?"

"If you ever do that again, it will be the last time."

"Cut the crap. You knew what you were supposed to do."

"You've let him manipulate you over the years."

"I like to think it has gone both ways. Name me any other reps who can call on him."

"Don't ask a question of me. It's your territory, not mine."

"Yeah, it's my territory and you don't know diddly-squat about the doctors in my territory."

"I have a job to observe your work and I am not happy with what I see."

"What a bunch of bull. If you have this attitude, I'll refuse to work with you anymore."

"You can't do that."

"You'll have to fire me."

"Give a good reason why I shouldn't fire you right now."

Stu noted nearly 10:00 a.m. on his watch. He looked up from it and began to drive out of the parking lot to another doctor's office where reps had their best luck at 10:00 in the morning.

"I'll give you seven good reasons. First, you knew the promise I made with that doctor, and you chose to ignore it. Also, I guarantee, you will never be let into that office again. You're supposed to observe and lend assistance if I ask for it. The next time you call me in the morning at the last minute to work with you, I'll tell you to go pound sand. Let's see, what number is next? Five, I am not a freshman rep. I have learned good judgement that comes from knowing my customers. You have not. Six, if you treat me like a kindergartener again, I will leave you to stomp in a fit by yourself. You can walk home. Lastly, and most importantly, you may have single-handedly ruined a relationship I worked on for a decade… all because you couldn't keep your trap shut."

A long silence commenced that lasted through four more doctor calls until lunch time.

"I'm not buying your lunch today."

"Thank God." Stu's comment was a sincere prayer. He was as enraged as Ben.

"You are the most negative person I know. You find fault with everything. You're not a builder. You're a destroyer. You're not a team player." Ben was trembling with rage.

"I don't fart, either."

"You'll hear next from Abbott, I promise you."

"You want me to call him for you? I have a cell phone handy."

Ben exited Stu's car, but failed to answer the question.

Stu reflected on what Ben shrieked in his rant that morning. The confrontation had built up over the last year, although at first it was subtle. Stu wanted revenge. He pondered his fate. He wanted to respond to his manager in a way that would make Ben feel foolish. He had never complained about the farting to anyone except his fellow sales reps. All the other Zombies found it disgusting, but they also liked his habit of leaving them alone in the afternoon. So, no one went up the chain of command to complain.

This was different. For the first time in his career, Stu feared having to work with his boss. Ben had poisoned the well. He decided the best solution was to somehow neutralize Ben in a way that would make him afraid instead.

He went home to share the events of his day with Ana. Stu found her finishing the placement of a few remaining items in their reorganized and cold garage. He drove his car in without worry of scraping against some Plushaut obstacle. Climbing out of his tricked-out Buick was easy, now that he could open the car's driver side door all the way. To his shock, his cases of samples stood stacked neatly by type and expiration date. His loads of giveaways rested on the shelves he had earlier installed to keep items off the damp cement garage floor. In one corner, Ana laid out by publication each of his shrink-wrapped bundles of scientific papers he used to discuss critical details of his products. He loved using them because he was a master at discussing statistical data in ways that his doctors found interesting and credible.

"You're home finally," Ana said with a satisfied sigh.

"You did all this while I was gone?" His boys charged out to hug him, their hands filled with little trinkets from his stash of giveaways.

"I most certainly did."

"You are a blessing. I can't believe you did this. It's cold in here."

"Not if you keep moving... so, what do you think?"

"This is wonderful!" Then with an impish addition he said, "It's so organized I doubt I will ever find a thing I'm looking for." The youngest, only eighteen months old, held in his hands a yellow squishy ball with Flofral printed in bold blue letters.

They both laughed as they shared a kiss. It was Friday, a time to unwind and think of things other than work. This evening it would be different.

Chapter Thirty-Two

"Ana, you've earned a night on the town... dinner and whatever you would like afterwards."

"Dinner will be wonderful." She looked at her husband, put her hands on his shoulders, and grinned. "Could we go to that place you talked about?"

"Where?" He kissed her more than once.

"You know. The place off Western and 63rd." She kissed him lightly.

"The Metro Wine Bar & Bistro?" He said it with his haughty voice in jest.

"The Metro. That's it."

"You better clean up then. You do that while I call for a reservation."

Stu first called Debbie, their trusted and always willing neighbor girl, to babysit the boys for a couple of hours. They loved for her to come over. She was a natural nurturer, even at fifteen years old, who knew how to keep them entertained. The boys were easy to handle, which made Stu slightly nervous. Boys were supposed to be ornery, especially when together melding three impish minds into one big mess. It was just after 5:00 p.m. when he called the restaurant. He knew it was a risk to call this late. Reservation times would be filling up by now since the weekend was starting. He managed to land the last time slot available for the evening at 6:30. He doubted Ana wanted to do more and would rather come home after dinner. That was fine with him. The cost of the dinner would be a business expense, since he was rewarding Ana for her day of labor for his benefit. He also knew that dinner would involve a discussion of his job. He needed her help and advice to salvage his career. Somehow, he would slip the receipt into his company expenses just to spite Ben.

Expense reports were tedious two-hour labors every Saturday morning. Enterprising reps finished theirs on Friday nights. Stu kicked himself each Saturday for waiting. When computers first came out, it didn't save time processing an expense report. It simply added another layer to the process. There would be no weekly expense accounting until in the morning for at least the thousandth time.

Stu had sweated out his dress shirt, despite the cold, after the stress of dealing with Ben. He walked back to their bedroom to remove his coat, shirt, and tie. He dropped his shirt in the dirty laundry bin and carefully hung up his sport coat and tie in his walk-in closet. He took delight in sneaking a peak at Ana, who showered nearby. He had never tired of looking at his wife, who to him got better looking each year. He had learned during their marriage to trust her judgement. Ana had that rare ability to take a situation, tear it down to its elemental parts, study it quickly, and put the puzzle back together. Then with the big picture pieces back in proper order, she could formulate a most perfect response to nearly everything. It was uncanny. Stu learned to problem solve from Ana because he lacked what she had—her intuition.

She looked through the steam in the shower at his blurry form and smiled, clearly enjoying knowing he idolized her and found her nakedness still an attraction. Exiting the shower, she dried off.

"We have a 6:30 reservation."

"Good job, Honey." She dried her back in full view of her man. "I didn't ask you. How was your day?"

Stu watched her as she dried herself energetically. He marveled that a petite woman of barely five feet in height could move boxes all day in the garage while fending off the boys and still have energy to do more.

"I may talk business at dinner, if you don't mind."

"Is that a good thing... or a bad thing?"

"It's a thing." Ana gave him a look like an English teacher who gets a dumb answer to her question. "Okay, it's more than a thing. I had an in-your-face battle with Ben in the parking lot of the Neuman Clinic this morning. I fear we managed to burn each other's bridges. It was a knockdown drag out."

Ana stood upright after drying her feet. "Did he hit you?"

"Oh, he wanted to, but no."

"Okay, so, tell me all about it while I get dressed."

Stu went through the events of that morning starting with Ben's anger about the video he didn't like. He mentioned his juvenile farting, his pressing Doctor Neuman with a close for more prescriptions, and his rage in the parking lot. He discovered in the telling that what hurt the most was Ben saying, "You are the most negative person I know. You find fault with everything."

"I've shared my opinions about what Plushaut could do better for almost fifteen years," he said. "I'm a natural problem solver. I see it. I solve it. And I share my thoughts with everybody. I think I'm being a loyal employee. I want Plushaut to succeed. How can Ben call that being negative?"

"Well, it's not." Ana pulled a green sweater over her head and stretched it smooth at her waist. "What do you want to happen?"

"I want to get even... revenge I guess."

"Not very healthy, don't you think?"

"Okay, I want healthy revenge. The kind that he can't brush off so easily."

"That's a tall order. The company doesn't want to hear a whining salesman."

"Remember my first drug, Flatulaide for gas and bloating? I could always present Fart-man with a bottle at our national meeting next month."

"That's lame. If you want constructive revenge, we need to think positively."

"I know we do. That's why I'll take your advice if you have any to share."

She was putting on her winter high heel boots. "Let's get to The Metro, enjoy our dinner without any business talk, and cleanse our minds of negative thoughts. I bet we'll have some ideas by the time we get home."

They thanked Debbie for walking through the cold to the house, gave a few minor instructions to her, and stepped into the garage. The three boys never bothered to see them go. Debbie was that special to them. As they backed out and proceeded to the street, temporarily removing the weight of an interesting day lifted the mood of both.

ARRIVING AT THE Metro, Stu opened the passenger door for Ana. She stepped out of his new Buick LeSabre, a company car a notch above the other reps. He was proud to drive it. It was a suitable car to take to a fine restaurant like The Metro. They arrived inside the door precisely at 6:30. A svelte young lady with short dark hair greeted them by name and led them to a cozy corner table near the bar. Ana chose the seat facing the wall. She knew Stu liked to face out into the room. It was something she remembered about wanting to watch out for anything bad that might happen. She suspected correctly that it had to do also with his enjoyment of beautiful women who might enter. As long as he admired her by his exclusive actions, she was content. Why else would she work all day in the garage for him? She loved him.

The Metro inside looked like something one imagined seeing in Western Europe. The textured light tan walls held framed posters of different French wines and paintings with landscapes of the French countryside. Roughhewn beams crisscrossed the lofty ceilings to lend support. A quieter area away from the bar nestled up a level on the east end. Tables for two and four lay arranged in a way that made them private, yet Stu would be able to greet friends if they appeared. The bar, with its Frank Lloyd Wright-inspired stained glass, fascinated Ana. She liked being close enough to hear the bartender vigorously shake Stu's gin martini and to hear the pop of the cork for her glass of England's Hush Heath Estate Balfour 1503 Classic Cuvée Brut.

They enjoyed the unrushed atmosphere as they sipped their drinks. Rarely did they go out to eat at fancy restaurants. There were already too many company dinner functions that they frequently attended.

They ordered crab cakes for a shared appetizer, a cup each of *Vichyssoise*, and a main course of salmon for Ana and filet of beef for Stu. By the time they finished those items, plus their mashed potatoes and broccoli on the side, dessert was no longer possible.

Stuffed to the gills, Stu paid the tab after calculating in his head an eighteen percent tip. They promised the *maître d'* they would come back. It was a cold but wonderful, calming evening that continued in the car on the way home. They drove in silence. Years before, they discovered that being together required no words. Spending time together in comfortable silence was a sign of marital happiness. In that calm, Ana's brain was churning out ideas.

Chapter Thirty-Three

THEY WERE STEPPING inside their house when Ana finally spoke. They were hushed the entire drive home.

"You need to rename what Ben calls your negativity. Instead, why don't you call them what they are... ideas and suggestions?"

Stu mulled that over while Ana paid fifteen-year-old Debbie and sent her on her way. The girl promised to call as soon as she got inside her own house, even if it was only a few houses away. Stuart junior, the oldest boy, remained half-awake in the den absorbed in a United States map puzzle that he put together and disassembled repeatedly.

Stu stepped into their traditional living room and plopped onto their red leather sofa that faced a fireplace they had never used. Christmas decorations included Santa figurines, a nativity scene, stockings under the mantle, and a six-foot Christmas tree ablaze with large strings of colored lights and hundreds of ornaments.

Ana joined him after checking on Stuart. "When Ben says you are being negative, you can correct him by calling them ideas and suggestions."

"But Ben will just ignore what I say."

"Then write them down."

"He'll throw them away."

Ana's eyes grew big, and her eyebrows raised. "I've got it. Write your suggestions to someone else. Perhaps you could copy them to more than one person."

"But I have several ideas."

"I know what would really intimidate him. Send him a letter and copy it to the region. Do about ten of those and he'll beg for you to stop."

Stu stood up to put a Christmas CD in their stereo player. Soon, a mix of carols and popular Christmas tunes softly filled the room with good cheer. Stu sat back down. His mind was generating an idea that he was trying to sort out into a comprehensive explanation for Ana.

"I know what I'm going to do. It will ensure that Ben will never mess with me again. It will take a lot of work, but revenge is mine and worth all the effort it takes."

Ana sounded a note of cynicism when she said, "Oh my, I can't wait to hear this."

"On my first day back to work... January second, I'm going to announce my first idea. I will say, 'this is number one of one hundred ideas and suggestions that I will offer Plushaut Uclaf employees in 1997.'"

"You sure you want to commit to one hundred?"

"I'm really angry."

"Well, after ten of those, Ben ought to be contrite. If you do ninety more by the end of the year, he'll be suicidal."

"All the better."

"Well, let's do it. I even have a few ideas I can add to your list. You sure you don't want to do maybe one a week?"

"Nope. One hundred is more intimidating."

"Okay, start making your list."

"My head already has the first ten lined up."

"Good. I've got *Dallas* recorded on the VCR. Let's go watch it and get our minds on their problems, not ours."

The next morning, after Stu filled out his weekly expense report, he wrote his first letter—Idea and Suggestion Number One, dated the beginning of 1997. He was now using an IBM PC with the latest word processing program, Word Perfect—a system that authors and publishers were beginning to adopt. With spell check to correct his chronic spelling mistakes, he tapped out his letter in record time.

January 2, 1997

Mister Ben Hodge

Dear Ben

To be honest with you, I get tired of our company's values that are counterproductive to our ethical selling. I am trying to help make Plushaut Uclaf a better company. In the spirit of "an environment in which each employee can contribute skills, talents, and ideas to a never-ending process of improvement and innovation in all aspects of our business," I submit the following idea.

To dispel any notion that finding fault is considered negative, from now on I will not call them criticisms or complaints, but, instead, Ideas & Suggestions. I intend to submit 99 more ideas and suggestions to Plushaut Uclaf to help improve the success and smooth operation of the sales force.

I encourage all members of our company to begin a campaign of submissions of forward thinking, positive ideas to make all members of Plushaut Uclaf happier and more productive. I am sure you would agree this is a positive step. I invite you to support and join me in my effort to make Plushaut Uclaf the best pharmaceutical company to work for in the world.

Success—One suggestion at a time!

Sincerely,

Stuart Roy

Senior Sales Representative

Plushaut Uclaf

Ana read his *Ideas & Suggestions Letter Number One* critically because that's what English teachers do. She pointed out a few sentences she would have written differently but declared it pure Stu Roy verbiage and gave her approval. Stu made a copy of his letter, signed the original, and stuffed it in an envelope. After addressing it to Ben Hodge and adding a stamp, he put it aside to mail on December 31st, assuring its delivery on the first day back to work on January 2nd.

Jimmy, Lorelei, and Four continued to work on their video for their regional manager. The three thought it was odd how Ben railed against their project but admonished them not to be negative. They learned from Stu that Ben was on the warpath. Thankfully for everyone, the Christmas break drew near. Christmas and New Year season was a time when the company was in a panic with their nine ninety-six campaign. It also was a time when doctors did not care about sales reps. Patients were cramming their insurance companies with last-minute calls and taxpayers were maneuvering their expenses to best put it to the IRS. All drug reps had left to do was call pharmacies and ask them to buy one last discounted order from Plushaut. What the company did not know was that these turnover orders died a slow death almost five years before. Good business practices, taught to a new generation of pharmacists, plus the growing influence of managed care, took sales reps out of the retail pharmacy picture almost entirely. Yet, the company insisted that drug reps make pharmacy calls—and the sales force simply faked them. It bothered none of the old timers to do that. Plushaut had directed the entire sales force to do the same thing when another company hired them to market their drug for one year. The sales force called themselves *Rent-a-Reps*. The contract specified that every physician on their provided list must be called on in person every four weeks for a year. The list for each rep was non-negotiable. The only way to make calls on every doctor on the list was to drive by and wave at the office door, talk to their gravestone, or tell the veterinarian he had to listen. When the company realized that the list contained non-existent, dead, incarcerated, and non-physicians, they instructed the sales force by word of mouth to fake it. The topic of having to fake calls to please the bean-counters would certainly involve one of Stu's one hundred ideas and suggestions.

Chapter Thirty-Four

PRIOR TO THE Plushaut Uclaf national meeting in late January, the company's USA president and chief executive officer, Jacques Alarie, Ph.D., sent a letter to the sales force. With a characteristic French flair, Doctor Alarie sent the letter in French, with an attached English translation. Wading through all the glittering generalities, ruffles, and flourishes, Jacques Alarie finally got to the only thing people cared about. The company achieved its nine hundred and ninety-six-million-dollar goal, exceeding it by fifteen million. Thus, he said, *"Notre entreprise est sauvée!"*

National Meetings were usually fun. Aside from a couple of days of agonizing zone meetings with roleplays, team builders, and endless award presentations, there was always one day to cut loose and enjoy the town. This year Philadelphia hosted Plushaut Uclaf. Stu had never been to the city, but he knew that it was a treasure trove of revolutionary history, with Independence Hall and the Liberty Bell being only two of hundreds of historical sites to visit. Some looked forward to running up the steps of the Philadelphia Museum of Art like Rocky Balboa. Stu, before he arrived with the other two-thousand salesmen, studied where the founding fathers met to create a nation.

His first impression of Philadelphia was shocking. Beggars and homeless were literally on every corner in the historic district of the city. Some held out cups. Some held out cups with pencils. No one spoke. No one looked at Stu. In his first morning there, he took a walk only to discover all the municipal buildings were covered with people sleeping on the steps. He knew it was a new world when during his sunrise walk, their leader announced it was time to wake up and fold their covers. The men and women dutifully followed directions. It was Stu's first experience with organized and institutional homelessness. What was once a tragedy was becoming an accepted and institutionalized way of life.

Ben received and read Stu's *Ideas & Suggestions Letter Number One* with contempt. When Ben called his regional manager on that first day, Abbott Wahl had listened and expressed his concern about Stu's attitude. But when he got his own copy in the mail from Ben, he altered his opinion. Rather than replying to his zone manager, he called Stu directly. For Stu, it was the encouragement he needed to press ahead with his plan to cram Ben's head full of a year's worth of advice. Facing Ben for the first time since that infamous day at Doctor Neuman's office no longer worried him. For the time being his instincts were correct—he was bullet proof.

He had already sent seven more suggestions to Ben, to Abbott Wahl, to a member of the Quality Assurance team, to Field Force Development, to two product managers, and to the head of Fleet Services. With each letter, he forwarded a copy to Ben for his review and irritation and to Abbott Wahl to further irritate Ben.

There were ultimately two highlights to the national meeting. Late in the morning on the first day of the meeting, the CEO, Doctor Alarie, introduced the raft video under dispute with a rare sense of humor. Alarie had decided to let his hair down. *Why not? We exceeded a billion dollars in sales.* This time speaking in English, he introduced the video, tongue in cheek, as what he was afraid was his fate after 1996. He presented it on the three jumbo screens in the arena filled with nearly three thousand salesmen and saleswomen, zone managers, regional managers, and directors. Secretaries and other staff assistants were also there, still working while the sales force sat in uncomfortable chairs.

The video's opening scene showed a placid river scene of Huck Finn riding a raft at sunset. The narrator, Benton Wickingham, IV, posed a question. "What Hollywood movie best describes 'We are all in the raft together?' *Huckleberry Finn*…? No, too tranquil."

The scene then dissolved into the image of Marilyn Monroe and Robert Mitchum on a raft in *River of No Return*. The river is terrifyingly turbulent. The narration continued.

"Not Marilyn Monroe! Too sexy."

The next scene was from *Apocalypse Now* with Martin Sheen on a Navy Patrol Boat in a journey upriver.

"Well, it's scary," Four said, "but it may never end."

The screen morphed into a clip from *The African Queen* as the big boat plunged down a waterfall and Katharine Hepburn cries out in fear.

"We're getting closer, but there's too much screaming."

Then a new movie faded in and the audience of salesmen began to laugh before the narration began. From *Ben Hur*, Charlton Heston sat chained with other galley slaves as they rowed toward a naval victory for the glory of Rome. Roman soldiers continued lashing oarsmen as flaming balls from unseen enemies came flying at them.

"Now we're getting closer," the narrator said over the laughter. What followed would be his last words. "But there's something missing. What would make it better? Okay… I know… yeah, that's it!"

The screen exploded with the sounds of two dueling banjos in an up-tempo performance. The opening scene revealed the roaring rapids on the Chattanooga River in northeastern Georgia. Two canoes plummeted down rapids in total chaos, shattering on the rocks. As the banjos continued their frenzied tempo, the video switches to a strumming country boy sitting on the river bridge then morphs into a scene of two nearly toothless hillbillies, reminding the audience, without direct reference, of a notorious rape scene vividly remembered by movie goers.

In a last clip set in slow motion, a surviving hillbilly in close-up slowly turns his head to the camera and looks directly at the audience, rotten teeth and all. The audience of salesmen erupted in applause, cheers, whistles, laughter, and shouts that required Doctor Alarie's intervention to quell. The swell of emotion from the crowd erupted again as he announced that they had surpassed the goal of 996 million dollars, and that the video was no longer necessary.

Just as the pandemonium began to subside, a booming bass drum followed by snares and tenor drums replaced the crowd noise. Curtains behind the CEO parted as he stepped quickly to the side of the stage. The entire marching band from a nearby university paraded onstage to Sousa's "The Stars and Stripes Forever." The crowd came alive again and stood up clapping to the lively pace of trumpets, trombones, baritones, and sousaphones. Clarinets and other wind instruments tried to outplay a lone piccolo. Following the marching band, came a group of local Philadelphians to dance the Philadelphia Mummers Strut for the amusement of the sales force. Fresh from the Mummers Parade of New Year's Day, they donned outlandish costumes that rivaled any costume seen at *Mardi Gras* in New Orleans. Many in the audience were puzzled by the weird gyrations and goofy steps they took. Suddenly, members of the sales force from the two Philadelphia zones and their managers stood up and joined the locals in demonstrating The Mummer's Strut. The tradition came out of defiance against a Philadelphia law banning dancing. The citizens developed a new way to walk, which looked a lot like dancing.

The marching band and the parade of Mummers stepped down from the stage, marched and strutted down the center aisle to the rear of the arena and out to the large entrance hall. The cheers and the clapping continued enthusiastically until the band hit their final notes, after which the drums beat a faint cadence to march the entire group of performers out of the building.

Stu took great pleasure in turning his head in the direction of Ben Hodge. He caught Stu's glance and winced ever so slightly. Stu laughed a jolly smile at his boss who turned away to stare into a blank wall. The sales force was rapidly heading out of the arena.

"Let's go eat lunch," he told his eight teammates sitting near him. "Lorelei, Jimmy, Four. Lunch is on Ben. Be sure and thank him."

Chapter Thirty-Five

"I THINK YOU should send some of your notes to people at higher levels." It was Ben who made it a point to sit next to Stu at lunch.

"Why would you say that?"

"Word got around at the home office that you are sending suggestions to the company. One or two people are hoping you'll send some their way... or at least spread them around."

"So now you like it?" Stu chuckled at the irony. "Next you'll be taking credit for that video you hate."

"Just take my advice. Spread them around."

It was obvious to everyone present that Ben had a tiger by the tale—that he was desperately hoping to ride to glory on the coattails of his sales rep who was getting positive notoriety.

It didn't hurt Ben's career to have the top salesman in the region in his zone. The second day of the meeting was the endless awards presentation. No one knew who the winners were, but Abbott Wahl notified Ben to be prepared. Ben did not know who, although his suspicions made him uneasy. Stu put his money on Four.

Plushaut awards were varied and complex. Trophies went to product award winners. Top region and top in the company awards were only verbal. No one could say why, except they had to be tops in product sales to stand a chance at the top awards, so they already had their trophies. There were awards for the top three regional Flofral sales winners in each of three categories—total dollars, dollar increase, and percent increase. The same awards applied to the top Destense drug reps in each region. To make it easier this year, each region had their own awards ceremony. It was a blessing, except to fill the time they encouraged each winner to give an acceptance speech. The sales force viewed the acceptance speeches, according to Jimmy, as a way to make it easier to hate the winner—unless it was them up on the stage. The company also added new awards for sales clubs, special duty awards, and best zone awards. It filled the day and made everyone's hands sore from clapping during the first hour. After that hour, the senior reps stopped clapping to prevent further bruising their palms.

The top regional salesman was almost always Bill Dooley, who remained in Finn Trottel's zone. It was easy to resent his yearly recognition because he made it so much about himself. The Zombies could not name a single friend he had in the company. Dooley liked it that way. This year, as expected, he collected four of six trophies before the morning was half over. Two other saleswomen won the other two trophies for each having the best percent increase for Destense and Flofral. Dooley's only comment was that they should have been his trophies.

"Those two little girls are new and took over territories that had next to nothing in sales. They could only win because the previous year they had a dollar in sales, then they sell a hundred dollars the next year and win my percent increase trophies."

For the sales force, they couldn't have been happier to hear him gripe. One of his Trottel teammates even slapped him on the back and called him a loser, which Dooley took literally and pitched a fit in front of everyone. But he still held visions of winning the regional and national titles again.

Stu more than once had upset his managers during his annual performance review. He and Four were always near the top, but Stu had never finished as number one in his region. He seldom won awards for top Flofral or top Destense salesman. But Stu had one claim to fame that he brought up with his managers each year. Plotting his ranking in his zone, he nearly always ranked second, while the number one performer bounced around to different people each year. Stu's claim to fame was his consistency and his ability to sell every drug at a high level, just not the highest level. Many other salesmen achieved their claim to fame by selling one drug extremely well. Stu liked to annoy the boss with these words.

"If I consistently finish in second place, it means that over an entire career, I will be best salesman of all times. Even better, nobody goes gunning for number two."

He was right, but it still irritated all his managers, including regional manager Abbott Wahl. Managers always encouraged their people to be the best. Stu argued, "By that measure, you would consider all other salesman below the best one to be failures."

Nonetheless, finishing number one got all the emphasis from the top all the way down to the lowliest sales rep. That was the dilemma when Abbott Wahl came up to announce the Top Region-Six Sales Representative for 1996. He began by talking about the value of having a work ethic that weathers evenly through both good and bad times. Then he bridged into an area that management would never mention.

"Yours and my raises come from selling Destense and Flofral." A spreadsheet of sales numbers appeared on the large projector screen behind him. "Our annual salary comes from all our products… the ones that we have and can sell, but don't emphasize. We forget how important it is to keep going with everything we sell."

He pointed to the screen above his head. There were no names, just rankings. Taking a laser pointer, he circled the first four awards, all won by Bill Dooley then projected over to the numeral one in the ranking column. He did the same for the two ladies who won for best percent increase. His next slide displayed the rankings of the winners for their four secondary products that made up about thirty percent of the company's revenue. All three winners, Dooley and the two ladies, ranked in the bottom half for every category.

"This is not to denigrate your success, but to show you how we rank the top regional rep."

Another slide came up, adding a new set of rankings in a row underneath the three trophy winners. There still were no names listed on the screen.

"This is an example of the ideal salesman that has learned to sell the entire product line. If every rep's numbers were like this, we would never have been in that raft together while chanting nine-nine-six!"

That brought a laugh from the audience and a few claps.

"This salesman's example does not rank number one in any category, yet because of this salesperson's sales of all six of our products he or she would be the top sales rep by a long shot. What we are looking for from all of you in 1997 is a consistent and steady selling of the entire product line, even if you don't win a trophy, your year-end evaluation will be based upon everything we sell, not just Destense and Flofral."

He switched to the next slide and a name appeared on the projected spread sheet. "This example is not a mythical salesman, but it is unusual to have a regional winner this year who has won no other award."

Stu looked over at Bill Dooley in the row in front of him, who gritted his teeth in frustration and turned to see Stu. "What the hell?"

The slide changed again. The name Stu Roy filled the large screen above Abbott's head. Mike Austin slapped him on the back. Charlie Ketter messed up Stu's hair before he could stand up. As Stu started to shuffle sideways to get to the end of the row of seats, Lorelei stood in his way to give him a rib crushing hug. He finished running past the handshakes, back slaps, and hugs to walk quickly up to the podium with Abbott. He stopped halfway up to stare dramatically at his name in three-foot-high letters. He allowed himself enough presence of mind to listen to the applause, which was loud and genuine—much more than just polite. That made him happier than anything else. When he reached the steps to the podium, Abbott Wahl reached a hand down and pulled him up the last steps. As excited as Stu, the regional manager extended a hand in the direction of the podium and took a step back. Stu was genuinely surprised by the turn of events. He was not expecting to speak to a bunch of salesmen who might hate him for certain after he opened his mouth. After years of experience talking to doctors, he had perfected one-liners he could employ in a pinch. He stepped to the mic and paused to look around at the crowd. He was disappointed to notice the spotlight on him made it hard to see anyone's face.

"I could do what a lot of winners do and thank a lot of people, but we would be here all night. Instead, I will leave you with the best advice I know to give." He cleared his throat for effect. "The less I say, the more you will remember."

He stepped back from the podium, squinting to see the crowd's reaction. While at first confused, they quickly caught that he was through and returned to an appreciative and rowdy applause which continued until he reached the row for his seat. After a few lingering murmurings from the sales force, Abbott Wahl added a few comments.

"Tonight, Stu will join his other eight regional winners on the penthouse floor at the nearby Marriott where he will stay the next two nights. Stu, you should have a good time there tonight… or at least, that's what I have been told."

Knowing and unknowing laughs filled the room. Stu again caught Dooley staring at him, the bitterness obvious in his expression. There was no more miserable person in the world at that moment. Jimmy Tomey, sitting behind Dooley's seat, couldn't help himself. In his final pronouncement before retirement, he bent over to speak into Dooley's ear.

"Hey Dooley. How does it feel to be a loser?"

Chapter Thirty-Six

AFTER SHARING DINNER with his region that night, Stu reluctantly left his friends to go for his reward in the Marriott Penthouse. Celebrating victory is hard work, as Stu was about to find out. First it was inconvenient to move to another room. There were two good things. The move was within the same hotel. The company occupied three other hotels to handle the size of Plushaut's meeting. Also, Mike Austin, Stu's roommate for the first two nights was thrilled to get the room to himself.

The downside was that in the company's quest to make his treatment special, it isolated him from his friends. Instead, it put him in close contact with several salesmen he did not know. He soon learned more than he wanted to about all of them. He would never describe them as towering egos, but it was clear that they had plenty of self-confidence. More than half had been top regional reps before. They took over leadership in teaching the newbies proper etiquette for their time up top in the penthouse. It was soon obvious that there were no rules or etiquette, only drinking, bragging, and comradery. Having all achieved their region's pinnacle of success, they became fast friends within the hour. One of the first topics discussed over the booze they shared around the fully stocked bar was how nice it was that Stu had bumped that S.O.B.

Dooley out of their party. The five returnees named Stu Man of the Year. From that moment on, he knew he belonged.

The night eventually started to drag until three winners decided to find the Cheetah Gentlemen's Club.

"How do we get there?" The three were asking each other. Stu gave the obvious answer.

"You get in a cab and tell him to take you to the Cheetah Club."

"Who's going with us?" When one of the freshmen winners volunteered, they were gone.

That left Stu with four other winners who spent the evening sharing bar snacks, unlimited drinks, and lots of stories of heroic sales calls, women, more women—mostly women. Stu had led a clean life, since Ana became his sweetheart. He told his standard joke about their being high school sweethearts. He held back the punch line for a while before revealing they were teachers when they met, not students.

Eventually, the five remaining at the penthouse bar became four and then three. At midnight, the four Cheetah party goers returned with their eyes wide with tales to tell. They shared no tales about pole dancers and lap dancers at the Cheetah Gentlemen's Club. Rather, they were animated in their descriptions of a skinny Laotian cab driver who got them to their destination at a high rate of speed while running every red light in Philadelphia. Their assessment of the Cheetah? Save your money. It was the B-team.

Stu became the third regional winner to call it quits for the night. As he left, he realized that he had forgotten to call Ana and tell her the good news of being named Top Region-Six Sales Representative for 1996. It was after 1:00 a.m., but once he got to his penthouse quarters, he called her anyway. As the telephone rang at home, boisterous laughter came through the walls of his room. He realized his room backed up to the bar he had just left. Ana picked up the phone on the fifth ring.

"Hello?" The voice was dreamy and slurred.

"Ana, it's your husband. Sorry to call so late."

At first Stu was only met with silence. Ana was not yet awake.

"Stu, is that you?"

"Yes, Ana. I had to call you. I'm the Top Rep in our region. I just got recognized this afternoon at our regional awards presentation."

"What's that noise I hear in the background?"

"That's some people in the bar that backs up to my room."

"What kind of room did you get?"

"A penthouse suite."

Ana was beginning to wake up. "Are there any Penthouse Pets up there with you?"

"Not yet, but how soon can you get here?"

"So, you won what again? Top Rep... which product?

"Top Regional Rep."

"The big one?"

"Yes, the big one... for the region."

"Well, somebody is having fun. I can hear them. Why aren't you there with them?"

Stu looked at the clock by his bed. "Because it's 1:27 a.m."

"That's only 12:30 here."

"Ana, are you proud of me?"

"Yes, I am." She sounded more awake. "What about Ben? Is he giving you a hard time?"

"No. Would you believe? He came up to me and encouraged me to write additional ideas to other departments in the company... to spread them out more. Apparently, word got out about what I was doing and... I bet... he wants to jump on the train and get part of the credit."

"Well, he can't hassle the top regional rep now, can he?"

There was an exhaustion driven pause to their sleepy conversation.

"I'm leaving now to go to bed."

"No, Stu. Go back to whatever noise that is and have some fun with the boys... it is all boys, isn't it?"

"It is… all boys this year. I think I'll stay in my room though and get some rest. Perhaps I can raise hell tomorrow for you."

"Okay, you do that. Good night. I love you."

"Good night, Lover Girl."

Chapter Thirty-Seven

OVER THE REST of the year, ideas and suggestions continued to flow from Stu into the various departments of Plushaut Uclaf. Ben began giving him ideas of which departments might benefit. Stu's ideas ranged from slogans that could help to sell certain drugs to repackaging of samples that would let them fit better in sample closets. He suggested adding a list of doctor specialties that were not on Plushaut's activity forms that reps filled out each week and mailed to their managers. Stu found that he called on a wider variety of specialist who could use Flofral for better patient care. He could not report them accurately until their specialty had a check box on the forms. He shared the idea to send out the official sales reps scheduling calendars by October, instead of December, since reps scheduled so many doctor call appointments six months in advance.

One issue that Stu treaded on carefully was a suggestion concerning vacation. Managers were intent on shaming reps into not taking vacation days. Their methods revolved around the theme of *"I am so important that I can't afford to take vacation. I am that valuable."* Stu would counter to the managers that *"I am so important that I can take off a whole month of vacation and my customers will sell for me while I'm gone."* There was some truth to it. Stu took data of his average three weeks in the field.

He compared that to his productivity in the combined total of the week before vacation, the week of vacation, and the week after vacation. Invariably, his three-week production including vacation was consistently higher than a full normal three work weeks. He suggested vacation eligibility be more clearly defined in the company benefits package. Some reps were not taking all available days off each year out of either fear or posturing for management's benefit. Lower management went ballistic over this one, much to Stu's amusement.

Ana suggested he submit one concerning company cars which need to have right side passenger airbags as standard features on all new company leases. She encouraged Stu to express concerns that the life of his division manager could be at risk. He needed more help than Ana could provide. He reached halfway with *Suggestion Number Fifty* in late September, which left him only three and a half months to submit fifty more.

On the Monday after Thanksgiving, Stu submitted *Suggestion Number Eighty*. The pressure was on him to pull twenty more ideas out of anywhere. He had less than three weeks to go. To add to the stress, Ana reminded him that the home office locked the doors for the year in mid-December. He polled his teammates but found that their ideas were not that good, and they wanted to talk too much. He needed the time to think. Lorelei, in the spirit of helping him reach his goal, wrote him a letter asking a question of how to best utilize Microsoft Word in her expense reports. Then she sent a question about spreadsheets. That gave Stu two suggestions he could document and help at the rep level. He discovered there was a wealth of ideas under his nose in the doctor's office. He pirated ideas from the promotional material of other drug companies. Now, in the last month of his quest for revenge on Ben Hodge, his best ideas were coming forth. Finally, on December 31st, Stu postmarked a letter to Plushaut Uclaf CEO Jacques Alarie, Ph.D., which summarized his findings from submitting ninety-nine previous ideas and suggestions to members of the Plushaut community. He stated that this would be his *Suggestion Number One Hundred* for him to consider. He first outlined the areas of the company where he focused his efforts. Then he outlined which efforts of his had gotten feedback and had shown success.

Now it was time to employ the best editor he knew, who would fear no wrath, and pull no punches.

"Ana, you're up."

Ana was not the only one to come into his office space. So did the three boys, who wanted to hear what had stressed out their father so much. All sitting down together on a sofa barely large enough to seat three adults, the family pile commenced his review.

"Can I mark on it?" Ana said.

"That's yours to write anything you want… hopefully a happy face, too."

Ana began to read. The fact that the three boys were turning the moment into a wiggly mess did not phase Ana at all. She read silently except for bullet point mumbles.

"Okay, what did not work well… um… action plan … committed managers… safety, okay… quality action… ha… you got QAT in there. That ought to get him riled… upper management… noncompliance to requests… apathy among reps."

Ana paused a moment to look at Stu and the cacophony of boys now wandering around the office. "Okay, now for ideas that do not work."

"Boys," Stu whispered. "Are you bored? You can leave or stay, but let Mom read."

Stu and Ana watched them escape in seconds.

"And what did not work well?" Suggestions made by reps to upper-level management." Ana chuckled, "You nailed that one."

"I've got ninety-nine examples to prove it."

"Okay… no success with groups and committees… ideas to the ignorant… being afraid to steal a good idea? Isn't that what we do with competitors? Okay… comfort and success… kills innovation."

Ana turned to Stu. "That's it. I like it."

"I don't think comfort and success have killed our innovation, has it?" He leaned over and planted a welcome kiss to her lips. She smiled back in a silent way that only committed couples can understand.

When Stu, Ana, and their three boys drove to the post office to mail the last suggestion, Number One Hundred, they went home to enjoy a night together on New Year's Eve like they hadn't had in years. It was looking like 1998 would be a good year.

TWELVE DAYS LATER, on a Monday morning at the Roy house, the home phone rang. Stu was not feeling like a go getter that morning and was running late. He debated whether to pick up the telephone. He didn't want to explain why he wasn't already headed out to work. But he was in an oh-what-the-hell mood and picked up the receiver on the third ring.

"Hello." He worried his voice sounded like he had only minutes before gotten out of bed.

"Is this Stuart Roy?" The male voice was unfamiliar. He almost cut it short, fearing it was a cold call for another credit card.

"Speaking," Stu replied curtly.

"Good morning, I'm sure you didn't expect this on a Monday." The voice sounded strange, like he was calling from a foreign country.

"Who is this?" He tried to be polite, but also careful.

"This is Jacques Alarie from Plushaut. I got your letter and I wanted to thank you."

"Doctor Alarie... this is a surprise!" He kept worrying that he spoke like a man just waking up.

"Yes. I wanted to call to tell you how impressed I was with your efforts. A whole year of work. I have talked to many people who know who you are now. We need more like you."

"Well sir, I try to be a loyal member of the company. I always see things we could do better. And it was a labor of love. I just hope I helped somebody."

"You did, I am sure... I know you are trying to get to work, so I won't keep you, but congratulations."

"Thank you. Doctor Alarie, I deeply appreciate the call."

"Bye-bye."

Stu dropped the phone. His heart pounded rapidly. He called to Ana. When she came into their bedroom, he simply said, "We did it!"

It was a triumph for Stu, but fame is fleeting. He was never able to confirm that Plushaut ever implemented a single idea or suggestion of his—and Doctor Alarie? He never put his words in writing.

Chapter Thirty-Eight

It was now the first year after the millennium, 2001. In the twenty years since Stu took his job with Plushaut Uclaf, the changes were enormous. He frequently quoted the words of seasoned salesmen who gave him good advice over the years. There were seasoned reps who hated their jobs and constantly grumbled about how their once great job was now awful. As a veteran pharmaceutical salesman, he still believed that it was a fantastic job. He was privileged to call on highly educated people all day long, with technical and scientific conversations, but unlike doctors, he didn't have to deal with body fluids. Now twenty years later, there were seasoned reps with fewer years under their belts than Stu who mimicked the disgruntled reps he met and avoided in 1980. It was the same mindset. Every twenty years this lousy sales rep job was the next generation's great one. Stu promised himself that he would never be a curmudgeon. He embraced change with enthusiasm.

The changes over that period involved many things. Physicians had less time to devote to salesmen. One story Stu loved to tell—an illustrative story from years earlier. In his first year Stu waited for a doctor to call him back to his office. The nurse came out to get him with the admonition, "Mister Roy, the doctor will see you now, but I'm sorry. He only has fifteen minutes to talk to you."

For Stu in the new decade of 2000, the average time available to discuss with a physician was less than five minutes. And that average period diminished with each passing year. The reason was simple. Doctors did not discuss science and medicine anymore. They did paperwork. Insurance, managed patient care, and federal government intrusions were destroying the art of medicine. Medical arts fell victim to drug formularies, uniform practices, and mountains of mandated records. Physicians and drug reps agreed on one thing. They both hated it. But Stu looked at the change and decided he would embrace it—not because he liked it, but because it was an opportunity to stand out. He devised several ideas to persuade doctors in less time. It was no longer a choice of what drug the doctor found most helpful. Now the best salesman was the one who was most helpful. A good drug rep became more valuable than a good drug.

Despite time being critical to a physician, Doctor Mac Monroe, M.D. used time itself to intimidate all drug reps. Charlie Ketter had recently picked up this doctor after a territory realignment. Christy Fowler warned him about one behavior that made sales calls difficult.

"Charlie, when you call on Doctor Monroe, be prepared for his egg timer. When you sit down at his desk, he'll slam his egg timer on the desk in front of you and say, 'You've got three minutes.' It's quite a distraction. I never can focus on what to tell him. You'll see what I mean."

Charlie learned a lot about intimidation while he was a college wrestler. When it was his time to call on Doctor Monroe, he got the egg timer treatment as expected. Without missing a word of his message, Charlie moved the timer to his right, behind a lamp, out of view of the doctor. In its place he put a peer-reviewed journal article he wanted Monroe to see. The doctor became the intimidated one, squirmed in his seat, and let Charlie spend all the time he needed. No word was spoken by either one of them about Charlie's actions. Charlie Ketter consistently performed at the top, demonstrating the reason every single day.

Sometimes being a good drug rep went awry. Years before, when Christy Fowler was new, she had an issue with a scientifically oriented physician of internal medicine. Doctor Emmerson Carter, M.D. was a product of the Mayo Clinic internal medicine residency program. He was a strictly-by-the-rules doctor—generic names only, no combined medications in one pill, an "I stand on my opinion" attitude, and incessant challenges at any statement a drug rep made.

Stu liked physicians who demanded proof for everything he said. It became a problem for Christy after she began calling on Doctor Carter. For Stu, he viewed Doctor Carter as a good choice as a personal physician. Knowing from experience that a doctor's objections should be treated as questions, he always welcomed them as selling opportunities. Stu, always confident that he had a better answer than his competition, wanted a doctor who demanded the best answers. Christy, one of the smartest reps in the company, was intimidated. Stu, after listening to Christy's discomfort, offered to work with her the next time she called on her problem doctor.

Doctor Carter was happy to see Stu the morning of Christy's appointment. She was surprised to see a new side of this physician. After sitting down with Christy, the two men chatted about where the other had been and how their families were. But time was critical even with friends, as Stu knew. He explained that he was on a ride along with Christy to see what she did that made her so successful. It didn't fool Doctor Carter, but it put Christy more at ease. This moment was the reason Stu joined her.

It was standard practice to place the most important drug in the number two position, which usually allowed the rep more time with a topic of most interest to the physician. For Doctor Carter, that drug was Lystrepto. He had his baptism of fire at Mayo Clinic when thrombolytics first came into wide use. Christy first covered Tapilon in the first thirty seconds. All went well—no objections. She bridged into the discussion of thrombolytics by mentioning how many antibiotics affected clotting factors at some point in therapy. Not the best bridge.

"We have to stop bleeding with some antibiotics," Doctor Carter said, "not dissolve blood clots. I miss the point."

"I just know that you see both frequently in the hospital," she replied.

"Yes, that is true."

"Are there any changes in protocol with thrombolytic therapy at this hospital?"

"What indication are you asking about? None for MI if that's what you ask."

"I was thinking more around deep vein thrombosis."

"We have a grant to study the merits of *urokinase* for DVT. It works surprisingly well."

Christy was shocked by this. *Urokinase* was not only difficult to produce, coming from massive volumes of human urine, but it was seldom used by hospitals after the introduction of *streptokinase* and *vePA*. Her self-imposed five-minute time limit rushed her sound judgement. That's when Christy's sales call hit the fan.

"But Doctor Carter," she replied, "*urokinase* is the worst choice you could make."

There was no recovery from that statement. It was the least helpful sales call of Stu's career. Doctor Carter stood up. Stu and Christy quickly followed suit. The doctor stared angrily at Christy, then looked down at her visuals on his desk.

"Young lady, why don't you and Mister Roy here leave my office so you two can discuss things." He turned and left them in his office. Christy's five minutes were up.

The trip to the parking lot for Christy was an agonizing walk of shame. Stunned and embarrassed, she asked, "What should I have said?"

"You could have asked him how successful *urokinase* has been. Doctor Carter said, 'surprisingly well.' I was curious why he was surprised. If you had let him explain, his answer to that question may have pleased you."

DETAIL MAN

ANOTHER CHANGE WAS the pharmaceutical industry's response to the new physician dynamic. At first Stu made sales calls every four to six weeks. Now Plushaut Uclaf had merged with an American pharmaceutical company. While Stu's job at Plushaut Uclaf had always stressed science, the new company, Connicut Labs of Hartford, Connecticut, was noteworthy for their marketing. Stu's teammates called them car salesmen. The industry called them successful marketing geniuses. Stu took this opportunity once again to adapt to change. With the merger came shocking changes.

"This sucks, men, but there will be a bucket load of changes." This was how Ben Hodge chose to start his first zone meeting after the merger. "I know you all are nervous. Who's getting fired? Will they merge pods with the car salesmen?"

Stu interrupted Ben, just to irritate him. "Maybe we can learn how to sell from them."

The meeting progressed at the speed of a slug. The information Ben covered was the same sermon he covered at each meeting. Only the personal stories of success he let reps share were of value. After lunch it picked up.

"TWO WEEKS!" It was Bill Dooley's reaction to Ben's first surprise, as if the voice of Bill Dooley wasn't surprise enough.

"That's what I said. We're dropping our four- and six-week cycles. We're going to two weeks and reducing the number of doctors you will call on."

"I'm not doing that," Dooley replied. "I've got doctors who depend on me."

"Depend on you to what? Die?" Charlie Ketter whispered.

Dooley didn't hear well. The wisecrack went over his head. He did, though, hear the laughter.

"We are also, Bill, beginning a hiring spree that will triple the sales force in the new company."

To everyone's joy, Dooley went into his sulking, noncontributing mode.

Stu raised his hand. "Won't the doctors get irritated at seeing us so much more?"

Charlie jumped in to answer. "I talked to some Connicut reps last week. They told me about their two-week cycle and how it worked. It was kinda funny. They said at first, doctors complained of the increased call frequency. After one of them missed seeing a doctor on his two-week rounds, he was surprised to hear the doctor say after four weeks, 'Where have you been?' He was not making idle chatter. He was miffed. 'I needed to see you last time and you left before I was ready.'"

That convinced Stu of a fundamental point. He had trained the doctor to expect him on a predictable schedule. Frequency was not the complaint. Unpredictability was the grievance. Better yet, that was the type of complaint drug reps dreamed of hearing.

A third change Ben discussed concerned managed care. Insurance and even hospitals were directing what drugs a physician could use.

"We're losing our ability to influence a doctor's writing habits," Stu said. Ben didn't like the inference that reps had no influence.

The insurance company won't let me have it was a phrase many doctors were saying. Now the patients were saying it, too. The doctors had simply given up resistance. They wanted to practice medicine more than they wanted to resist mandated uniform practices.

"The art of practicing medicine began to morph into more paperwork and less hands-on medical care several years ago," Christy said. "Why do you think they have no time for us now?"

That started a discussion that might have lasted all day, if Ben hadn't put a stop to it.

SEVERAL CHANGES AFFECTED Stu and the other Zombies or Boomers directly. With new management after the merger, Zones reverted to the old district name. That meant no more Zombies for a nickname. It was back to Boomers, which had always been the official name. Not only had the company survived the threatened millennial apocalypse, but they had learned to embrace being managed by Americans.

Connicut Labs had an undeserved reputation. They proved it at their first national meeting in January 2002, where they welcomed Plushaut Uclaf reps into their world. There were certainly no stuffed shirts in Hartford, Connecticut.

Jacques Alarie, Ph.D. retired from the company. The new CEO of Connicut-Plushaut Labs was a dynamic workaholic by the name of Harold Porter. Since the year was 2001, Plushaut reps assumed the zany national meeting would capitalize on the movie, *2001: A Space Odyssey*. Connicut was notorious for their wacky themes for their big meetings each year. But instead, they turned to a more recent movie that came out in November. So, with the name Harold Porter, the theme for their annual meeting was *Harold Porter and the Sorcerer's Stone*.

Harold Porter introduced himself to the crowd dressed in a student's black robe and white collar, goofy glasses, and a prominent zigzag scar on his right forehead. He looked ridiculous, of course. Harold Porter looked more like Rubeus Hagrid in school clothes and a magic wand, than he looked like a young Harry Potter. But that was all part of the circus atmosphere that constituted the management style of a company that was successful, good to its people, and to everyone's surprise, was greatly admired by their customers. As Stu would eventually learn, it was to be a decade of great fun and greater challenges.

"Mike, tell me you're joking," Stu said.

"I'm afraid it's no joke. We're going to the pod system, and you are now partnered with Bill Dooley."

Stu, in uncharacteristic fashion, exploded with a series of curse words filled with scatological references and other words descriptive of messing up his life. Mike Austin was impressed.

"You gotta look at it this way, Stu. You have me in your pod. We have Lorelei as number four. That's three against one. You're not alone."

The pod system was a further escalation by his new company to get further exposure to doctors. Where once a doctor spent fifteen minutes with a rep on a call every six weeks, now four reps would spend one minute with the same doctor in a rotating two-week assault. There was no more science in their calls, only sound bites. Stu wondered, like all the others, why one needed a degree to do this. He had always prided himself on being innovative to meet the changes in the industry, but now he would have to cooperate with three others to form a unit strategy. He had had that experience in high school playing football, but he never had to deal with Bill Dooley in the huddle.

In some ways he was lucky. Dooley was the best salesman the company had ever had, despite everyone from customers on down intensely disliking him. Stu remembered two more episodes where drug reps slugged him in a parking lot. A few clinics banned him from entering, but he ignored them. The staff and doctors were always too polite to stop him. Stu predicted that half of his own sales calls might be to apologize for Dooley's behavior.

The only good news was that everyone shared the same doctors and the same success. Lorelei called it communism. Mike preferred the term Three Reps and a Babe. Stu called it The Pod People. Bill Dooley called it a non-starter. He was angrier than all of them combined.

Other good news was that Connicut-Plushaut Labs kicked Fart-man Ben Hodge upstairs to the new home office in Hartford. At least there, as low man on a very tall totem pole, he would be forced to curb his bad habits. Finn Trottel retired, but Stu and several other veteran reps from his early division manager years, refused to go to his retirement party or to congratulate him. They had not forgotten his duplicity of turning back money allocated for pay raises that instead went to reps in other divisions. Lance Layton, an original Land Runner in Finn's division, took the reins as the new Boomer District Manager. Lance, with his booming bass voice, sounded more like a commander than a manager when he spoke, but the Boomers under him were happy he was leading.

One miracle of longevity extended his record as the region six manager, Abbott Wahl.

The Pod People held their first planning meeting while in Hartford during the national meeting. As expected, Bill Dooley remained defiant. He would not cooperate in any coordinated strategy with his pod mates. The others suggested laying out what strengths they had and didn't have. They discussed dividing up their talents by message with different messages for selling the same drug to the same doctors. The three agreed that only one member of their pod should call on some doctors. Dooley erupted at that in a fit of flailing arms and curses.

"I'll call on any doctor I want to. You can't stop me."

"What about that doctor in your old territory who said he would never write another script made by Plushaut until you left or died?" It was Mike, feeling his past managerial oats again. "He's in our new territory now."

"He won't stand a chance. Just stay out of my way."

"We can't stay out of your way, Bill. We're supposed to be a team," said Lorelei.

"You can just all go home. Stay out of my way. I'll handle it without you."

THAT NIGHT OVER several beers the three-member pod formulated its strategy. In the morning, the Pod People were to present their plan to a group of managers from both sides of the merged company.

"What do we tell them about Dooley?" Lorelei's question was directed to Stu and Mike.

"Say nothing," Mike replied.

"Our problem is that he is the company's darling… a super salesman," Stu said, "and even if we explain our predicament, we won't get any help. He's bullet proof in the eyes of the company."

"What do you think he's going to do tomorrow?"

"Hopefully, shut up and pout."

"Stu's right, Lorelei. He'll be pouting on the inside, but that's what he does."

"When I played football in high school, we had a monster man. We could call Dooley our monster man, you know, the guy on defense who roams where he chooses based on his experience at reading an offense."

"Let's call him that. He might even like it."

"Ha! He will never like anything," Lorelei said, "but it might just shut him up."

"Which one of us is going to present this plan tomorrow?" Stu pointed a hand at each of them.

"You are," Mike replied. "You're the teacher and it's one of your strengths." Lorelei nodded her agreement.

The three looked up to see their new manager, Lance Layton approaching their table.

"What are you guys doing working at the bar? It's past midnight... and where's Dooley?" His deep bass voice already attracted attention at the table nearest them.

"Dooley has a few issues with the team concept," Mike replied.

"What Mike means is he's not a team player and refused to participate," Stu said.

Lorelei was smart enough to shut up.

"Guys, I know I'm new at this, but I can tell you that if there's divisiveness in your pod, your buddy Dooley will not get the blame."

"What? You want us to wake him up and tell him to cooperate?"

"If you must, the answer is yes. Make it work tomorrow in front of the managers or they'll be on your ass like a Lone Star tick."

Chapter Thirty-Nine

THE CONTENT OF business plans made sense only ten percent of the time. The rest was just fluff and glittering generalities. This year's exercise centered around a third iteration of sales accounting. When Stu joined Plushaut Uclaf in 1980, sales crediting was subjective. No one really knew who deserved it. The game for sales reps was to induce physicians to prescribe, but there was no way to measure prescriptions. The only measure possible was to count the purchased drugs by the pharmacy in the town where the doctor worked and wrote scripts. That data could only be collected from the wholesaler. The problem with the system was twofold. Many pharmacies attracted patients from other towns and even other states, which meant a sales rep often got credit for someone else's sales efforts. The other problem was the wholesaler that did not share their distribution data. In that case, no one got credit for their sales efforts. Many reps simply quit calling on towns and doctors where no or little sales credit was possible. All the Boomers did that, which Finn and Ben hated, because they received credit for their district's total sales. Finn, especially, was fudging figures on sales reps to reward his favorite salesmen. Considering who called on the non-credited doctors, Finn concocted their sales figures out of his head.

Things got better in the mid-eighties when companies emerged that would buy the data from wholesalers and sell it to drug companies by zip code. Now, sales reps learned exactly where a prescription came from down to the zip code on the doctor's prescription pad. Even wholesalers that earlier refused to cooperate with the old system happily accepted payment for their data. The downside to this crediting was that in zip codes with more than one doctor, no one could be sure which doctor wrote the prescription. The upside? It was the first truly helpful data for sales reps. With the data they received, they also got data on sales of their competitors. Overnight, managers either awarded reps with the title of Super Salesman or publicly flogged them with a cane made of humiliation. To Stu's delight, he again became a hero of the company.

In the new millennium, a third way to count drug sales emerged that left little doubt about a sales rep's efforts. The new system collected data on each individual doctor. No longer did a zip code matter. Prescriptions, written off a doctor's permanent office address listed on their prescription pad in Stu's territory, were his alone. More flogging commenced, but it helped a rep more effectively call on the big fish, not the minnows. Reps now knew how many prescriptions a doctor wrote each month broken down to individual drugs. Better yet, reps knew exactly what competition existed when calling on an individual doctor. The downsides were worth the pain. Competitors had the same data and could focus their efforts against Connicut-Plushaut products. Doctors didn't like it, claiming it was an invasion of their privacy. That was true, but the law only prohibited knowledge of patient data, a rule that reps strictly followed. Lastly, the new data along with the growth of managed care made pharmacy calls less necessary. Where years before pharmacies were the best sources for knowledge of a physician's writing habits, now with the data available, reps had ninety percent accurate information.

With this new system to account for Stu's sales efforts, his *One Hundred Ideas and Suggestions* began making more sense to upper management. To Stu's surprise, and without attribution, the company's marketing department began implementing some of his one hundred suggestions.

With this new knowledge possessed, there was renewed energy in three-fourths of Stu's pod as they prepared for their presentation that morning.

───────────

STU, MIKE, AND Lorelei entered the room just before 10:00 a.m. to present their proposal. Bill Dooley was not with them. The three came around a large conference table to greet the three managers. There was one familiar face. The other two were managers of the old Connicut Labs.

"Thank God for Abbott Wahl," Lorelei whispered to her pod mates as they took their seats.

"Where is number four?" The question was from a Connicut manager, a lady about fifty with a pleasant smile and a dressed-for-success outfit. It was clear from the start that she was in charge.

Stu answered first. "Bill said he might be a little late. He had a customer on the phone. You know how he is."

"That's our boy!" Abbott Wahl said. "That's the rep we were talking about."

"Oh, I see," the lady replied, "your scorched earth sales representative."

The door opened. Bill stood briefly to look suspiciously at the occupants. Abbott hailed him with a question.

"Did you make the sale?"

"What sale?" Bill replied. He came closer to take his seat.

Abbott looked over at Stu, who was smart enough to learn from Lorelei and kept quiet.

"Well, I see we are all on time," the lady said. "Let's get started. Who will go first?'

Stu stood up quickly before Dooley could blurt out something and said, "I will speak for our pod, as we all agreed beforehand."

He glanced hopefully toward Dooley who gave no response. That is what Stu needed.

"Last night our group talked about the unique strengths each of us brought to the table. We asked around the table… what was our best asset?" Stu tried to get a feel for the true interest the managers had for his introduction. "Mike Austin, a former district manager, told us that his number one strength was his personal relationships that he develops quickly with doctors. With so many me-too drugs out there now, relationships are more important than the drug itself."

The third manager nodded his head in agreement. This man carried the rugged features and square jaw of someone who was no nonsense. His nod was a significant encouragement for Stu.

"Lorelei Lolly told us that her best asset was closing the sale. She is tenacious. She is comfortable with that silent wait that often turns doctors from 'maybe" to 'yes, I will.'"

"Is that all you can do, Lorelei?" the lady manager asked.

Lorelei didn't have to say it, but she was also imperturbable. "Of course not, but we only asked for one strength. We only have fifteen minutes allotted to sell you on our plan. We could go overtime but that would just sound like bragging."

"And what do you think, Mister Dooley?"

"She's a fine closer. Yes, ma'am."

Lorelei was not through. "And one more asset I have, ma'am, is no fear of confrontation. If you are going to call Bill, Mister Dooley, I want you to address me with similar respect as Missus Lolly."

Without hesitation, she replied with a delighted smile, "Point well taken."

Stu took this opportunity to return to the subject. "My own best asset is the difficult doctor… the one the rest of the group dreads calling on. Usually, they use intimidation by word or action. They also like to bully salesmen with technical replies. I'm good at confronting such individuals head on. I don't back down and I can match them in a clinical discussion. I rather enjoy the challenge. Many of those same individuals are now our good customers… and our friends."

Abbott couldn't resist. He glanced at the other two managers. "I would absolutely agree there."

"And lastly, we have Bill Dooley... the legend... and we have him in our pod. Bill said his greatest asset is best stated this way." Stu turned to speak the words directly to him. "'Get out of my way.'"

Laughter came from everyone, including The Legend himself. Stu continued.

"When I played high school football, we had a position we called the Monster Man—the guy on defense who roams where he chooses based on his experience reading an offense. He was unpredictable, which forced the offense, or in this case our competitor, off his game. That is what Bill Dooley, the Legend, does best... and we don't want him to change."

"Monster Man... I like that," Dooley said. From the tone in his voice, it was apparent to all others in the room that he was hearing the term for the first time.

"The next area we covered," Stu said, "was how do we take advantage of these assets to our best advantage?"

Stu began listing the several scenarios that might arise. Dooley sat expressionless and bored through the rest of the presentation. All he cared about was hearing himself called The Legend.

"Let's suppose we have a doctor who agrees with what we say. I have convinced him clinically. Mike has developed a good one-on-one friendship, including lunch or some after work socializing. Bill has monstered him to death. Yet, he still isn't writing our drug's name on the script pad. We have Lorelei, the closer. We give her the task to focus on the doctor we have convinced but who hesitates to change his practices.

"It could be the doctor who wants to help us out. He says 'yes' to Lorelei, but only 'I promise' to the Monster Man and invites Mike to his backyard barbecue. Just one problem. He's worried about drug interactions. My job then is to focus on him in clinical terms.

"Or there is the doctor who prescribes because he likes the rep. Get Mike, our pod's social animal, on the problem.

"There are some doctors who will always talk to a rep, say the right things to us, and never write for us. That's tailor made for a rep who can go in and scare the hell out them, like Mister Dooley can.

"Our pod consists of four seasoned reps. Rather than conforming to the usual approach of tying each doctor to a common pitch, we propose tailoring each doctor to a specific sales rep."

Stu continued until his fifteen minutes were up. The managers gave the four a thank you nod and rubber-stamped their pod's proposal. They hurried them out to make room for the next pod.

"Well, that was a total waste of time," Dooley said after the door closed behind them.

"We could have presented it while drunk and they would have approved it," said Lorelei.

"I like that Monster Man bull you called me."

"Good, but you could have been there with us last night when we decided on things," Mike said. "You put us on the spot this morning."

"It worked for me."

"Okay, Monster Man." Stu said. "Thanks for coming."

Chapter Forty

THERE IS A theory that goes, *your name determines what you become.* It's likely that a man in the Army or Navy named Baker or Bacon will be a natural for kitchen police or KP. There were doctors who were destined to go into a specialty defined by their name. Doctor Emde was an M.D. Doctor Junk became a urologist, while Doctor Beavers went naturally into obstetrics and gynecology. Doctor Cutter became a general surgeon. Doctor Booze became an alcoholic. Doctor Strange was indeed.

Doctor Malcolm Strange was a fun call once Stu got used to his odd quirks. He was a control freak. He had strict rules of calling on him. Rep appointments were strictly enforced with only two per year allowed. After twenty years on the job, Stu had a good idea what doctors went through. He told anyone who complained about Doctor Strange's appointment schedule that, if he were a doctor, he would have the same arrangement.

When Doctor Strange noted that Stu was his sales rep appointment, he was gracious, inquisitive, and grateful for his efforts and samples. Any other time during the year, he refused to acknowledge any salesmen in his presence. Even Fart-man Ben Hodge could not have gotten him to look up.

Stu came in for his bi-annual rep appointment at 8:00 a.m. only to find his friendly receptionist replaced by a new lady in her middle thirties. She was equally friendly with the added quality of being more of a take-charge person. Stu imagined the possibility of a clash between Doctor Control Freak and Missus Take Charge. Stu dismissed the possibility, since he knew that Doctor Strange was dating a young drug rep who now sported an engagement ring. No doubt, his attention to details declined. Stu introduced himself.

"Good morning! You're new to the office. Where's Joyce?"

"Joyce retired three months ago. I took her place." Stu noted her nametag read Tammy Steel, a name about to turn ironic. "Are you here to make an appointment?"

"Today is my appointment, but I could make another one, if you like."

"Not until you see Doctor Strange. Those are the rules."

"Okay," Stu replied. *Joyce would never follow that rule.*

"Now, before Jane calls you back, let's cover the rules for talking to Doctor Strange...."

Stu interrupted. "You know, I've made over forty calls on Doctor Strange in the past twenty years. I know his rules."

"All fifteen of them?"

"All fifteen, yes."

"All right. Have a seat and Doctor Strange will be with you in a moment."

When first seen years ago, Doctor Strange had four rules. He kept adding rules nearly every year. Now with fifteen, Stu was disappointed to learn there was not a number sixteen to entertain him as he waited.

Stu took a second look at Tammy. "Did you used to work at the Fagan brother's office downtown?"

Tammy perked up. "Why yes, I did."

"I bet that was fun." The two medical doctors constantly fought in the office, disagreeing with everything—even the words Stu said to both in the same room together. Stu enjoyed the call, like he did the fifteen rules, solely for its entertainment value.

"I had to leave. They started fighting each other over money."

"Was that recently?"

"Oh, no. That was five years ago. I worked for Doctor Tate for four years, then a year with Doctor Price."

Stu called on all the doctors she mentioned, but only vaguely remembered seeing her. Doctor Tate was a low priority psychiatrist that Stu would only call on if he ran out of doctors to see. He called frequently on Doctor Price but never met Tammy there. Stu concluded she must have worked in the back.

Within minutes Jane called Stu back to see her doctor. He checked with the nurse for any samples the doctor needed. After six months, he needed everything in abundance. Stu got back to the office and made his highly productive call on the man. They parted as pals, but once out the door, Stu became invisible to him as was the routine.

After he left the office and got in his car, he wrote up his call, including information on Tammy, the new receptionist. Details like what she shared often came in handy in later calls. Office staff always appreciated reps who remembered their names and tidbits of their interests. With time on his hands until a call at 9:30, he sat in the car trying to remember Tammy at Doctor Tate's psychiatric office. All he could remember was that he left on his last visit before he was able to call on Doctor Tate because two Oklahoma State Bureau of Investigation officers were talking to another lady in the office. The mention of $25,000 came up as the three chatted without concern for Stu's being present.

Now he was curious. He checked his calendar. He had an appointment in two days with the other doctor Tammy mentioned, Doctor Price. He decided that Doctor Price and he were tight enough that he could mention the name of Tammy just to see how he reacted. He called Ana at home to share with her that he was going to be Sherlock Holmes for the week.

Ana, not sure what was up, decided to play along. "Is this roleplay, dear? How should I dress?"

DOCTOR PHIL PRICE was a new internist with a practice that started disappointedly slow. Stu liked calling on him and tried to boost his practice as much as possible. It was one of the under-appreciated aspects of what drug reps could do for a new physician's practice. They could arrange for them to be speakers at dinners the company sponsored. Dinner talks got a doctor's name in front of the medical community. Golf tournaments introduced doctors to each other, which was excellent for referrals—unless the doctor was caught fudging his card. There were many ways a rep could help without spending money. Today it was Stu's turn to receive.

"Phil, I have a personal question I need to ask you." Stu's call was routine and short. Doctor Price had his feet propped up on his desk after sharing his concern for a lack of patients coming to his office. His office and the waiting room were both lacking in furnishings or décor of any value.

"Ask away."

"Did you have a receptionist named Tammy Steel?"

The reaction was swift. Doctor Price put his feet back on the floor, sat up straight in his inexpensive office chair, and uttered words under his breath that Stu only guessed at. His long dark hair fell across his face. His next words were clear enough to make Stu wince. Finally, he asked the obvious question.

"Why do you bring up that little trollop?"

"She works at Malcolm Strange's office as a receptionist."

"I fired her about four months ago."

"What for?"

"When I interviewed her for the job, she had this sob story. She had three young kids and needed the job to support herself and her little darlings. She seemed so desperate… so I hired her. Almost immediately I started noticing certain things missing… mostly cash. Some patients pay me in cash. I guess that's better than in eggs or chickens." Doctor Price began to grit his teeth. "I finally paid for an audit, which found that there was almost five thousand dollars missing from the books… most of those cash payments in just eight months. I checked on her kids, only to learn she has no kids."

"So that's when you fired her?"

"No. At first, I called the police to see about arresting her or just suing her. You know what they said? It'll cost you more in lost business if you sue and we can investigate the embezzlement, but it won't get your money back. It's not a top priority for the police."

"So, then you fired her."

"Then I fired her." He gritted his teeth once more. "But my attorney advised me not to tell the truth if another person calls for a reference. She could sue me."

Stu shared his conversation he had with Tammy two days before. He described for Doctor Price the Fagan brothers, who began fighting over missing money, the visit of state investigators at the psychiatric office, and the year she spent at his office.

"There seems to be a pattern, Phil."

"I hadn't heard about the Fagans or Tate hiring her. You're right. There's a pattern."

"We need to do something to let Strange know."

"He's an odd duck, isn't he?"

"Yes, but you're a doctor. Could you call him? He won't see me for six months."

"Like I told you, Stu. I can't. She might sue me."

"I hate to see one of my doctors getting robbed."

"I should have known better to hire someone with the last name of Steel."

For the next week Stu and Ana talked over the implications of helping Doctor Strange. He couldn't call the office. Tammy would answer the phone. He couldn't wait for his next appointment. It was six months away. He had a friend from high school in the neighborhood who was an attorney. He called him one night and gave him a short synopsis of his dilemma. Stu had only one question.

"Do I risk liability if I inform the doctor?"

"I'd let him know. Then it's up to him. Just let him do all the dirty work. You stay out of it."

So, Stu managed to get Doctor Strange's address and telephone number. At first, he decided to mail him a letter but stopped when he remembered a television show where a letter was evidence that got a character in trouble with the law. He worried that making a call and leaving a detailed message on the doctor's answering machine could end up as evidence also. He decided that a simple call would be his only answer, but no one would answer the telephone. It always went to his answering machine. So, he left a message.

"Doctor Strange, this is Stuart Roy. Would you please call me back? I have something vitally important and urgent I need you to know. Please call me back," and he left him his telephone number at home.

He waited a week and tried the call again. "Doctor Strange, this is Stu Roy again. I'm sorry to disturb you, but I have some information about your practice that you need to hear from me away from the office." Again, he left his home phone number. A week later, he again had no return call. Stu was determined to save the man from this woman.

Ana suggested her own idea. "Isn't he getting married to a rep you know? Call her."

He had a business card for the woman, but when he called her, the number was out of service. Checking around, he learned she quit her job ahead of the wedding. Out of desperation, Stu hatched a plan to visit the doctor's house, early in the darkness of morning. He grabbed a non-pharmaceutical notepad from Ana and jotted his message to the engaged couple.

Doctor Strange,

I apologize for leaving this note at your house, but it is vitally important that you or Janie contact me. Janie will understand the information if you prefer that she call me back. You will both be grateful. Please, it's in your best interest.

Stu

He left Monday morning more than an hour before sunrise and drove five miles to his spacious house overlooking a small lake. Parking two houses away, Stu quietly left his car. He held the note in one hand while he blocked the glare of a streetlamp with the other. The day before, he had executed a Sunday drive by their house to get a sense of where best to leave his note. He knew Doctor Strange drove a white Lincoln Continental. He made that his target.

The morning was crisp, but no frost appeared. He had checked the weather the night before, fearing the note might be lost if Doctor Strange turned on his windshield wipers. The house was dark. Doctors were notorious early risers. Stepping carefully down the sloping driveway, he was relieved to see the Lincoln. It had only now occurred to him that the doctor could have garaged it overnight. Stu was lucky this morning. He cautiously leaned over the windshield, grabbed the driver's side wiper, and slipped the note under the rubber blade as securely as he could. A gentle breeze convinced him to more securely attach the note farther toward the center portion of the wiper. He was satisfied with his effort and left to get home and shower for work.

EIGHTEEN HOURS LATER, near midnight, Stu's home phone rang. He answered it in the dark from his bed. Ana was instantly alert. They were both hoping it was Doctor Strange.

"Hello." Stu tried his best but sounded half-awake.

"*Stu, this is Doctor Strange. I got your note. I'm curious why you called me?*"

Stu knew that it was vital he get straight to the point. It was his only chance.

"Doctor, thank goodness you called me back. Are you aware that your receptionist Tammy Steel has worked for three other offices where embezzlement occurred?"

The silence was agonizingly long. Stu could hear the heavy breathing of anxiety on the other end. Finally, in a succinct fashion that only Doctor Strange would find normal, he spoke.

"*That's interesting. I had a lady work for me ten years ago that embezzled over one hundred thousand dollars from me. Thank you for letting me know. Good night.*" The phone call was over—Stu's mission complete.

Stu hung up his phone. Ana rolled over to him. The question came through in her body language. "We did it, Ana. He thinks I'm a hero. I'm just sure of it."

It was five and a half months later that Stu learned from Doctor Strange that Tammy Steel was now working for the State of Oklahoma at the medical school.

Chapter Forty-One

THE LAST NAME Strange should have been Bill Dooley's because nobody could figure out this enigma of a man. He had managed to marry five different women. It proved the adage that there are always several someones for everyone. He never talked at all about his current wife. He had a daughter, but few knew she existed.

"Have you ever seen his house?" Benton Wickingham, IV sat across from Stu at a booth at a local diner. Outside it was dreary with a chance of rain. The two were sharing their frustrations before going to work.

"I have no idea where he lives," Stu replied.

"It's a sad dismal place for a man so revered."

"Revered? You mean revered by those who don't have to deal with him."

"His whole life is selling and being left alone. His salary and bonuses exceed many district managers."

"So, Four." Stu wanted him to get back to his original question. "You've seen his house?"

"Yeah. It's a dump. I went to exchange some samples with him. When I got to his house, he wouldn't let me in… seemed upset that I was there."

"I hear he keeps everything in a locked storage unit."

"I see why. He lives in a house about the size of this diner. It's tiny. He could afford a mansion."

Stu started smiling as he listened to Four. The weather was now a light sprinkle with dark clouds rolling in from the southwest.

"Dooley is the biggest tightwad in the world," Stu said. "Remember when we had those last territory realignments?"

"Don't remind me."

"I brought lunch to the Sharpe brothers' clinic to introduce myself. They walked into the kitchen and went into shock. Big brother looked at me and said, 'What? No more baloney sandwiches?'"

"Dooley brought baloney to a high-powered clinic like that?"

"Yeah, and they asked if I was Dooley's replacement. When I said yes, they both seemed overjoyed."

"That's a good sign."

"Not really… Four, their prescribing habits went away after Dooley left."

From the outside window, heavy rain started. The downpour's roar on the glass caused all of the diners to look up in surprise. Stu turned to Four who gave a slight nod.

"Ma'am," he said to a passing waitress. "Could we have more coffee?"

When Plushaut and Connicut merged, the managers from both companies in Oklahoma convened a joint sales meeting. On the first day each salesman and saleswoman got to say something about themselves, including their favorite hobby. When it was Dooley's turn, he stood up. He always wore the same dated and tired polyester suit. His collection of wide ties had not changed in twenty years.

"My name is Bill Dooley, and my only hobby is selling drugs." Then he sat down.

The Pod People were unhappy. Four people were now calling on the same doctors and selling them the same drugs. The three sane members of the pod discovered that the arrangement gave doctors a new item to discuss. When Bill Dooley was the lone company salesman to call on these doctors, they had no recourse but to follow his wishes or he would badger them to death. It was easier to do what he wished. But now, the doctors had recourse. They could complain to the three other members of his pod—and they did so in buckets.

"I've got a solution maybe we can all agree to," Mike Austin said. "If there is a personality conflict between a doctor and one of us, let's agree to stop calling on that doctor."

Lorelei, trying to put a positive comment to the new pod system, said, "That is one of the advantages of the pod system. We all have doctors who view our presence as unwelcome. Let his favorite rep call on him exclusively."

All agreed but Dooly.

The Monster Man mandate was another issue. There were some rules the pod agreed to for strategic purposes. Some promotions would work for one doctor, but it could cause conflict with the entire medical community, such as aggressively selling against a hospital's strict formulary. That might make doctors view the entire Pod's promotions as unethical. Stu offered an alternative he hoped would appeal to Dooley's ego, using a football metaphor.

"Hey, Monster Man," Stu said, calling Dooley by his new nickname. "Are you good with pulling your hits, if the target is out of bounds?"

"What does that even mean? I won't slack off for anybody."

The Pod People were in trouble.

ONE OF THE hospital drugs originating from the Connicut Lab side was now promoted by the pod. It was an injectable 2nd generation cephalosporin antibiotic used primarily in the hospital. It succeeded in receiving FDA approval, while Plushaut's PLU-919 failed. The pod had great success selling Tapilon (*cephotapin*) in the hospital for the specific indication of primary treatment of nosocomial or hospital-acquired pneumonia and for surgical prophylaxis. Dooley had gotten one of the last remaining shot doctors to use it liberally on his patients in his clinic. The hospital's infectious disease doctors went ballistic.

"Tapilon (*cephotapin*) use in the community setting will promote further bacterial resistance and hurt this and other antibiotic's chances of being effective in future years," read the hospital's letter to Plushaut's president.

Since Tapilon was the darling antibiotic of the Connicut side, knowing that four Plushaut salesmen were wrecking Tapilon's reputation, put them all in trouble.

Lance Layton, the new district manager and once coworker with the pod, told Dooley as well as the others, "The driver of the getaway car gets hanged, too, not just the bank robber who kills the teller."

It got even worse. Stu scheduled a lunch at a clinic of four doctors, where the biggest writer, Fran West, D.O., was not a fan of Flofral, but his internal medicine partner, Jeff Haskell, M.D., used Flofral successfully on many of his elderly patients. The pod's stated objective was to get the two doctors together at lunch and lure Doctor West's partner into explaining why he found Flofral so valuable.

Unfortunately for Stu, Dooley called him.

"Can I tag along at your West and Haskell lunch?" The skinflint took every chance for a free lunch.

The clinic was a relaxed environment. The doctors were always accessible. The nurses liked Mike and Lorelei, as well as Stu.

"Okay, Bill, but you have to be a fly on the wall today. This is my appointment with a very specific goal. Since it's my money paying to feed the clinic, it's under my rules of conduct."

Dooley agreed to the rules and made it on time. He looked at the lunch Stu provided in the doctors' conference room and was visibly agitated.

"How much did you pay for this spread?"

"A lot." Stu replied. "The quality of my meal reflects the quality of my doctors." Dooley failed to respond, only scooped up a plate of fine food and sat down to eat.

Fortunately, the moment came when both doctors came in together. Things were lining up well for Stu. As they ate, Stu talked to them. He first brought up the merits of Tapilon for treating hospital acquired infections. Then he came to the subject of Flofral. Stu asked Doctor Haskell a question.

"You use a lot of Flofral successfully. Why do you like it?"

The stage was set. Doctor Haskell started to answer the question. Doctor West was listening carefully. Visions of success and sizable bonuses filled Stu's head. Some of the most successful sales calls for Stu were when he shut up and let the doctor do all the talking.

"You know the biggest reason I use Flofral," Doctor Haskell said, "I have...."

And then it happened.

"I'll tell you why," Dooley said, interrupting the doctor. He began his irritating sales pitch, but no one was listening.

Doctor Haskell stared daggers at Dooley. He knew what his role was to be. The moment was lost. He looked at Stu and knew why he looked so disappointed. The chance for glory and sales success vanished because Bill Dooley thought he could do it better than a doctor.

THE POD AGREED to a meeting of grave importance for 4:00 p.m. on Monday. They chose a sleepy café near Baptist Hospital on the northwest side of Oklahoma City. It was 4:30 before Dooley joined his other three frazzled teammates. He was in a foul mood. That only made an unpleasant meeting more so.

"I wanted to make one more call before I got here," he said, putting his own interests over the pod, even if it meant the weekend would have to wait for an extra thirty minutes.

"Okay, let's get started," Stu said. He was becoming the natural leader of the pod, much to Dooley's unhappiness. "We were going to compare our calendars and share lunches, but since you were late, Bill, we already divvied them up among the three of us."

"What dates do you have for me?"

"None... sorry."

"So, you guys went behind my back and decided to keep me from joining you, is that it."

Mike was ready to start his weekend. "Get here on time, Dooley, and you might get a slot to share."

"Okay, I had some lunches to share, but I don't think I will."

No one reacted because no one wanted to share anything with the Monster Man. The meeting only got worse from there. At 5:00 p.m., Stu announced he was going home to see Ana. Lorelei and Mike stood up to leave. Dooley began raising his voice.

The other three ignored the tantrum and hastily exited the café ahead of him. Unfortunately for Stu, Dooley soon caught up with him before he could get inside his car. Other customers in the parking lot took note of the angry words coming from Dooley. One woman got back into her car, waiting for them to leave.

"Get out of my face, Dooley," Stu said, anger swelling up. "You have broken your promises too many times for me to give a damn!"

"I don't have to listen to you or anybody else for that matter. I'm the best in the world, but now you are ruining it for me. You go behind my back and block my access to doctors. I can't wait to let Lance and Abbott know what you're up to."

"I'll call them now for you, if you would like."

"Don't be a smart ass. They know you're a troublemaker. And now, you're in my way."

"Then back off if you think I'm in your way. I'm backed up to my car about to punch you in the mouth, if you say one more word."

Dooley looked confused, before he realized he had backed Stu up against the car. It unnerved him. He pictured a punch to the face as his fault for not paying attention. His rage abated, which gave Stu time to carry out his first threat. Pulling from his pocket a cellphone, he punched in a number with his speed dial. Compared to ten years before, cellphones were now an indispensable tool for many things. Stu put his phone to an ear and waited for the other end to answer. Finally, a voice answered.

"Hello, Abbott. Stu Roy here. I've got Bill Dooley with me. He wanted to talk to you." Stu handed his cellphone to Dooley. "Here Bill. Tell Abbott Wahl yourself."

This technique had worked for Stu before. He looked forward to the fun. Dooley grabbed the phone in an automatic reaction. He immediately regretted taking it.

"Abbott Wahl, my ass. What jerk did you call for this set up?" Putting Stu's cellphone to his ear, he made a quick assumption who it was and growled his words, "Who is this? Mike, if this is you, I'm tired of this team bull crap you three are cramming down my throat. I don't need you. I don't need Stu or that bitch Lorelei. Lance and Abbott can kiss my ass, too. You got that?"

He paused to hear Mike Austin come clean with his charade. He did not wait long.

"*Bill, this is not Mike. I'm the man you want kissing your ass. I'm sorry, but that's not going to happen.*"

"Who is this?"

"*This is Abbott Wahl. Now if you have an issue with your pod, I suggest you settle it or I'll be kicking your ass, not kissing it.*"

Dooley turned beet-red-faced, but he wasn't finished. "Who is this, really? Abbott Wahl, my ass."

"*Give the phone back to Stu. I want to talk to him.*"

"Here," Dooley said. "Your little bastard friend wants to talk to you again."

Stu took the phone back. He, too, was angry—so much that his laughter from Dooley's confusion wouldn't come out.

"Yes, sir."

"*Stu, I've heard people complain before, but to be honest I didn't believe it… until now. Tell me what's going on.*"

"Abbott, I'm in the parking lot with him now. I don't think it's a good idea to discuss things until he leaves the area."

"Well then, tell him to get the hell out of the way. I've got a weekend to get to."

Stu turned to Dooley, who was already moving back in confusion and worry. "Abbott wants you to get the hell home, so he can enjoy his own Friday evening."

Dooley, with what remained of his dignity, turned and headed for his own car four spaces away. Stu waited while he got in his car, backed out, and gunned it too fast out of the parking lot. He went past with screeching tires and a thick smell of burned rubber.

"He just left," Stu said.

"I heard."

"Sir, I apologize for calling you like this. I needed someone to know what was going on."

"I take it then, that this is not the first time."

"No, sir. Far from it."

"Tell me in a nutshell what he's been doing."

Stu proceeded to explain the hostility to any teamwork. Breaking promises about cooperation. Disparaging remarks toward Lorelei. Doctors who complained to his pod partners about his behavior.

Stu also covered the less motivating aspects of working with a negative and insulting personality—how the team's weakest link of optimism was bringing the pod's success down.

"But I remember you said, and I quote, 'he's ours and you can't have him.'"

"I lied. I wanted to show him we valued his help. In truth, he refused to join in any meeting. We three alone had to plan our presentation to you and the other managers in Hartford."

"Okay, I'm glad you told me. Go start your weekend. We'll talk again."

"Thank you, Abbott." They disconnected.

Stu drove straight home to Ana. His triumph filled him with adrenalin and other hormones after his battle of words with Bill Dooley. He told Ana as much after dinner. After playing outside with the boys until dark, Stu made sure they were prepared for bed. They were exhausted from the vigorous play. Dad was not. It was around 9:30 that night that Mom and Dad conceived their fourth child—a girl.

Chapter Forty-Two

SELLING TAPILON FOR hospital infections became a whole new adventure for the Connicut-Plushaut Labs sales force. The amount of training required to learn about this arena was like getting a second master's degree. It was a jigsaw puzzle of six dimensions. The first dimension was the myriad infective bacteria. Next was the array of antibiotic classes and all their subgroups. Then there were endless ways to become infected in the human body. Physicians had as many opinions as there were options to treat an infection in the hospital. The hospital itself interfered with all the other dimensions by attempting to coordinate all the others. The last dimension was the array of sales reps who competed against each other as warriors, both within and without the company. It was the only product category that consistently caused animosity among salesmen. Stu called it the drug with a dick. For some of the men, Tapilon became the proof of the size of their manhood. If a sales rep sold at elite levels, he was a man among men. If he didn't, managers sent threatening letters to that rep. Any women who became Tapilon super-saleswomen became a man among women. Stu found their behavior amusing.

For a while spending money became seemingly limitless. An ethical gray area meant that the term bribery and research funding became one.

The same with many of the antibiotic speakers who often chose their antibiotic choice by which company provided the most recent monetary grant proposal to their hospital.

The one aspect of the new arena that Stu and Ana liked was the number of opportunities they had to entertain physicians and their spouses. Ana became a happy and willing asset to help Stu sell Tapilon ethically. For the first time that Stu could remember, doctors with spouses became their friends, not just their customers. Wives and husbands of physicians brought more humanity into the two sides. It switched the dynamics of every office call that followed for the rest of Stu's career. These experiences brought the two sides closer to feeling like peers, not adversaries.

In time Stu could disagree with most physicians about the uses of his product line and be a problem solver for them. Once, he said something that had landed him in trouble. He told a cardiologist, "You may be an expert in cardiology, but I'm an expert on Destense." For a moment he feared the man would ask him to leave. The doctor didn't agree to his premise, but in later calls, the doctor listened far better than before. Ana joked that he was listening for another chance to throw him out. Stu countered that he was just that great of an asset to him. They were both right. The cardiologist had a long memory but admired Stu's standing his ground.

More often than Stu would wish, he had to advise a physician to stop using his drug. A highly potent topical steroid called Grandicort 0.2% Steroid Cream was highly effective but could cause the skin to atrophy if applied too frequently.

Doctor Johnston often shared his unorthodox family practice treatments with Stu. Years before he was an understudy of Franz Joseph Steuben, D.O., shot doctor and occasional sales rep tyrant. He liked teaching and Stu was always open to learning new things in medicine. Doctor Johnson looked at the tube Stu held in his hand and told him a new use he discovered for Grandicort.

"I had a married couple come in last month. She complained of pain during intercourse. They were both distressed. I did the usual workup on her. I asked her about vaginal dryness, ruled out a yeast infection, and checked off all the usual causes. I gave them some medicine to try."

Doctor Johnston reached across his desk and picked up a sample tube of Grandicort.

"I had one of these next to my telephone, so I told them to try this as a sex lubricant and called in a prescription for them. They called me yesterday and sang the praises of me and your cream."

Stu was appalled. He had visions of an atrophied penis and severe vaginal wall thinning. He thought of the occlusive environment in the poor woman where the effects of the steroid cream would multiply.

"Is this a one-time therapy?" Stu asked.

"No. The wife is the one who called me. They're having sex all the time now. Sort of making up for lost time."

Stu raised his hand to stop him from talking. "I suggest that using Grandicort in this manner is a bad idea. Have you considered the prolonged use of something this potent and how it could harm them both over the long term?"

The doctor became pensive. Stu waited.

"I thought of that myself, but until you reminded me again, it slipped my mind. Old hubby might be somewhat bothered if his manhood shrank permanently."

"I'm more worried about his wife. Grandicort can't get out. It's like an occlusive dressing inside."

"You have a point. Too much of your stuff and she won't feel anything at all."

"There won't be anything left."

"So now what do I do? I could have them use it once a week maybe."

"Oh, please don't. If you insist on using a steroid cream, I'd stick to the lowest strength hydrocortisone. Even that, too, makes me shudder."

Doctor Johnston began to laugh. "It sure made them happy though."

"Yes, it did. Another success story for my fine, fine product line."

THERE WERE ALSO times that Stu had to use extraordinary means to stop a doctor's shenanigans. Christy Fowler, the young baby-faced Stanford graduate who was pals with heart transplant pioneer, Christiaan Barnard, M.D., came to Stu for assistance. Now happily married, Christy remained stunningly beautiful after ten years of selling pharmaceuticals. It was hard for doctors to avoid the comments they made when she first met them. The men of the Boomer District admired her refusal to exploit her beauty. She preferred to earn it, but there was no getting around it. Good looks sold.

"I'm having trouble with a couple of doctors," Christy said, "and I'm wondering if you could give me some advice."

"Let me guess… Doug Rice and Blaine Richards?" It was funny how many times doctors who sat alphabetically next to each other in medical school ended up as partners. They were both notorious philanderers.

It was the morning before a golf outing that occurred way too often to suit Stu. Connicut-Plushaut Labs invited as many as a hundred doctors to play golf after hearing a well-respected specialist talk for thirty minutes during lunch. This time the topic of choice was the treatment of hospital acquired pneumonia. The solution for the sales force was Tapilon. The theme on the golf course was rarely either one, but golf was truly a powerful salesman—and Stu hated the game.

"Rice and Richards. You guessed it. I got a call from Doctor Richards last night," she said, sitting across from Stu in the elegant hospital foyer at Mercy Health Center. "Did you invite him to the golf tournament tomorrow?"

"No, remember? We had to restrict the number for budgetary reasons. We can't have more than seventy-two players."

"But we invited Doctor Rice?"

"Yeah, and I knew that was going to be a problem. I wasn't in charge of invitations."

"Well, Doctor Richards wants to come anyway."

"He can't."

"That's what I told him last night. Then he said some very disgusting things to me. I'm glad my husband didn't hear what he said. I think he might do something. That's why I asked to meet you."

"May I ask... what did Richards say?"

Christy blushed so visibly that even Stu noticed it. "He said that he had a brother visiting from out of state. He's a gynecologist. He told me that his brother and Doctor Rice would be willing to give me... a free pelvic exam."

"Oh, Christy... that's bad. What happened next?"

"I told him that he was disgusting, and I would hang up on him... but he went on to say that if I didn't invite him to the golf outing, he would call you in the morning."

"I haven't heard from him."

It was if the doctor could hear them. Stu's cellphone began to chime. He answered it with a hello, then turned with a smile and a nod to Christy.

"Yes, Doctor Richards, this is Stu Roy. What can I do for you?"

"Christy told me last night I was not invited to the golf meeting. I want to be invited to come today."

"We're full right now. I suppose you could come and hear our speaker."

Christy started to giggle at the suggestion. Rice and Richards almost always arrived for these golf outings after the speaker was through.

"I figured you could get me in."

"Here's the deal, Doctor Richards. After what you said to my partner last night, I will make sure we never invite you to another golf tournament."

"Why? What did I say?" He sounded like a twelve-year-old caught red-handed by a stern teacher.

"Don't give me that. You know exactly what you said to her."

"No I didn't. Tell me... tell me what I said to Christy!"

"You said your brother and Rice would be happy to give Christy a free pelvic exam... nobody is going to talk to one of my partners like that."

"Oh... yeah, I guess I did say that."

"And furthermore, I will advise Christy to never call on you as long as you're in practice."

"I'm sorry, I shouldn't have said that. I'm sorry. Can I come to the meeting and apologize to Christy?"

"Doc, the never-get-invited part has already started. You want someone to talk to in your office, it will have to be somebody else."

"I don't think you are being fair. Doctor Rice is going. I was going to ride with him."

"I'll tell you what I'll do, Blaine. You see reps at 8:30 in the morning. I'll be there Monday morning at 8:00 a.m. sharp. We can talk face to face. How's that?"

"I don't think that will be necessary."

"You look for me... eight o'clock sharp... I'll be there waiting for you." Stu ended the call without another word. Christy was aghast.

"I can't believe you told him that."

"Well, he shouldn't mess with our reps. And I will tell Lance or Abbott or anyone you want that I insisted that you should never call on those two again."

"I'm glad you mentioned both. Doctor Rice is almost as bad. He's always hitting on me. I tell him I'm not interested... that I'm a married woman... but he keeps pawing me and making little comments that gets me squirming."

"You're off the hook from now on."

"But I'm ruining our pod's chances for a good year."

"Some things are more important, Christy. Besides, if I get a chance, I'm going to put it to Doctor Rice." He crossed the fingers of his right hand. "We are just like this. He'll never know it's coming."

It was late afternoon at the golf course of Oak Tree Country Club north of Edmond, Oklahoma. It was a long golf cart ride back to the clubhouse. Stu had maneuvered himself onto the foursome with Doug Rice. They shared a cart for eighteen holes together. The ride back without anyone around was a perfect setting for a story Stu wanted to tell him. Rice had already spent four hours talking about women he found hot, including Christy. It was easy for him to mention her again.

"Is Christy back at the clubhouse?"

"I think she may be, but I never checked her schedule." Stu slowed down the speed of his cart to allow more time for conversation.

"I'd like to know her schedule. I could have something waiting for her. What a babe. Um… um!"

Stu agreed that Christy was indeed a looker.

"That reminds me, Doug, of a story my brother told me when he moved to Kansas City. You know it's a town with a heavy Italian-American population. It was part of the mob back in the nineteen twenties and thirties. My brother had this affinity for Italian women. He met a young lady at work… very attractive… who showed some interest in him. So, one day he asked her out on a date. The next morning when he left his apartment for work, there were two men standing by his car. It was clear that they were waiting for him.

"'You asked my sister for a date yesterday, right?' My brother said her name and asked if that was his sister. The other goon stood by quietly as he replied, 'We are Italian. You asked one of our own on a date. You don't look Italian.' My brother agreed that he was not Italian. The man continued, 'Then let me give you one piece of advice… don't fuck with our women.' Then they turned around and walked away."

Stu let that sink in for a few seconds. Doctor Rice said nothing. He was mulling over the story as they bounced their way to buildings ahead.

"Doug. When it comes to you and Blaine Richards, interacting with our sales reps in Connicut-Plushaut, I want you to know that the same thing goes for me… don't fuck with our women."

Chapter Forty-Three

STU ALSO HAD firsthand experience in saving a life. It was Saturday evening. Stu and Ana had steaks on the grill in their backyard. The children were happily playing together with a soccer ball on a freshly mowed lawn. Stu worked up a sweat to make the yard look perfect. The weather was perfect for an outdoor picnic. Being outside, he didn't bother to clean up after his labors. It was a rare coming together of good weather, happy children, and some extra expensive steaks Ana had saved for a special weekend. But Stu heard the telephone ring inside.

"Don't answer it," Ana said, but Stu compulsively went inside to take it.

Not waiting for him to come back outside, Ana attended to the grill while simultaneously setting up the picnic table with plates, utensils, and all the fixings. She was taking steaks off the grill when Stu came back to join them.

"I have to go. A doctor has an emergency, and I must take him Lystrepto."

"Where?"

"Clinton. They're out of stock. I need to pick up some from another hospital... take it to 'em."

"That's a hundred miles away. Can you eat first?"

"No. It's an emergency. With Lystrepto, time is muscle." Stu smiled at his use of the slogan he often employed in selling to doctors.

"What happened?"

"I didn't ask. It could be a heart attack or deep vein thrombosis. If it's the heart, I must move fast."

"All right then. I'll save your steak for you, but it won't be as good."

Stuart listened intently to their hurried conversation and added his voice. "Can I go with you, Dad?"

Stu looked at Ana. Her expression told him what he needed to know. "I need to make two phone calls first. Eat while I do that, then be ready to jump in the car. I won't wait."

"Yes!"

"Bathroom first, young man." His mother based her admonition on previous experience. "I'll make a plate for you to take in the car."

While everyone worked to get ready, Stu first called Deaconess Hospital and got approval to pick up and borrow a box of twelve vials of Lystrepto. That amount would cover treatment of any indication the patient required. Next, he called the highway patrol headquarters, explained the urgency and asked for either a ride in a patrol car to Clinton or permission to speed on I-40.

"We don't have a patrol car for that purpose, but if you are reasonable, you can increase speed. I will let units know. Don't overdo it."

He described his car and gave the dispatcher his license plate number. "I'm talking ten to twenty over the limit… on I-40 only. Is that okay?"

"Don't overdo it."

"Thanks." He hung up and called Stuart. "Let's go!"

Stuart led the charge to the garage with Ana close behind carrying an armload of plates with food, utensils, drinks, and napkins—lots of napkins.

"Honey, I made a plate for you, too… Stuart, you take care of Daddy's plate until he's ready."

They were backing out of the driveway as Ana stood waving. Stu glanced at the banquet she had prepared for the two of them in wonder. *How did she do that so fast? How is Stuart going to handle this… this cornucopia?* Then he looked at the pile of napkins Ana left with them. *Oh, I get it.*

They stopped at Deaconess Hospital to pick of the Lystrepto. It was good to have good relations with the staff in the pharmacy. Back in the car, they headed five miles south for the interstate highway. Turning to the west, as Stu merged with light traffic onto I-40, he turned to look at a grinning Stuart.

"You ready to put the pedal to the metal?"

With a nod of the boy's head, because his mouth was already full, Stu floored it for both their benefits.

"We're off!"

The 85 mph drive was uneventful except for the food they both spilled and smeared over the passenger seat. Stu didn't care. It was a company car that was already scheduled for replacement. He never saw a trooper on the road. He had secretly hoped to get a hundred mile an hour escort, but it was not to be. Pulling into Clinton Regional Hospital's parking lot, they jumped out with their life saving drug, and hustled it back to the pharmacy.

"Oh good, Stu. You're here. I'll call Doctor Hatch and let him know," Linda said. The middle-aged pharmacist seemed remarkably unhurried, considering it was a life or limb situation. But then, it was Doctor Hatch, not known for his speed or urgency. When she got an answer, she handed the telephone to Stu.

"Hello, Doctor Hatch?"

"Yes, Stu. Did you bring the Lystrepto?"

"Yes, sir. I brought the whole box of twelve vials... I didn't know what we were treating, so you have enough to treat a deep vein thrombosis, if that's what you have."

"No, I don't need that much."

"May I ask you what we are treating tonight?"

"A young lady was brought into the E.R. about six o'clock yesterday with a hematoma on her cheek."

Stu's mental red flags began to wave vigorously. This emergency was more than a day old. If time were muscle, the advantage of early treatment was now past. A hematoma was not a typical indication for such a complex drug as Lystrepto.

"What are the circumstances of this hematoma?"

"*It resulted from a serious auto accident yesterday. I need to help her save her pretty face from permanent discolor.*"

Stu's heart skipped a beat or two. He pondered how to explain it to Doctor Hatch that he was proposing one of the dumbest and most dangerous uses of a drug that was possible. He gathered his thoughts, remembering that being honest and upfront had always served him well.

"Doctor Hatch, I can't give you the Lystrepto you asked for."

"Oh? Why's that?"

"Because she has been in an accident. If you give her any hemolytic agent like Lystrepto or *vePA*, your patient will bleed to death from any source of bruising or trauma. Besides, treating a hematoma with the same agents would be a dangerous use of the drug. I'm sorry."

Stu looked over at Linda, who was listening to one end of the call with sudden interest. Her expression of shock and embarrassment was evident. A pharmacist, as well as the doctor, should have known this information. Stu knew that he had not left that out of his sales calls. It was too important a point.

Doctor Hatch had the last word on the subject, "*Thanks,*" and hung up.

Stu turned to his son, who had been polite and quiet the whole time. "Well, Stuart. We get to take the drugs back home with us. We are done. You ready to go?"

Stuart only shrugged his shoulders. He sensed the disappointment in his dad. Stu was planning this to be his heroic effort to save someone's life. He had wasted his time. Looking back at Linda, Stu shared his frustration.

"What a disappointment. I thought I was saving a life, but all I did was miss an outside cookout with my family."

"Stu, I'm sorry," Linda replied, "but you're not looking at the big picture. You came to help us save a life. Instead you stopped us. You saved her life, thank God. I'm grateful you came."

"Yeah, I guess you're right," he said as Stuart joined him in the hallway. "I did save a life tonight."

Chapter Forty-Four

It was June when Stu called on a new dermatologist for the first time. It was hard for new physicians to get residency in dermatology. Medical professionals limited available slots. Medical students had to be at the top of the class. Many doctors wanted into that specialty because of its frequent description. *Dermatology, where no one gets better and there are no emergencies.*

The receptionist was a short plump lady who appeared to be close to sixty years in age. She greeted Stu warmly when he put in a card. He introduced himself and then asked her name.

"My name is Ginger." She looked at his card. The dark splotches on her neck and wrinkles on her face gave evidence of her age and possibly a lifetime of cigarette smoking. "Mister Roy. Thank you for coming. We don't see many drug reps yet. My doctor has been frustrated. She has no samples to give out. She had tons at the med center when she was still a derm resident."

"Would I have known you from any other clinic?"

"No, this is my first job since my first baby was born. You look familiar, though. Did you go to high school here in Oklahoma City?"

"Yeah." Stu pointed outside the entry door. "The one two blocks from here."

"Oh, me too! What year did you graduate?"

Stu always made a point to make believe any woman was younger than he was. "Oh, I graduated way before your time. I'm in the Class of 1968."

She didn't laugh like Stu expected. She was pleased by what he said. Stu wanted the joke to end there, but she had to ask him a potentially fatal question.

"That's nice of you to say. How old do you think I am?"

It wasn't the question that would be fatal, but the answer would be. He didn't want to try for accuracy by guessing sixty years old. She might be hurt that he knew she looked her age. He thought of lowballing it to fifty, but somehow that seemed a cop out. Either go for accuracy, he decided, or go for the ridiculous. He determined an age that a teenager might believe was a real guess, but a sixty-year-old would consider humorous. How could he lose?

"I am going to guess…." He bit his lip while lifting his eyes to the ceiling in a pose of make-believe calculation, "…I'd say you're twenty-one."

Ginger looked surprised but pleased. She broke out in a big smile.

"You're close. I'm twenty-six. Class of 1995. Go Bears!"

Stu knew he dodged a bullet. This new wisdom added to his comfort in an uncomfortable situation. After work he shared with Ana his observations.

"I will always tell a woman she looks to be twenty-one. If a woman is sixty, she knows you are joking, but she is still flattered. No harm done. If she's thirty to forty, she may believe you mean it. She is pleased. No harm done. If she's seventeen, she is thrilled because all teenagers dream of being twenty-one someday. I can't lose with this plan."

"So how old am I?"

"Do you want me to lie?"

"You should never lie to your wife."

"Okay… you're twenty-one."

It was years later that Stu called on fifty-eight-year-old Frances Welty, M.D. for the first time. It was a normal clinic, with uncomfortable vinyl waiting room chairs. Some showed signs of wear with cracks running the length of the seat from front to back. The end tables held generous stacks of magazines for patients to read while waiting. While he sat, until a nurse called him to the back, Stu sifted through the magazines for something of interest to read. The only thing he found interesting were the dates on the issues. Some of the magazines were sixteen years old. He thought of the collectible Life Magazines he had seen in antique shops. These might be valuable.

A middle-aged and tired nurse called him back. She introduced herself as Sarah.

"Is this your first time to see Doctor Welty?"

"Yes." He looked around discreetly at the walls and counters of the lab and kitchen to his left. They were stacked to the ceiling with medical journals, piles of mail, drug rep giveaways, file cards, sales visuals, empty boxes, empty glass bottles, packing material, plastic packaging, and even toilet paper spools. Sarah turned Stu to the right into a hallway stacked with more journals on the sides of both walls. *Now I know what going through the eye of a needle is like.* She directed him to a door on the right, a less crowded room.

"The next time I'm here, this must be where I go, right?"

"Yes, this is our rep room. You're welcome to lay your information on the counter and Doctor Welty will be right with you."

Stu sat in a chair next to an enormous pile of file cards and visuals, now nine inches high, spreading out like the ash of a volcano. It threatened to spill off the counter onto the floor. He shoved it back which steepened its slope. He looked on the top of this stack. To his surprise he found one of his own visuals on top. It had only been a month since the company realigned sales reps' territories. Christy Fowler, who seldom had stories to share at meetings, previously had called on Doctor Welty. This was a remarkable story she should have told him.

Stu started to check what competitive papers and visuals he might glean from the pile. It was a gold mine of treasures for a drug rep to discover competitive visuals, research papers, and assorted useful information. He pulled the items carefully out, laying them to one side. Sarah stuck her head in the door to chat. After some small talk, he asked her if he could take his small collection and place it in his bag for keeps.

"Oh, please, please, please do. You can see she won't miss it."

"Thank you. I had noticed that there might be some extras."

To Stu's surprise, Sarah began to share her doctor's story. She was a child survivor of the Warsaw Ghetto during World War Two, saved by Catholic nuns who sneaked her to safety in a suitcase. Later coming to America, Frances Welty managed to do well as a student, ending up in medical school. With a chance to move elsewhere, she elected to stay in Oklahoma and practice family medicine.

Stu was honored years later when Doctor Welty shared her story with him in a quiet moment of reflection and friendship between a Christian drug rep and a Jewish physician. She was a hoarder because she never lost sight of the potential value of even a tiny scrap of paper. She spent her whole life preparing for the next Holocaust.

After ten years of calling on Doctor Welty, she died at the age of sixty-eight. The victim of a heart attack, Stu went to her Sunday morning funeral at the Jewish cemetery in south Oklahoma City. He admired her toughness and her story of survival and achievements.

As the cheerful sun tried to bake the mourners, Stu, wearing a yarmulke as a gesture of honor and reverence, stood in line with other mourners to offer a shovel of dirt to bury a person, forever wounded, but honored for still achieving a rich and happy life.

Chapter Forty-Five

IT WAS A slow devolution, but calling on retail pharmacies became less valuable over twenty years. What Stu did with pharmacies in the 1980s did not apply anymore. Back then, a sales rep could sell directly to the pharmacist. The rep could get information about a physician's prescribing habits—what drugs he liked, how many total prescriptions he wrote in a month, or if he was writing scripts for a new drug. Reps could learn if the physician was an early adopter of new medications or a conservative writer who waited a year to see if the drug was good or bad.

Then the chain stores began restricting a drug rep's access to the pharmacist. Managed care took over pharmacy management. Costs at the retail pharmacy became irrelevant because insurance copays were the same for every patient and every prescription.

Sales reps knew this, but the management did not. Lance Layton knew because he only recently left the field. Abbott Wahl, should have known, but he did not. The director of sales—there was a new one every six months—continued to insist on actions impossible to do for five years.

The small-town pharmacies had another problem. The older physicians, a part of a small town's community, were dying off. Pharmacists were without a doctor, patients, or drug reps. Stu knew there was no reason to call on them, but they were friends that he missed seeing.

Stu had a new area added to his call territory, Hollis, Oklahoma, 180 miles from home. As far southwest as was Oklahoma, it was a dead-end town with only one way in or out. Hollis was an arid and barren area of land, where cotton bolls scatter across the roads in good years. This day was hot.

The rule for any new town is to first head to the pharmacy. The first store sold more limeades than pills. The second pharmacy asked Stu, "Why would you come here?"

"It's my first time to be in Hollis. I always want to go first to where the money is."

"Ha! There's no money here. Our doctors don't prescribe. I don't know what they do... maybe send their scripts to Altus to get filled." He changed the subject abruptly. "You be sure and try out our new restaurant just one block west of here. You can't miss it. It was the first hotel built in town. We've restored it. You can still rent rooms upstairs. That's where the whorehouse was... way back when."

"That will be helpful to know. What can you tell me about your doctors?"

"They all want to see you at noon, which will be hard, since they all have separate offices... and don't call on Doctor Tower. That's all I'm going to say about him."

The third pharmacy was in the heart of the small downtown district on the main drag, blocks away from the town's only stoplights. It was well-maintained, still looking like a real pharmacy. Stu parked his car directly in front of the entrance. He was surprised to see an attractive woman open the door and greet him.

"You're the only man in town in a suit, so I had to find out your business in Hollis."

Stu laughed. It was his kind of humor. And it was true, all the other men seemed to prefer jeans or overalls.

"I guess I'm the new kid in town." He pulled out his business card and handed it to her. She introduced herself to him as Anita.

"Connicut-Plushaut Labs?" She read aloud. "When did they merge?"

"Oh, a couple of years ago."

"Well, we don't get a lot of news here… out in nowhere."

"I thought I better check with the pharmacies before I went to meet your doctors."

"Have you been to the other pharmacies, yet?"

"Yes. They're pretty small. You do most of the business, I presume?"

"Nobody is surviving out here… did they tell you about Doctor Tower?"

"Yes."

"What'd they say?"

"Don't call on him, but I don't know why."

"Well for starters, you don't want to be there when there's a drug raid."

"You mean like the police?"

Anita pumped her thumb upward. "Go higher… like federal. It has to be really bad if they come out here."

"So, they've raided the office of this guy?"

"Not yet, but we've all been interviewed by them. So have all the doctors, including him… we're just waiting."

"So, what doctors should I call on?"

She went through the whole list. "There are three regular family doctors, plus the hospital-built clinic for circuit riding doctors who set up shop one or two days a week. They come from towns that are a hundred miles away."

That was outside Stu's territory, which meant he would not get credit for their prescriptions. Anita talked a little about herself. She was in her thirties, an age Stu found to be the acme of beauty for a woman. She took care to wear makeup, fix her hair, and dress smartly. Other women he noticed in small towns wore jeans and tee shirts, covered their hair with a ball cap, and spent too much time in the sun. Anita was different.

"I'm only in Hollis because of my husband." Her voice dropped to an unanimated tone as she described him and her location. She sounded lonelier with each word she spoke. Stu looked at his watch. Noon approached, the prime doctor call hour.

"I better go meet your docs... minus Doctor Tower. Thanks for the information. You've been the most help of all."

As Stu walked to the front door of her pharmacy, she followed him. He turned in a farewell nod, but she spoke again.

"So, where do you go to make calls after this?"

"Well, it's a hundred and eighty miles to Oklahoma City, so depending upon how long it takes me to see your doctors, I might stop in Altus on the way out or just head straight for home."

"That sounds good. I might share with you something else." She looked serious and sighed before she continued. "My advice to you is to not bother calling on these doctors. The farmers are broke. We're in a drought. The town has no money. The doctors don't write prescriptions."

"Okay."

"And I'll ask a favor of you. Before you leave town, would you come back by here... and would you take me with you?"

Chapter Forty-Six

BILL DOOLEY WAS not getting any better at being a team player. Upper management gave Stu a dressing down because of his supposed negativity. Even Lance, who should have known, was piling on. Abbott, despite his own experience dealing with the man, sent word that he, Stu, was the object of discussions about termination. It was a maddening time for the three victims of their pod.

Stu was not known for bending over and taking it from management. He began again his hundred ideas and suggestions in the middle of the year, vowing to send in another one hundred. Beside himself with anger, he tried to stay under the radar as he mailed more letters to the Connicut-Plushaut management team. It was all new stuff for the Connicut wing of the company, who had missed out on Stu's earlier one hundred.

More of Dooley's injurious behavior prompted Mike to begin writing letters documenting the myriad actions that wreaked havoc on his four-member pod. He too received threats of disciplinary action for his alleged negativity. Stu got further blame for fomenting Mike's activities. Lorelei stepped back and observed all the men, documenting the behavior of all three. Thus, she took on the role of arbiter between the sides—Dooley's and everybody else's.

Lorelei took Stu and Mike aside, which wasn't hard to do since Dooley never was in meetings. She suggested a mediation session. Her plan, which required that they be in the know, was to conduct a face-to-face meeting. In front of all four, she wanted to list behaviors she wanted Mike to improve. Then she proposed chewing Stu out for some minor infraction. Finally, she would do the same to Dooley, by listing the legitimate issues she hoped to suppress in him.

"You're not going to like what I say about you two, but remember, it's all a bunch of made-up bull. Just go along with it. We've got to make him think we're not targeting him. He will think I am laying equal blame on all of you."

"It sounds complicated," Mike said.

"No, it's not. All you must do is take a few insults that don't matter… and then look hurt or mad or… I don't care what. Just let Bill think I'm giving everyone a good spanking."

After they agreed to Lorelei's plan, Mike and Stu looked at each other with trepidation. They knew their jobs were unjustifiably on thin ice as they were. This, they agreed, could be a disaster.

"Can you act insulted after hearing fake accusations from Lorelei?"

"Not only could I, but it might just make it more real if I hurl a few criticisms back at her."

"We don't have to tell. Her reaction would be more real. Surely, she'll know we're kidding."

"That could make Mister Monster Man want to defend her. He'd be more willing to listen to her."

"I could hurl those insults with you," Mike said.

"No. Don't. We don't want to gang up on her. That might backfire."

That evening, Lorelei called the three men and offered to meet them at her house on Wednesday morning at 9:00 a.m. Bill Dooley was first to accept, a factor totally unexpected. Stu and Mike agreed. Stu had underestimated Lorelei's abilities as a go-between. Wednesday's meeting results might be unforeseen.

BILL DOOLEY SAT in the favorite chair of Lorelei's husband—the best seat in the house. It was Wednesday morning, and he was fifteen minutes early. He fidgeted with his car keys to the point of distraction to Lorelei. Otherwise, he sat still, looking smug. He knew that Lorelei wanted to help heal the rift in the pod, but he was in no mood to give an inch. After all, he was the fair-haired boy loved by management and feared by both peers and competitors. He liked thinking that doctors feared him as well.

"Can I get you anything, Bill?" Lorelei asked him from the kitchen. "Coffee, juice, water?"

"Nothing."

She now knew his disposition and was not happy. She tried to lighten the mood.

"Have a good day yesterday? Who did you see?"

"Not really."

"I called on Doctor Steuben yesterday. He has another new partner with him. He seems to be a nice man. He's Doctor Crowder's son. You heard the father retired?"

"Of course I have."

She gave up and opened the front door, so she could see through the glass storm door when the other two men arrived.

"My husband just took up golf. He says it's addictive and he is kicking himself for not trying it earlier. Are you a golfer?"

"No."

"Ever tried it?"

"I hate it."

Lorelei stepped back into her kitchen. She wanted to hide. Dooley wanted her to, also. He sat still and sulked. He liked to sulk. It made people fear him, or at least feel uncomfortable around him. It gave him control in any small group. He was used to getting his way. Lorelei knew Dooley would attempt to dominate everyone but her—unless her husband left. Then he could give them all hell.

There was a knock at the door. It was Mike. Stu was a minute behind, parking in the street, when Lorelei shouted to Dooley.

"Bill, could you get the door. I think it's locked."

Dooley stayed where he was, simply staring at Mike on the other side of the glass door. Mike turned to Stu as he walked up to join him.

"Are we locked out?" Stu asked.

"Yes and no. I'll knock again and maybe Dooley can get out of his easy chair and let us in."

Stu glanced through the glass and spied Dooley. "Oh, I get it."

Mike knocked again and rang the doorbell. "Come on, Dooley. Let us in."

Both men found humor in the situation and simply shook their heads in resigned disbelief. Dooley remained where he was. A fit and well-dressed man crossed in front of him.

"I'll get it!" he said.

Opening the door, the man held out his hand to the two. "Hi. Come on in. I'm the no-good bum who just married your pod partner."

"Bud, right? I'm Mike. Glad to meet you. This is my side kick, Stu."

"Come on in, guys. I gotta leave for work in a few minutes, but I was hoping to meet all of you."

As the men stepped inside, Bud turned to Dooley and extended a hand. "So, you must be Bill."

Dooley did not stand up. He offered a limp and unenthusiastic hand to Lorelei's husband. Bud grabbed his hand in an unintentionally knuckle cracking grip and shook. Dooley's face winced with the pain.

"Sorry," Bud said quickly.

Dooley remained silent, so Bud tried to make up for it. "Lorelei said you might be the only golfer in the bunch."

Lorelei came flying out of the kitchen and grabbed Bud's arm. "I was wrong about that. Come in here a minute. I need you to help me with something."

Mike and Stu, now left alone with Dooley, jockeyed for seats in the small living room. Their combined furniture made for a tight fit, but with plenty of seating. Mike chose the seat farthest from Dooley, while Stu chose to sit next to the Monster Man. He turned to him.

"Golf. Thank God Lorelei rescued all three of us. Not my game. I don't get it. How about you?"

"Yeah."

"I like driving the golf cart, though," said Mike.

Lorelei was getting no help from her husband. That was not his intention. He only wanted to meet the others. So, instead of letting him hang around, she kissed him on the lips and told him to go to work. As Bud departed into the garage, she picked up a tray of cups and saucers with coffee, cream, and sugar. Placing it on a coffee table she asked Mike and Stu if they would like coffee or something else. They both declined, leaving the coffee service as a prop to proper etiquette.

Lorelei took a seat between Mike and Stu, consciously trying to avoid Dooley's feeling surrounded. While Mike, Stu, and Lorelei sat upright in their upholstered armchairs, Dooley halfway lay in a slouch, which got worse at the speed of a glacier. It is a principle of selling to first begin a conversation with idle chatter. Lorelei did her best to begin the meeting that way.

"So, what was your day like yesterday, Stu?"

"It was rather rough…." Dooley cut him off.

"Are you making a sales call? Or can we cut to the chase?"

All three men looked at Lorelei. This was her idea—her show. She didn't miss a beat.

"Well then, we'll get started. Okay with you, Stu?"

"Sure. Let's go."

Lorelei was the only one in the room who showed no signs of tension.

"Okay. Let's go," she said with a sigh of genuine regret. "It makes me sad to see you three at odds. I feel like I am caught in the middle. Besides breaking my heart to see such fighting, it's weighing on our efforts to do the best job the company expects. We have managers after us. Even some of our doctors are asking me questions about you all."

She picked up a typed sheet she brought in with the coffee tray. "I have a list of complaints that I have on all of you."

"Oh boy! Here it comes," Dooley said with a derisive tone to his voice.

"Okay first up… Mike," she said.

Dooley watched Mike swallow hard. The slightest smile cracked upon Dooley's face, as Mike displayed a what's-coming-next expression.

"I have a list here…."

"A list?"

"Mike, it's a short list… calm down. But I do want you to consider how your conduct affects our success."

"Hurry, will you?"

"Number one. I'm bothered by the way you smirk and turn to Stu whenever Bill is speaking. You don't listen. Instead, you whisper to Stu. That's rude. It gets noticed by others outside the pod. Do you think you can give Bill the courtesy of stopping that?"

"I don't think I do that…."

"Yes, you do," said Stu. "She's right."

As Dooley's smile got bigger, Mike's expression became defensive.

"Okay. Go on. What's next?"

"Number two. One of our doctors… I won't say who… complained to me that when he asked you about Bill, you weren't very complimentary."

"That was Doctor Stanley and all I did was nod in agreement to what he was saying."

"You're saying that you can't just listen. Do you have to reinforce a notion about your partner? It became my problem, too, because you couldn't be loyal to your teammate."

"Okay, fair enough."

"Number three. I've read your notes on our computers. I don't see anywhere where you have followed up with Bill's suggestions after each of his calls. We need to work in tandem on our calls to reinforce each other's efforts."

"Okay, I can do that. That one makes sense."

"What about the other two? Will you work on those?"

"Bill, I'll start listening to you and being more respectful when I talk to doctors. You do have the greatest work ethic in the company. I couldn't do it. That's what I need to say when a doctor brings you up. So… I'm sorry. I'll do better."

Lorelei turned to Dooley. "Bill, do you accept Mike's apology and his plan for future actions?"

"Of course… and it's about time."

Mike's anger began to rise, but he kept that evidence in check for the moment.

"All right, are you ready, Stu?"

Stu wasn't sure he was, now. The examples she used for Mike's spanking were trivial in his estimation and not worthy of complaints. *What bull is she planning for me?* Simply thinking it made him mad. He looked at her with an I-dare-you stare.

"Okay. Number one. You spend too much time talking to me about Bill, when you need to solve your own issues first."

Stu turned red in the face. It might have been a good reaction to convince Dooley it was not a con job, but her words angered him. He remained stoic. She continued.

"I get tired of this constant whining about things out of our control. I prefer to hear solutions, okay?"

"I can do that."

"Okay. Number two. You…."

"Can I ask how many you have for me?"

"Just two more. Secondly, you're leaving too many samples in some of the offices. Sometimes we need the clinics to be out of samples so they will need to see us. We can't make a sales call if we're not needed." She turned to Dooley. "Right, Bill?"

"Dead on." Dooley was starting to enjoy this meeting.

"That makes sense… and easy to do."

"Then lastly, you try to run our pod meetings rather than let each of us have a chance. You're not my district manager. Quit trying to take control of things. We might all be happier."

Stu did not see this one coming. His anger grew intense as he reflected on his efforts to bring order to their pod meetings that Dooley had made a shambles. No one else had taken leadership. He couldn't think of when he had either. Her complaint was a total fabrication designed to win Dooley over. Nevertheless, Stu was sent beyond angry to apoplectic.

"Where in the hell did that come from?"

"Well, you did let me lead this meeting, so we may be making some progress."

Dooley finally jumped in. "I like Lorelei's leadership. She should conduct more of our meetings."

"So should you, Bill." She turned to Stu. "Are you going to take this to heart, Stu? Let me hear it."

Stu sat simmering. He did not expect to hear Lorelei say those things. Knowing that she said to be prepared, Stu still resented her words, fabricated or not. *Did she mean it? Have I ever done these things? Where did she ever get such ideas?* Deep down in his soul, he feared that she might be right. He continued playing Lorelei's charade.

"I can do better. I'll start improving myself, not my partners. Samples? Yeah, you're right. I can leave fewer of them. And if I've been too bossy, I'm sorry. I'll learn to let you three take the lead. I didn't know I was doing that, and I apologize." He looked at Dooley as he spoke.

Dooley had a broad triumphant smile across his face. Stu was seething, which gave him great pleasure. He turned to Lorelei.

"Is that it? Are we done?"

"Not quite, Bill," she replied. "Let's talk about you."

"What? Me?"

"Well, I said we need all of us to stop certain things… and you're part of all of us."

"I'm not going to sit here and listen to a list of a dozen complaints about me."

"Only one, Bill. Just one. Will you listen to me for a minute?"

Dooley stood up and inched toward the front door. "I don't have time for this. I've got calls to make."

"Number one, Bill. That's all. You need to attend our meetings… like now. You're leaving when we need your input."

"Okay, here's my input. You called this meeting to fix issues with our pod. You did, so we're done."

"But Bill, we all have issues we need to address. Me, too, I will add."

"I'm out of here. I have work to do. You have wasted an hour of my time. Stay away from me and we will get along fine."

"But Bill…."

Dooley stepped angrily outside, hurried to his car, and sped away.

The three sat together dumbfounded. Murmurs and mumbling were merely comments of incredulity. Finally, Stu spoke.

"Is anyone going to believe us if we tell them what just happened?"

"Oh, hell no!" said Mike.

"I thought we had a good plan," Lorelei whispered to Stu.

"What is with this garbage you two said about Mike and me? That was totally unneeded!"

"That was our plan, remember?"

"Still, what you said was a steaming pile of bullshit!"

"It wasn't for you, Stu. It was for him."

Mike, who was less sensitive to make-believe, tried to calm Stu down.

"Stu. Just remember. It was an act."

"Well, it failed, and I'm a terrible person."

"No, you're not," Lorelei said. "We tried something, and it didn't work, but we will try again… and quit taking what I said personally. It was meant to soften up Dooley, not to get you all riled up. Quit being so sensitive."

"Now you say I am too sensitive. Is that item number four?"

That question broke the ice. The three laughed together.

"At this stage, no one can do it, except Bill himself," Mike said. "What are the odds of that?"

"Not good," Lorelei said grudgingly.

"We may be doomed," said Stu.

Lorelei, always a superb image of calm, quietly turned to each of them. With a chuckle, she reassured them.

"Coffee?" asked Lorelei.

Chapter Forty-Seven

To the surprise of the Boomers and the entire company, Connicut-Plushaut Labs purchased a third company, a smaller pharmaceutical innovator named Kappa Legend. This recent startup drug company had worked under the radar for several years developing a new therapy for a disease no one knew they had. Connicut-Plushaut Labs CEO, Harold Porter, announced the acquisition of Kappa Legend and described a new chemical entity with revolutionary capabilities. The concept was so esoteric that even he had trouble explaining it to the sales force. That was a bad sign.

It is difficult to sell a drug to a doctor who is unaware of the disease it hopes to reverse. When the complexities of a new chemical agent complicate the simplicity of marketing and sales, it's a red flag.

What Stu's company was doing was concentrating, not on its FDA-approved indication, but on its side effects? Like Seward's Folly after purchasing Alaska, Harold Porter paid the price for ice and got the value of gold.

A side effect can be bad, but often it is beneficial. Antihistamines were experimental antidepressants, before they found their niche in treating seasonal allergies and hives.

In the case of KL-101, in double-blind placebo-controlled studies of 425 patients, an amazing fact emerged. Seventeen percent of the patients in the placebo group came down with the common cold. The group that received the actual chemical KL-101 suffered no infections. Follow-up studies confirmed their earlier findings. Was this the long-sought cure for the common cold? Harold Porter was betting on its becoming a blockbuster.

Kappa Legend was cheap to buy. The development of a new indication for KL-101 was not.

After one year on the FDA fast track and a billion dollars, Connicut-Plushaut Labs introduced Rinitistas (*stasovir*), the first proven prevention and cure for the common cold. The company was the darling of the news magazines, television hosts, and doctors, who were the first to take it themselves.

That left Harold Porter with a dilemma. He had three high flying drugs at the same time. Flofral was the successful entry from Plushaut Uclaf. Tapilon was Connicut Lab's darling antibiotic. Kappa Legend's newcomer, Rinitistas, deserved the biggest push. The CEO, already known for the unorthodox, announced the new strategy at the Connicut-Plushaut Labs Annual Meeting in Orlando, Florida, in Disney World, where the company occupied two hotels in the park.

"Ladies and gentlemen, this year I'm announcing to you our sales force... a novel campaign. With the pressures to reduce drug prices and the additional yearly increase in the costs of bringing a drug like Rinitistas to market, we cannot afford to lose market share of our other two big hitters, Flofral and Tapilon.

"Tonight, I am announcing the order of priority for selling our terrific array of products.

"The number one priority for 2003 is... Rinitistas... Tapilon... Flofral.... All three are the most important products. We're going to sell them all."

For Stu it left a bitter taste in his mouth. It forced him to recall the year he had the highest sales for the year in the region without being an award winner for any single product. Back then he did sell them all. He prioritized all his drugs as equally important. Look where it got him—three nights with no sleep in the penthouse next to the raucous award winners and their honor bar.

The net result for the year was a free-for-all. Each of the three legacy companies tried to prove their drug was the winner by focusing primarily on their own innovations. It turned into a disastrous year for the company. Bitter or not, this was where Stu would shine—and he did.

Chapter Forty-Eight

THE POD'S CONFLICT with Bill Dooley continued to worsen. Not only did they have the stress of their uncooperative partner, but the pressure from management remained. No one in the company, except for Stu, Mike, and Lorelei knew the score. Somehow, Dooley had to go—or they would lose their own jobs.

After the national meeting ended, Abbott Wahl convened a meeting of his region in Oklahoma City. Reps from other states had to drive in for the one-day meeting to share their pod's plans. It was a stressful time for everyone. Hints that the company stock was falling made Connicut-Plushaut Labs a target for acquisition. Costs of research and marketing forced companies to merge or take over rivals.

Everyone in Connicut-Plushaut Labs remained uneasy. To add to the stress was the last-minute announcement that two directors from Hartford were coming to take questions at a town hall scheduled in the morning. It was a time when positions lacked stability. Many people cycled through jobs only to disappear.

At 8:00 a.m. on Monday, ninety sales reps and their managers took their seats at several tables in the large meeting room. Lance Layton glanced at his district of ten members, *or was it nine?* He stared directly at Stu.

"Where's Dooley? Anybody seen him this morning?"

Stu shrugged his shoulders. "Who knows? We can't control him."

Lance frowned at the words Stu used. *More divisiveness.* "Mike, do you know? Has he called anyone?"

"He hasn't called me...." Mike replied, then turned to Lorelei in a whisper, "...as if I give a rat's ass."

Lance looked uncertainly at Lorelei. "Lance, I don't have a clue where Bill is."

"This is just great," Lance said with sarcasm. "This won't impress the big dogs who showed up. Where is that SOB?"

Regional Manager Abbott Wahl interrupted Lance's panic and quickly brought the meeting to order. He said a few opening remarks about the fun he hoped his sales reps had over the weekends. Then he quickly introduced his two home office director guests who were pressed for time to make their next flight. Each man gave introductory remarks of a forgettable nature, then took questions. There were plenty. Their answers came directly from the corporate guidelines every rep read years before—unsatisfactory responses to serious questions.

At 8:20 a.m. the doors to the meeting room burst open. A red-faced, agitated Bill Dooley made a disruptive entrance. He strode forward to Lance's group of Boomers. Without any awareness of what business the region was conducting, he began a rant.

"I don't know why you had to start so damn early! I've been stuck in traffic, and I don't want anyone to say anything."

No one did. The room froze in silence from the shock. The home office guests were taken aback. Abbott Wahl began a gesture toward him but cut it short at the next words from Dooley.

"I've gone to meetings for almost forty years, and I have never been late... so I won't stand for anyone telling me... or making jokes...."

That brought the first sound of a titter behind him. He turned around like a cornered wild beast.

"...or making comments behind my back!"

"Bill...." Lance said.

"Let him go," Stu whispered. Dooley turned to face him next.

"You think you can get me fired. Is that your game? I'm going to announce to everybody in this room what a sick person you are. This pod of people right here... they're a disgrace. They'll try to use anything they can to blunt my success."

Dooley paused to catch his breath. His rapid breathing was an audible indication of his rage.

"I've tried for years to be successful, and I'm not going to let this stupid meeting, or the poor leadership, stop me from being number one again. I won't share my sales with anyone!"

He was out of breath again, which gave Abbott a chance to take back control of his meeting.

"Bill, we are in the middle of a town hall meeting with these gentlemen up here. Would you please take a seat?"

Dooley grabbed the back of a chair that Abbott assumed was the prelude to his taking a seat. Instead, Dooley leaned on the chair back in a semi-stooped position.

"Then I have a question... who the hell is responsible for these changes to the way we do business? I don't share my work... never will. And as for this new way we sell with all our drugs being number one priority... they should know that I have always made everything I sell number one. That is copying me. I should be getting payments for the idea, instead of having you home office weenies steal it from me."

Abbott answered first. "I think there are many advantages to...."

"I give up my vacation to work for this company, but do you expect me to carry this dead weight around with me?" He pointed at his three pod mates. They remained still and silent. Each of the three had the same thought. *Keep talking, Dooley. Keep talking.* Lance briefly sought to get him under control, but his first step brought renewed fury.

"You're probably going to try to get me for being late, but I dare you to try. I don't put up with grief from my wife and I sure as hell won't put up with you all." Looking up at Abbott and the two visitors he added. "You all need to get your act together so I can go back to work... and no mention of my lateness! I'm the best you will ever have."

The region's salesforce, still silent, watched Dooley take his seat. An uncomfortable moment was broken by the footsteps of Abbott when he stepped back to join the other two guests at the front.

"All right. I think we can continue now. The lady who asked the last question. I'm sorry, but I forget who asked it. Could you please repeat the question for our panel?"

Abbott next turned his gaze at Stu, then Mike, and finally Lorelei. All three hoped with some confidence that their boss's boss finally understood.

The meeting continued throughout the day without another word from Bill Dooley, who still believed he had set the record straight. His breathing soon returned to normal, but his face never changed to a normal color. Lorelei feared he would have a stroke. Stu and Mike expressed no concerns.

That evening, Stu got a telephone call from the region's office.

"Stu, Abbott Wahl. I'm calling you for two reasons."

"Yes, sir." Stu said, always on guard for unforeseen surprises.

"I understand now what you have been going through. Also, I want to apologize for doubting what you told Lance and me. I thought that phone call you arranged a while back was just a fluke. I was wrong. I want you to know that."

"Thank you, sir. I'm sorry you had to see that. My pod has tried very hard to make it work."

"Well now, you don't have to worry about us. It will be difficult to make changes, you understand, but you must make do the best you can... any way you want to do it."

"Bill would maybe like being fired from our pod. Can we do that?"

"Any way you want it. I'll make it happen."

"Thank you, Abbott."

"I've gotta go now and talk to your pod mates. You take care."

Abbott hung up. Stu heaved a stress relieving sigh. "Ana? Ana, where are you?"

He searched all over the house for his wife. He would not yet enjoy the moment until he could share it with the woman he loved.

Chapter Forty-Nine

THE FIRST HALF of the year was the best time anyone could remember. Having three number one priority drugs translated to no rules of engagement from on high. The pods were in control of their own success. The savvy pods in the company turned the lack of direction into an opportunity to innovate. Unique approaches were everywhere. The conversations on the company's voicemail system allowed a good idea to be shared in a forwarded message to the entire sales force. While some sent ideas or shared success stories to boost their own egos, most were in the spirit of helping everyone. Some kept their best ideas secret. That was the case for Stu's pod of three plus one.

The team knew how important relationships were to sell a drug. With two agents perceived to be more or less equal, doctors supported the drug rep they liked more. Bill Dooley was a salesman that physicians might respect but didn't like. It caused problems when selling Rinitistas. Often doctor's objections to using a new drug, until it was proven safe and effective, were reinforced by Dooley's aggressive actions. Stu stumbled on an idea after an encounter with a physician who had dug in his heals because of Dooley.

"I'm sorry, but your partner has poisoned the well for me."

"But you are missing a great chance to be a hero to your patients, if you can stop their head cold overnight."

"I wouldn't give Mister Dooley the satisfaction."

"But you're hurting Mike and Lorelei as well as your patients with that approach." Stu paused to create the right words to use. "Let's try this. Instead of thinking of Rinitistas as Dooley's drug, I want you to think of it as my drug."

"That will be hard to do."

"I have an easy solution. Instead of calling it Rinitistas, why don't you call it Rinitistu's… Stu's drug!"

The doctor found it humorous. He agreed it was a good memory device and, after some thought, he agreed to prescribe the miracle cure for the common cold—Rinitistu's.

Stu pursued this strategy with the help of his partners. Their message to every doctor was that they should write Stu's drug. "Think of it as Stu's drug… Rinitistu's but prescribe it as Rinitistas." It began to blunt Dooley's negative effects on many physicians. It even had a humorous side to it when one physician took the plan so much to heart that a pharmacist called him to request that he spell the name of the drug properly. Stu would never get a greater compliment than this degree of loyalty.

Work was fun again. Dooley left his partners alone. The other three enjoyed the best sales figures of their careers. They achieved at the midpoint of the year the highest sales of Rinitistas in the nation. Then came the phone call.

"*Have you listened to voicemail this morning?*" It was Lorelei.

"Not, yet. I'm too busy feeding four kids," Stu said.

"*There is an article in The Lancet that has gotten a couple of U.S. Senators riled up. They are calling for hearings to talk about some deaths reported in patients taking Rinitistas.*"

"You're joking, surely."

"*Listen to your voicemail. We need to meet. I'll call Mike right now.*"

"Okay, call me back."

The issue in *The Lancet* was a tempest in a teapot that soon got out of hand. Two senators of opposite political parties had joined forces "in a spirit of bipartisanship" to address the safety of products in the pharmaceutical industry. They demanded nearly perfect safety records for the industry. One death occurred in a patient who took Rinitistas. *The Lancet* report was in the Letter to the Editor column, written by a physician well-known for reporting negatives about any drug not yet gone generic. Simon Tiger, M.D., wrote that an *eighty-one-year-old female patient took twice the recommended dose of Rinitistas. Subsequently, the patient experienced respiratory distress and died in the emergency room.*

There were several factors that Stu could object to. The dose was inappropriate but likely not a factor. The dose of Rinitistas was based on the maximum therapeutic benefit, not on any need to limit any adverse effects. A second factor had for years been an irritant to him. The FDA required evaluators to report every side effect. The lady was taking a pill to counter the upper respiratory distress of a severe common cold virus. Doctor Tiger claimed respiratory distress as a possible cause of death. Stu could paraphrase him better. *The virus didn't cause respiratory distress. The drug did.* So why was she taking the drug? The doctor also claimed that a death so early after launch was a clear indication of its high fatality risk. In the first six months since its launch, Connicut-Plushaut Labs sold prescriptions to half a million patients. This was a good start for a new drug that treated a previously untreatable condition. Doctor Tiger claimed that a death rate of two in a million patients for any drug was unacceptable. The two bipartisan U.S. senators in Washington agreed.

Weeks went by. Stu's drug once more got pushback from physicians. It turned into an albatross around his neck which affected his success with the other two number one priority products. With increasing frequency, Stu listened to a familiar message from his doctors.

"I'm sure it is a fine drug, and I will still use it, but patients watch the news and read their newspapers. They don't ask for it now. When I suggest they try it, they are reluctant."

"It doesn't seem fair, does it?"

"Nothing is fair in my line of work. Without sick people, we'd both be out of a job."

"I think the real losers are the patients. They don't deserve this."

Senate hearings at the end of the year commenced with a condemnation of both the FDA and Connicut-Plushaut Labs. CEO Harold Porter testified before a senate committee, trying to defend the research and development process of his company. He also defended the FDA's approval process and its fast-track process for approval of critically important drugs. Porter's time before the panel was an unpleasant experience he would never forget nor forgive.

A subcommittee in the FDA revisited the approval of Rinitistas, voted to leave the status of the drug unchanged, and reiterated its safety. But a new month brought new obstacles—and a second reported death in the news. Journalists were on the hunt.

The two bipartisan senators and their large entourage made a visit to the FDA headquarters at the White Oak Campus in Silver Spring, Maryland. They made it clear to the FDA approval committee members that an annual budget review was in the works. That was the FDA kiss of death. With over a billion dollars spent, Connicut-Plushaut executives chose to put Rinitistas out of its misery.

More than one doctor made an interesting observation.

"Under this FDA, it would be impossible to get aspirin approved as a prescription for any patients or any uses."

Bean counters still had to add in the after-costs of manufacturing, sales, and marketing. Another good drug was dead and gone forever—and patients still wondered why their prescriptions cost so much money.

THE PHARMACEUTICAL INDUSTRY changed rapidly with new restrictive federal laws on the sales force. The industry shared blame by building up sales forces that tripped over each other while calling on fewer doctors. Managed Care turned physicians from healers into paper pushers.

Regulators banned dining with a physician's spouse. It had been a treat for spouses, who were often the glue that made the dinner a good business investment. Federal laws sucked the joy out of personal relationships.

Regulators soon banned dining completely. Giveaways, those little trinkets which functioned to keep the name and spelling of a drug in view, got the axe.

Companies ordered their salesmen to destroy or trash their supplies of penlights, ear thermometers, blood pressure cuffs, stethoscopes, tissues, umbrellas, lotion, key rings, windshield shades, clocks, stress balls, paperweights, antimicrobial wipes, and rolls of exam paper. Drug samples appeared likely next on the chopping block.

Stu was relegated to calls of plain vanilla on a tiny tasteless cone. Paying thousands of sales reps to do less was not sustainable for the industry. He evaluated his prospects for the sunset of his career with sadness. He wanted to quit before he became like the older reps he used to avoid—those bitter old souls constantly griping about their jobs and praising the good old days. If he could only hang on a bit longer. He decided to reinvent himself and again learn to make it fun—just a little while longer.

ONE SOLUTION TO Stu's unhappiness came in an unexpected call. It was never what he hoped would happen.

"Stu, this is Lance. Sit down for this one."

"I'm sitting down. Tell me it's good news."

Lance laughed nervously.

"I'm sure you'll agree it's not what we wanted to happen. Bill Dooley passed away this morning. He developed a headache. It grew in severity. He stroked out while making a call."

"Were you working with him?"

"Yeah, I was with him when it happened. I told him earlier he should go home, but you know what a hard-headed S.O.B. he is."

"How's his wife taking it?"

"I don't know. She seemed upset obviously... but I've gotta say, she might be relieved. At least that's what Dooley himself used to tell me."

"Well, I'm sorry for the guy. Even as miserable as he was, he deserved to die after enjoying a little retirement or something."

Lance was laughing into the phone. "What do you think his last words were?"

"I hope I can quote them. Tell me."

"He said, 'I've never been to a doctor or taken a pill in my whole life... and I'm not going to start now.'"

Chapter Fifty

BILL DOOLEY DIED without a will. Missus Dooley had no access to his bank accounts or to any important records. She was a wife who tuned her husband out completely. That worked well since he worked even in his sleep. It did not serve her well, if she could not find their marriage license, any checkbooks, or a warranty deed to their house. She lived in a small house with little furniture or possessions. Calling Social Security offices to get help, they turned her away when she could not produce Bill's Social Security number. Out of desperation, she called the only man she knew who may have been his friend.

Jimmy Tomey retired nine years before. He was the first Boomer Stu met that first afternoon in the parking lot before his first division meeting. Jimmy was always helpful, showing kindness in the same manner to everyone, including Bill Dooley, when they both worked for Finn Trottel. The seemingly heartless Dooley confessed to his wife that Jimmy was kind to him. Rare for him, he included words of appreciation. For Missus Dooley, her call to Jimmy was a wise one.

The Dooley funeral was on a Saturday when there were no competing public events to prevent a large crowd of reps, doctors, pharmacists, and spouses from attending. Missus Dooley asked Jimmy Tomey to officiate a secular occasion. Dooley never talked about church.

Now it was clear that, like not going for a doctor exam, he had never been to a church either.

Stu arrived at the funeral home fifteen minutes early, as was his habit. He signed the guest book, noting that he was number eleven. He looked around the lobby for others, but only a poorly dressed man of thirty walked past him. The man failed to acknowledge his presence. He followed behind him into the funeral chapel. The space could easily fit two hundred people. No one else sat inside. Stu returned to the lobby to wait, fearing he was in the wrong location.

A hand firmly clasped Stu's shoulder. Stu turned his head around and smiled.

"Jimmy Tomey! How are you, old man? How's retirement?"

"Retirement is still good."

"I'm beginning to think about it myself."

"You're still working? Why did I think you retired?"

"I look old to you, I guess."

"Not at all. I do feel a lot of pressure here. Everyone else here are Bill's relatives, mostly his in-laws... I'm sorry to ask, but they want me to say some kind words about Bill... and I'm glad you're here because I don't know what to say."

"You mean we're it... as people from work? I was afraid I was in the wrong place."

"I'm afraid we're it."

"Well Jimmy, we are salesmen. We can come up with something flattering to say about old Bill."

"So why are you here?"

"Because I feared no one else would come. He was my partner, you know."

"You had to work with him?" Stu nodded. "That must have been awful!"

Stu laughed briefly then got down to business. He looked at his watch. Jimmy had a pen and a sticky notepad with Flatulaide printed on it.

"Okay, you have about seven minutes, so jot this down. Bill had the most impressive work ethic of any rep in Plushaut Uclaf. Forget the other company. Just use Plushaut." Jimmy madly scribbled it all down word for word.

"Next... he was the most successful pharmaceutical salesman in the history of the company. That is true by the way... for sure. Doctors would comment that he always seemed to be in their office."

Jimmy laughed at the last sentence. He knew Stu meant it as a double entendre. Dooley's habit was to constantly get in a doctor's face. It only seemed like he was always in their office.

"How about... he inspired everyone to work at a higher level? Every doctor, nurse, and pharmacist knew his name. He brought out the leadership potential in others. That's enough to fill your time."

Jimmy stayed focused on his notepad. He looked up at Stu.

"What can I say about his wife?"

The question hit them both the same way. They broke out laughing together.

"I don't know what to tell you to say there. All you and I know about her likely came from him, Jimmy Boy. I'd keep that to myself."

"I do remember that he told me his 401k account was all in cash. He always put in the maximum."

"Well, the 401k option began the year I was hired, so he has at least twenty-five years of hoarding money tax free to make quite a nest egg of cash for Missus... what is her first name anyway?"

"I don't know either. I better find out before I get up there to speak."

Jimmy quickly headed to the family room to get more information. Stu moved to the chapel. He found a seat on the left near the back. He wanted to count how many were there. As much of a problem as Dooley was to Mike, Lorelei, and him, he bowed his head in a prayer for his soul in heaven. He ached for his family's grief, that they had to see so few people in attendance. He read the obituary provided at the door. It turned out to be only bullet points of his life—date of birth, birthplace, date of death, mother, father, and the name Julie, his daughter. It told a sad tale of a colorless life.

The family came into the chapel to the soothing sounds of recorded music. By now there were four people to stand up and pay respects to the family. Jimmy came in behind the family, walking up to the front. He took a seat behind the podium and patiently waited while the women of the family tried to arrange seating for a couple of grandchildren. Stu counted twelve family members. The music faded away. Jimmy had his moment and stood up to give his opening remarks. The soprano voice, singing "How Great Thou Art," intervened. He sat down again, looking carefully at the order of service. Stu glanced at his own copy. The unexpected solo hymn was not on the program. Jimmy waited as the singer sang the slowest version ever performed. It gave Stu a chance to glance at the photograph of Dooley on the front of his folded obituary. Dooley's portrait was of a dower looking man wearing a T-shirt at a Plushaut national meeting emblazoned with an overused theme, *Tapilon Kills Bugs!* Even in death, he tried to sell.

Jimmy stood up again and waited for the final notes of the hymn to end. Since he had to wait for "How Great Thou Art," he decided to offer a prayer in defiance of Missus Dooley's secular wishes. His invocation was tasteful and preciously short.

"...Amen. Thank you for coming to celebrate the life of William James Dooley. Bill led a full life of devotion to his family and his career. We spent many days together as fellow salesmen in the pharmaceutical industry. You can't work with someone for twenty-five years without getting to know them extremely well. He was unique in his drive to excel. We were peers in the same company, not competitors... thank goodness. Bill demonstrated a work ethic, the marvel of his fellow salesmen within the company, Plushaut Uclaf. He was feared by his competitors. He was an unrelenting powerhouse in the industry. Doctors would comment that he always seemed to be in their office."

Jimmy paused. He began to choke on something. Stu started to choke also. Both tried their best to suppress a laugh that would be highly undignified. Jimmy practiced his breathing to mask his feelings. To the family, he might have appeared to be crying. Upon recovering his composure, he continued.

"He inspired everyone. Every doctor, nurse, and pharmacist knew his name."

Missus Dooley was certain now that Jimmy was crying. Jimmy held his hand to his face and remained silent until he recovered his dignity.

"We talked on occasion about planning for the future. Bill planned well and shared with me that when he died, his wife would be a millionaire."

Missus Dooley's head shot up. She stared a laser beam of attention toward the podium. Now she listened to something of interest. She focused her grief to his words.

"We all have that hope, but I think with his success in life, he may have achieved his goal."

Missus Dooley beamed with pride as she sat up a little straighter in her seat. Her husband, she decided, was a good provider after all.

"Let me summarize my feelings about my friend, Bill Dooley. I am pleased to say that this man is a former colleague of mine. May we all rest in peace."

He put his hand once again to his face as recorded bagpipes began droning "Amazing Grace." As he stepped down to take a seat, Stu put both hands to his face from the back of the chapel. He kept his face covered that way for an uncomfortable length of time. Soon his laughter subsided, and he regained his composure.

Later in the day over too much beer and looking back on Bill Dooley's career, Jimmy and Stu agreed they were happy that Bill Dooley was a former colleague of theirs. They clinked their beer mugs and together said, "May we rest in peace."

Chapter Fifty-One

A MONTH AFTER Bill Dooley's funeral, the pod had a new member, Nora Chase, fresh from college graduation. The pod was at first apprehensive that Lance had hired the exact opposite of Dooley—unmotivated, overly friendly, and too needy. To the delight of everyone in Lance's Boomer District, Nora was fearless, brilliant, and capable. However, she was young and had a lot to learn. Lorelei became her mentor. It wasn't long before the two women came to a pod meeting with a great tale of an awkward question Nora asked some nurses. She was already comfortable enough to tell the embarrassing story on herself.

"We went to see Doctor Castle, a podiatrist, on Classen Boulevard. Bill's notes said that the best time to see him was just before noon. So, Lorelei and I get there about ten minutes early. I grabbed things, filled my bag, and we go in there, right?"

She had a beautiful smile that melted the hearts of Mike and Stu. She was of the generation that was taller than the women of even twenty years before. She had medium length curly chestnut brown hair. She dressed tastefully, which helped male doctors pay attention to product visuals rather than thighs or cleavage. She laughed as she told her story.

"I walked into the most marvelous smell of lunch. I didn't know they let reps bring them lunch. It's such a small office. Well anyway, I walked in. I noticed Lorelei making a face. I didn't think much of it. I thought maybe she was a vegan or something."

"I may become one," Lorelei replied.

"So here we are. Lunch smells so good. I handed my card to the nurses standing at the reception desk. They look like they are not happy to see another drug rep. I try to be friendly, okay? So, I dramatically give a big whiff of the lunch that's cooking. I gave them an 'um... um!' They had a funny look on their faces when I did that. I thought I better be quick and clarify my silly comment, so I asked them. 'What's for lunch? It sure smells good!'"

Mike was catching on fast. "Oh no. You didn't...."

"They started laughing at me. I was so confused and embarrassed... and Lorelei, my buddy, was stepping back laughing her... you-know-what off. So, I turned back to the nurses and just simply asked them. 'What did I say?' You know what they said?"

"I know what they said," Mike said. Lorelei was laughing again. Stu still didn't have a clue.

"'That's not lunch, sweety. Doctor Castle is in a room burning calluses off a patient's feet.'"

Nora laughed harder than anyone. It was easy to like someone who enjoyed who she was. The team cemented quickly. It was time to show the company that they were number one because of their team, not because of one super salesman who had sucked the joy out of his own life.

THE YEAR WAS 2008—three years after Nora joined Connicut-Plushaut Labs as a Boomer in Stu's pod. Changes in the industry came at a rapid pace. Physicians Assistants and Nurse Practitioners were taking over many responsibilities once the sole tasks of physicians, especially in the rural areas of Oklahoma. Drug samples became the next hot topic in Congress. In his nearly thirty years in pharmaceuticals, Stu was seeing a slow creep in restrictions and requirements to account for drug samples. He got inspired from his earlier one hundred ideas and suggestions and sent another letter to CEO Harold Porter. What could he lose? He was of retirement age.

Connicut-Plushaut Labs
Hartford, Connecticut
Harold Porter, CEO
July 22, 2008
Dear Mister Porter,

In the spirit of sharing ideas and sharing observations from a veteran rep in the trenches, permit me to make the following historical observations.

Sampling has evolved into an arithmetic nightmare. Twenty-eight years ago, I gave out samples. That's it. Twenty years ago, I reported the number of samples I left. Fifteen years ago, I counted how many samples I had. Ten years ago, I subtracted the number of samples I left from the number of samples I had in my possession and reported the result. Eight years ago, I had to explain why the result did not match the count of samples I had in my storage closet. This year I now must include the lot numbers of samples I have minus the lot numbers of samples I leave. It's like evolving a simple formula $a-b=c$ into a convoluted formula $(a+b+d+c+f+e+m+w+?)-(l+p+u+j+?)=audit$.

Now in high school, a grade of 92 on a math test got you a grade of "A." In the real world, as we learn constantly, "A" ain't good enough. Bean counters expect near perfection.

In my 29 years of experience as a pharmaceutical salesman, if my computer can generate a number, there is someone in the home office who wants to count it, then beat me over the head with it. My only question is who will count it first - the company bean counter or the federal bean counter? They are now both telling me that my numbers are wrong. Since they both already seem to know the answer, I sure as hell wish they would give it to me, saving me all that trouble.

Sincerely,
Stuart Roy
Oklahoma City

There was talk that the next Congressional ban would be drug samples. Some reasons made sense. First, of course, was that nobody could count. Also, samples left in a car's trunk in the summer could bake all day at the same temperature as a slow-cooked barbecue brisket. Samples were poorly accounted for in the doctor's office. Petty theft in clinics was common. Even drug reps would borrow a sample occasionally. Stu had done that, but always asked the doctor first. Competitive samples often made good visuals when comparing them to his line of products. Salesmen from different companies occasionally traded samples for personal use. Some of the tiny samples of creams and ointments cost more to manufacture per tube than the actual prescription size.

Salesmen had persuasive arguments for continuing drug samples. It was often the only hook that got a drug rep any chance to talk to a doctor. Patients benefited immensely from the option to try out a drug for safety and effectiveness before they paid money for the prescription. It benefited a doctor to give samples to a patient so they could compare two or more competitive drugs. The patients could choose the drug that worked best for them. It meant less work and worry for the doctor.

The saddest part of a changing industry was the thirty-year dwindling value of the job as a pharmaceutical salesman. The days of fifteen to thirty-minute consultations with physicians were over. A detail man became a pharmaceutical salesman became a drug rep. The only title left was deliveryman, but now with an empty trunk and no samples, that title was not descriptive.

Nora in her first three years had learned a lot and seen a lot. A great storyteller, she loved to bring a new one to every meeting. In her relatively short tenure, she understood the momentum of changes and knew how it affected her own joy of working. She had adapted in her life the same values as Stu had shared with her about his own growth in the job. Don't be a grouch as you get older. Learn to adapt and innovate to make the job fun. Don't hang around negative people.

For Stu, it was becoming true that his job had less fun to it. He was getting close to the point of the job being just a job. He had vowed to retire while he was having a good time. Nora's optimism served to extend his career a few years more.

Chapter Fifty-Two

It was the twilight of Stu's career in late 2009. Christmas time was no different than the other thirty Christmases Stu worked. Doctors didn't care to talk shop. They wanted to just talk. That was okay with Stu because he didn't care either. He determined that 2010 would be his last year. He kept it to himself. Mike Austin was suspicious. Lorelei was certain. Nora knew because Lorelei talked about her intuition. Ana was concerned if they could afford for Stu to retire. Stu told her that one more year and the job would no longer be fun. It was time.

The company was a buyout target. Drugs in the pipeline that showed promise were dashed on the rocks of an overly cautious FDA. Connicut-Plushaut Labs stock was down. Other bigger companies were licking their chops. The company realigned all the reps' territories, hoping that stirring the pot would pay dividends. For many of Stu's doctors, who over time relocated, were now having mini reunions with him. One was unexpected.

Selling his office building and electing to move to a small office downtown near historic Saint Anthony's Hospital was tyrant, mentor, and shot-doctor Franz Joseph Steuben, D.O. His relocation changed all the data for whales and minnows. He was curtailing his practice. Once the biggest writer in several counties, he was now a minnow. Out of curiosity, Stu put in a card one afternoon. His waiting room was empty. He had a single nurse, the longtime and tolerant Martha, who doubled as his receptionist. Within minutes Doctor Steuben called him back to his office. Stu had never been in Doctor Steuben's office. He bet he was the first rep to have the privilege.

Stu was surprised by the plain walls, modest desk, and disorder in his workspace. It contrasted with his meticulous clothing—charcoal slacks with crisp seams, open collar white dress shirt, and white leather shoes—a habit from his Navy days.

"Come in here, Stu." He marveled that the man remembered his name. "I've been here for a year, and you are the first detail man to come see me."

Steuben's behavior was so out of character, Stu used caution in answering.

"I'm surprised to hear you say that."

"Well, all you old timers have retired. Those kids they hire these days do what they are told. I don't count for much anymore."

"They have no clue what they're missing." Stu decided to be more bold. "Reps used to be terrified of you."

"Not you, apparently."

"No, not me. I rather enjoyed the experience once I knew the rules."

Doctor Steuben quietly chuckled at the comment. "I was a busy man until I fell down a flight of stairs."

"I heard about that. I didn't know it affected your practice."

"It taught me a lesson."

"What was that, sir?"

"Stop drinking. Stop chasing women. It was grand while it lasted, but it began to make me tired. Know when to hang it up, son."

Stu reflected on his admonition. He already knew when he was going to hang it up.

"But you're still here. You aren't out of it, yet."

"Yes, but I'm looking back, not looking forward."

Steuben's comment intrigued him. "Looking back... any regrets?"

It was a bold move. To his surprise, Steuben smiled as he mulled over how to answer. Stu realized that no one had ever had the guts to ask him that question.

"Interesting question... yes, I have regrets, but I don't dwell on them. I was not the most loyal husband." He laughed in a way that meant he didn't feel sorry for the women in his life or regret how he used them. "Those were good times. Now my pecker has retired."

Stu smiled at the coarse reference, remembering in earlier years how this doctor every so often referenced some bawdy activity during his weekend. Suddenly, he realized that the man, after thirty years of being called on, viewed him as a friend. By all measures of conduct over that time, Stu never considered that Doctor Steuben was glad to see him on those sales calls.

"I've always wanted to ask you something. What's your story? Where did you grow up?"

His eyes brightened. He was ready to talk, after years of unrelenting focus on his medical practice.

"I was the youngest of six brothers and sisters in Ohio. We all worked hard from an early age. My father labored to bring food to the table, while Mama corralled us, motivated us, and fed us. Dad expected us to work and promised he would give each of us a college education, if we earned it." His eyes got glassy with emotion. "He put us all through college. I got my pharmacy degree, then a scholarship to osteopathic medical school through a Navy program. I finished at the top in medical school... even got a Ph.D. in pharmacology... went into the Navy for six years, then opened my practice where you first called on me."

"Korean War?"

"That was the era, but I spent my time on a ship in the Mediterranean, going from port to port all over Europe, Asia, and Africa. I had a hell of a good time, but I knew someday they would assign me to a ship in some hellhole part of the ocean and I would lose the perks of those port calls."

"Were you married at the time or were you an out-of-control single man?"

"Navy is not a place for a married man."

"Any children?"

He grinned like a kid caught in the act but proud of the deed. "Eight children from five different women."

"Married five times, eh?"

"The best one was number three. Can't remember what went wrong with that one."

"Are you talking about wives or kids?"

"Wives... wives. My kids are all grown. I produced three doctors, two pharmacists, two navy officers, and a stay-at-home mom."

"Scattered all over the country, I assume."

"If they want to see me, they must come here. I was always too busy to travel to them. They are independent... don't see me a lot."

Stu let his guard down completely.

"If I knew all of this about you, I wouldn't have been so afraid of you all these years."

He grinned again. "Yeah."

"You see many patients here?"

"Probably ten percent of what I used to see. I can't give shots to patients anymore... not like I used to do."

"HMOs. Managed care. They've ruined both of our careers."

"You even have samples anymore?"

"We do, but I don't carry them in my car. You sign a slip and they mail them to you."

"Well, send me some."

"I can't."

He looked at Stu with those penetrating eyes he remembered from years before.

"You can't?"

"I can only arrange sample deliveries for a list of doctors given to me by the bean counters in their ivory tower in Hartford, Connecticut. I have no choice."

"Well, you can't change things… I know. Everything is out of our hands anymore."

Stu waited a moment in case he wanted to add more. It was time to go.

"Doctor Steuben, I guess I've been here long enough. This has been a real pleasure getting to sit down with you like this. I enjoyed the whole thirty years, and you were a part of the fun."

"Likewise, son." His smile was warm with a hint of sadness. "Come back to see me. I'd like to hear your story. Thanks for coming to see me."

They shook hands. As Stu walked out of his office, he spoke a few words to Martha. She had a loyalty to her doctor that was common for many nurses and their older doctors. They often became like a platonic married couple, arguing and shouting at each other one minute, then defending each other the next.

"Martha, good to see you again. Thanks for letting me break through the gate into the back. What a contrast."

Martha smiled. "I'm so glad you came. Doctor Steuben is very lonely right now with just a few patients who insist on him only. He has this office open only because of them. You will never know how much your visit will lift his spirits. God bless you, Stu."

Chapter Fifty-Three

WHILE ALL CHAOS reigned in the industry, CEO Harold Porter launched a training program based on a new way to approach sales. Stu already knew it. He learned it from experience. The premise was that there are four basic personality types among doctors. A dozen companies jumped on the bandwagon with their own names for the four categories. Stu had given them his own pet names—*Touchy-Feely-Needies, Frat Boys, Eggheads,* and *Space Cadets.*

Stu summarized a second aspect of Porter's training program as, *find out what the doctor wants and give it to him.*

The training became more complicated than Stu's succinct phrases. He lived by his own pet motto, *the less I say, the more you remember.* Stu more aptly described their personality training as, *the longer the training goes, the more confused we will be.*

Of the four personality categories, Stu found the *Touchy-Feely-Needies* the worst to call on. As a rule, these doctors would tell Stu anything that would make him happy. They needed sales reps to like them. Their conversation would go like this. Assume Doctor Jones writes none of Stu's drugs.

"Doctor Jones, what do you think of Flofral?"

"Stu, there's no better drug on the market. I use it all the time."

Unlike the *Touchy-Feely-Needy* types, the *Frat Boys* didn't care what they prescribed. They had the loyalty of a dog in heat. Doctor Jones's encounter with the sales rep would be open and honest.

"Doctor Jones, what do you think of Flofral?"

"Good stuff. If you want me to write some for you, I'll be happy to do so."

Eggheads were tough calls. They thrived on data, science, and peer research. They were slow to adopt a new concept. Calls on them required a good knowledge of the technical. Make a mistake and a rep could lose his credibility. Doctor Jones would respond in this way.

"Doctor Jones, what do you think of Flofral?"

"Mister Roy, I studied that paper from Annals you left me about *heptoxifylline*. Don't talk to me about that paper again. The design of the study is all wrong. I don't believe any research with a validity of only 0.05%. You show me one with 0.01% validity and we can talk. I also checked in your package insert to see what the most prevalent effects are. I disagree with those findings. I sometimes wonder what the FDA is thinking because *heptoxifylline*, in my clinical experience, does not work that way. I studied under Mayhew at Cleveland Clinic, and he is the one who drew me to the attention of that mistake in *heptoxifylline's* package insert... but so far I'm very pleased with its efficacy and safety."

The *Space Cadets* were the weirdest of all. They were future oriented, loved chrome and glass, black and white décor, and made no sense when they talked, which was usually rapid. Stu, who had never made sense of them, decided they were all schizophrenic or in a permanent bipolar manic phase. They espoused wild theories, fast cars, hot nurses, and fifteen seconds of time for a sales rep. Stu couldn't figure them out, but he sometimes envied them. If Doctor Jones was a *Space Cadet*, the call would go like this.

"Doctor Jones, what do you think of Flofral?"

"Sure."

Giving the doctor what he wanted was another simple bit of advice that took a couple of days of training before people got totally confused.

Find out what the doctor wants and give it to him sounded clear enough to Stu and the rest of the Boomers. There were a few corollaries. *Give it to him if it's not illegal, immoral, or unethical.* That issue was no problem for members of the Boomers, who had a reputation in the company of being rules driven. But those other pods had never had a Bill Dooley in their midst to set the standard of what not to be. For the Boomers, a two-hour review would be overkill. Instead, it took up two long and wasted days.

In all enterprises, change over time must be addressed with innovation. The work the company did teaching sales skills was a clue to where the company was headed. Their new emphasis was not on introducing a new drug, but the preservation of sales of the old. It looked like a race within the FDA between new drugs being approved and new drugs being pulled off the market. The scientific findings by the medical researchers mattered less than the opinions of congressional crusaders around drug safety, cost, and profit. The phrase, "we're not out to kill people for profit," did not fit well into a sales call, but drug reps were on defense. Good drugs left the market. It angered Stu to see a new drug from any company get pulled because the safety was not better than a generic of a less effective class of drugs. Stu's Rinitistas was not the only drug pulled from the market for a death rate of one in a million. In 2008, there were 37,423 traffic deaths in the United States. The death rate for 304.1 million citizens was 123 deaths per million. No one clamored for the recall of automobiles. The fun was gone from being a pharmaceutical salesman. The government, by congressional proxy, deemed sales reps as unwanted.

With those dreary thoughts bouncing around in Stu's head he slowed his pace in the last few weeks of his planned retirement. He disliked the increasing number of offices that further limited his access to their doctors. He sat in a multi-specialty office near Baptist Hospital when a rep from a competing drug company walked in. Barry Tanner was a competitor and friend of over twenty years.

"You mind if I put in a card?"

"Go for it, Barry. There are only two here this afternoon... Sanford and Greaves. Payne and Lester are gone this week. I don't know if you call on any of the others."

"Seen either one yet?"

"I saw Greaves. He seems to be in a foul mood today. I'm waiting for Sanford."

"How long a wait?"

"Not bad today. I'd try it, then sit down and tell me what's new."

Barry went to the receptionist, chatted and flirted for a minute, then joined Stu to wait.

"Done any good today?" Stu asked.

"Yeah, kind of an interesting day. There's been a lot of doctor turnover in offices around here."

"Who?"

"You call on neurologists?"

Stu shook his head.

"Well, anyway, they built their own building way north of here near Edmond. They moved out last week. Word has it that if you're in a car wreck with a head injury, you better hope it's near their new office because they're not always in the other hospitals anymore. They're holding out for some ungodly sum of money for being on call."

"Who's in those offices now?"

"There's one doctor in there so far. He came from somewhere outside of Oklahoma City. I've never heard of him before. He's fairly old... maybe sixty-five, just a guess."

"Who is he? Maybe I know him."

Barry pulled a card from his shirt pocket. Stu noticed another trend now more widespread. His friend did not wear a coat, just slacks, dress shirt, and a tie.

"Let's see here. I never called on him, just picked up his card. He's a family doctor by the name of Trevor Addicus, M.D. You know a Doctor Addicus?"

"Yes! Yes, indeed I do."

Thirty minutes later after chatting with Barry, Stu went into the back to talk with Doctor Sanford, an egghead/space cadet, who for thirty seconds listened without visible emotion to Stu. He left to see another patient with a one-word answer.

"Okay."

Emerging from the back, he passed his friend, waved, and moved quickly outside to his car. He was heading to the old neurology building to see his old buddy, the once methamphetamine-addicted Doctor Addicus.

Chapter Fifty-Four

STU GREW AMBIVALENT as he sat in his car. Ironically, he again was in a Chevy Malibu, like he drove thirty years before—the first and last time he called on Doctor Addicus. Some events in a person's life burn indelibly into their conscience. There were few days in his career that Stu had not thought of that day. He feared the doctor behind the desk was dying as he frantically gripped the edge. He stupidly gave his sales pitch to a possibly dying man. There were rumors of his days that followed. Doctor Addicus disappeared, leaving him as only a crazy story to tell other sales reps while waiting to see doctors.

One question going through Stu's head was what if this was possibly Doctor Addicus, the son. He had to know for sure. In some ways, this would be closure for him. Like class reunions, this would give him a chance to see if he made a success of his life. As he pulled into the expansive parking lot, he parked among several cars—more than he expected for a one-doctor office.

The three-story building, built with a limestone exterior and accents of other stone, had an arched doorway with a heavy oak door. Stu entered an ornate marble-floored lobby with rich oak molding from floor to ceiling, framing an exquisite array of wall murals. The doctor's office was to his left on the first floor.

Stepping through the door of Doctor Addicus's waiting room, he was surprised at the contrast in style. His office was spartan, unlike the ornate crown molding and beautiful marble of the buildings entrance. His guess was these were furnishings he bought from the neurologists. It was an eclectic mixture of lamps, tables, and chairs that had seen better days. To his inner joy, the office looked busy. Seven patients waited for a nurse to call them to the back. At the counter were two nurses and a receptionist. Stu came up, placed a card before the receptionist, and gave them an introduction.

"Hi, I'm Stuart Roy. It's my first time here, but I called on Doctor Addicus years ago. I'm hoping I came at a good time." He turned his head around to the seven patients. "It looks like he has a successful practice already."

An older nurse looked over at him. "You called on him before, you say?"

"Yes, ma'am."

"How long ago?" Stu recognized her and broke into a smile.

"Your name is Mary. You were there… about thirty years ago."

"Oh my!" Her face turned red with apprehension.

"Well, that was a long time ago. It must have been memorable if you remember my name."

"Yes, ma'am, it was… is there a best time to see him?"

"Well let me see…." She looked at his business card, "…Mister Roy."

"Please, call me Stu."

"Okay, Stu. If you come back at eight o'clock tomorrow morning, I know he will be glad to see you. He hasn't seen a drug rep in a long time… I doubt if he will remember you, but I will tell him you're coming."

"Look for me, Mary… and good to see you again."

STU CAME TO the clinic door fifteen minutes early. He waited until 8:00 a.m. before Mary unlocked the door to let him in. She paused with him briefly to offer a word of advice.

"Stu, he is not the man you may remember. His career is back on track and he's still a very good physician."

"Thanks for letting me get another chance to talk to him."

"Well, come on back." She led him briskly back to the offices of Doctor Trevor Addicus, M.D. for the second time in three decades.

Stu did not see the man he first met so long ago. Where once there was a young dark-haired man slightly overweight, here was a man with wavy-silvered hair, gaunt face, and the body of a runner. He didn't stand up. Rather he greeted Stu in the imperious manner of a man above Stu's station. Somehow his behavior made Stu happier. Addicus was no longer the man Stu's manager, Finn Trottel, told him about when he said, "He is known to do what detail men tell him to do." Instead, Doctor Addicus addressed him like any other doctor did—short of time and impatient to get on with his day. His first words, though, shocked Stu.

"Stu, I understand you used to call on me years ago?"

"Yes, sir. It was 1980 on my first week in the field as a brand-new drug rep."

Doctor Addicus's expression changed to one of reflection and sadness. "I'm afraid I don't remember anything from back then. I started my practice again in 1985, after some time away from medicine. I went to the Oklahoma Department of Mental Health and Substance Abuse Services, then about ten years ago I got an itch to go back into private practice. I've been in Yukon for the past eight years... decided to slow down with an office here, but you saw yesterday. My patients followed me."

Stu got confused. "That's a long time to be there. Were you in therapy or...."

"I counseled addicted doctors and dentists."

"I see. Forgive me for being confused."

"It's been a passion for me ever since my time away from medicine to help others. I still work at the Department of Mental Health. I'm an adviser with Substance Abuse Services. I also do counseling of doctors and dentists for a private drug and alcohol rehabilitation home just east of here. You can add the work I do at the Oklahoma State Medical Association as a substance abuse counselor. Then I have my private practice."

"I'm exhausted hearing your list of duties."

He laughed at Stu's comment, but it was a controlled laugh, like someone who remained keenly aware of each reaction he had. Doctor Addicus knew the truth. Every day for him was a battle to hold back the demons.

"I've found keeping busy is my salvation. I've become a religious man, who believes Jesus Christ saved me, but I wake up every morning and pray to him a promise that I will stay clean for just one more day. I've prayed the same prayer for at least... oh, twenty-five years or more."

"Well, sir, it's a pleasure to see you again and know that you are doing so well."

Doctor Addicus looked at Stu with a grudging smile. "So, what do you have to sell me this morning?"

Stu laughed before he spoke. "I may have a few drugs I didn't sell in 1980."

BACK IN HIS car, Stu wanted to write up his call, but the computer he used for work was nothing more than a time stamp for doctor calls. Doctor Addicus was not on his list of doctors he was paid to call on. The time spent selling Doctor Addicus would be of no benefit to his paycheck and yearly bonus, but for his soul it was a big payday. Stu had gone full circle in his career and was back with a single doctor who had such a significant impact on him. First, a drug addict profoundly opened his eyes to the human condition that could be so self-destructive. It toppled his image of all doctors being in ivory towers. Then, there he was with the same human, who was not the same person at all. It gave him a feeling he did not quite yet understand. He couldn't put a word on it.

Stu made a mental list of the many encounters with people that fit that same word. Some ended with it, but most did not. Bill Dooley did not. Stu doubted that Rose Astor the Disaster qualified. He still could not grasp the right description or the word. He also recalled Doctor Lane who treated people from his jail cell. Finn Trottel taking salary away from his reps, simply to impress others. Cissy Bordon, who ended rep careers like Lizzy Borden ended lives. Would Ben Hodge, The Fart-man, ever grow up and quit his childish antics? Hollywood Bill Brighton's Quaalude writing frenzy landed him in the El Reno Federal Reformatory for half a decade. Although he tried to get back into a medical practice, he was a broken man. Stu had known philandering doctors, alcoholic drug reps, and home office personnel who had nearly brought Plushaut Uclaf to ruin.

While most doctors, managers, pharmacists, drug reps, nurses, and competitors were good friends and honorable, Stu's memories kept coming back to the lost souls he knew. He worried for them. Finally, the word came to him. It possibly applied to him as well. He had had his moments of regret in his career. He thought again of the two biggest changes for the good he so recently encountered after calling on Doctors Steuben and Addicus. They were the two greatest examples for Stu of one reinventing a lost soul and allowing room for forgiveness.

There was a place left in the world for anyone to find the word—*redemption*.

Chapter Fifty-Five

STU SAT QUIETLY on his comfortable living room sofa with Ana. The children were all there with grandkids in tow. He had spent the past few hours reminiscing with them about his career, the people he met, and the challenges he faced. He was surprised with himself how much he enjoyed telling them of his challenges, not his triumphs.

But he thought also about the metaphor of the squeaky wheel. Everyone complains of the squeaky wheel on the wagon, but they never praise the other three wheels that give them no trouble. In thirty years as a pharmaceutical salesman, Stu worked with the other ninety-nine percent of the medical profession that conscientiously worked unbelievable hours day after day for the benefit of mankind. He always hoped a doctor would call him for advice—and occasionally they did. It was a moment of considerable pride for him to know he had made a difference for a patient.

The whole family, grandkids and all, were visiting them at home. By now their dream home, that thirty years of work brought them, was big enough to accommodate the entire brood of children, spouses, and their offspring. Stu told them at breakfast that his story was not yet finished. He wanted to tell them the reasons why he took pride in what he did for thirty years. It wasn't a career that got Stu his own statue. He got no medals for heroism. No one would ever nominate him for any hall of fame. He turned down all offers to be a Who's Who for anything. He was only a single man in a vast cog of a wheel that kept the world turning for the betterment of mankind—and he got paid good wages to do it. He sat his family down after breakfast and asked them to listen for one more hour.

"At the end of thirty years, I now have friends who are glad to say hi when I pass by. That is a treasure worth more than gold. You remember that."

Stu watched the grandchildren twitch and wiggle on the floor in front of him. He told all the children that if they wanted to leave, they could. The youngest ones left to find more important adventures, while the older grandchildren and their parents stayed.

"I learned that doctors are just like the rest of us. They have a special skill, just like a plumber, a lawyer, or a drug rep. Each has a position to make the world a better place. I want you to know that whatever career you choose, do it to make a difference for others."

He looked at his family. He knew he had lost a few already to their daydreams. It was the same with doctors he had called on. Not everything he said in his career was effective. Over time, he realized why he called on the same doctors every two to six weeks and repeated the same thing for thirty years. At some point in that time, a doctor would have an epiphany—the same message Stu had repeated for years. He shared with his family how he did not get credit for the information. Someone else would claim credit. But Stu knew that it had been his work that enlightened the doctor. His message to his children was simple.

"My goal was not to get credit, but to make a difference in the doctor's practice. If I was honest with him and he believed me, he would reward me. Sometimes it's okay to let someone take the credit. My goal was not to become a hero, but to make a difference."

That night the children were gone, back to their own homes and their own dreams for the future. Ana sat close to him. They talked about their future for the hundredth time. The days of doing expense reports every Saturday morning were over. Stu vowed to continue getting up at

5:30 a.m. every morning. But he could read his newspaper at his leisure. He could stay in his bed clothes if he desired. But he was a creature of habit and convention. He instead chose to dress in time to go to work—if he had any.

He shared with Ana his worry that the younger members of the Boomers would not enjoy their careers as much as he had. He worried they would become the grouchy old sales reps he always strived to avoid. Mike Austin was still at it, as well as Lorelei Lolly, now Lorelei Schultz, and Benton 'Four' Wickingham, IV. They were the best hires Mike ever made. They remained dynamos in a group of high achievers in Lance Layton's district of Boomers. Christy Fowler took advantage of moving to a new startup pharmaceutical company with a much bigger paycheck, thanks to the glowing endorsement of her pod mates. Soon after that, she married a *Space Cadet* physician. After only one month with Christy, he started making more sense. The pod reclassified him as a *Frat Boy*. Charlie Ketter, college wrestler and another top performer, found another pharmaceutical company to work for. His goal was to have twenty years with each company before he retired. The other newer sales reps in the Boomers and in Region Six didn't have a lot in common with the old timers. Stu had trouble remembering their names.

As he talked with Ana, he confessed that in his early days he had read many of the older reps all wrong. While they once appeared to be too confident of their abilities, now he admitted their feelings were now also his. He finally knew why.

Salesmen successfully sold pharmaceuticals to doctors in many ways. There was the hard charging drug rep whose customers wrote his products just so he would go away. A salesman could be a robot that chanted his memorized sales pitch so frequently that his doctors repeated it in their sleep every night. Then there was the pharmaceutical salesman who got to know his customers and became friends with everyone, including his own competitors. The hard charger lasted maybe five years before he flamed out. The plodder and the rep who learned how to be both a friend and salesman could last twenty or thirty years.

Over time these men, and later women, had earned the respect of their customers. Stu said it best, when he corrected a doctor's perception of his job as a pharmaceutical salesman.

"I get to surround myself all day long with highly educated people, but unlike you, I don't have to deal with body fluids."

The doctor responded contritely, "If you put it that way, you make your job sound pretty good."

It was a good job and it paid well, but certainly nowhere close to a doctor's income. Stu and Ana were frugal whenever possible with four kids to feed. At some point they bought an empty lot for their dream house and waited until the future shined upon them. The day came sooner than they expected. When construction on their house began, a competitor of Stu's approached him one day in his booth at a state medical convention.

"I heard you're building a house in that new neighborhood in Edmond. I know several doctors who live there."

"I noticed that, too. Who would have thought? I hope they don't move out when they learn a detail man is moving in next door."

"Yeah, you might scare them."

"I've talked to some of them. I promised I wouldn't throw file cards out my car window when I drive by their houses."

"If you don't mind me asking, how much of a house are you building? What's it costing you?"

"A little over four hundred thousand to build... we hope... we already own the lot. It's about thirty-two hundred square feet on an acre."

"How can a drug rep afford a house that big?"

"My wife is filthy rich."

"Oh? Did she inherit a bunch of money or something?"

"No, she's a schoolteacher."

Stu watched the wheels turning in his competitor's head. He muttered something not in the English language, but remained puzzled, until he walked away to another display booth. It was because of their early frugality that Stu and Ana could now live like a doctor.

It was hard on him, realizing there were people in his medical career that he would no longer see routinely. He was under no illusion. The doctors, nurses, pharmacists, and other sales reps would soon forget him. His name might come up, but there was no drug rep memorial to commemorate his journey in their arena. Only God and Ana would know and remember his good deeds. That was okay with Stu.

Easier to remember, but wanting to forgive and forget, were the nefarious deeds done to him by men and women in the same arena. Why did Finn Trottel, such a good manager, shortchange their paychecks? Why was Bill Dooley so hostile beginning on day one of Stu's career? How could Fred McAnich, a good rep, fall from grace and leave in disgrace, but his two paramours, Cissy Bordon and Rose Astor, kept their jobs? When did allowing men to become alcoholics become an obvious corporate mistake? What motivated Ben Hodge to act like a twelve-year-old? Then there were the philandering doctors. For Stu, he tried to practice forgive and forget. He never lost faith in the possibility of human redemption.

His joy in retirement was knowing that ninety-eight percent of doctors, nurses, pharmacists, and drug reps were honorable people whose efforts did wonders for the patient. Stories of good doctors, though, are boring. Fortunately, there were everyday stories of hard, conscientious work, unbelievable hours, and late nights. They often worked boring hours being away from families and getting little sleep. A challenging case was a gift to a physician. Physicians like Doctors Hull and Crowder, who eradicated Stu's pneumonia, performed what to them was just another routine day of work when he came for help—just another day of treating sick patients. They were part of a vast evolution in medicine that crept along one day at a time.

DETAIL MAN

A new acquaintance once asked Stu what he did for a living.

"I'm a pharmaceutical salesman."

"I hear it pays well. Have you seen the cost of drugs in your industry? It's shameful."

"So, what do you do for a living?"

"I am a university professor."

"Wow! Have you seen the cost of tuition these days? Isn't that shameful?"

Stu determined it was a reply that worked for any job. "Nearly everything in life costs more money, but people still complain about it, then demand it."

Twenty years before, Stu stood in line waiting at a small-town physician's office to open. There was a cold but sunny early morning winter sunrise. A dozen patients waited patiently, quietly chatting. A man behind Stu began to berate him.

"Here's another one of you peddlers who will make me wait while you take up all Doctor George's time. Why don't you go to the back of the line, so us people can see the doctor first? Let's make you wait and then see how you… you in your fancy suit and your bag of over-priced snake oil likes it, huh?"

Stu was about to respond with some brief words of kindness, when an elderly man in front of him turned around and confronted the man.

"Sir, this gentleman in front of you in the fancy suit, as you say, happens to be here for our benefit. He educates the doctor. He'll leave us samples we can try for free. Why, he's worth every penny they pay him." He looked at Stu. "Isn't that right, son?"

Stu nodded. His defender turned back to the man. "This is an honorable man who deserves our respect. He stands out here in the cold with us. He has a job to do, just like you have, I'm sure."

The man at the back of the line backed off and remained silent. Stu thanked the other man profusely. Never again in thirty years did he ever hear a patient explain his value to others. Stu savored the moment for his whole career. The only other person that reminded him that his job had worth was Ana.

"I'm proud of you," she said, taking his hand in hers. "You learned to speak to doctors on their level. You saved some lives and helped many doctors. You earned their respect. You faced down bad elements in the company and outlasted them. You taught doctors how to save money and time. And you now have a thousand friends in medicine."

Even if no one else ever said it, Stu knew his years of labor helped people have better lives. Not every job is heroic, but what stories he could tell? And his job was so much fun.

Epilogue

THE YEAR WAS 2024. Stu and Ana Roy were now sharing retirement together. The mornings were quiet and less hurried now. Still getting up like clockwork at 5:30 a.m. each day, the couple enjoyed that first fresh cup of coffee together for the thousandth time. Things in medicine continued to evolve, but they learned more of the new system at each doctor's visit.

The practice of medicine was different. Primary Care Physicians rarely treated Stu hands on, except for taking his blood pressure and pulse, listening to his heart and lungs, and perhaps hearing his bowel sounds. The doctor's stethoscope was the only instrument he ever used on him.

Another change was the laptop computer that his family doctor studied with deep concern. Stu often wished he would look at him with equal attention. On one visit, Stu mentioned concerns to his doctor about the lack of the usual routine checks most men dreaded. After some further discussion about why Stu expressed concerns, his doctor had him lower his trousers to conduct a check for a hernia. The young doctor seemed nervous. His hand trembled as he searched for the spot that makes all men rise on the tips of their toes with discomfort. Stu had no such reaction. The doctor declared him in good shape. He had missed the mark. Stu remained silent. His doctor did not know what he was doing—but his computer skills were superb—and he knew how to refer Stu to a specialist for every issue he had.

The whole world now was run by the decisions of Medicare, insurance companies, drug formularies, clinic managers, and hospitals. Stu's era was gone forever. Was it a better system? Stu thought not, but he would adapt. He always had. What else could he do?

About the Author

Kent McInnis is an Oklahoma-born chronicler of people, places, and good times. He lives with his wife, Cheryl, in Oklahoma City. He served as an Air Force jet instructor pilot during the last five years of the Vietnam War. For the next 33 years he worked in the pharmaceutical industry for Hoechst Pharmaceuticals which evolved through mergers into Sanofi-Aventis. After retiring in 2008, Kent assumed the position of Chairman of Westerners International, an organization with chapters on three continents, dedicated to making the study of Western American history fun – "no stuffed shirts allowed." He stepped down nine years later to return to writing full time.

Kent is the author of the Sierra Hotel Trilogy about the life of an air force pilot during and after the Vietnam War.

In his spare time Kent travels by car with Cheryl to see America at ground level, visit their three grown children, and savor the joys of freedom in this great country.

Find Kent at kent@mcinnis.us or on Facebook.

Author's Note

Growing up surrounded by myriad animals from dogs and rabbits to ducks and lizards, I dreamed of becoming a veterinarian for the Oklahoma City Zoo. After earning a Zoology Degree at Oklahoma State University, I found my goals suspended by the needs of my local draft board. Five years later with a need for employment, I was lucky to find a job where a zoology degree was valuable. The pharmaceutical industry hired salesmen to enter a doctor's office and persuade them to alter their prescribing habits. After several years of honing my skills, physicians, nurses, pharmacists, and hospital personnel became not just customers but friends. When I met my soon to be wife who worked in a pharmacy, she commented that she found detail men to be an elite group of professionals. My own opinion of the profession changed because of that comment. For whatever reason, her comment made me have more fun at work. One day when a doctor complimented me by asking why I didn't consider going to medical school, I had a ready answer. "As a pharmaceutical salesman I surround myself all day long with highly educated people, but unlike you, I don't have to deal with body fluids." He replied, "The way you put it, it sounds pretty good."

Acknowledgments

It is mandatory for any credit first going to my parents who taught me how to tell a good story with good grammar. I am always inspired by my English teacher and librarian wife, Cheryl, who told me when I had doubts about my career that she was proud of me. I add a thanks to my editors, Casey Cowen, Amy Cowen, Dennis Doty and Anthony Wood, who make editing a fun exercise. There are too many friends in the industry to thank, instead they collectively go by the titles of Hoechstlings, Tornadoes, and The Party Van. You know who you are. Finally, I thank the thousand physicians, nurses, pharmacists, hospital workers, and competitive drug reps who have shared their lives with me for four decades. I call them all my friends.